DEATH CHORUS

DI JAMIE JOHANSSON BOOK 4

MORGAN GREENE

ALSO BY MORGAN GREENE

DS Jamie Johansson Prequels
Bare Skin
Fresh Meat
Idle Hands

The DS Johansson Prequel Trilogy Boxset

———

DI Jamie Johansson
Angel Maker
Rising Tide
Old Blood

Death Chorus
Quiet Wolf

To those who help make Jamie real.

DEATH CHORUS

1

BLACK WINGS CHURNED AROUND HIM, claws snatching at his skin, beaks gouging, cries cutting the heavy summer air.

He threw his hands around his head, beating them away, running as hard as he could through the forest.

Tears streamed from the boy's eyes, lungs burning like cold fire.

His feet crunched in the undergrowth, pine needles and twigs snapping under his heels. The air was soup, the smell of pine sickly and sweet. Choking him. Pollen drifted down, hanging in the moonlight. He streaked through it, the straight trunks flashing past, heart thundering in his throat.

The boy's breath was ragged as he came up the rise, scrambling forward, fingers stained with the loamy earth.

At the top, he stumbled, then lost his footing, landing on his side, tumbled forwards, down, down, down, until he came to rest at the bottom in a panting heap.

He stared up through the swaying canopy, the night black and endless above, starless.

Everything hung still for a moment, and then, all around, they exploded from the trees.

There was a roar of shimmering bodies jostling for space, an impenetrable river of crows swirling and screaming, their calls echoing and building until they deafened him.

He held his hands to his ears, screwed his eyes closed and rolled onto his side, curled up, feeling their wings pounding his skin, their beaks pecking and pulling. The boy let out a scream. Long, raw, until his throat ached.

And then there was nothing.

Silence.

He opened his eyes slowly, skin slick with sweat, and looked around.

They were gone.

He was alone.

He pushed himself to his knees, and then to his feet, staggering a little, the cool, damp earth matted in his hair. He cradled his arm instinctively – he wasn't sure if he was hurt – and blinked himself clear.

The boy turned slowly, looking for any signs of the one chasing him, and stopped, staring up at a gap between two trees on the hill.

A shape hovered there, cut out against the dim yellow moon behind.

The boy swallowed, mouth dry.

And then, before he could run, there was darkness.

2

Detective Jamie Johansson didn't really like having a gun pointed at her.

Especially not before her morning coffee.

She held her hand out, meeting his cold, amber eyes, and steadied her voice. 'Give it to me,' she said. 'Give me the gun. Now.'

Hati stared back, standing on her bed, the SIG Sauer P226 semi-automatic pistol held firmly in his mouth.

Jamie took a tentative step forward, holding the bath towel around her with her left hand. A pool of drips was quickly forming around her feet.

She couldn't even take a shower without this dog making her life a waking nightmare.

Hati flinched, lowering his head, growled, and readjusted his hold on the gun. He glanced at the open door to Jamie's right that led into her living room.

'Don't!' she warned, turning her hand over and into an authoritative point.

If Hati had fingers, this was the time he'd show her the middle one.

He launched himself forward, the ragged, three-legged hound scarpering off her bed, right for the door.

Jamie leapt to tackle him, missed, and landed with a painful grunt.

The dog lurched forward awkwardly, claws scrabbling on the polished boards, and disappeared around the corner towards the kitchen.

Jamie sat back and pushed heavy strands of wet blonde hair from her eyes, sighing. At least the gun wasn't loaded. Actually, that might be better. At least then there'd be a chance he'd blow his fucking head off and finally give her some peace.

No, no, he was just a dog. It wasn't his fault, as much of a cold, aggressive, biting, growling, pissing, thieving asshole as he was.

That'd teach her for picking up a stray from the side of the road.

Her phone buzzed on her nightstand and she stood up and walked over to it. The office – Kurrajakk Polis HQ. Generous as that term was. It was Jamie, a twenty-three-year-old *polisassistent* called Minna, and a grouchy old *kriminalkommisarie* called Stig Ohlin. Her boss. In nothing except title.

'Johansson,' Jamie said, holding the phone to her ear.

'Hej, är det Inspektör Johansson?'

'Yes, Minna,' Jamie replied in Swedish. 'If you call my phone, and I answer "Johansson", it's me.'

'Okay,' she said, laughing nervously. 'I, uh, Ohlin called me, told me to come in early.'

Jamie pulled the phone from her ear and checked the time. Shit, yeah, it was barely seven. She'd already been up and done her daily ten-K, but most people would be just pulling their faces from their pillows right now.

'What's wrong?' Jamie asked. For Ohlin to be up before ten, it must be serious.

'There's an, um, I don't know how to … uh …'

Jamie sighed. The kid was sweet, but she was going to make a terrible officer. If anyone else had applied for the job, she was pretty sure they would have given it to that person instead. 'Just say it, Minna, your probation period is over.' It wasn't, but there was no real hope of finding a replacement.

'Someone's dead.'

Jamie did a double-take. 'Sorry, what did you say?'

Jamie had been with the department for nearly four months now, and the closest thing she'd had to an actual case was a local who'd had his car stolen. By himself, the night before. When he was drunk. 'Did you say that someone's dead? Like a crash, or an accident?'

'Like … someone *killed* someone, Ohlin said. A boy – something about a tree, and … and … birds … and he was …' Her voice was cracking.

'It's okay, it's okay, just breathe,' Jamie said, looking around for her boots.

'He wants you out there. Right now.'

Jamie was nodding to herself, heart beating fast. 'Send me the address, I'll head right over.'

'I can't send you an address …'

She paused the boot hunt and waited for the hammer to drop.

'… it's in the middle of the forest.'

3

JAMIE KEPT TELLING herself that this was just a misunderstanding. A blip. Some sort of accident that *looked* like murder. Come on, this was Kurrajakk. People didn't get killed here.

It was the whole damn reason she chose the place.

She sighed, fingers drumming on the faded steering wheel. The road ahead stretched through endless pine forests, the jagged tops waving slowly around her. The sky was that flat mottled grey she'd come to know so well, the road straight and unmarked. It'd been here for a hundred years but had never had a name.

Jamie spotted the back of Ohlin's car ahead, pulled in behind it and killed the engine. She stepped out of her beat-up SUV and down onto the gravelly verge. Twenty miles down the road there was another village, but they were the only polis department for eighty miles around.

Ohlin's car was parked behind another she didn't recognise. He'd been *kriminalkommissarie* in Kurrajakk for fifteen years now, and had only been promoted to that position because the previous *kriminalkommisarie* had died.

That was kind of how it went around here.

Though Jamie didn't choose it for the career track.

She sighed, straightening her belt and hip holster, and waded through the grassy ditch at the side of the road before climbing up the hill and into the trees.

She massaged her bandaged right hand with her left, wondering if getting her gun back was really worth getting bitten, and followed Minna's painful instructions.

Head up the hill until you find a stream, then follow that for a bit. Ohlin's in the forest already.

Yeah, except there's a thousand hectares of forest out here. And a stream every hundred metres.

Jamie grumbled, moving upwards until she came to a sad little summer-dried trickle of water. She stared down at it, then set off again, wondering how far she'd get before she had to decide she was going in the wrong direction and turn back.

Mercifully, she heard Ohlin's hacking cough after a few minutes and homed in on it.

The undulating ground was soft and thick with a blanket of pine needles. She followed the boot marks in the bank ahead, and when she reached the top, saw she was standing on the rim of a bowl.

But it wasn't the natural landscape that drew her eye, it was what Ohlin and the other man were standing in front of.

The sinkhole was about thirty metres across and ten deep. The bottom was flat and lined with wide, natural stone slabs. Small cairns had been built on some of them, and in the centre there was a huge tree stump that had been ground flat. Ohlin had his back to Jamie, his bulk apparent, an easy identifier. He was wearing a white shirt that hung over his belt. It was tucked in and made him look like an overstuffed builder's sack. He had blotchy, rolled arms that were crooked at the elbows, his hands buried somewhere in his soft flanks.

Except Jamie's eyes weren't fixed on him, but on what he was standing over.

The body was mostly obscured from where she was standing, but on the left she could see bare feet, black with dirt, and on the right, a head. The head of a teenage boy. It lolled backwards off the stump, hair hanging below it, matted and tangled with pine needles. The eyes stared blankly into the sky, the mouth forced open.

And sticking from it, Jamie could see the tail of a crow.

Her skin was immediately prickling. She moved quickly down the slope, the sound of the cascading brush under her heels enough to alert Ohlin to her presence.

He turned, his wide, red face, mostly covered by a thick black and grey beard, a mix of angst and frustration. *'Du tog din tid,'* he said, his voice that same old rasping, lawnmower tone it always was. You took your time.

'Vad hände?' Jamie asked. What happened?

He sniffed sharply, then hawked and spat a dubiously-coloured lump of phlegm into the undergrowth. 'Someone killed a fucking kid,' he grunted.

Jamie stared down at the yellow-brown chunk of mucus. She didn't think telling him this was a crime scene would make a blind bit of difference. Nor would she get a straight or useful answer from him if she asked anything else.

Ohlin didn't like his job. He also didn't like Jamie. And he especially didn't like it when a body turned up, it seemed. She'd barely seen him the whole time she'd been here. He didn't come into the station, he didn't attend cases, and he didn't answer his phone either. At least not to her. Everyone in town knew him, knew he was the only police officer around, and they all had his number.

She figured the guy standing next to him – he had to be in his sixties, wiry, with a long beard, an ear-flapped cap on, and a hunting rifle over his shoulder – had found the body, and called Ohlin directly.

And now Jamie was here to take the whole thing off his hands, so he could go back to his armchair and whatever else he did with his days.

Drink, by the smell of him every time they crossed paths.

'Okay,' Ohlin said, nodding and turning to the hunter. He offered a swollen red hand and the hunter shook it and nodded, then turned away.

'Hey,' Jamie called automatically. 'I need to speak to—'

Before Jamie could stop him, or even finish, Ohlin was facing her, that same hand now held up in front of her. 'Jakob would prefer to be left out of the report,' he said. 'I'm inclined to oblige him.'

Jamie narrowed her eyes. 'And why would we do that? He was the person who discovered the body.'

Ohlin wasn't budging, his deep-set eyes bloodshot and puffy. 'Things work a little differently out here than in the city.'

Jamie set her jaw. *He's your boss. He's your boss.* She kept repeating it in her head.

'So do your job – which last time I checked, was following my orders.'

'I thought my job was to catch criminals?'

He offered her a wide, toothy grin. 'Then it's your lucky day, isn't it?' He stepped sideways and revealed the stripped body on the stump behind him.

Jamie felt bile rise in her throat at the bloody sight before her.

She let her eyes move across the body as Ohlin sidled away. 'CSTs are on their way up from Lulea. Think you can hold the scene till they arrive?' He didn't bother turning round to speak.

Jamie didn't bother to answer.

'Oh, and Johansson?' he said, already out of breath and no more than a quarter of the way up the slope. 'Keep an eye out for your new partner, he arrives today as well.'

Jamie did turn now. 'What did you just say?'

Ohlin paused and leaned on a tree, panting. 'He was supposed to start next week but, considering the circumstances, I moved the date up.'

'Partner?' Jamie didn't even try to keep the disdain from her face. 'I don't need a partner,' she said.

He looked up the loamy slope like it was the last stretch to the top of Everest. 'I think you do,' he said. 'It'll help put my mind at ease.'

Motherfucker.

Did he really think so little of her policing skills? Had he even bothered to read her history? And now he was, what, sticking her with a babysitter?

Jamie drew a slow breath, trying to let the anger drain away.

It wouldn't budge, a hot lump burning in the pit of her stomach.

'Guess I forgot to mention it,' Ohlin said then, shrugging. His eyes drifted down to her side. 'What happened to your hand?'

'I—'

'You know what, I don't care,' he said, starting back up the slope. 'Try not to fuck this up,' he called, nearing the top. 'If you need anything, your new partner has my number.'

'I have your number,' Jamie yelled, watching him disappear over the brow.

But he didn't stop, or respond.

And then she was alone, bandaged hand throbbing, balled into a tight fist.

She hung her head, sighed, and turned slowly back to the body, only one word coming to mind.

Fuck.

4

THE SUN CLIMBED behind the trees, weak through the cloud, but enough to fill the natural bowl she was in. Still, the place was dim, cold, and silent, the air in there heavy, making her chest tight. It made her skin tingle, goose-pimple, like the trees themselves were watching.

Jamie shook it off and walked in a slow circle around the body, inspecting everything.

In a way, she was glad Ohlin had pissed off, given her space to work. And whoever this new 'partner' of hers was, she was happy to be doing the initial walk-through without him. No doubt Ohlin had pitched her as some jumped-up city-dweller who thought she knew everything.

The guy had never left Kurrajakk.

And he wouldn't know correct police procedure if it kicked him in the balls. Which Jamie was pretty close to doing herself.

She paused and looked down, crouching on one of the stone slabs, her lightweight trail boots squeaking as she did.

The surface was covered with lichen, loose pine needles.

She pulled a pair of nitrile gloves from the pocket of her

polis-issue bomber jacket. It was September, summer in its final throes, the weather already beginning to turn and cool as the sun sliced an ever-lower arc through the sky.

Between her toes, she could make out carvings in the stone.

She brushed the needles aside, pushing them further and further back until she'd cleared the entire slab. It was filled with markings – curves and crosses and dots. Old. Roughly done. Deep. Runes. Norse runes.

She lifted her head, looking over at the stump again. It was white, all but petrified. How old it was, she couldn't say.

Jamie approached slowly, trying not to look at what was on top just yet, and searched around it, seeing more markings, more carvings.

At the sides of the bowl where the trees started, she could see flat stones stood up, laid against the trunks, camouflaged by moss and algae, but apparent to her now. There was no doubt in her mind that this was a ceremonial site of some kind.

She let out a long, rattling breath, the dead quiet of the forest enough to put a sheen of damp sweat on her skin. The trees had even stopped moving. Everything was still. No birds, no animal calls, nothing. As though the entire forest was afraid to make a sound.

Jamie stood straight, her hand finding the grip of her pistol at her hip, and turned in a slow circle before coming back to the half-naked boy in front of her with a crow stuffed in his open mouth.

She stared down at him for the first time and took it in.

He was flat on his back, his shirt missing. He was wearing shorts, but his feet were bare – Jamie tilted her head – dirty, his heels especially. Dragged, she thought. Backwards, through the forest. But the pine needles and dirt between his toes told her he'd been running, too.

Not fast enough, apparently.

She shook her head, grimaced, and then checked the ground around the slabs at the sides of the bowl. There were no tracks except her own and Ohlin's, no signs of the boy's clothing either. Nothing to suggest how he'd got down here – of his own volition or otherwise.

She looked at his position, draped over the stump. Then she looked up. It was like he'd fallen right out of the sky.

Was the body transported here after the kill? Had he been brought here alive and killed?

Jamie stepped closer, sniffed the air over the boy, detected the sickly-sweet smell of stale sweat. It was strong. He'd been running, definitely. He'd not made it easy on the killer.

Way to go kid, she thought abjectly. Good for you.

She let her eyes move up his legs. Scratches there – brambles, undergrowth. Over his shorts then. Denim, fitted. She saw nothing to indicate that he had a phone or wallet on him. She reached down, patted his thighs to double check. Empty.

Her eyes continued upwards, over the flat, well-muscled stomach, the thin line of hair tracing to his naval, and towards his protruding ribs. He was athletic, he worked out, she could tell that. Strong, fit. His jaw was angular, his face once handsome, the thin nose, symmetrical features, medium length, wavy brown hair enough to send the local teenage girls wild, she guessed.

At least, he would have.

Jamie clenched her jaw again to stop her lip from quivering, the scent of sweat drowned in the stench of blood.

She let it in then, the real horror of what had been done to him.

All across his body – one every square inch – were nicks.

Deep, gouged cuts that looked like they'd been done with a sharpened teaspoon. Down through the skin, right to the muscle tissue. The edges of the cuts were peeled back, shining red in the way that only raw flesh can.

Blood had run from them, soaked his entire body. It had pooled on the stump beneath him, seeped into the grain of the wood, and run into the earth around, staining the greyed needles black.

Jamie leaned in closer, checking his fingers, his nails. They were dirty. It looked like he'd been digging, or scratching in the earth. But she couldn't see any signs of defensive wounds, nothing to suggest he'd clawed or punched at anyone.

She exhaled, covered her nose with the crook of her elbow, and drew a slow breath, eyes moving up his arm to the face, the mouth – the crow.

The bird wasn't small. Its entire front end had been forced between his teeth, pushing them apart until the skin on his cheeks stretched beyond its natural limits, distorting the shape of the boy's eyes.

His lips had rolled back slightly, showing the incisors digging into the feathered body of the bird. Its wings jutted out at odd, awkward angles, its legs stiff and splayed above it, tail like a black wedge pointing at the sky.

It was as though the thing had dive-bombed the boy, flown straight down his throat.

She could see the misshapen oesophagus above the Adam's apple, knew that the head and beak were down inside it. Jesus Christ, she hoped he was dead before that happened at least. If not, it would have blocked his airway, suffocated him.

She could see the dark veins in his eyes, around his dark

brown irises, knew the pain and the spike in blood pressure that had caused them to swell and burst like that.

Jamie pulled herself away, breathing slowly, steadying herself ready for everything that came next.

But no matter how far she walked, she couldn't get the stench of blood and death out of her nose, or the image of what she'd just looked at out of her mind.

She had no idea what had led to that boy's death, but she knew one thing – that stripping a boy half-naked, laying him on a ceremonial altar, cutting into his flesh a hundred times, and then ramming a bird down his throat meant one thing.

She was dealing with a real fucking psychopath.

5

It was two hours before the first sounds of the CSTs echoed over the rise.

Multiple sets of footsteps crunching through the forest, voices, grunts and moans about dragging heavy equipment through the woods.

Jamie had gone over the site a dozen times now and was sure she'd not missed anything. But the CSTs would do their work, the coroner would remove the body, then a pathologist would do the autopsy. And then they'd get some real answers.

She got up from the log she was sitting on at the top of the ridge above the crime scene and circled around to intercept them.

'*Hålla,*' she called, raising a hand.

There were five of them, all in white overalls unzipped to the waist and hanging loose. Three men, two women, carrying hard-shell suitcases, cameras, goggles dangling around their necks.

The one at the front, a guy in his late forties with a round head and hair that stuck out behind his ears, laid down his silver case, wiped the sweat from his domed forehead, and returned the wave. *'Kriminalinspektör Thorsen?'* he asked.

Thorsen? Who the hell was Thorsen? *'Na,'* Jamie said, a little indignant. *'Kriminalinspektör Johansson,'* she said, extending her hand. 'Jamie Johansson.'

'Oh,' he went on, 'we were told that we'd be greeted by Detective Thorsen, from the Kurrajakk Polis. Are they … here?'

'This is my scene,' Jamie said, putting two and two together. 'Ohlin's got his facts wrong. This is my investigation, and you'll be reporting to me.'

The guy looked back at her, measuring her cold stare, the surefooted answer. 'Well alright then. Torbjörn Forss,' he said, smiling briefly and offering his hand. 'Show me where the dead body is.'

Jamie shook it quickly, then glanced over her right shoulder and dipped her head that way, down into the site.

The technician leaned around her, let out a low whistle. Even from here, what they were walking into was apparent. 'Suits on,' he called behind him.

Everyone began lifting and zipping up their overalls. A quiet had fallen among them, the smiles and laughter that had accompanied them up the hill now gone in the face of whatever the hell it was that waited below.

'Did the coroner come with you?' Jamie asked, trying to break the mood.

Torbjörn Forss, the lead crime scene technician, shook his head. 'No,' he said. 'He won't be far behind, though.' He chuckled to himself. 'His name's Vardeman. Göran Vardeman. Real charmer.'

Jamie rolled her lips into a line. 'Great, I can't wait.'

Forss zipped up his suit and pulled his hood up, glancing

back at his crew. They all nodded and gave thumbs, and then headed down towards the body.

'Hey,' Jamie called after them.

Forss looked back.

'If you, uh, find a big chunk of yellowish-brown, phlegm-looking, uh … you know what, never mind.' She waved it off.

The tech nodded slowly, not really understanding, then carried on.

She watched the crew disperse across the site and begin setting up.

Thorsen. Was that the name of her would-be partner?

She'd promised herself she wouldn't do another one.

Her track record with partners wasn't great. For them at least.

Thorsen.

Yeuch, she hated him already.

An hour passed before a short, stocky guy with long grey hair that seemed to be thinning on top, and square glasses that magnified his eyes, came ambling up the hill from the road. He was limping, holding a rolled-up windbreaker in one hand and carrying a satchel over his shoulder. He hauled himself up, glancing at Jamie when he got about halfway.

'Don't worry, I don't need any help,' he said. 'Not like I've got a bad knee or anything.'

Jamie sighed. 'You must be Vardeman, the coroner.'

He got to the top, did a faux bow. 'My reputation precedes me.'

'Yeah,' Jamie said. 'Something like that.'

He squinted up into the trees, looked around a bit, then back at Jamie. 'Well, this place is a real shithole, isn't it?'

'It's a forest.'

'I'm not a fan,' he said, reaching level with Jamie. 'What happened to your hand?' He nodded to her bandage.

'I ...' she said, shaking her head, '... burnt it on a pan.'

'Well, that was a bit stupid wasn't it?'

'You want to just get to work?' Jamie asked hopefully.

'You got any prelim for me?' he asked, readjusting his glasses and squinting down into the scene.

'Young male, late teens,' Jamie said, following his eyes. The techs had now set up a tent over the body and were busy laying out evidence markers. 'Looks like he was stripped and posed, laid flat on a tree stump. The body has multiple wounds made with a small blade, and ...' Jamie didn't quite know how to say the next part.

'Well, spit it out,' Vardeman said.

'He's got a crow shoved down his throat.'

'A live crow?'

'Well, it's not alive anymore.'

'Interesting.'

'Is it?'

'More interesting than the car crash I attended yesterday.'

'Nice to see you enjoy your work,' Jamie added.

Vardeman shrugged and headed carefully down the hill. 'It has its good days. Are you coming?'

'Sure,' Jamie said, casting around for any sign of 'Thorsen'. Nothing yet.

She flexed her bandaged hand a few times and then followed Vardeman down towards the tent.

He left a strong smell of cheap aftershave in his wake, the grey polo shirt he was wearing tucked into his black chinos, which seemed to be tightly belted and very high around his waist.

She didn't deign to ask why.

He paused at the door of the tent and fished in his chest

pocket for a pair of magnifying clip-ons for his glasses, then dumped his satchel and threw his windbreaker around his shoulders. It was waxed, black, and had the word '*OBDU-CENT*' across the back. Coroner.

He pulled out a metal clipboard, took a pen from his top pocket, licked the end of it, and started making notes on the paper in front of him. He scribbled quickly, pausing every now and then to look up, his eyes large and terrifying behind his glasses.

A few minutes later, without warning, he ducked through the door of the tent.

Jamie followed him in, the smell of blood mixed with whatever scent he was wearing enough to make her nose burn.

'Christ,' Vardeman said, looking down at the boy on the stump. He waggled his pen at him. 'You weren't kidding about the bird.'

'Why would I have been?' Jamie asked.

He shrugged. 'Some people have got a weird sense of humour.'

Jamie blinked, not knowing quite what to make of that comment. Or the man who made it.

Vardeman leaned over, his hair spilling around his collar and over his shoulders. 'Marks look to be deep, but wide – gouged almost. Never seen knife wounds like this.'

'What do you think it is?'

'I don't know,' he said, looking up at her. 'I just said that.'

'Right,' Jamie said, closing her eyes. Just breathe.

'Hmm,' Vardeman said then, standing and making more notes. 'We'll have to take him back to Lulea for the examination. Not much else to do here.'

'You don't want to look at anything else?'

'What did I just say?' He stopped writing and looked at her. 'Are you in charge here?'

'Yes, I am,' Jamie said.

'Thorsen, right?' He raised a bushy eyebrow.

Jamie just walked out of the tent. Fucking Thorsen.

She looked up, hearing voices, and saw the technician she'd spoken to earlier – Forss – speaking to a man she didn't recognise.

He was tall, maybe six feet one or two, with light brown hair, a narrow, strong face with a pronounced nose. He was in a woollen jacket, jeans, black boots, and was gesturing to the surrounding area, speaking quickly.

Jamie approached, knowing who it was without asking. 'Thorsen,' she called.

He paused, turned to face her. 'And you're Johansson,' he said. 'You want to tell me why there's no cordon set up? Why there're no officers on the road directing traffic? Why nobody's answering their goddamn phone?'

Jamie stopped short of the big man, measured his lean build and wide shoulders, then narrowed her eyes. 'No one's set a cordon up because I'm the only one here, and I couldn't leave the scene to go and get anything. There are no officers on the road directing traffic because firstly, there *are* no officers *to* direct traffic. And secondly, because there's no traffic. And the reason why no one's picking up the phone is because the girl who works at the station and is paid to answer the phone probably isn't there, and Ohlin … well, he never answers his phone. Does that about cover it?'

He stepped towards her. 'What kind of operation are you running here?'

Jamie held fast. This guy could get out of her face any time he liked. 'The kind that prioritises finding killers over having pissing contests about who's in charge.'

He looked at her for a second, then snorted. 'Yeah, no contest. It's just a good thing I'm here now.'

Thorsen moved past her and stepped into the tent without another word.

Forss stared at her.

After a second, Jamie sighed. 'Don't you have work to do?'

He pulled the corners of his mouth towards the points of his jaw, the kind of look that usually came with a 'Yikes'. Thankfully he didn't say it, and instead did get back to work.

Jamie hung her head back and stared into the still canopy, the grey clouds hanging motionless overhead.

It was going to be a long day.

6

JAMIE DUCKED back inside the tent to find the coroner going over the body for Thorsen. In more detail than he'd offered her. A lot more.

Thorsen had his arms folded, eyes fixed on Vardeman, face stern. He didn't even look at Jamie.

After the coroner had finished, Thorsen turned to her, blocking her way to the body, arms still folded. 'Secure the area, set up a cordon, then go back down to the road. If you don't have anyone else to do it, you need to be the one directing traffic. I don't want an accident fucking up my investigation or some idiot wandering up here off the street.'

Jamie raised her eyebrows. 'I don't know what you think is going on here … Thorsen, right?'

He didn't move or even blink.

'But this is my investigation, and this is my town. Now Ohlin may think that bringing you in was necessary, but I assure you, it wasn't.'

'No?' He scoffed a little. 'Because he asked me to come a week earlier than I was supposed to so that this wasn't botched from the start.' He looked her up and down. 'You're just some big-city detective who couldn't hack it out there. Who buckled under the stress, so you requested to be transferred somewhere like Kurrajakk, where *nothing ever happens.* Well, does this look like nothing?' He pointed behind him at the boy mounted on the stump. 'It's a different world out here, *detective.* And you're a long way from Stockholm. So either fall in line, or stay out of my way. Because there's a killer out there, and I intend to catch him.'

Jamie gritted her teeth, trying to pick that apart. Some big-city detective buckling under the pressure? He couldn't be more wrong. But was she going to stand here and defend herself to this guy? No, screw that. Screw him. She didn't need this shit. But he was right, there was a killer out there, and they were standing here measuring dicks.

'Listen, Thorsen,' she said, lowering her voice a little, stepping closer so she was under him as much as in front of him. She lowered her head, not bothering to meet his eye. Not giving him that respect. 'I get it, okay. I know how this may *seem,* how Ohlin painted it, but all you're proving to me right now is that you care more about your ego than anything else.' She did look up now. 'So let me just say this, just the once, because I'm not going to waste my breath a second time. The reasons I'm here are none of your *fucking* business. But if you think I'm about to roll over and let you shit all over this investigation ...' She trailed off, laughed a little, shook her head. 'You and Ohlin can suck each other's dicks for all I care, but you're not in charge here. And the faster you realise that, the faster we can just get on with this, okay?'

She met his eyes now, grey and lifeless as the sky, let that fester in the air for a moment, then turned away.

'You know,' he said, as she walked through the door, 'I was about to say the exact same thing.'

Jamie paused but didn't dignify his comment by turning around.

Once she was out of the tent, she steamed towards Forss, pulling a card from her pocket. 'Hey,' she called, holding it out. 'Call me when you finish up, I want to know the second you're done and the body is removed.'

The tech lowered his camera, reached out and took the card tentatively. 'Are you leaving?'

'Yeah, I have work to do,' she said flatly.

'Okay. Is … is Inspektör Thorsen staying?'

'I don't know.'

'Should I just let *him* know when we're done?'

Jamie's expression answered the question.

'I'll just call you,' he said.

'Good answer.'

She gave him a curt nod and then headed up the slope, feeling her heart beating behind her eyes, in her ears.

Jamie was halfway back to her car when her phone started buzzing. Had Thorsen gone running back to Ohlin already? Reported her to teacher?

She glanced down, saw it was HQ. 'Johansson,' she answered.

'*Hålla, Inspektör Johansson?*'

'*Ya, Minna,*' Jamie said, sighing. 'What is it?'

'I just got a call from a Christian Nordahl,' she said.

'Okay?' Jamie slowed up.

'He says his son went out yesterday evening and hasn't come home. His phone is off, and his friends haven't seen him.'

Jamie stopped altogether, surrounded by the silent forest. 'What's he look like?'

'He's seventeen, a hundred and seventy-five centimetres, athletic they said, plays lots of sports, brown hair.'

'Shit,' Jamie said, hanging her head. 'Alright, send me their address, I'll head there now.'

'Was the … body, I mean … is it … him?' Minna asked, stumbling over the words.

'Just send me the address,' Jamie said, and then she hung up.

She glanced around, the weight of the forest heavy on her shoulders, and headed for the road, quickening her pace.

7

JAMIE PULLED UP OUTSIDE THE NORDAHLS' house and got out of the car.

The air was cool, the sky darkening, the clouds thick and brooding now.

A slow breeze wound through the outer reaches of Kurra-jakk. The town wasn't big. It had a central cross where two linking roads intersected, a few shops and restaurants along it, a small lower school and a high school that covered the whole municipality, a local hospital, the Polis station. But otherwise, it was just a few looping residential streets, the thousand or so houses spread out across a wide area. They were mostly bungalows or modest two-storeys, surrounded by pale grass that slept under snow for more than half the year.

Jamie walked up the concrete-slab path to the house and knocked, surveying the place. It was in good condition. One car was on the drive, a ten-year-old Volvo estate that had seen better days.

The door opened in front of Jamie, and a middle-aged man with lined eyes and dark hair looked out at her. He pushed his square glasses higher on his nose. 'Oh, I was expecting Ohlin,' he said, looking at Jamie.

'Ohlin's indisposed,' Jamie replied. 'Kriminalinspektör Jamie Johansson.' She offered her hand and he took it tentatively. She thought it was in bad taste to say how useless Ohlin would be if he was here. She was just glad Thorsen wasn't. She needed a clear head going into this, and having him bumping shoulders with her for room was only going to muddy things. Jamie didn't really care if he was a good investigator – if he was here, in Kurrajakk, then something had gone wrong for him. She'd requested to be here by choice, but she doubted Thorsen's reasons were along the same lines. So either he was running from something, or his knight in shining armour act was a thinly veiled demotion and being banished to Kurrajakk was a punishment. Ohlin wasn't charming or pleasant enough to get anyone to agree to anything by asking nicely. But whatever was going on with that would have to wait.

Because there was a man standing in front of Jamie, and she was about to tell him his son was dead.

'Christian Nordahl,' he said, 'please, come in.' He proffered her the hallway.

She nodded and stepped inside, walking through into the living room.

'Can I get you a coffee, tea?' Nordahl asked.

'Coffee would be great – black is fine.' Jamie stepped around the room, checking out the pictures on the wall, on the mantle. She had little doubt in her mind that the man making her coffee was the father of the boy in the woods – she could see the resemblance – but she had to be sure.

She paused, homing in on a family portrait. The father, Christian Nordahl, his wife, and their son. He was maybe a year or so younger in the photo, his hair shorter, but it was him alright.

Jamie felt her stomach knot itself up …

'Inspektör,' he said from behind her.

Jamie turned, taking the coffee from him.

'What happened to your hand?' he asked.

'Oh, jammed it in the car door,' Jamie said, waving it off. 'It's nothing.' She shook her head and took a sip of the coffee. 'Thank you.' She looked at Nordahl. He appeared a little tired, but mostly worried. 'When did you last see Felix?' she asked, clutching the steaming mug.

'Uh, around seven, maybe,' he said, shaking his head a little.

'He went out at seven?'

'No, I did.'

Jamie had to be careful not to make this into an interrogation – especially with what she knew and what Christian Nordahl didn't. Namely, that his son was dead.

'He didn't text you to let you know he was going out?'

He shook his head. 'No, he has his independence. But he usually lets us know he's alright – especially if he's staying out all night. It's not like Felix to not stay in touch.'

Felix. Felix Nordahl. The boy. Jamie took another sip. 'Minna told me Felix is seventeen, is that correct?'

He nodded. 'That's right, yes.'

'And this photograph here,' she said, gesturing to the portrait. 'Does he still look like this?'

'His hair is a little longer, a little wavy. And he's been going to the gym – at the school – so he's a little bigger now, more muscular, you know? He plays a lot of football, hockey in the winter. He's quite good,' he said, smiling proudly.

Shit.

'Mr Nordahl,' Jamie said, lowering her cup and clutching it in both hands. 'I'm afraid I have some bad news.'

Nordahl stiffened, eyes twitching.

'Is your wife here?' Jamie asked.

'No, she's at work, at the hospital, she's a nurse,' he said quickly. 'What's wrong? Is it Felix? Do you know something? Is he alright?'

Jamie steeled herself. This was always horrible. 'This morning I was called to attend the discovery of a body in the woods.'

The colour drained from his face.

'I went out there, and I believe that it is your son, Mr Nordahl. I'm sorry to—'

'Body?' The word came out shaky and thin. 'He's ... Felix is ... is he ... ?' He shook then, threw his hand to his mouth, and ran into the hallway. A door banged against the wall and then Jamie heard a toilet seat hitting the cistern, Christian Nordahl emptying his stomach into the bowl.

She swallowed, drew a slow breath, then took another sip of coffee. It was good, hot, burned her tongue. She embraced the pain, took another sip, waited for him to come back.

He stumbled into the hallway, steadying himself on the wall.

'Mr Nordahl,' Jamie went on.

He didn't look up, kept his head hung, fist balled at his vomit-moist lips.

'We'll need you to formally identify the body once it's been removed and—'

'Get out,' he said.

Jamie stopped talking for a second. 'I know this is hard—'

'Get out!' He roared it then, exploding into a tearful rage, hands flailing. 'Get out! Get out!'

Jamie swallowed, crossed to the kitchen and put her mug down. She reached into her jacket and set a card down next to it. 'I'll be in touch. Call me if you need anything in the meanwhile. My card's on the counter.'

She headed for the door, not looking at Christian Nordahl, who'd now collapsed back against the wall, pinching the bridge of his nose, sobbing, eyes rammed closed.

Jamie let herself out and exhaled long and hard, pausing on the walk.

She sank forward, resting her hands on her knees for a moment, and then straightened, filled her lungs, and carried on. There was nothing she could do for him right now.

Nothing except her job.

Jamie got into her car and cranked the key, pulling off quickly. She accelerated hard towards the main cross and slowed, checking left and right. She knew where she was heading next.

The engine whined as she downshifted, and then complained as she pulled off, the old clutch slipping. Something flashed in her peripheral and she stood on the brake instinctively, the car rocking heavily on its springs, stopping dead.

A woman in her sixties slapped her hand on the front wing of the car and then came to the window. Jamie didn't recognise her. She had wild eyes and even wilder hair, wind-blown and big, white. She drummed with both hands now, pressing her face to the glass.

Jamie leaned across the passenger seat and wound it down awkwardly, the old SUV equipped with an old-fashioned roller instead of power windows.

'Konstapel, konstapel' the woman said breathlessly. She was wearing a tatty zip-up fleece, and Jamie could smell the beer and cigarettes on her breath. And it was barely eleven in the morning.

'Inspektör,' Jamie corrected her tiredly. *'Hur kan jag hjälpa?'* How can I help?

'Is it true?' she asked, holding on to the sill. 'Is he back?'

Jamie narrowed her eyes. 'Is who back?'

'Kråkornas Kung,' she said, as though it was obvious.

'The King of Crows?' Jamie repeated back.

'Yes!' She nodded, gripping the car. The whole thing wobbled slightly. 'Jakob said a boy is dead!' The woman turned and pointed down the street.

Jakob. The hunter that Ohlin had refused to bring in. The one who found the boy.

Goddammit.

'He was killed, by the King of Crows! Just like before!'

'Before?' Jamie shook her head. Cars were beginning to back up behind her, but none dared beep at the blue and white liveried, siren-topped polis car. 'Before when?'

The woman's eyes flitted around and then she lifted her head, her neck folding down into itself. She glanced over her shoulders, then at the sky, eyes wide and mad.

Crow calls began to fill the air, a flock circling above.

The woman covered her head like they were attacking her, pushed herself away from the car, and started running for cover.

Jamie stepped out onto the street, hand on the grip of her pistol, staring into the sky. There were dozens, no, hundreds of them, all spinning and wheeling in a vortex. Right above the cross.

The woman was fleeing, squawking.

'Hey,' Jamie called after her. 'Who's the King of Crows?'

She didn't answer.

'How many people did Jakob tell?'

But she was already gone.

'Fuck,' Jamie muttered, walking out into the intersection. A few cars had stopped, their occupants looking up at the spectacle overhead.

Jamie strode out, hand fastened on her weapon as the cries above rose to fever pitch.

Her boots crunched on something and she stopped, looking down.

She grimaced, her heel squelching as she shifted her weight and lifted her foot, seeing a strange clump of pinks and purples and browns. They looked like … 'Guts,' Jamie muttered, backing up a little to get a better look at what she was standing in.

Tiny guts, entrails, innards, a few thin bones that she'd stepped on. Animal remains, squirrel or rabbit maybe, but there was no sign of the body, just a bloody smear of offal on the asphalt a metre long.

Jamie looked up again, into the eye of the hurricane of black wings above, wincing at their collective scream.

And then they stopped, as suddenly as they started, and dispersed, peeling off in layers and swooping low over the roofs of the surrounding buildings back towards the trees.

Jamie lowered her eyes, heart beating shallow and fast in her chest, and looked at the cars and people surrounding her. They were all standing behind their open doors, watching her, looking at her for some sort of instruction or reassurance.

She cleared her throat, swallowed, and then found her voice. 'Everything's fine,' she said loudly, waving people back into their cars. 'Just some roadkill. Nothing to worry about.' She smiled briefly, turning in a circle so everyone could see just how fine everything was, and then struggled to hold onto it as she headed for her car, the sweat on the underside of her jaw and the back of her neck cool and clammy.

8

JAMIE PULLED in at the high school, unable to shake off the feeling of unease that had settled into her bones, and left her car at the curb in the drop off zone.

The school taught students from first grade, seven-year-olds, right through upper secondary, to the age of eighteen. The students were in their classes now, but she hoped she'd be able to catch a teacher. One of Felix's.

Jamie pushed through the double doors and into the entrance hall. The school was relatively small and, like the rest of Kurrajakk, pretty tired. It had been built in the sixties or seventies, the Soviet Bloc influences apparent, and hadn't been updated much since.

She headed up the front desk, a woman in her forties there tapping away on a computer. She had deep, red hair, almost burgundy, and dark, stark lips. She looked up at Jamie.

'Halla,' she said, glancing at the badge on Jamie's jacket. *'Kan jag hjälpa dig?'* Can I help you?

'Yes,' Jamie said, leaning on the counter. 'I'm looking to speak to a teacher of a certain pupil. Felix Nordahl?'

'Felix Nordahl?' She repeated the name back, raising her eyebrows. 'Can I ask what this is about?'

'An active investigation,' Jamie said diplomatically. 'I just need to check some facts, find out some information, and I was passing by.' She brushed it off, acting casual. There was no need to raise suspicion or come out and say that he was dead. She wasn't technically allowed to, anyway, until the body had been formally identified. Though there was no doubt in her mind now that it was Felix Nordahl in the forest.

The woman began tapping on her keyboard and Jamie stepped away from the counter and arched her back out. It popped and cracked, and she let out a little sigh of relief. The last two years had aged her. But she guessed that with a track record like hers, it wasn't surprising. Her body looked like an Etch A Sketch that had been thrown down the stairs. Crisscrossed with scars from knives, bullets, fists. Kurrajakk was supposed to be a way to leave all that behind. But she guessed she couldn't run from her past any more than she could from her future.

She was just thirty-eight. But she felt ten years older.

And the dog sure as shit didn't help. Panting, growling, scratching at her door in the night. Like living inside a Kubrick flick. She couldn't remember the last time she'd had a decent night's sleep. Not since she'd arrived. And not before, either.

'Inspektör?'

'Yeah,' Jamie said, looking up.

The woman was holding a sheet of paper up for Jamie. 'Here, Felix Nordahl's schedule. But I can see here that he's been marked absent from his first two classes, so I don't think he's in today.'

Jamie took it and turned it over, scanning down the list for whatever classroom was closest.

'What happened to your hand?' the receptionist asked then.

Jamie looked down at the bandage, a few spots of blood beginning to show through. 'Uh, cut it on some broken glass,' she said, lifting the paper. 'Thanks for this.'

She turned and walked away before the woman could ask anything else. The CSTs would be finishing up with the scene soon and the coroner would be removing the body. Then there was Thorsen to contend with. And by the time he got his bearings, she wanted to be out in front of this thing.

Jamie walked quickly through the corridors, pausing at each class that Felix was in. The first three were occupied by other students, but number four was empty apart from a teacher. Jamie knocked and pushed through the door without invitation.

A thin guy with a bald head looked up. He was in a white, short-sleeved shirt that looked unironed, and a grey striped tie whose width told her it was probably older than any of the kids he taught.

'*Hålla,*' she said, holding up her badge. 'Kriminalin-spektör Jamie Johansson, Kurrajakk Polis. Got a minute?'

The teacher stopped marking the papers in front of him and sat up straighter. 'Of course. Is everything alright?' he asked, fixing his tie knot.

Jamie cast her eyes around quickly. By the maps and photos on the wall, this was geography.

'Felix Nordahl,' she said, not wasting any time. 'You teach him?'

He nodded. 'Yes, Felix is in my second-grade class. An eleventh year.'

'You know him well?' Jamie perched on the corner of a table in front of his desk, rested her hands next to her hips, knuckles around the edge.

'Well enough, I think. He's less interested in geography than he is sports or girls, but he does alright.'

Jamie took note of that. Sports and girls. The former rarely caused problems. The latter was a different story. 'Would you say he's a good student?'

'Is there something wrong? Is Felix in some sort of trouble?'

'I can't talk about that,' Jamie said, keeping eye contact, 'but I'd appreciate it if you could answer my questions. It would really help me out.'

He raised a hand. 'Of course, my apologies,' he said politely. 'Anything I can do to help a polis officer … Felix is naturally smart, charismatic. He doesn't try especially hard, but he does well enough. He's got a good mind for facts. I've never had a problem with him. Never heard of him getting into any trouble. He's never caused me any, I know that. He's relatively quiet, but popular enough. He has a few close friends, I think. He sits with a boy and a girl and they're always talking.'

'What are their names?'

'Um,' he said, looking at the desk, eyes wide, as he tried to recall. 'Hugo Westman, and … Olivia Söll … No, Sundgren. Olivia Sundgren.' He nodded, confirming it to himself, and Jamie.

'Great, that's really helpful. Do you know where they might be now? Are you able to look that information up for me?'

'Sure,' he said, smiling at her. He put his pen down and turned to the computer on the corner of his desk. 'So is Felix okay, at least?' He glanced over at Jamie. But she was keeping her face straight.

'As I said,' she repeated, standing, 'I can't say anything at this point. I'm just trying to gather some background information, eliminate some options, get a sense of things, you know?'

'I understand,' he said. But he didn't, because that was the kind of bullshit line that didn't mean anything. There was nothing to understand.

He jabbed the enter button, then squinted at the screen. 'It looks like Hugo and Olivia are … oh, they're in the same class. English Language. E-12.'

'Thanks, you've been a big help,' Jamie said, nodding and heading for the door.

'Wait, inspektör,' he said, getting out of his chair.

Jamie turned to see him walking towards her.

'It's Mr Ledman,' he said, rubbing his palms on his thighs awkwardly. 'If you need any more help, I mean.'

'Thanks, Mr Ledman, I'll bear that in mind.' She reached out for the handle.

'It's just, I mean …' He trailed off.

Jamie had one hand on the door handle now and was staring blankly back at him. 'What is it, Mr Ledman?'

'I don't know if this is inappropriate, or anything,' he began, grinning nervously, 'but I haven't seen you before – around town, I mean. And there isn't often a new face in Kurrajakk, so I was wondering if, you know, one day, you might let me buy you a cup of coffee, as a welcome to the—'

'Yes, Mr Ledman,' she interrupted, offering the briefest, most platonic smile she could muster, 'it is inappropriate.' She let the smile slip intentionally. 'And I'm also here in the course of an official investigation—'

'But … after?' he asked, ever hopeful, holding his hands palm-up like he'd just finished a tap routine.

'I'll call you if I need any more information,' she said, avoiding the question. 'Thank you for your time.'

'But you don't have my number,' he said, following her to the door.

'I'll find it,' she called over her shoulder, making sure not to look back.

Jesus Christ, of all the classrooms she could have chosen.

Jamie sighed, feeling his eyes on her, and then upped her pace, hoping to hell the next classroom was a very long way away.

9

JAMIE KNOCKED ON E-12, thankful it was on a different floor, and caught the eye of the teacher standing in front of the board. She kept speaking, meeting Jamie's eye with a questioning look, and then stopped when Jamie held her badge up to the glass. She told the class she'd be a second and came into the hallway.

She looked terse, an older woman with thick hair, dyed and side-parted into something that looked like it could be screwed off.

'Yes?' she said quickly.

'Kriminalinspektör Jamie Johansson,' Jamie said, putting her hands on her hips.

'Inger Holm,' the woman replied.

'I need to speak to two of your students, Ms Holm. Hugo Westman and Olivia Sundgren.'

The woman seemed surprised. 'Hugo and Olivia? What did they do?' She looked genuinely concerned.

'Nothing,' Jamie said, shaking her head. 'I just need to speak to them for a few minutes. Do you mind if I pull them out of class?'

'Is this to do with Felix Nordahl?'

Jamie narrowed her eyes a little. 'How did you know that?'

'The three of them are always together. And Hugo and Olivia didn't know where Felix was this morning,' she sighed, 'and that in itself was strange. So you arriving, asking about them …' She shrugged a little, then shook her head. 'Is he alright? Did he do something wrong?'

'I can't talk about it,' Jamie answered truthfully. 'I'm just trying to build a timeline here.' She was trying to sound as casual as possible, but the woman in front of her was clearly intelligent. And perceptive.

Holm nodded slowly. 'There's just a few minutes left of class, would you mind if we finished, or is it pressing?' She watched Jamie closely.

Jamie smiled back. 'No, it's fine. Finish up. But could you ask Hugo and Olivia to stay behind? Is your classroom in use after this?'

'It's not,' she said, not seemingly thrilled with her students being questioned in her classroom by the police. But she didn't deny Jamie. 'I'll do that. When the other students have gone, you can come in. I don't want to cause a stir.' She paused, eyeing Jamie. 'You know how teenagers can be. I'd rather there not be any more drama than necessary.'

Jamie nodded. 'Of course. Thank you.'

Ms Holm turned around and went back, her apology to the class echoing out to Jamie before the door closed. She let out a long breath and walked in a tight circle. Drama. Damn. If Jakob was already telling people, spreading rumours about the … *King Of Crows* – whoever the hell that was supposed to be – then it wouldn't be long before the whole town knew. Word spread fast here. Like wildfire. Much as she hated that saying. And once news of the killing got out, it would consume the entire town.

Before that happened, before people started talking and conjecturing and getting themselves into a frenzy, she needed to know where Felix Nordahl was before he was killed and who might have wanted to kill him. If the killer got wind of the body being found before Jamie could close in on them, then they might run.

The bell sounded overhead and before Jamie could get out of the way, a flood of body-sprayed teenagers with trendy hairstyles swept over her.

She shouldered and swam through the crowd, keeping her hand firmly on her pistol, until she reached the wall.

They flowed past, laughing and talking, and then as fast as they'd come, they were gone. Jamie blinked a few times, got her bearings, and then crossed the hall to Ms Holm's classroom and entered.

Sitting in the middle of the room were two teens. Both around seventeen. The boy was Hugo Westman. Tall, thin, with a chin lined with tiny spots and scraggly hairs. The girl was average height, with long, dark, thick and wavy hair. She had strong features, and near enough glared at Jamie as she entered.

Ms Holm was standing on the far side of the room, arms folded.

'I'll remain here for your questions,' she said, answering before Jamie even asked. 'This is simply an informal interview, correct? You won't mind if I stay just to make sure my students are being represented in the absence of their parents or legal counsel – they are technically minors, after all.'

Jamie hated having the law quoted back to her. Almost as much as she hated the assumption that she was about to lay into these kids in some way.

'Of course not,' she said politely. 'As you said, this is just an informal conversation.'

'Where's Felix?' the girl asked suddenly.

Olivia Sundgren. Jamie looked at her for a second, then deflected. 'We're in the early stages of an investigation currently, and I'm not able to divulge any specific details. But I'd really appreciate your assistance in order to give us the best chance of bringing it to a swift resolution.'

She glared at Jamie unabashedly now.

Jamie didn't like lying to them, and she certainly didn't like withholding the fact that their best friend was dead. 'When was the last time you heard from Felix Nordahl?'

'Yesterday afternoon,' Olivia answered quickly. 'Where is he now?'

'Was that in person or over the phone?'

'Text.'

'What was the conversation about?'

Olivia looked at Holm now. Jamie glanced at her too, just in time to see the woman give a subtle shake of the head.

Olivia sat upright. 'I don't think I have to answer that.'

Jamie's nostrils flared as she drew in a breath.

She leaned back against Holm's desk, massaging her bandaged hand. It was throbbing.

'No, you're right, you don't have to. You have your right to privacy. But I'd really appreciate it if you would tell me. It would be really helpful to …' Jamie trailed off, looking at Hugo Westman now, who was staring at his crotch. His hands were down there, too, tapping away on his phone.

He was licking his lips, mouth slightly parted, breathing quickened.

Fuck.

Jamie knew it was coming a moment before it did.

His head shot up, eyes wide. 'Is Felix dead?' he demanded.

Wildfire.

Jamie held fast, considered her options.

Olivia looked down at his screen, read the messages coming through there, then turned on Jamie too. 'He asked you a question,' she snapped, rising out of her chair, hands on the table. Her voice was shaking, eyes filling.

Jamie's throat tightened. 'Early this morning, a body was discovered, which we have reason to believe ...' – her voice caught in her throat a little – 'may belong to Felix Nordahl.'

'He's dead?' Olivia practically yelled. 'And you're just sitting there, asking us when the last time we spoke to him was, pretending like he's still alive, while you – while you ... knew ...' She broke then, shattered into a sobbing mess, and sank back into her chair. She turned, burying her head in Hugo's shoulder. His bottom lip was quivering, hands in fists in front of him as he stared at Jamie.

Fury. Fury in his eyes. She knew that look. She hadn't killed Felix, but there was no one else there.

Ms Holm walked towards Jamie. 'I think this is over,' she said abruptly, showing Jamie the door. 'If you have any further questions, you can direct them to the school or to Hugo and Olivia's parents, and I'm sure they'll be glad to arrange something.' She had one hand on Jamie's arm now, the other pointing at the exit, herding and pushing in equal measure.

Jamie let herself be guided out into the corridor.

Ms Holm closed the door behind them. 'Is it true? Is Felix Nordahl dead?' she asked, keeping her voice low.

The corridor was empty. A break, she thought.

'I ...' Jamie began, sighing and dropping the diplomacy. 'We haven't had an official confirmation of his identity yet, but I'm fairly certain that the body we found belongs to Felix Nordahl.'

'Fairly certain?'

Jamie met her eye. 'It's him.'

'What happened?'

'I can't discuss that.'

Ms Holm snorted. 'When I go back in there to console those two kids, whose best friend has just died – which they had to find out from God knows who – what am I supposed to tell them?'

Jamie gritted her teeth. 'You can tell them that … that we're treating Felix's death as suspicious, and gathering as much information as we can before we release any more details.'

'Murder?'

'It looks like,' Jamie said. The woman was relentless.

Holm nodded. 'Suspects?'

What was she, a detective? 'As I said, it's still early in the investigation. We're fact-finding, compiling evidence, constructing a timeline.'

Holm shook her head dismissively. 'And calling in help, I hope? A murder in Kurrajakk? It's unheard of.'

'We're more than capable of handling the situation,' Jamie said, half diplomatic, half sick and goddamn tired of having her competence questioned.

The woman's eyes burned into Jamie. 'Hubris will help no one, inspektör.'

Jamie let out a long breath, tried to let go of the frustration building in her guts. 'You can tell Hugo and Olivia that I'll be contacting their parents in due course, and they will be expected to come to the station for questioning.'

'I'll see that they are informed. And *prepared*.'

Another snipe? Jamie needed to get out of there. The

paths ahead were sprawling and splitting, and the town was gearing up to tear itself apart. She could feel it in the air.

'Thanks,' Jamie said, giving a quick nod. 'I appreciate the cooperation.' She headed off then, could feel Holm's eyes on her back.

She slowed, paused, something occurring to her, and looked back. 'Have you lived in Kurrajakk long?'

'My whole life,' she answered, looking at Jamie questioningly. 'Why?'

'Have you ever heard of *Kråkornas Kung?*' Jamie took a step closer.

Holm seemed a little taken aback. 'I, um, yes,' she said. 'It's a local legend. A ghost story my grandmother used to tell me – that mothers told their children in the old days.' She held her finger up. 'Don't go into the forest on your own, or *Kråkornas Kung* will get you.'

Jamie rolled that over in her head.

'Of course, it was just a story – back then we still had wolves, bears moving through these woods. It was just to scare children, to keep them safe.'

'So you never heard anything about the King of Crows being ...'

'Real?' She raised an eyebrow. 'No. I think a half-crow, half-man creature that stalks the forests at night, flying at the head of a murder borders on the fantastic, don't you think?'

'A murder?' Jamie asked.

'A murder of crows. A flock. It's what it's called.'

Jamie sighed. 'Perfect. Well, thank you anyway. You've been a big help.'

'Why do you ask?'

Jamie offered a shrug. 'No reason, just something someone said.'

'Oh,' Holm said, nodding slowly. 'Well … good luck, then.'

Jamie gave another nod, keen to be out of there.

She turned, walking fast.

A murder of crows.

You couldn't write this shit.

10

BY THE TIME Jamie got back outside, the wind had picked up.

It was cold and chaotic, blowing in turbulent little gusts that pulled her hair all around her head. She shielded her eyes from it, brushing it over her ears as she headed towards the curb, stopping when she spotted Thorsen leaning against her car, arms folded.

His was parked behind – a mid-model BMW with big, sporty alloys. It'd be useless come November when the snow started piling up. She hoped he wouldn't be there that long.

He was standing with his feet crossed, heavy charcoal-coloured woollen coat billowing around his legs. He watched her come.

She said nothing as she approached.

'They cleared the scene,' Thorsen said as she got closer.

Jamie lifted her chin in acknowledgement but didn't speak. She couldn't even be bothered to get worked up about them not calling her like she asked.

'I couldn't get hold of the station,' he added. 'I drove by, but it was all closed up.'

'Yep,' Jamie offered, stopping. Thorsen was leaning against the driver's door.

'I can't get hold of Ohlin, either,' he added.

'No surprise there.'

Thorsen drew a sharp breath. 'I checked into you.'

'Great. You mind?' Jamie pointed at the drivers' door.

He didn't move. 'I called down Stockholm, I know a few people down there.'

'I bet.'

'Spoke to your old partner, Anders Wiik?' He inflected it like Jamie should have been impressed by his detecting skills.

'Uh-huh.'

'He was, uh,' Thorsen began, looking down for a second, 'shall we say, *impassioned,* about you.'

Jamie found that hard to believe. If there was one thing Wiik wasn't, it was prone to emotional responses.

'He gave me a *brief* overview of your experience-set.'

Jamie held back a smirk. 'Bet that was a pleasant conversation.'

'He's convinced I'd be lucky to have you as a partner.'

She knew Wiik. They'd worked well together. Had something good going. But their paths had diverged, they wanted different things. Still, he was one of the few people in the world Jamie actually trusted. And liked. And she was fairly certain she could visualise how that phone call had gone. And that there'd been a lot more expletives than Thorsen was letting on. Wiik didn't take well to guys like him.

'Honestly,' Jamie said, 'I don't give a shit what you think – of me, or this town, or anything else. A kid is dead, so you'll have to excuse me if proving my competence to you isn't high on my priorities list right now.'

Thorsen's lip curled. 'He said you wouldn't take any shit.'

'That much he was right about, now would you mind moving?'

He stepped out of the way for her. 'You know,' he said as she climbed in, 'two heads are better than one.'

'So I've heard.'

His hand shot out, stopped the door from closing.

Jamie sighed.

'And if we've got no help here, we should work together, don't you think?'

Jamie laughed now. 'Maybe you should have thought about that before you tried to hijack my crime scene.'

'I was under clear instructions,' Thorsen said defensively, his knuckles whitening around the door as he fought Jamie to keep it open.

'Oh, Thorsen,' Jamie said, shaking her head, 'that's something a big-city detective would say.' She met his eyes now. 'And you're a long way from the city.'

He released the door, grinning to himself, at his own words parroted back to him. 'That's good,' he said, 'funny.'

'I thought so,' Jamie answered, and then slammed the door. She cranked the ignition, wheeled out of the car park, and left Thorsen standing in the rear-view.

He was right, two heads were better than one, but not if they spent the whole time butting together.

An hour ago he was convinced he could solve this himself, had told Jamie to get the hell out of his way.

Well, now he had his wish.

Except he didn't know this town. He didn't know Kurra-jakk, or the people, or what made this place special, and strange. And dangerous.

But Jamie did. She'd spent four months here, learning it, learning its ways.

And she had the trail now.

She just needed to see where it led.

Jamie pulled in at the side of the road just beyond town, and killed the engine. She grabbed her work bag from the passenger seat and got out. She needed space to think, and she didn't want to risk being intercepted by anyone else raving about *Kråkornas Kung.* She scoffed a little and shook her head, dumping the satchel onto the bonnet of the SUV. She pulled out her laptop and opened it, resting it on the warm steel.

Jamie laid her phone down next to it, activated the hotspot, and stopped, looking around.

The wind was still blowing, but she was sheltered by the trees on the side of the road. There was no one around, no sound except the creaking of the waving pines, and yet, she felt eyes on her.

She scanned the tree line, saw nothing except vertical shafts of black shadow between the gnarled trunks. Then she spotted them, the glinting back eyes, like little lumps of jet, staring down from the canopy. Crows. Watching her from the treetops. Dozens. Silent. Like sentinels at the edge of the forest.

She shook her head again, told herself to get real, focus. Jamie pulled up a fresh browser and headed for Facebook. A seventeen-year-old kid, smart, athletic, close friends, handsome. He'd be popular. And what seventeen-year-old wasn't all over social media these days?

She searched for Felix Nordahl and found his profile quickly. It was set to private, but she could see his profile photos. The first was of him playing football, a snap from the sidelines. She clicked through to the next one – a picture of him at a party somewhere. Maybe a little drunk. But hardly incriminating. He was, by the look of it, in a field, or maybe the woods. No one else in the background. She checked the date. May this year. Next one. He looked different, younger. A photo taken in the mirror. He was throwing up a gang sign with his other hand, pouting at the camera. It was dated three years ago. And that was it.

Shit.

She clicked his friends list. Just shy of 200. Not a lot, but Kurrajakk was a small town. She found Olivia Sundgren quickly. Her profile was also set to private. And the only photo she had was her profile one, which showed her over a birthday cake with a sparkler in her mouth like a Parisian cigarette holder. She was staring off to the left.

Jamie sighed, went hunting for Hugo Westman. She couldn't even find a profile for him.

The laptop she was on was her own. They didn't even have them at the station, and the desktop there was older than the car she was driving. And that was saying something.

She didn't have the manpower for this, or the software. She needed to call in the cavalry.

Jamie lifted her phone and scrolled through her phone book. When she found the number she wanted, she dialled, listened to it ring.

'*Hej,*' came the answer, bright as always. 'Jamie,' she said.

'Hallberg,' Jamie replied, already feeling relieved. 'How are you?' She'd worked with Julia Hallberg in Stockholm. She'd been Wiik's partner before Jamie had arrived, and even her partner for a while. She was one of the smartest people Jamie knew, and hands down the best researcher. It's why Europol had wasted no time snapping her up. If there was anyone who could dig up something useful on a couple of social-media reclusive teenagers, it was her. Jamie just hoped she had the time.

'I'm good. It's great to hear from you,' she said. 'What do you need?'

Jamie laughed nervously. 'What makes you think I need something? Can't I just call to catch up?' She'd always seen Hallberg as a girl – ten years her junior, full of enthusiasm and energy. It was like Jamie was looking into a time-warped mirror. And now, just four months after they'd parted ways, it was like she was speaking to a whole other person. Like Hallberg had suddenly grown up, flung herself into seriousness and adulthood.

'You could ...' Hallberg said slowly. 'But I figured you would have done that by now if you intended to.'

'Yeah, sorry about that,' Jamie said. 'Things have been ...' She looked around the empty road. It'd been five minutes and a car hadn't driven by. 'Hectic ...'

If Hallberg knew that was a lie, she said nothing about it. 'Honestly, don't worry – what can I help you with?'

'You sure you've got the time?'

'For you, always,' Hallberg said.

Damn, way to make her feel like a piece of shit, Hallberg.

'I've got a seventeen-year-old kid turned up dead – nasty one.'

Hallberg listened intently.

'Taken into the woods, hacked up ... bird stuffed in his mouth. Choked, or suffocated, it looks like.'

'Jesus,' Hallberg said. 'I thought you picked that place because it was quiet.'

'It was supposed to be,' Jamie sighed.

'Okay, so what can I do?'

'I've checked out their socials, but the victim and his friends have their accounts set to private, and I'm spread thin.

I need to know what they've been doing, who they've been with. Any information I can get.'

'No problem,' she answered. 'Just send me their names, I'll get right on it.'

'Just like that?' Jamie was impressed.

'Well, I say *I* – I'll have one of my guys get right on it. I'm snowed under here.'

Since when did Hallberg have 'guys'? Now she was really impressed. She was all grown up. 'What're you working on?'

Hallberg chuckled through closed lips. 'Come on, Jamie, you know how it goes, I can't tell you that.'

'Right, right,' Jamie said. 'You happy, at least?' She stared out into the mottled grey sky, drowning in the solitude of the place.

'Yeah,' she said, 'I am. Thanks – I wouldn't be here without you.'

'Oh, no, I didn't mean it like that,' Jamie said, turning around and leaning on the car.

'I know,' Hallberg answered. 'Just wanted you to know that.'

Jamie bit her lip.

They were quiet for a moment.

The crows continued to watch from above.

'Okay,' Hallberg said then. 'I've got to get back. But send me those names, and I'll have something for you as soon as I can.'

'Will do. You're doing me a big favour here, I really appreciate it.'

'Of course, and Jamie?'

'Yeah?'

'Look after yourself.'

'Always do,' Jamie answered.

'Yeah, I don't know if that's true. Just be careful.'

'Always am.'

'Okay, now I know that one's a lie.' She laughed, said, 'bye,' then hung up.

Jamie lowered the phone and stared up at the black, beady eyes above her, wondered if a gunshot would echo all the way back to town from here.

And then she decided that she should probably save the bullets.

After all, they were just harmless birds, right?

11

JAMIE WAS on her way back to town when her phone started ringing. She picked up, not recognising the number.

'Hålla, Kriminalinspektör Jamie Johansson,' she said.

'This is Lovisa Nordahl,' came a curt, shaky reply.

Felix's mother. Christian Nordahl's wife.

Jamie waited for her to speak again.

'I'm … I … Christian said …' She started, her voice crumbling. 'What did … Is Felix … is he … ?'

Jamie clenched her jaw, downshifted, and put her foot on the floor. The revs climbed, the SUV hauling itself back into the low-slung outskirts of town. 'Mrs Nordhal,' Jamie said, 'Are you at home?'

'I … . yes,' she answered quietly.

'I'll be there in a few minutes.' Jamie hung up, flicked on her blue lights, weaved around a slow-moving estate car, and then swung the SUV through the cross in town, back towards the Nordahl's house. She kept the siren silent. No need to cause any more panic.

Inside two minutes, she was stopping outside the Nordahl's house and walking up the front path.

The car that had been on the drive before was now gone, but the front door was open.

Jamie paused, leaned inside, looking into the dim interior. She knocked lightly on the frame. 'Mrs Nordahl?' she called softly, her hand finding the grip of her pistol.

A woman appeared around the corner, in nurse's scrubs, holding a tissue under her nose in one hand, her cheeks bright red, eyes swollen. 'Inspektör?' she asked, holding her elbow with the other.

Jamie nodded, released her gun, and stepped inside. 'Mrs Nordahl,' she said, moving slowly. 'I'm so sorry.'

She shook her head, then sobbed.

Jamie pushed the door closed behind her. The coroner wouldn't have managed to get the body back to Lulea yet, which meant that they wouldn't have been called to make a formal identification. The lab would have had to speak to Jamie first – or Thorsen – and then they'd call the Nordahls to let them know. But she doubted Thorsen had already had word, then been and done that. So where Christian Nordahl was, Jamie didn't know. But his wife was here, had come here from work. He'd called her, she'd rushed back, they'd argued, he'd left. That was Jamie's guess. They'd both be angry. No, that word wouldn't even come close. They'd be in ruin. Jamie could see the woman in front of her was. A shell of whoever she'd been before the phone call that would change her life forever.

Jamie stepped into the living room for the second time, spotted her cup on the counter where she'd left it before.

She heard Lovisa Nordahl walk in behind her, and turned to see her standing just a few feet away.

'Did you see him?' she asked, eyes fixed on Jamie, searching her face.

There was a time for diplomacy, and there was a time to be a human being. 'Yes,' she said. 'I saw him.'

'And he was …' She began to shudder.

Jamie nodded. 'I'm sorry.'

Her jaw was quivering, but she held herself together, clenching the tissue in her fist, allowing the tears to roll freely. She was a nurse, faced death every day, but nothing could prepare you for the death of a child. Of a brother. Of a father.

'How did he … die?' The word sounded strange coming from his mother.

'Right now,' Jamie said softly, 'we're treating his death as suspicious.' We. That was rich. It was just her. There was no one else. 'I'm trying to put together a timeline for where Felix was yesterday. I spoke to his friends, who said they heard from him yesterday afternoon. And he was found early this morning, and was likely …' She searched for another word for *killed*. 'It was likely that the incident leading to his death occurred sometime during the night.' She took a breath, watching Lovisa Nordahl take it all in. 'We've had a forensic team from Lulea go over the scene, and a coroner is taking Felix back to Lulea as we speak. Once they arrive, they'll let us know, and we'll be in touch. You'll have to formally identify Felix, but I can arrange for someone to pick you up and—'

'No, no,' she said, shaking her head. 'That's … that will be okay … just … what happened? Tell me.'

Jamie was glad for that part to be out of the way. 'We're not sure what happened to Felix yet, but we'll know more after they've run some tests, investigated a little further. I'll keep you updated every step of the way, though. Okay?'

She dabbed away her tears now. 'Thank you,' she said, sniffing.

'I'm sorry to press, but is there anything you can tell me about where Felix was last night? Who he might have been with?'

She shook her head. 'No, I don't know – I was working from twelve until twelve. When I came home, I went straight to bed, as I was back in work this morning.'

'Do you know if he was in the house when you got back?' Jamie asked hopefully. Yesterday afternoon to *sometime during the night* was a big, vague window to be working with. And Kurrajakk wasn't *that* small of a town.

'I don't know, I didn't check,' she said. 'Christian said that he went out last night – about seven, but that he didn't hear from Felix before he went to bed.'

'And what time was that?' Jamie asked, filing all of this away in her head.

Her phone started buzzing in her pocket.

She ignored it.

'I don't know – he usually goes up about ten, ten-thirty.'

'Is it usual for Felix to be out late?'

Nordahl nodded. 'Yes, we're quite lenient with it. He's usually very good – doesn't come home drunk, is never loud, he's never caused any problems at all. His teachers have always said so, too, that he's a nice boy. Who would want to hurt him?'

That was something Jamie didn't have an answer for.

Her phone buzzed again.

She took stock of what she knew. 'Where is your husband?'

'He went out for a drive, to clear his head,' Lovisa Nordahl said. 'He'll be back soon.'

That wasn't uncommon. It was difficult to face a trauma like this, difficult to face each other, too. This would test their relationship, their marriage. Probably break it. It did most.

'He told my colleague at the station that Felix went out yesterday evening, but his friends – Hugo Westman and Olivia Sundgren – do you know them?'

Lovisa Nordahl nodded.

'They said they hadn't heard from him since yesterday afternoon. Is there anyone else he could have been with? Anyone else he's likely to have been with?'

'I … I don't know,' Lovisa said, the realisation dawning on her face that she didn't actually know that much about her son. 'I've only ever seen Hugo and Olivia, heard him talk about them.'

'Did he have a girlfriend maybe? Felix was a handsome boy, he couldn't have been short of options.'

She smiled weakly, then shook her head. 'No, he never mentioned anything, never brought anyone home. He was more focused on sports, school, than that. He wanted to go to the city – Stockholm or Gothenburg, to university next year.'

Jamie's phone buzzed again. Shorter this time, a text or email.

She put her hand on her thigh to quieten it.

'Okay,' Jamie said, 'thank you, that's a big help. I'll have some more questions, but I was wondering if you'd mind if I looked around Felix's room? He didn't have his phone on him, no wallet, or any identification, so I was hoping I could check around, and …' Jamie looked over towards the stairs.

His mother nodded. 'Yes, yes, of course,' she said, following Jamie's eyes. 'It's the top of the stairs on the right.'

'Thanks,' Jamie said. 'I won't be long.' She pulled her phone from her pocket and checked what all the buzzing was about. Two missed calls from Hallberg and an email from her. Jamie clicked the email and opened it.

. . .

Jamie –

Tried but couldn't get through. Looked into Felix Nordahl's account. Facebook hasn't been updated in weeks, but found a linked private Instagram, got around the block. Most recent photos attached.

Nothing on Westman or Sundgren yet. Will keep you updated.

Hallberg

Jamie smiled to herself. Hallberg was good.

She opened the attachments and scrolled through them, stopping on the stairs. They were timestamped from within the last week, newest to oldest. Four pictures. One was a photo of Felix standing on a rock, silhouetted against the setting sun. Two days. The next two were of Felix in the forest. There was a fire in the background, other kids around, drinks in hand. In the first one, he had his arms around Hugo Westman and Olivia Sundgren. They all looked to be having a good time. Felix was in the middle, Hugo was taking the photo.

And the next one, he was staring right into the camera, with Olivia Sundgren kissing him on the cheek, her face screwed up.

It looked late, they were lit by the firelight.

They were both dated Saturday night just gone. It was now Tuesday morning.

Jamie paused, staring at the image.

Felix Nordahl was sweating, grinning wildly, eyes wide, his pupils massive.

She knew a kid on drugs when she saw one.

Her eyes lingered on that photo for a second or two longer, then she moved on to the last one.

This was different. A different girl. The lighting was dim – it was close to dark. They were out of town somewhere. It looked like the hills. Lots of exposed rock. There was a girl in his arms – she looked younger. Fifteen, sixteen maybe. She had her eyes closed, was languishing in his arms as he pressed his lips to the side of her head. He looked emotional, eyes wistful and clear, staring over her head. She looked sad, lips pursed.

This one was dated a week ago.

Jamie couldn't make much sense of the photo without context. She'd ask Hallberg about the caption later. For now, she needed to keep going.

Jamie stowed her phone and carried on up. She'd call Hallberg back when she could. Before she'd checked the email, she hadn't really had much idea what she was looking for, but now she did.

The door creaked open and Jamie was faced with a typical teenager's bedroom. A single bed on the right-hand side, a dark curtain hanging over the window. Laundry all over the floor. A plate with some leftover food on it. The smell of a teenage boy, all sweat and breath and stale deodorant.

Jamie stepped inside, pulling gloves from her pocket, and put them on. She opened the curtains first, letting light flood into the room.

She turned back then, taking in the rest. There was a desk opposite the bed, next to a wardrobe. On top of the desk, there was a laptop. Jamie opened it, was met with a lock screen. She'd have no chance cracking it here. It would need to be removed, taken to Lulea, and brutalised in their crime lab. Jamie moved on, no point wasting time now. She found school books, notepads, paper. The drawers were rife with old school stuff and electronics – Gameboys and phone chargers. She sighed. Nothing.

The wardrobe was filled with clothes and Jamie patted down the pockets of the jackets, found some old receipts from the store in town, a lighter – she reminded herself to ask if he smoked, but she doubted it – at least not cigarettes. Maybe a joint while he was out with his friends. The toxicology would tell her if there was anything in his system.

Jamie moved on, going methodically, moving the dirty laundry on the floor with her foot. Nothing stuck out – other than the fact that teenage boys weren't clean creatures.

The bed next. She pulled back the covers, looking for anything to suggest he'd been having sex there. How serious was this thing with the girl from the photo? Jamie saw the telltale signs of activity, but that told her nothing. He was a teenage boy, after all. Those kinds of marks didn't tell her whether a partner had been there with him.

She went to the bedside drawers now, pulled the top open. Socks. She rummaged through them, found what she expected to. A couple of condoms in the bottom. Was there a wastebasket in here? She saw one by the door, went over, stared down into it, grimaced a little, and then knelt, lifting a few tissues out, moving some crumpled up paper, until she found a little parcel of toilet roll the same size and shape as a used condom stuffed back in the wrapper and tossed away.

Okay, so he *was* sleeping with her. Or someone else. But his parents didn't know. Odd. Why not tell them? Lovisa Nordahl was out at work a lot. It'd be easy to get past her. She'd have to ask Christian Nordahl if he knew. And if he did, why he was keeping it from his wife.

Too early to make any assumptions.

The other two drawers in the bedside unit were uninteresting. Underpants in the middle one. Knick-knacks in the bottom. Old stocking fillers that had no home anywhere else, and odds and ends that would clutter up any space they were put in. So they were stuffed in here instead. Who didn't have a drawer like that?

Jamie stood back, fearing that the room was going to offer her nothing at all.

Her eyes moved upwards then, to the bookshelf above the bed. It ran the entire length of the wall, was filled with books. On the left it was fiction – teen fantasy books, some thrillers and military action books. SAS soldiers and CIA operatives out to save the world. Her eyes traced them for anything that stuck out. Then she reached the sports section – autobiographies, memoirs, greatest moments in sports, encyclopaedic stuff. He was into sports. It made sense.

Her hope waned further.

Then came the school stuff. Lined up. English – Shakespeare plays, a poetry anthology. Maths – algebra, trigonometry. Science – biology, chemistry, physics … Tomes. Big books. So big they practically hung off the end of the shelf. Jamie stared up at them. They were in the far right corner. The top corner of the room. On your right as you walked in. You'd have to close the door and turn around to look up at them. Jamie checked the soles of her boots for dirt and then stepped up onto the bed, drawing level with the spines.

She looked at them more closely, could see that the layer of dust present on the other school

books was wiped off these. They'd been moved recently. Jamie reached up and over, running her hand down the tops, back towards the wall, pausing when she felt space.

The other books were butted right up to the wall itself. These ones weren't.

She hooked her fingers behind, pulled the books forward

slightly, heard whatever was pinned there slump down onto the shelf.

Jamie removed the books carefully, heart fast in her chest, and dropped them onto the bed. They landed heavily, bouncing, making the whole bed move up and down.

But Jamie was still, eyes fixed on the find in front of her.

There, lying on the shelf, were three rolls of banknotes bound by rubber bands. And next to them, a bag of red pills in a ziplock bag.

And not just a few, either.

Enough to sell.

Enough to make real money with.

Jamie held her breath.

Enough to get killed for.

12

JAMIE DESCENDED THE STAIRS, the rolls of banknotes in the pocket of her jacket, the bag of pills hidden, pinned under her arm. Until she knew the lay of the land here, she didn't want Felix Nordahl's mother to make any assumptions. And she definitely didn't want to suggest her son was dealing drugs – even though that's exactly what she thought.

When you found a bag with hundreds of pills in it and rolls of small notes hidden in a seventeen-year-old's bedroom, there weren't really a lot of other things it could be.

Jamie cleared her throat as she hit the bottom step, and Lovisa Nordahl rose from her stool at the kitchen counter. She wiped off her cheeks and came over, running her tear-soaked hands down her thighs.

'Did you find anything?' she asked.

Jamie offered a brief shake of the head. 'Nothing to suggest where Felix might have been or who he was with.'

'I'll … I'll have a look through when I can,' she said, nodding.

'Don't push yourself,' Jamie replied, swallowing. Damn, in any other city, there'd be grief councillors she'd refer her to, there'd be officers who could call in and check on her, there'd be a hundred options. But now, all she could do was just say, 'and call me if you need anything. I'll come right over. I can't imagine how hard this must be.' She reached out, put a hand on Lovisa Nordahl's shoulder. 'I'll find out who did this.'

She nodded again, lips bunching into a quivering purse.

Jamie exhaled, pulled her phone from her pocket. She didn't want to ask, but she couldn't leave without knowing. She held it up for Lovisa, the photo of Felix and the mystery girl on her screen. 'Do you recognise this girl?'

She squinted through puffy eyes. 'When was this taken?' she asked.

'A week ago.'

Lovisa Nordahl shook her head. 'I don't. No.' Her expression became conflicted. 'Did he … is that … Felix had a girlfriend?' She shook her head and looked at Jamie for answers.

She had none.

'I've got to get back,' Jamie said, pushing her phone into her pocket. 'There are questions I still need answered.' She began moving towards the door. 'But I'll update you as soon as I have anything. Is there anyone I can call in the meanwhile, to come over? Is there somewhere I can take you?'

'No, it's okay, my mother lives …' She pointed up the street. 'Not far. I'll call her and … and tell her.' Her lips began shaking again, the tears coming.

'You have my number,' Jamie said, looking away. 'Call if you need anything.'

And then she was gone, out of the house and down the path.

She couldn't stay any longer. There were threads to pull on, and a crater left in the lives of everyone Felix knew.

And it was Jamie's job to fill it.

. . .

She made a judgement call. Jamie needed to go back to the station, put the drugs in evidence, get the crime lab to come and pick up a sample, but first, she needed to know who the girl was.

She pin-balled back towards the school, driving fast.

She blinked, cars and buildings flashing past, her vision blurring suddenly.

She blinked again, dragging the back of her hand across her eyes, feeling her knuckles coming away wet, a stabbing pain in the back of her throat.

Jamie balled up her fist and beat it on the top of the wheel. The pain bolted up her arm and she ground her teeth. Spots of blood began to soak through the bandage.

Jamie swore and rolled down the window, breathing through it.

By the time she got to the school, the wind had dried her eyes and a cool anger had taken hold.

Jamie dumped the pills and the money into her satchel, closed the flap and stepped from the car, heading for the front door. Thankfully, Thorsen had left, so she was alone.

She checked her watch. It was after midday now, and by the students she could see milling around, walking to and from the building, sitting on the grass, eating, she guessed it was lunchtime.

Jamie weaved through the bodies, most not even noticing her, a few seeing the emblazoned jacket and moving out of the way.

Inside, the interior was warm with breath. She headed for the front desk again. The same woman with the dark red hair and harsh lips looked up. 'Back again?' she said lightly, offering a small smile.

Jamie nodded. 'I need to see a teacher – Ms Holm. She teaches English.'

The receptionist looked apprehensive.

Jamie did probably look pretty determined. 'She's not in trouble, I just need to ask something I forgot earlier.'

'Oh,' she said, laughing it off. 'Of course, she's probably in the staff room as it's lunchtime.'

'And where's that?'

The woman leaned up over the desk and pointed down the main corridor. 'All the way to the bottom, take a left. It's on your right, you can't miss it.'

Jamie thanked her and started walking.

'Inspektör?' the receptionist called.

Jamie paused and back-pedalled.

'Is it true …' the woman began, 'that a student is …' she lowered her voice, looking more interested in getting an inside scoop than concerned that a teenager might be dead. She trailed off, registering the look in Jamie's eyes.

'Straight down and then left, yeah?' Jamie confirmed.

She nodded sheepishly in response. 'It'll be on your right.'

Jamie knocked the top of the reception desk and set off for a second time.

The corridor was busy with students. The older boys were mostly taller than her, the girls the same height. They looked her up and down as she passed. The pretty girls, the popular girls. Jamie set her jaw, her make-up-less face, her plaited, low-maintenance hair, her unisex long sleeve and bomber jacket prime fodder for their judgement.

It was like university all over again.

And the boys were even worse, leering, feigning offering their wrists to be cuffed, looking her up and down in another way, whistling, winking.

She kept her head down and ploughed on, hand on her hem, pulled tight over the grip of her pistol. She took no chances. Not ever.

Jamie forged through the throng towards the staff room, hung a left at the end of the corridor, and found the room.

She didn't bother knocking, just pushed straight in, and searched for Ms Holm. She spotted her at a table in the back, with two other teachers, and headed over.

'Ms Holm,' Jamie said, appearing at her shoulder.

The other two teachers on the table looked up. Holm turned around to face Jamie.

'Inspektör?' She put her knife and fork down, wiped her mouth with a napkin. 'What can I do for you?'

'I was hoping I might ask you another question. Some new information has come to light.'

'Of course.' Ms Holm gestured to an empty chair and the other two teachers leaned in to get a better handle on the situation.

Jamie wasted no time, sat, and pushed her phone across the table to Ms Holm, the photo of Felix and the girl already on screen.

'Do you recognise the girl with Felix in this photograph? Is she a student here?'

Ms Holm picked up the phone and studied it. 'She looks familiar, but I can't recall her name – she's maybe an eighth, no, ninth year?'

She turned the phone to show the other teachers. A balding man, and an older, slim woman with glasses.

'Ah,' the man said, 'yes, she's in my class. A new ninth year.' He nodded to confirm it to himself. 'She was in the first week or two of term, but I haven't seen her the last few classes, I don't think. I'd have to check the registers.'

Jamie's blood ran cold. Hadn't seen her? 'What's her name?' Jamie asked quickly.

'Viklund. Lena Viklund.'

Jamie nodded. 'Ninth year. That makes her ... fifteen?'

He nodded. 'I believe so, ninth years turn sixteen during the year.'

Jamie thought on that. Seventeen-year-old boy, fifteen-year-old girl. 'Do any of you know Lena Viklund's parents?'

'I think,' the woman with the glasses said now, 'that I met her father last year at a parents' evening. I don't know about the mother.'

'How did he seem?'

Holm jumped in, perceptive as ever. 'The kind of father who might object to his daughter seeing an older boy?'

Jamie looked at her to see if she'd answer her own question.

She didn't.

'He seemed fine, nice enough, I think,' the woman with the glasses said.

'Did anyone know about their relationship?' Jamie cast her eyes around the table.

The biology teacher spoke again. 'These kids ... they get together and break up so frequently. We do our best not to involve ourselves in these kinds of things.'

The woman in the glasses looked away, laughed a little. 'That's putting it mildly, it's like working in a rabbit hutch.'

She was right, Jamie would have much better luck asking Felix Nordahl's friends about Lena Viklund. But she doubted she'd get an answer from them about the next part.

'What about drugs?'

'What about them?' Ms Holm asked.

'Does the school have a problem with them?'

The teachers exchanged glances.

'What kind of drugs?' the woman in glasses asked.

'The kids smoke a little bit of cannabis every now and then,' the biology teacher said lightly, shrugging. 'We catch them sometimes at the far ends of the playing field, behind the equipment shed. But it's only a handful, and most of the time the field is under snow, so it's only really every now and then.'

'What about pills?' Jamie asked, looking at each of them.

The lady in glasses looked down. The biology teacher opened his hands and laid them on the table. Ms Holm folded her arms.

That said it all.

'Is it a big problem?'

'No,' Ms Holm said then. 'It was one bad egg that tried to spoil the whole bunch.'

'Felix Nordahl?' Jamie asked.

Ms Holm looked confused. 'What? No, Felix was … no. It was last year. A twelfth-year. Mats Flygare.'

The biology teacher shook his head.

'Mats Flygare?' Jamie confirmed. 'He was selling pills in school?'

Ms Holm drew a sharp breath, seemingly unhappy to be talking about it. 'It happened quickly – swept through the school late last spring. A few students were caught with them in their bags, a few others had to be removed from classes for acting erratically, and one girl even collapsed. Had to be taken to hospital.' She snarled then, angered by it, obviously.

'Where did Mats Flygare get the pills from?'

'That we don't know,' Ms Holm said. 'When that poor girl came around, she named Mats Flygare as the source and it was dealt with quickly. He was removed from the school, and we haven't seen him since. I don't even know if he still lives here.'

Jamie tugged at her bottom lip with her teeth. Her first thought had been that the drugs came from Flygare, and maybe Felix was his new route into the school. But if he wasn't in town anymore, maybe Felix was the new dealer, replacing Flygare.

'How was it dealt with, do you know?' Jamie asked.

Biology chimed back in now. 'Ohlin came in, pulled Mats out of class, and manhandled him out of the building. It was a big thing, the whole school was talking about it for weeks.'

'But you never heard from him afterwards?' Jamie pressed.

Everyone shook their heads.

Great. Now she just needed to get hold of Ohlin, and hope that he didn't kill Flygare. No, he wouldn't do that, would he?

Jamie put her phone back in her pocket. 'Thank you, that's everything I needed.'

Holm put her hand on Jamie's arm as she rose. 'Do you think Mats Flygare had anything to do with Felix's death?'

Jamie could see the angst in her eyes. 'Do you?'

'He was a difficult student. Difficult home life, from what I gathered. But murder is a big step from drug-dealing.'

'It is,' Jamie said, letting Holm's hand fall as she stood. 'But we'll explore every avenue, and when I find Mats Flygare, I'll be sure to ask him.'

Holm sighed. 'Felix was a good student.' The other teachers nodded their agreement. 'Promising. He wouldn't be mixed up with Mats Flygare. He had intentions of going to university, of leaving Kurrajakk, making something of himself. Not enough do, but he was getting out of here.'

And dealing drugs would be an effective way to make money. She felt like saying it, but didn't. 'I'll find out who killed him. You have my word on that.'

She looked at each of them in turn, took out a card and

left it on the table. 'If any of you have any more information, you can reach me on this number.'

She moved towards the door, rolling his name over in her head. Mats Flygare. She needed to find him.

People had been killed for less than a bag of pills and a few rolls of cash. And if Felix Nordahl was planning to get out of Kurrajakk, then that would mean Flygare's distribution channel into the school was about to dry up.

She wondered how he would have taken that news.

As she pushed through the front doors of the school for the second time and headed for her car, she knew there was only one way to find out.

Jamie got in, peeled away from the curb and gunned it back towards the station, ignoring the pale sky and the growing flock of crows circling above the town.

They wheeled slowly, as if waiting for something.

Jamie just wasn't sure she wanted to find out what.

13

JAMIE DROVE beneath a cloud of black wings.

She pulled up outside the station and killed the engine. 'Shit,' she breathed, kicking the door open and stepping down onto the pavement.

Thorsen's car was parked in front of her.

Jamie walked in through the glass-panelled door, satchel over her shoulder, and looked around.

The room was sizeable but dated, not decorated since the 70s when the building was built. There were four desks set up in the points of a square, and at the back there were two small offices. One was Ohlin's, the other empty. It was supposed to be Jamie's but it hadn't been cleared since Ohlin took over as the Kommissarie, so it was still full of his predecessor's junk, and fifteen years' worth of files, boxes, and other garbage. Jamie hadn't needed an office since she'd arrived, so hadn't even bothered to try and get it sorted.

She could see Thorsen moving around behind the blinds, no doubt making a nest for himself as the new self-appointed cock of the roost. Emphasis on *cock*.

On the left of the room, a door led out to a corridor with

two cells and two interview rooms. And on the right, there was a small kitchen, bathroom, and evidence room.

Minna, the twenty-two-year-old desk clerk, beamed up at Jamie. She had short, gingery-brown hair, freckles, and round, wire-framed glasses. 'Inspektör Johansson,' she said, grinning now. Giddy almost. 'Did you know we had a new detective?' She looked over towards the office.

'I heard,' Jamie growled.

She lowered her head a little. 'Handsome,' she said, half-under her breath, then gave Jamie a thumbs up.

Jamie closed her eyes to hide the fact that they'd just rolled into the back of her head. 'I need you to look something up for me. Two somethings, actually,' she said, coming forward. She stooped over Minna's desk, pulled a post-it pad with a doodle of a misshapen cat on it towards her, and lifted the top page.

'Mats Flygare. And Lena Viklund.' She turned the paper around with the two names on it. 'I need their details, okay? Address and contact. Now, Viklund is a minor, so I'm not sure if her details will show up – but her father's also going to be called Viklund, and I doubt there's going to be more than one Viklund living in …' Jamie stopped talking, seeing the girl's blank, borderline pained expression. 'Ohlin did show you how to look up public information on the directory when he hired you … didn't he?'

'I …' she started. 'I just answer the phone.' She laughed nervously then.

'Jesus Christ. You know what?' Jamie stripped the paper off the stack and crumpled it in her hand. 'I'll do it, don't worry.'

'Oh no, my drawing,' Minna said, the disappointment clear on her face.

Jamie separated the sheet with the names on from the

doodle and handed it back to her. She flattened it out on the desk in front of her, smoothing down the corners.

Jamie felt her fist tighten around the remaining sheet. She's just a kid. It's not her fault.

Minna looked up then. 'What happened to your hand?' she asked.

'Nothing,' Jamie said, teeth grinding. 'Burnt it on the stove.'

'Looks painful.'

'You have no idea.' Jamie stared down at the girl in front of her. 'I've got some evidence to log, don't suppose you know where Ohlin keeps the forms?' It'd been four months but she hadn't had to log anything yet. Really not very much happened in Kurrajakk.

Minna bit her lip.

'I'll find them, it's okay. You just … stay here, answer the phone if anyone calls.'

'Now that I can do,' she said brightly.

Jamie thought it best if they end the conversation there, and went towards the evidence room instead.

She headed through the kitchen, past the toilet, towards the steel caged door that kept the safe.

There was a handle and a lock. Shit, she didn't have a key. Jamie filled her lungs to call out to Minna – and then two things occurred to her. Firstly, Minna wouldn't have a key. And secondly …

She tried the handle.

It wasn't locked.

'Figures,' Jamie muttered, pulling it open and stepping inside.

There was a clipboard hanging on a nail inside the door with some blank log forms pinned to it, and a stack of clear sealable bags covered in dust sitting on a cardboard box below. Jamie reached down and picked one up, shaking the dust off, and then lifted the flap of her satchel to get the pills out.

'What's that?'

Jamie turned at the sound of the voice to see Thorsen standing in the doorway. He filled it completely, his tall, lithe frame making his head touch the top. He had his fingers through the mesh above his head suspending him there, his eyes fixed on the bag in Jamie's hand. They looked practically silver in the harsh lighting. They were grey bordering on blue. Duck egg. That's what they called it. He was a tall son of a bitch with duck-egg eyes.

Jamie restrained a smirk and then collected herself. 'Drugs,' she said plainly. 'Pills found in Felix Nordahl's bedroom.'

'Felix Nordahl. That the kid's name?' he asked, keeping the comment casual. He swung back and forth, his leather boots creaking as he did.

Guess he wasn't as in command of the investigation as he thought.

'Didn't know that?' Jamie said lightly, dropping the pills and rolls of cash into the bag and sealing it.

He shrugged. 'I didn't go to the school just to find you. But I figured it was pointless to head in and ask the same questions twice.'

Jamie pulled the clipboard towards her and took a pen from her inside pocket. 'Surprised you trusted me to ask the same questions you would.'

He smiled to himself now. 'I think we got off on the wrong foot.'

'And whose fault is that?' Jamie sighed, filling in the fields quickly.

'Look, I've worked small towns before. And I've met

detectives who take them on lightly. I jumped to a conclusion.'

Jamie looked up at him. 'Those natural police instincts of yours serving you well.'

'Hey, it was Ohlin who said that Kurrajakk was in a mess. That it needed me.'

'Your own fault for believing him.' Jamie jabbed the form with the pen to dot the literal 'I', and then pulled it free of the clip.

'I left a good job in Lulea to come out here,' Thorsen said, as though that made up for the way he acted.

'Then you're twice the fool,' Jamie answered, tossing the pills onto the nearest shelf and heading for the door.

Thorsen back pedalled

'This is serious,' he said. 'A boy is dead. You're going to want my help.'

Jamie stopped, the both of them crammed into the little kitchen.

She didn't want his help. But it was never a bad thing to have someone watching your back, and with a killer on the loose – maybe the guy she was about to go and see next – a buffer might come in handy.

'So you and Ohlin know each other?' she said, sighing and turning to the cupboard on her left. She pulled out a dusty glass, rinsed it in the sink, and then filled it with water.

'My father does,' Thorsen said.

Jamie glanced over. He must be forty. Probably close to her age. Maybe slightly older. 'Your father was a detective?'

'Yeah, he and Ohlin worked together years ago. Owed him a favour, I guess. He asked him, he asked me, you know how it goes.' He shrugged it off.

'I do,' Jamie said flatly.

'Your father a detective, too?' he asked, searching for some common ground.

Jamie took a long draught and then put the glass down, meeting his duck-egg eyes. 'No. Now come on, we've got work to do.'

14

JAMIE PULLED off the main road and headed down a pot-holed track.

The old springs on the SUV squeaked and groaned as the car hobbled through the forest. The road curved gently, and after a minute, they were totally surrounded by trees. Tall, rising pines that blotted out the already-dimming sun.

It was early afternoon now, but autumn was looming, and the sunlight hours were shorter here than in the south.

Jamie moved the wheel back and forth, guiding the vehicle between divots, right hand at her lips, pad of her thumb rubbing the crook of her index finger.

'What happened to your hand?' Thorsen asked. They'd driven in silence up until that point.

Jamie straightened her fingers and looked down at it, all spotted with blood and throbbing steadily. 'Mauled by a bear,' she said quietly, letting her eyes go back to the road. There was a growing unease settling over her. The windows were open, but the usually vibrant forest was utterly quiet.

Bird song always punctuated the air. The distant sound of

screeching deer. The rustle of rabbits, squirrels, mice in the undergrowth.

But there was nothing.

Just the throaty, chugging of the old engine. And Jamie's heart in her ears.

'A bear?' Thorsen seemed surprised. 'You get bears up here?'

They did, but Jamie'd never seen one. There were only about three thousand in all of Sweden, and they stuck mostly to the mountains and the remote forests. Still, firearms were endemic in Kurrajakk. Rifles. Shotguns. You could never be too careful.

She nodded. 'Mhm.' She glanced over. 'Better keep your safety off,' she added, nodding to the pistol hanging off his ribs.

He was wearing a white shirt rolled to the elbows, his sinewy, veined forearm laid on the central arm rest as his pale eyes scanned the trees. 'I'll keep that in mind.'

They rolled on.

The house swam into view a few minutes later. Mats Flygare's place.

His parents still owned it, but his mother was declared deceased eight years back, and there was no other information on his father. So what they were to expect, Jamie didn't know. Neither had any tax filings to their names, but both collected *Bostadsbidrag* and *Försörjningsstöd.* Housing allowance and a type of welfare for those who can't afford a reasonable standard of living.

As Jamie killed the engine, she had to concede that the second one was fair.

The house wasn't a house, but a mobile home. A long, discoloured metal tube set on bricks.

A rusted steel pipe rose out of the ground before it and

hooked over, dripping water into a wide brown puddle, an old-fashioned pump handle on the back of it.

There were three weathered solar panels laid on the roof, and a small wind turbine held upright by pieces of wood and rope. Wires stretched down towards the house.

'Jesus,' Thorsen said, leaning forward to take it all in. 'What a dump.'

Jamie reserved judgement. 'There's not a lot of work out here, but there's a lot of land. You'd be amazed how many people live like this.'

'I'm sure I would be,' Thorsen said. He looked outside at the muddy ground, let his eyes move to the leaking well-pipe, and then down at his leather shoes. City-boy shoes.

'I've got some wellingtons in the back if you can squeeze into a six.'

He sort of half sneered, then opened the door and stepped out with a squelch.

Jamie didn't think he needed to know she'd specifically swung his side in next to the boggiest looking part of the forecourt.

She stepped down onto gravel and headed for the house.

Thorsen did his best to tip-toe through the quagmire, and then got up onto the path himself, holding his hands up like a gibbon.

He took one look at Jamie's clean boots and sighed. 'Mature, really.'

Jamie shrugged and motioned him on. 'Let's go, I want to get over to the Viklund place as soon as we can.'

They headed toward the door, the quiet still hanging around their necks like a noose, and Jamie approached the milk crate being used as a front step.

She paused, listening for any sound of movement, and then turned her head, searching the space in front of the house. No car, no vehicles she could see. And they were a few miles outside town.

No lights on either, no TV sound or music.

Place looked empty.

Jamie stepped up onto the crate, felt it bend under her, and knocked a few times.

The door would swing outwards, so she dropped back down to give it space.

Her heel hadn't even touched the ground when the door exploded above her, right where her head had been a half-second earlier.

Shards of plastic and insulation fibre shot into the air like an oversized party-popper, covering Thorsen in dust and showering the windscreen of her truck in fragments.

Jamie's ears were ringing as she hit the ground, landing hard on her side, and rolled instinctively underneath the raised mobile home.

She looked out, stars dancing in front of her eyes, and watched Thorsen scramble back towards the SUV on all fours, sliding in behind the rear bumper in a cloud of gravel dust.

Fuck, that shotgun blast had nearly taken her damn head off. It would have if she hadn't stepped down.

It was definitely supposed to.

What was he, waiting in front of the door with the gun in his hands?

Jamie opened and closed her mouth, trying to click her jaw and un-pop her ears.

She pulled her pistol from her hip and held it in front of her face, pulling back the slide and flicking the safety off.

'Johansson!' It was Thorsen. 'You dead?'

'Not yet,' Jamie called back over the whistling in her ears, blinking herself clear. She took a deep breath. 'Mats

Flygare!' she yelled. 'This is Kurrajakk Polis! Put the weapon down and come out slowly with your hands in the air.'

There was no response.

Jamie rested her forehead in the dirt, catching her breath. She moved out here *not* to get shot at. She'd been there, done that, had the scar on her belly and back to prove it. And she didn't feel like repeating the experience.

'Mats Flygare!' she yelled again, looking over at Thorsen, who was peering around the corner of the car, own pistol in his hands. 'You've got five seconds!'

Thorsen edged forward, then got up to a knee, resting his wrists on the bumper, muzzle trained on the door.

He looked at her, then shook his head.

No sign of Flygare.

Jamie crawled forward a little, then pulled herself up into a crouch. She put two fingers in front of her eyes, then pointed to the door, signifying for Thorsen to watch it. She motioned around the corner with her head then and he gave a brief nod.

Jamie could see the focus in his eyes, the steadiness of his hand. She didn't know what his story was, but he wasn't one to balk at a little gunfire.

She got to her feet and scuttled around the side of the trailer, keeping close to the wall and low, moving quietly.

If there was a back exit she wanted to make sure Flygare wasn't trying to …

Shit.

Ahead, at the far end of the house, Jamie could see a window was open and moving, hinged at the top. It widened and then a pair of legs appeared in the gap.

Jamie took off, kicking stones out behind her, losing her footing before finding her stride.

A body dropped from the window, hit the ground, and darted into the trees.

Jamie drew level with the window, skidded, and then cut into the woods after him.

The stony hardstanding gave way to thick brush and exposed roots.

Footsteps sounded ahead. A dark shape moving between the trunks.

Jamie pressed on, fighting her way deeper into the forest.

She heard the distinct metallic click of a hammer being pulled back and spun right behind a trunk.

A report rang out, echoing through the trees, and the wood reverberated between her shoulder blades, buckshot flying through the branches around her.

Jamie took a breath, plunged around the corner, and closed ground, pistol up.

There, a shape.

A few more steps.

She picked him out of the gloom, a man, scrawny, doubled over a double-barrel, fumbling smoking shells from the weapon, fishing in his pocket for fresh ones.

'Stop!' Jamie yelled, breaking into a sprint as he managed to get one into the shotgun. He looked up, eyes wide, decided not to bother with the second, snapped the weapon closed.

It flew upwards, hammer clicking back, and then breathed fire.

Jamie dove forward, lost her grasp on her gun, heard the whizz and zip of the shot fly overhead, peppering the canopy.

She was on the ground then, scrambling forward, all but on him.

The stock whistled through the air, the shotgun a better club than it was a firearm at that range.

But it was heavy, and Jamie was too close already.

She drove her shoulder into his gut and pushed him backwards.

The shotgun hit the ground, his lips puckering as he expelled the air in his lungs.

But Jamie was lighter than him, and felt his hands on her ribs before she could get him off his feet.

He took hold of her jacket and twisted her free, nearly throwing her clean onto her back.

Jamie stumbled, staggered, but stayed up, finding balance just in time to see Mats Flygare coming at her, all top-lip hair and bloodshot eyes. He looked like he hadn't slept in days.

A wide, telegraphed hook came around from his right and Jamie ducked it easily, putting a hard jab into his solar plexus, right below his sternum. He made a strangulated squeak, winded, and moved back a step. He fought worse than he shot, but he was clearly tasting his own product, and recovered quickly, brushing the pain off.

Jamie wasn't big, but she'd put a significant portion of her life into making sure she knew how to handle herself.

He came forward again, hands raised, going for her throat, and she put the heel of her boot into him centre mass, forcing him back, giving herself space to put him down properly.

And then Thorsen was there, breathing hard, hair wild.

His long, lithe arms came down over Flygare's head and locked around his chest, pinning his arms to his sides.

Jamie called out a second too late, watching as Flygare recklessly threw his head backwards, the crown of his skull connecting with Thorsen's nose.

The sound was dull, a muted thud immediately drowned out by Thorsen's voice as he let loose with a stream of profanity, throwing his hands to his face to catch the falling blood.

Flygare righted himself, searched for Jamie again, but by the time he found her, it was already happening.

The heel of her boot cut the air in a flat, high arc, and impacted right on his cheek.

He spun towards the ground and landed face down in the bed of browned pine needles, his hands lying limply at his sides, nail-bitten fingers and pink palms to the sky.

Jamie turned back towards the two men on the ground and pushed the loose strands of hair off her forehead, wiping away sweat with her sleeve.

Flygare was down, groaning softly, clinging to consciousness.

Jamie stepped over him towards Thorsen, who was trying to get up off his ass, and offered him a hand.

He took it and she pulled him up, his white shirt now splattered with red. He was pinching his nose, eyes watering, chin slick and crimson.

'That asshole broke my nose,' he growled, glaring down at Flygare.

Jamie put a boot in the middle of his back and pulled his hands up behind her heel, slipping a pair of cable cuffs out of her jacket pocket and over his hands, pulling them tight.

She took a fistful of the baggy, cigarette-holed hoody then, and dragged the boy to his feet. 'I wouldn't worry, it was crooked anyway,' she said, shoving him towards Thorsen and hunting around for her pistol.

He caught him by the scruff of his neck and frogmarched him groggily towards the car, mumbling something about his shirt, still pinching his nose.

Jamie found her weapon and ejected the round from the chamber, finally catching her breath.

She slotted it back into the holster, pocketing the loose bullet, and then looked for the shotgun.

It was lying against a tree and she went over, taking it in her hands.

The thing was practically an antique. But it hadn't stopped Flygare trying to kill her with it.

She broke it over her knee and then let it hang loose at her side, her eyes climbing the sap-slathered trunk to a limb about six feet overhead.

A single crow sat there, looking down at her, cocking its head, translucent lids flashing over its black eyes every few seconds.

'What are you looking at?' she asked it.

But it didn't answer.

It just sat. And watched Jamie.

All the way back to her car.

15

BY THE TIME they reached the station, Flygare had fallen into a stupor. Whether he was coming down off the drugs or Jamie had just given him a concussion – or both, probably both – they didn't know. But even when Thorsen pulled the back door open, nose stuffed with tissue, and slapped him a little to wake him up, he just sort of groaned, and turned away, eyes half closed.

It wasn't a pained groan, more a *get off and let me sleep groan.* Jamie had seen it before – trying to move addicts off streets. Their buzz had tailed off, and they were crashing. Two days with no sleep would hit pretty hard when the drugs stopped doing their work.

'Let's just get him in a cell,' Jamie said. 'I'll have Minna call the hospital, see if we can't get a doctor out here to check on him.'

Thorsen dragged him from the car and all but carried him inside.

If only for that, Jamie was glad he was there.

And despite wanting to, she found she couldn't take any pleasure from Thorsen's face. His nose had swollen now, eyes blackening by the moment. She wasn't sure if it was broken – if it was, he had a high pain threshold. If it wasn't, then Jamie would be surprised. Flygare had really caught him.

Minna stood up out of her chair in surprise as they dragged him in. In the four months Jamie had been there, she'd not arrested anyone. Not put anyone in one of the cells. There'd been no need.

'Who's that?' she asked as Thorsen took him in and shoved him down onto one of the cots.

He immediately flopped onto it, curled up and faced the wall.

'Mats Flygare,' Jamie said, folding her arms, watching as Thorsen closed the door with a clang. It locked automatically. 'Don't suppose you know where the key is for that?' she asked Minna, lifting an eyebrow.

She just smiled nervously, then shook her head.

'Of course not.' Jamie sighed, rubbed the back of her neck. 'I need you to call the hospital, tell them we've got a suspect in here that needs looking over – possible concussion, substance abuse. See if they'll send over a doctor. Can you do that?'

'Uh …'

'Just nod, Minna. I'll write it down for you.'

She nodded.

'Good,' Jamie said, looking at the girl. 'If we're going to do this properly, we'll need a warrant to search Flygare's house. And it's not like it's going anywhere. Do you know which judge Ohlin contacted when …' She stopped talking. Why she even began in the first place, she didn't know. God, she missed Hallberg.

'I can make a call,' Thorsen said then, appearing in the doorway to the cell corridor. His voice was high and nasally.

'I know a few judges back in Lulea. I'll get one of them to sign off on a warrant.'

Jamie nodded.

He was proving his usefulness by the minute.

'In the meanwhile,' Jamie said, glancing back at Minna, 'we're going to head over to Lena Viklund's house, see what she knows about Felix. If he wasn't with his friends, I bet he was with her.'

Minna stared blankly.

Jamie just shook her head and walked away.

Thorsen caught up with her at the curb. 'Hang on,' he said, touching her elbow and heading for his car.

Jamie lingered, watching as he opened the back door and pulled a bag to the edge of the seat.

He unzipped it and then took off his rib holster and unbuttoned his shirt.

Jamie turned away, leaned on her SUV and looked up.

No crows for once. That made a nice change.

'Hey,' Thorsen called.

Jamie turned, seeing him buttoning up another white shirt, his flat, defined stomach poking through the undone hems at the bottom.

'Got any water?' he asked.

Jamie turned back to the car and opened the back door, reaching into the emergency duffle in the footwell. She always carried it – road flares, water, protein bars, foil blankets. Getting caught out this far north came with serious consequences.

She pulled out a fresh bottle and tossed it to him. 'You know there's a bathroom right inside?'

He unscrewed the cap and emptied a little onto a flannel he'd gotten from his wash bag. 'And risk another conversation with Minna?' His eyes flitted to the station. 'I'm good.'

Jamie walked over a little. 'She's nice enough. Not the sharpest, mind.'

He leaned forward, peeling the wads of tissue from his nose gingerly. 'You can say that again.'

A heavy chunk of congealed blood landed in the gutter between the car and curb and splatted on the dry tarmac.

He started sponging the blood from his lip and chin with the flannel. At least his nose looked to have stopped bleeding now. And it wasn't broken by the shape of it. But damn close.

'How'd she get the job, anyway?' Thorsen asked, stooping to check his face in the wing mirror.

Jamie shrugged. 'There wasn't exactly a queue of applicants.'

'Small towns.'

'Yep.'

Thorsen stood, kneading the flannel between his bloodied hands. He looked at Jamie, looked like he wanted to say something. Then just wrung the flannel out instead, and tossed it back in the car.

'You ready to go?' Jamie asked.

He slung his holster around his shoulders. 'After you.'

'Alright, but you're the one knocking on Viklund's door this time.'

He made a little 'humph' laugh noise, cracked a smirk. 'Whatever you say.'

Jamie caught herself smiling, then promptly wiped it from her face as she reached the driver's door. 'You got extra tissues? I don't want you bleeding all over my car.'

'I won't. I promise.' He held his hands up.

Jamie tried not to meet his eye as she climbed into the driver's seat, but she could feel him watching her.

She cranked the ignition, eyes fixed on the horizon, and pulled away from the curb.

The town was still around them. Stiller than usual.

Not a person on the streets.

Jamie's brow furrowed as she watched the darkened shops and buildings go by. They were usually still open at this time.

Neither of them spoke as they drove, the town thinning at their flanks, and then they were into the forest once more, the car swallowed up by the gathering dusk.

16

'So how much did Wiik actually tell you?' Jamie asked, keeping an eye out for the Viklund house.

It was on this road, but a house only cropped up every quarter mile or so, and they were tucked back, shrouded by trees. She checked her watch – three. Shit, it had been a long day already, and there was still a way to go.

Jamie wound down the window and took a few deep breaths of cool, pine-laced air.

Thorsen rolled his head side to side. 'Not too much,' he said. 'But he seemed pretty annoyed to have your ability questioned. He said you'd been involved in the Imperium scandal.'

Jamie glanced over.

'Don't worry, he told me you were on the right side of it.'

'That's one way to put it,' Jamie said, rubbing her midriff where the scar from a bullet wound still shone. It never stopped hurting.

Thorsen laughed a little. 'Said you were the most deter-mined detective he'd ever worked with.'

'Is that right.'

'And the smartest – he said it'd be in my best interest to listen to your instincts when it came to a case.'

Jamie smirked to herself. It'd taken Wiik a while to learn than himself.

'And then he said that I shouldn't get too attached to you.'

Jamie looked over and saw that he was watching her again. Studying her.

'What'd he mean by that?' Thorsen kept his eyes on her. 'He didn't really expand on it.'

She raised her shoulders in an exaggerated shrug, stuck out her bottom lip.

'You churn through partners quickly or something?'

She didn't feel like lying. 'Not exactly by choice.'

'So by chance then?'

'How about we just focus on this case, huh? I'm sure you're going to be wanting to jet off back to Lulea as soon as you're done here now that you know Ohlin's full of shit.' Jamie blinked a few times, trying not to get sucked in by the hypnotic throb of the passing trees.

'Humph.' He smiled to himself. 'Yeah, probably. Hey, I think this is it.' He leaned forward, pointing out the window at a mailbox on the side of the road. It was a square box sat on an old fence post.

Jamie read the number. 'Yeah, this is it.' She swung the SUV down off the road and onto the track leading up to the house.

It was a square two-storey with a rough white exterior and a stone-tiled roof, small windows, exposed, gnarled wood holding up the front porch.

An unkempt grass frontage showed off a rusted pickup truck, a cobbled together chicken shed, and a rotting wood store. There was a man standing in front of it, splitting wood on a log with an axe. He was a smallish man with broad shoulders, a strong, rounded trunk, and thickly haired forearms. He had dark hair and an unkempt beard, shaded, deep-set eyes, and thin lips no more than a cut in his face.

He put the axe on his shoulder, watching the SUV pull up.

Jamie stepped from the car, the smell of freshly cut wood thick in the air. 'Gunnar Viklund?' She held up her badge.

He nodded, putting one dirty boot up on the stump. It was caked in mud, his jeans splattered too.

As Jamie got closer, the smell of raw sap was replaced by sweat. It was beaded across his forehead, soaking through his white vest and wetting his hairy shoulders.

'We were hoping we could ask you a few questions.'

'Haven't seen you before,' he remarked, putting another piece of wood on the log and winding up. 'Where's Ohlin?'

'Retired,' Jamie said without skipping a beat.

She caught Thorsen narrowing his eyes in her periphery, but he kept quiet.

'There was an incident last night – a boy was found dead.'

'A boy?' Gunnar Viklund looked up but didn't stop chopping. The axe came down swiftly, split the wood clean, firing two separate pieces in opposite directions. 'Local?'

'Yeah,' Jamie said, looking up at the house. It was dark. 'Is your daughter Lena Viklund?' She already knew the answer.

'What's Lena have to do with this?' He stopped chopping now.

'Are you aware that your daughter was in a relationship?'

'A relationship?'

Thorsen jumped in now. 'She had a boyfriend.'

His lips curled down. 'The Nordahl boy.'

'Yes,' Jamie said. 'So you were aware?'

He nodded slowly. 'Aware, but I didn't approve. It's the reason I sent Lena to Malmö.'

Malmö? That was at the southernmost point of Sweden. As far from Kurrajakk as you could get without falling off the end. 'You sent your daughter to Malmö?'

'My aunt lives there. I didn't want her spending time with Nordahl,' he went on. 'Did you know he was involved in drugs?' His hands tightened around the handle of the axe, twisting with a low groan.

'We're looking into Felix Nordahl,' Jamie said, skirting the question, watching his knuckles around the smooth wood. 'But any information you have would be useful. What makes you think he was involved with drugs?'

Viklund shook his head then, tsked, seemingly amused by Jamie's play-dumb attitude. 'About a week ago, Lena came home late – she was … *on* something. She wouldn't say what. But she was acting strangely, so I took her bag from her – there were drugs inside. A bag with pills in it.'

'What colour were they?'

'Red, I think,' Viklund said. 'She wouldn't tell me who gave them to her, or why—'

'How many were there?'

'I don't know. Dozens, hundreds?' He shook his head again. 'I didn't count. Didn't have time to. We argued.'

'What did you do with them? Are they still here?'

'No, I flushed them down the toilet.'

Jamie's jaw flexed. Nordahl gets a new batch of pills to sell, he can't keep them at home, gives them to Lena for safe keeping. Her father finds them, flushes them, Nordahl's now in the hole with Mats Flygare. They get into it … A picture was starting to form.

'What happened then?'

Thorsen was watching Viklund like a hawk.

He drew a slow breath. 'She screamed at me. Told me I didn't know what I'd done. Told me she hated me. Told me she was going to run away from here. With … with the Nordahl boy.'

'And then?'

'She disappeared.'

'Disappeared?'

'Only until the next day. She wouldn't answer her phone, texts, nothing. Then she came back, crying. She wouldn't talk about it, wouldn't tell me what happened.' He sighed. 'She's always been a good girl – good in school, quiet, not many friends. Then, this summer, suddenly she's coming home late, alcohol is disappearing from the house, she was changing. Drinking, taking drugs.' He grimaced. 'Throwing her life away. She's barely fifteen, for God's sake,' he said, putting the axe down and leaning forward on it. 'Her mother died, about five years ago, now – it's been difficult since, for her. They were close. So alike. Looking at Lena … It's like looking at Alma …' His lip quivered a little and then he buried it, standing upright and sniffing. 'I've done my best, but … she's getting to that age.'

'Take your time,' Thorsen said then, his voice rich with compassion, eyes soft.

Jamie couldn't help but feel like he was a different man suddenly. Did he have kids? A wife? A daughter?

Viklund let out a long, shaking breath, the hardness he was trying to hold onto fading fast, a broken father in its place. 'I called my aunt. My mother's sister. She works at a school there – I didn't know what else to do. I told her the situation, and she offered to take Lena in for the year, and we could go from there. So I made the arrangements, and sent Lena down there.'

'I'm guessing she didn't take that very well?'

He shook his head.

'Malmö is a long way from here,' Jamie said.

'That's why I chose it. I didn't want her running back here.' He looked stern, but didn't seem worked up at all.

'How did she get down there? Did you drive her?'

'I drove her to the train station in Jokkmokk. The ticket ran through Boden, Umeá, Sundsvall, Gävle, Uppsala, uh …' He looked up, racking his brain. 'Then down to Stockholm, and on to Malmö from there.'

He knew the route. 'And when was this?'

'Almost a week ago. Last … Wednesday, I think. I can find the receipt for the ticket if you want? I think I still have it.'

Jamie nodded. That was six days ago. 'Sure, that would be helpful. She arrived safely?'

'My aunt said so. Lena wouldn't speak to me. Still won't.'

It all seemed to fit. Lena hadn't been in school for the last week. And the timestamp on that photograph with Lena was dated seven days ago. She'd double check, but she was pretty certain. Last Tuesday. The night before she was being shipped out. The evening that she came home, argued with her father, then disappeared, running back to Felix. The next day, when she came home, he put her on the train to Malmö.

'We'd like to speak to Lena. Could we have her number?' Jamie asked.

'I have her phone here,' Viklund said, pointing to the house. I didn't want Nordahl contacting her down there. I wanted it to be a fresh start. I gave my aunt some money to get her a new one.'

'Do you have the new number?'

He shook his head. 'We're not exactly on speaking terms at the moment – but in time she will see it's for the best.'

Jamie reserved judgement on that. A father's best intentions didn't always work out so well for the daughter. She knew that much from experience.

'We do need to speak to her,' Jamie pressed.

'I can give you my aunt's number if you need it.'

'That would be great. And we'll also need Lena's phone if you don't mind.'

'Of course, anything I can do to help,' he said, laying the axe down now. 'You said a boy was dead, didn't you?' he asked then, his expression changing, becoming almost pained.

'That's right,' Jamie said, playing her cards close to her chest.

'And you think the Nordahl boy is involved? That Lena may know something.'

'Maybe,' Jamie offered. 'We're just information gathering at the moment.'

'I wouldn't be surprised if he did it,' Viklund said, rubbing his calloused hands. 'I only met him the once, but I could see it in him – he wasn't what everyone else thought. He was clever. Manipulative. And he wasn't afraid of hurting people.' He started towards the house then.

'Why do you say that?' Jamie called after him.

He paused at the door frame, leaned against it, hanging his head. 'Lena may have thought it was love – but let me ask you this. What does love have to do with convincing a fifteen-year-old girl to sell drugs for you? What does love have to do with keeping her out all hours, and … and forcing her to …' He steeled himself, screwing his eyes closed. 'I'm not stupid,' he said then, looking up. 'I know what boys want. And I know what Lena was ready for, and what she wasn't. I saw the marks, I saw her change. It wasn't love. What that boy was doing to her – it was as far from love as things get.'

He went inside, leaving the door open.

Jamie could see Thorsen breathing hard, fists balled at his sides.

She remembered Felix Nordahl's room, the condoms. She remembered the waste basket, what was in it. Is that where Lena had gone that night? Is that where she'd escaped to?

Teenagers could be difficult. Every detective, every officer, every parent knew that. She may have thought she was in love with him. But if he was plying her with drugs, with alcohol, sleeping with her ... and she was just fifteen ... and only just by the sounds of it.

By all accounts Felix was smart, nice, well-liked. By Viklund's estimations, he was the opposite.

And buried amongst all this was Flygare. Were the crows. Was *Kråkornas Kung*.

Jamie looked around. There were no crows here. No sign of the king.

Viklund came back out then, smartphone in hand. 'Here,' he said, handing it over. 'I don't know the passcode, though.'

Jamie took it off him, clicked the unlock button. The screen remained black. Dead battery. She put it in her pocket. 'Thank you.'

'And this is my aunt's number.' He offered a piece of paper. 'My number's on there, too, if you need to reach me.'

Thorsen took it from him.

'Is there anything else you want to know?' Viklund asked.

Jamie met his eyes, measured him. 'Just to be thorough, where were you last night?'

'At the Moose's Head.'

'All night?' Jamie asked lightly, as though it were purely formality.

He nodded. 'Yep, from about six until ...' He sucked air

through his teeth. 'Closing, I guess. Things were getting hazy by then.'

'And what time does the Moose's Head normally close?' Thorsen interjected.

'Oh,' Viklund said, sighing, rubbing the back of his neck. 'Twelve, one maybe? I'm not sure.'

'And people can place you there?' Thorsen again.

'About a dozen, I should think,' he said, laughing a bit.

Jamie knew that the Moose had a dedicated crowd that closed it out every night. And Viklund was seemingly a part of that crowd.

'And how did you get home?' Jamie asked then. 'You drive?'

'It wasn't the sort of night for driving,' he answered. 'Left the car there, Olof brought me.'

'Olof?'

'Englander.'

'He wasn't drinking?' Jamie raised an eyebrow.

'Didn't ask,' Viklund answered flatly.

Jamie took that in, nodded. She was the extent of the patrolling police force, and she didn't feel like whiling away her hours outside the Moose at gone midnight. Though if she did, she thought she'd catch more than a few people driving when they shouldn't be.

She sighed. 'Thank you,' she said. 'I think that's all for now.' Jamie started to turn away. 'But we may be in touch.'

He nodded, going back to the axe. He picked it up, wiped the sweat from his head. 'I hope you catch him, if he is responsible, the Nordahl boy,' Viklund said then. 'I hope you nail him to the fucking wall before he hurts anyone else.'

Jamie offered the briefest of smiles, then laid a hand on Thorsen's arm. But he wouldn't budge.

She looked up at his face, his eyes fixed on Viklund. 'It's Felix Nordahl who's dead.'

Jamie turned quickly to catch Viklund's reaction, ignoring the instant anger at Thorsen revealing that.

Viklund processed that slowly. 'Oh,' he said, leaning on the axe. 'I'm not saying I'm happy the kid is dead,' he added then, without being prompted, 'but if he was doing to others what he'd done to Lena … this town will be better off without him.'

The blade rose and fell, sending two shards of wood flipping into the shaggy grass around him.

Jamie thought on that, gave him one final nod, and then headed for the car, Thorsen in tow.

They climbed in in silence, Jamie wondering why he'd decided to break procedure like that. Then she backed up, turned, and then pulled out onto the carless road, leaving Viklund in the rear-view, the darkened forest at their back, the darkened sky ahead.

A half a mile later, Thorsen spoke. 'What do you think?' he asked, voice low, brow furrowed. He massaged his wide jaw with his hand.

She sighed. 'I think there's more to Felix Nordahl than we think.'

'And what about Viklund?'

'What about him?'

'Father finds out his fifteen-year-old daughter is sleeping with an older boy. The drink. The drugs. The late nights. It's motive if I've ever heard it.'

'He's got an alibi.'

'We don't know when Felix Nordahl died.'

'We will soon,' she said. 'Autoposy will give us time of death.'

'Mmm.' More a sound than a word.

'You think he's lying?'

'Don't know. Fathers and their daughters,' he said, shaking his head. 'Doesn't take much.'

'That why you told him Nordahl was dead?'

Thorsen leaned on the window sill, said nothing, just stared at the road.

'Let's ask around, see what we can find out about him,' Jamie said, not leaping to any conclusions. 'We've still got Flygare in a cell, and we need to figure out how this bullshit about *Kråkornas Kung* fits into it somehow.'

'*Kråkornas Kung?*' Thorsen asked, raising an eyebrow. 'Who's the King Of Crows?'

'Just some local ghost story,' Jamie said dismissively. 'A half-crow, half-man creature that watches over the forest, commands a legion of birds.'

'That explains the crow in the mouth,' Thorsen said, sighing and rubbing his eyes. 'But not why someone would go to the trouble.'

'No, it doesn't,' Jamie said. 'It doesn't explain anything. It's just smoke.'

'Someone trying to cover their trail?'

'Trying to make this look like something it's not.'

'And what's that?'

Jamie pursed her lips, letting the word form on her tongue. It came naturally, instinctively. She let out a slow breath, watching the last of the light fade from the sky.

'Revenge.'

Jamie shifted down, eased the SUV up to the limit, and headed for Kurrajakk.

They drove the rest of the way in silence.

17

By the time Jamie and Thorsen pulled up at the station, it was dark, and Minna was locking up to leave.

They both jumped out, leaving the engine running, and headed her off.

'Hey,' Jamie called.

She jolted, keys jangling in the lock. 'Oh, inspektör,' she said. 'I didn't … I mean, I didn't know if you were coming back.'

'What happened with Flygare?' Jamie squinted into the lightless interior.

'I rang the hospital like you asked – and a doctor came over with a nurse. I managed to find the cell key, and he checked him out. He started reacting, shouting, trying to get out of the cell.'

Jamie tensed, hoping to hell she wasn't about to say that he'd escaped.

'The doctor managed to hold him, and the nurse sedated him.'

Jamie breathed a little sigh of relief.

'He looked him over, gave him fluids, stayed for a little bit, and then left.'

'So he's still here?'

'The doctor said he'd sleep until morning, probably,' Minna added. 'And my shift is over ...'

She couldn't expect the kid to stay all night. She nodded. 'Okay, you head home.'

'You want me to leave it open?' Minna looked down at her key in the door.

Jamie weighed it up in her head. 'No, it's okay,' she said, 'if he's out, we won't be able to talk to him. And so long as the cell is locked, he's not going anywhere.'

Thorsen cupped his hands over his eyes and peered inside. 'I can stay if you want. In case he comes to.'

'No,' Jamie said, sighing, 'it's fine. It's been a hell of a day, and this is the safest place in Kurrajakk. We'll pick this back up in the morning.'

Thorsen nodded. 'Too late now to petition a judge anyway, I'll put a call in, but best case it comes through by breakfast. We'll search Flygare's place, see what we can turn up, then question him from there.'

Jamie had to agree. That sounded like the best course of action. 'Where are you staying?'

'The Kurrajakk Inn,' Thorsen answered.

Stupid question, really. It was the only hotel in town.

'Until I can find a place, at least,' he added.

Did he really intend to stay here? Jamie knew why she chose Kurrajakk, but now that Thorsen knew the truth, why wouldn't he want to go back to Lulea? Euch, she was too tired to open that can of worms right now.

The three of them stood there for a few seconds, then Minna spoke. 'So, can I go now?'

Jamie nodded. 'Sure, Minna. Make sure you get home okay.'

'I will,' she said, smiling. 'See you tomorrow.'

Thorsen gave her a little salute and Jamie put her hand on her shoulder as she passed.

When it was just the two of them, Thorsen leaned back against the window. 'So, there anywhere decent to eat around here?'

'There's the Moose's Head – they do a decent reindeer burger. But otherwise, you might want to just stick to the hotel.'

Thorsen looked off towards the main cross, visible in the distance. There were no cars moving, no people walking around.

'Jesus, this place is quiet,' he said, lowering his voice a little.

Jamie looked in the same direction. 'Yeah, but not usually *this* quiet.'

'Kind of weird,' Thorsen said.

Jamie didn't nod, didn't agree. But she definitely didn't disagree.

'Okay,' she said then. 'I'm going to go.'

Thorsen pushed his hands into his pockets, gave a little dip of the head.

Jamie climbed into the SUV, looked at him through the gap between the door and the frame.

'Drive safe,' Thorsen said.

Jamie gave a restrained smile, then closed the door and pulled away.

He came forward to the edge of the curb, looking after her.

She watched him shrink in the rear-view.

All around her, the town held its breath.

Jamie slowed up at the red light on the cross and glanced both ways. Everything was dark, everything shut up for the night. Hell, it was barely five. Had the whole town fled without her noticing? Where the hell was everyone? Usually by this time, commuters were heading home, the after-work drinkers heading to the Moose. People would be on the streets.

But today, there was nothing.

Jamie stayed there, fingers drumming on the wheel long after the light had turned green.

Eventually she sighed.

Add it to the growing list of questions mounting up in her head.

It was late. She needed food. She needed to decompress.

She just hoped Hati hadn't shit all over her bed.

Again.

18

J AMIE WALKED into her modest bungalow, tucked away on a dead-end road at the edge of town.

She was surrounded by trees on all sides, the house invisible unless you were on the drive. There'd been a sign with a number on it, a mailbox on the road. She'd taken them both down, didn't bother trimming back the vines and plants shrouding the entrance.

You wouldn't know it was there unless you were really looking. Just how Jamie liked it.

She pushed the door closed behind her, listened to it latch, and then set her keys down on the old side table with dog-gnawed legs. She removed her holster, and set it down next to them.

The faint odour of dog urine drifted from somewhere inside. There were two lights burning – a lamp in the living room, and the extractor-hood light in the kitchen.

A low growl rumbled from deeper in the house.

Jamie stepped into the open arch to the open plan kitchen-living room and looked in. It was reasonably sized, backed by floor-length windows that stared out into the wilderness behind the house.

Hati picked his head up off the sofa and stared at her, sitting on a bed of pillow fluff. The destroyed carcass lay in the middle of the floor.

Jamie sighed. 'Alright, asshole?' she asked.

He let out a dismissive moan and then put his head back between his paws.

She left him be – it was just easier to, and then walked through the tired house towards the kitchen, her stomach tight and empty.

It had been built in the seventies, and the exposed wood, stippled ceilings, and long, hanging light fixtures attested to that. She'd bought the place cheap. It'd been unoccupied for the best part of a year before she did, the previous owners dead, their children living away, not knowing what to do with it.

Almost poetic that she let go of one estranged parent's place only just to acquire another. Or was it ironic? She didn't know. She'd sold her father's house in Stockholm, the fire-ruined husk that it was, and bought this instead. She could have bought it three times over with the money. Strangely, the housing market in Kurrajakk wasn't what you might call buoyant.

Jamie reached for the pot of coffee on the counter, cold since that morning, and poured out a half cup, heading for the microwave.

Hati watched her, whining from his throne.

'Yeah, yeah,' she said opening the microwave, 'I'll do it now, just let me get a coffee first.'

He grumbled, then barked, the noise deep and harsh.

'Fuck, fine,' she said, shoving the cup inside, setting it to run and going to the top cupboard, the only place she could keep his food that he couldn't get at it. She pulled down the bag, walked over to the big steel bowl, and topped it off.

The dog sidled down off the sofa with his one missing front leg, and hopped over the bowl. He lowered his nose to it, took one sniff, and then turned away.

'You're kidding?' Jamie asked, scoffing.

Hati walked over to the doorway, looked over his shoulder, lifted his tail to show Jamie his testicles and arsehole, and then sidled out of the room.

The microwave beeped and Jamie took the coffee out, shaking her head. She lifted it to her lips, felt it burn, and then pulled the cup away. 'Fuck,' she muttered, going for the sink.

She ran the cold tap, pushed her mouth under it, and then stood up in front of the window above it, hands either side of the bowl, and stared out into the darkness, wondering, for the first time since she'd moved in, if someone was out there, staring back.

It was nearly nine when Hati started barking.

Jamie didn't hear it at first. Headphones in, fists plunging into the heavy bag suspended from the beam in the garage, all that filled her head was *thud, thud, thud.* Left hook, right hook, jab, jab, jab, back up, shift weight, round house to mid, round house to mid, other foot, spinning kick.

Her heel hit the plastic coating and a bolt of feedback shot up her calf.

The years of Tae Kwon Do had numbed her feet to the point she barely felt the impacts anymore.

Jamie pivoted back to neutral, breathing hard, and rested her hands on her knees. She winced, standing straight, rubbing the bullet scar on her stomach. The punching was fine, but kicking hurt. She knew it always would. She kept massaging her flank, listening to the blood receding in her ears. Her heart slowed and she lifted her hand, pulling open the velcro wrist cuff on her gloves with her teeth. The bite she'd had from Hati was throbbing underneath.

She heard him then, and paused.

Jamie spat out the strap, pulled the headphones from her ears, and shook the glove free of her hand, undoing the second one and heading for the door to the house.

Hati was a dickhead, but he didn't do a whole lot of barking.

Jamie stepped into the hallway, and raked her forearm across her head, wiping away the sweat.

Hati was standing in the entryway, three feet from the front door, barking right at it.

She neared him and slowed.

He twigged, turning, and bared his teeth.

Jamie raised her hands. 'Hey, it's just me, okay?'

He flattened his ears to his head, whimpered once, and then turned back to the door, letting out a low, sustained growl.

The hair on the back of Jamie's neck stood up and the breath she'd just caught disappeared from her chest. Her heart was beating fast as she reached out for her holster, eyes fastened on the front door.

Hati was moving forward and back now, barking and barking.

Jamie tightened her grip on the pistol, pulled back the slide to chamber a round, and then trained it on the handle. Her left hand came free and stretched out for it.

She felt Hati's flank against her leg as he pedalled backwards and then sank behind her, still growling.

Her fingers opened, tingling.

Not far.

A bang rang out and Jamie froze, wheeling around, the noise echoing from the living room. Hati exploded into a flurry of barks and reared up onto his hind legs, spraying saliva everywhere.

Someone was hammering on the window.

Jamie ran to the corner and pressed herself against it, heart in her throat, and then spun out, covering the entirety of the glass with her weapon.

She stood there, framed in the archway, eyes roving back and forth across the window. But nothing moved.

Just glass, then darkness. Silence. What the hell?

Then it happened.

The briefest flash of movement.

Then a bang.

Jamie jumped, stepped back, nearly fell over Hati who was standing right behind her.

He growled, hobbled out of the way, and Jamie staggered into the wall behind, gun still raised, trying to figure out what the hell was happening – what was hitting her window. What she was supposed to be aiming at.

Another bang. Then another.

More flashes of blackness outside.

Hati ran in, barking wildly again.

Jamie recovered herself and pushed forward, brain working intensely, and listened as more bangs rang out.

She lowered the gun slowly, wincing with each impact, realising that there wasn't someone outside beating on the window …

Light from the lamp to her right spilled through the glass, illuminating the first foot or so of moss-covered patio, and now that she was close to it, she saw what was making the noise.

Birds.

Crows.

Hurling themselves against the pane.

She looked out into the sky, saw no stars, nothing except a sea of ink. Thud. Another one. Thud. One more.

Jamie let the pistol hang at her side as she counted them off in her head, watched some fly away instantly, others fall to the ground, flounder, then take off again. And a few just twitch and flap and then fall still, their little eyes glazing over as they died. Broken necks, broken spines, wings at odd angles, legs in the air, tiny talons curled up in the cool summer air.

'What the fuck?' Jamie muttered, looking down at Hati. He looked back at her, hackles up like the spines of a cactus.

She headed for the front door again, each bang on the glass sending a shiver down her spine, and tore it open, stepping out into the heavy air.

The smell of the pines was layered over the house, but it was laced with something else. Something sweet, and sickly. Fragrant and rotting.

She stood on the front step, looking into the night. But saw nothing.

Hati, who'd usually bolt the second he had a chance at an open door – the reason Jamie had to keep him inside – stayed back over the threshold.

He snorted, then lowered his head, sneezed once. Twice. Then whimpered and backed up down the hallway.

Jamie looked over her shoulder. He was standing next to her closed bedroom door, panting, whining.

'You know you're descended from a wolf, right?' she said, locking eyes with him.

He laid down, continued whining.

'Coward,' she muttered, forcing her lungs to take in the thick air.

Jamie looked out over the cracked asphalt driveway, past her sleeping patrol car, into the trees beyond, squinting into the utter darkness, struggling to make out anything except the tops of the pines.

The distant thunk of the birds hitting the glass at the side of her house continued to ring in the darkness.

She kept her breathing even, eyes focused, and reached behind the doorframe, fingers spidering up the wall until she felt the discoloured plastic switch. She flexed the fingers of her right hand around the pistol, now slick with sweat, and then she flipped the light on.

The security light above the front door came to life, flooding the drive with brilliance.

Jamie didn't know what she was expecting – but it wasn't an eruption of black wings and bodies.

She threw her arm in front of her face reflexively as hundreds of crows all took flight simultaneously, calling and screeching as they fled back into the woods, shaking the trees as they went.

It was a moment of carnage, of pure chaos and heat, and then they were gone, and silence returned.

They must have been covering the entire driveway, her car, the house.

Jamie was practically panting as she stepped down onto the drive, the air still rotten with the stench of death. Her nose tingled, the metallic tinge unmistakeable. Blood.

She could see it then, glistening on the bonnet of her truck.

Jamie approached cautiously, pistol still held tightly in her hands.

She looked down at the black, congealed liquid, splattered and smeared across the faded paintwork. Tiny claw marks and bird footprints tracked all over it. Odd feather and wing imprints. Her brain couldn't make sense of it. Of what she was seeing.

A fizzing had developed behind her ears, her mind struggling to get a handle on this.

She was in gooseflesh then, bathed in a cold sweat. Jamie swallowed, a weight on her shoulders like she'd never felt, a million eyes all watching her. Breathing ragged, heart pounding, eyes bulging from their sockets.

Her feet were heavy, gun rattling in her grasp.

Jamie charged inside on blind instinct, slammed the door, and sank back against it, dropping the pistol between her knees, holding her fingers up in front of her face.

She looked at them, jolted again in shock, her hands covered in blood. Her head hit the wood behind her and when her eyes refocused, her hands were clean.

'Jesus,' she breathed, voice strange and quiet, alien in her ears. She shook her head, swallowed, mouth dry, let out a long exhale. 'Get a fucking grip, Jamie,' she said, louder then.

She stayed there for a few minutes, Hati watching cautiously from the end of the hallway, and then she got up, wobbling forward on unsteady feet.

Jamie felt exhausted and wired at the same time, sick and half asleep. Her vision was blurred around the edges. She was just tired. That's all it was. It was a long, disturbing day, and she'd barely eaten, barely drunk anything. She needed sleep. She needed it.

She got in the shower a minute later, and cranked it as cold as it would go. The sensation on her skin was distant, the white noise comforting. When she regained focus, she didn't know how long she'd been under the water, but her fingers had pruned and she was shivering.

Jamie turned it off and stepped out, drying herself roughly with a towel.

By the time she stepped into her bedroom, Hati had already taken up residence on her bed.

She never let him sleep on it. Never let him in the bedroom even. Not after the shitting incident.

But tonight …

'Good boy,' Jamie said, heading back into the hallway quickly. She double-checked the door was latched, then locked it. She moved quickly, checking the back door, then the garage door. Locked too.

There was nothing she could do about the windows in the living room. They didn't open, but there were no curtains either. Nothing to stop anyone looking in.

Back in the hallway, she went over to her gun and picked it up off the carpet where she'd dropped it. It felt heavy in her hand. There was still a bullet in the chamber. This time she didn't eject it.

She weighed it, looked at the holster on the side table, then decided she'd rather have it with her.

So she took it. Into the bedroom. Put it on the bedside table, closed the bedroom door, drew the blinds, and then climbed into bed, cold and still shivering, sweat beading up in the small of her back, around her jaw.

Her eyes settled on the handle of the bedroom door, the sound of Hati's small, quick breaths enough to keep her on edge.

After a while, she rolled onto her side, looked at the loaded gun in front of her, and let sleep come.

She didn't know when, but at some point during the night, it did.

And it was even worse than being awake.

19

JAMIE WAS no stranger to nightmares.

But last night was a whole other beast.

Her eyes dripped open sometime around dawn, the covers a tangle around her exposed legs. The bed was drenched in sweat, and she could smell it on her skin, a ripe and sharp tang in the thick air.

She sat upright, feeling the hair at the back of her neck sodden and matted, and squinted around. Hati had fled to the corner of the room and was curled up in a tight ball, nose tucked under his back leg.

He opened one eye as Jamie got to her feet, the loose t-shirt and shorts she was wearing damp and cold.

A frame of light bled in around the blinds and when Jamie pulled them back she was greeted by a bleak and wet morning. Rain had started falling during the night, and everything was heavy with droplets, shining like pearls clinging to the undersides of the tree branches and blades of grass. It had cleared the air, along with whatever had been smeared across the bonnet of her SUV. She could see it from here, the paint faded, but clean.

Had she imagined that? No, she hadn't.

There was a noise next to her and Jamie looked down. Hati was at her side.

She reached out, laid her hand on his head.

The moment it touched, he twisted around and snapped at it.

She reeled back just in time, the clap of his teeth enough to make the bite mark already on her hand twinge.

He stared up, teeth bared, huffed, and then walked away.

'You're feeling yourself again then,' Jamie said, turning to watch him go.

He stopped at the door and gently butted his head against it.

'Yeah, yeah,' she said. 'Alright.' As she walked over, flashes of her dreams played like a slideshow behind her eyes, gnarled shapes and sensations of falling and flipping, of choking and drowning, of screaming breathlessly and clawing through endless water, never reaching the surface.

Her throat was tight and she squeezed it, wondering if she had called out in the night. If that's what had frightened Hati off the bed.

Out in the hallway, the air was cooler, the warmth of two bodies in the bedroom enough to raise the temperature in there.

Jamie padded towards the kitchen, pausing to check the windows in the living room.

She stepped around the old armchair and scanned the ground. She counted three crows lying on their backs dead.

'Jesus Christ,' she muttered, shaking her head, and then went towards the kitchen. Hati was already at the door, waiting to go out.

She dumped the used filter full of grounds into the bin and refilled the coffee machine, set it to run, and then grabbed the slip lead and dog treats off the shelf next to the door.

She put a single treat on the tiles and then laid the loop of the lead around it like a snare trap, the other end in her hand.

'Hey, dickhead,' she called, kneeling and beckoning the dog over.

He came begrudgingly, eyed the treat cautiously, then bent down to snatch it up. Jamie whipped the lead upwards with a short, sharp movement, and it jumped onto his neck and tightened just before he could pull away. He tried anyway, growling and complaining. But calmed after a few seconds.

She wished she could just let him out, but he wouldn't come back, and she didn't trust him not to bite someone else. Sure, he was a jerk. But he'd been beaten, broken, abandoned at the side of the road. When she'd found him, he'd been limping along the shoulder, one leg up and lame, dumped out of a car, covered in bite marks, bleeding, one of his jowls hanging off, ear in two halves.

She guessed he'd been a fighting dog.

And that he'd lost. Served his purpose. Outlived his usefulness.

It'd taken her thirty minutes and an entire box of bran flakes to coax him into the boot of her car.

And she'd been regretting that ever since.

The vet had offered to put him down – said it would be best. For him. For her. For everyone.

But somehow, Jamie couldn't bring herself to.

She opened the door and he pulled forwards, dragging Jamie onto the step. As he sniffed around in the long grass just outside, Jamie looked into the trees beyond, saw nothing moving. No birds. Nothing. No sound either, save the pattering of the rain.

The air was cleaner, crisp this morning.

A new day.

A better one, she hoped.

As usual, she was wrong about that.

It was just before eight that she got the call.

She answered, not recognising the number. *'Hålla, Kriminalinspektör Jamie Johansson.'*

'Hey, it's Kjell.'

'Who?' Jamie asked, brow furrowing.

'Kjell Thorsen,' he repeated.

'Oh,' Jamie said. Kjell was his first name then. She'd not even asked. 'How did you get my number?'

'I took a card off your desk,' he said quickly, out of breath, 'but that's not important. You need to get down here.'

'What? Why? Where are you?' She was dressed already, standing in the kitchen, a dog-poo bag sitting on the counter in front of her with a dead crow in it.

'I'm at the station, but listen—' He paused, taking a breath.

Jamie tensed for it.

'It's Flygare. He's gone.'

Jamie closed her eyes. Fuck.

'But that's not the weird part.'

'Of course it isn't,' Jamie said, putting her coffee down.

'I don't know how to explain it … it's …'

'Something to do with crows, I imagine,' Jamie said, grabbing the poo bag and heading for the door.

'How'd you know?'

She pulled it closed behind her and stepped down onto her drive, glancing at the misshapen package in her hand. 'Just a wild guess.'

20

JAMIE DIDN'T NEED to ask what had happened.

As she pulled up, she could see plainly that the doors had been ripped right off the hinges. One lay flat on the ground in front of the entrance, the glass smashed and scattered everywhere, the other hanging at a strange angle, clinging onto the bottom bracket, all stretched and twisted.

On the ground, Jamie could see a few little black bodies, a few loose black feathers scattered around, like daubs of ink on the rain-wet pavement.

Thorsen was standing in front of it all in a long coat, hood up, arms folded, his BMW stretched across the road to try and block traffic from rolling through the scene.

Except there wasn't any.

Jamie slotted her car in so the bumpers formed a V, protecting the doorway, and got out.

Her boots crunched in the glass, the rain pattering on the shoulders of her leather bomber jacket. She could feel it cold on her scalp. She hoped it would wash away the previous night.

'Jesus,' she muttered, approaching Thorsen.

He looked at her, raised an eyebrow. 'You okay?'

'Don't I look it?'

He clicked his teeth together, eyes roving her sleep-starved, pale face. 'Just a question.'

The answer was no, she was not okay. In fact, she felt like shit. She'd never been hungover, because she'd never been drunk. In fact, she didn't drink at all. But she'd seen her father plough through entire shelves of liquor, and by the way he described his hangovers, she didn't feel too far away.

Just a bad sleep, that was all. A long day, and a bad sleep.

But there was no time for self-pity now.

'There even any point asking what happened?' Jamie asked.

He shook his head. 'If I had to take a guess, I'd say someone looped some chains through the handles of the door, attached them to a truck, and …' He lifted one hand from the knot of his arms and pointed down the street, made a little whistling noise.

'And the birds?'

He just lifted his shoulders, looking down at them.

She didn't have an answer for that one either. 'You been inside?'

He nodded.

'And Flygare's gone?'

He nodded again.

'Any signs of forced entry on the cell?'

He shook his head now.

'Someone with a key?' She looked up at him.

He looked back.

'Minna,' Jamie said then. 'Shit.'

They both turned in unison, ready to race over to her place, but stopped before they even got going.

Minna was standing between their cars, hand clutching

her handbag at her side, eyes wide. 'Oh my god,' she said, looking at the gaping hole where the door used to be. 'What happened?'

'Minna,' Jamie said. 'Are you okay?'

'Yeah, of course, why?'

She looked back at the doorway. 'Flygare – he's gone. Someone let him out of his cell. And as you had the key, we thought—'

'I didn't have the key,' she said. 'It was on my desk.'

Thorsen stepped forward now. 'You left the key on your desk?' His voice was harsh.

'Yeah, I thought … that if you needed to come in early to speak to him, that … that …' The girl's eyes began to shine now, well up.

Jamie sighed. It was like scalding a puppy. 'It's okay, Minna, you didn't do anything wrong.'

'Didn't do anything wrong?' Thorsen snapped, turning on Jamie now. 'She left the fucking cell key on her desk! Flygare could well have been the one who killed—'

'We'll find him,' Jamie said then, shutting him down. 'We'll find him, okay?'

Thorsen was seething, but he nodded eventually. Though he still wouldn't look at Minna.

Jamie needed to think, walked in a tight circle.

After a second, she headed inside, trailing droplets. She needed to see for herself. Needed to figure out their next move.

Inside, things were relatively normal. Save for the dead crows. Minna's desk was at an odd angle, a few pens on the floor. It looked like it had been shunted out of the way in a hurry. And now there was an open path between the front door and the cells.

Had it been moved on the way in, or out? Had the person

who'd broken Flygare out moved it? Or had Flygare been fighting him, kicked it out of the way as he'd been dragged past?

Was it a rescue, or something else entirely?

Jamie stepped over the bird corpses and into the cell corridor.

Nothing seemed out of place. Except the smell. The harsh scent of old bleach mixed with a newer one of mould was an uncanny and unforgettable mixture. But now, layered on top of that was a smell that made Jamie's hairs stand on end. That same sickly-sweet odour from last night. It was faint, barely detectable, but enough for Jamie to put a connection between the two events. What happened outside her house last night, and what happened here weren't two freak incidents. They were linked – by a ten-lane goddamn highway.

'Anything?' Thorsen asked, appearing at her shoulder.

'No,' Jamie said, pushing back out and heading across the room. 'You check the evidence lockup?'

His silence was enough to tell her no.

She didn't even need to go in to know the drugs were gone. The second she got around the corner into the kitchen she could see the cage open at the end of the corridor, the place still filled with dusty boxes. But the bag she'd thrown onto the nearest shelf, filled with bright red pills, was missing.

She hung her head. 'Fuck. They're gone.'

Thorsen said nothing, just walked into the middle of the room and sat on one of the desks, watching Jamie.

She came out, rubbing her temples with her freshly-bandaged right hand.

Jamie looked down at Thorsen. 'You get anything back on that warrant for Flygare's?'

He sucked air through the corner of his mouth. 'Nothing

yet. I sent an email across last night, left a message first thing this morning.'

'We need to head to Flygare's anyway. If he's out, and there's anything there he didn't want us to find, then that's where he'll head. Maybe we'll get lucky and catch him.'

Thorsen nodded, getting up. 'I also put a call into the lab in Lulea, asked for someone to come up and collect a sample of the drugs we recovered to analyse them. They should be on the way.' He looked at her, as though waiting to be told he should cancel it.

'Good,' Jamie said, already moving through the gaping doorway and heading for her car. 'Let's just hope we can find some by the time he gets here.'

'And if we can't?'

She opened the passenger door and grabbed the oddly shaped small black bag she'd brought from home, throwing it to Thorsen. 'Then at least we have this.'

He caught it, grimacing. 'A bag of dog shit?'

'It's not dog shit.'

'Then what is it?' he asked, holding it up by the handle, trying to make sense of the strange corners.

'It's a dead bird.'

He sighed, lowering it. 'Think I would have preferred dog shit.'

Jamie didn't bother with the sirens or the speed limit. The town was still a graveyard, still empty. It was well before nine, but no one seemed intent on leaving their houses that morning.

Her phone rang and she answered it. 'Minna,' she said, pre-empting the standard confirmation of identities. 'Got a pen?'

She'd elected to head for Flygare's and brief Minna on the way rather than stand there and waste any more time.

'One second … Where are my … ? Why are they on the floor?'

Thorsen looked over at her. Jamie closed her eyes. She's all they had.

'Okay,' Minna said then. 'Found one.'

'I need you to find the numbers for Hugo Westman and Olivia Sundgren's parents,' Jamie said, elongating the names so she'd definitely catch them. 'We need to get them down to the station as soon as possible for questioning, okay?'

'What about the door?'

'Westman and Sundgren first. Then, once they're on the way in – find someone to fix the door.'

'Who?'

'I don't know, Minna,' Jamie said. 'You're going to have to use your initiative, okay? But Westman and Sundgren *first*. The door isn't important.'

'But what if someone tries to rob us?'

Thorsen closed his eyes.

'I think it's a little late for that, Minna,' Jamie said. 'Just … do what I ask. We can sort out the doors later. And Minna?'

'Yeah?'

'Don't leave the station til we get back, alright?'

'But I usually go home for lunch.'

'I'll bring you a fucking sandwich! Now make those calls.' Jamie hung up, her head throbbing.

'She's … something,' Thorsen said.

'She's an idiot,' Jamie added, stepping on the accelerator. The engine whined, heaving the SUV forward.

Though Jamie didn't think it would be fast enough, no matter how quickly she drove.

And as usual.
She was right.

21

THEY HAMMERED DOWN THE TRACK, the tyres fighting for grip, and then Jamie hit the brakes, locking all four of them up.

The car juddered to a stop, skidding into the drive at an angle, sending a cloud of dust rising through the rain.

They both exited, weapons in hand, and made for the open door of the mobile home.

Jamie and Thorsen slowed, and then without being asked, Thorsen took the lead. He paused at the threshold, then stepped up inside, turning to face the interior.

He gave a little nod that it was clear, and then Jamie followed him, seeing the one thing she hoped she wouldn't.

The place was a mess. Not just because Flygare was a slob, but because someone had been through there looking for his stash. Everything was upended, the cupboards opened and emptied all over the floor. The bed at the back had been flipped over, the mattress carved up with a knife. Even the light fixtures had been ripped down, and in one place, behind an armchair lying on its side, the wall had been torn off, exposing the insulation behind. The plastic veneer curved outwards, and Jamie made a beeline for it, lifting the flap.

Behind it, some foam had been hacked away, making a space.

She glanced back at Thorsen and he nodded slowly in agreement, then swore under his breath.

This was Flygare's hiding place – where he stored his drugs and his money. And it had been cleaned out.

Had they pulled that panel off by chance? Or known to look there? Had Flygare done it? Told the person who had where to look?

Thorsen walked through the rest of the trailer, moving things with the toe of his boot.

That warrant would be worth shit now.

Damn. Why hadn't they come last night? She should have. Viklund could have waited.

Jamie cursed herself, let out a long breath, hands on her hips.

The air was close on account of the rain, thick and saturated with moisture. And in here, the smell was nothing short of horrendous. It smelt like pretty much every other drug addict's house she'd been in. A mixture of sweat and urine and other bodily fluids.

But there it was again, faint, but unmistakeable. She lifted her head. 'Thorsen, do you smell that?'

He pulled his head out of the tiny bathroom. 'Shit and piss?'

She shook her head, going to the door, stepping down onto the drive. She took another breath, trying to separate the smell from those around it. But she couldn't put her finger on what it was.

Thorsen stepped down next to her, followed her lead,

opening his large, still-swollen nostrils, turning down the corners of his mouth. 'I don't smell anything.'

Jamie sighed. 'I don't know if I do, either. Last night it was … I mean, I was …'

'You were what?'

'Nothing,' she said, swallowing and clearing her throat. 'Just a rough night.'

'Want to talk about it?'

She looked at him, at his black-ringed, grey eyes.

He didn't seem like he was making fun of her.

'No,' she said. 'It's fine.'

'Sure?'

'Yeah,' she said, holstering her pistol and heading for the car. 'Come on, we should go.'

'Where?'

Jamie stopped halfway to the car, feeling the drizzle soaking through her hair. 'I don't know.' She glanced back. 'But we're not going to accomplish much standing here in the rain.'

'Doing anything's better than nothing, I guess.'

'That the Lulea official polis slogan?' she asked, climbing in.

He feigned a laugh. 'Funny.'

22

JAMIE MOTORED BACK towards the main road, the wipers slapping lazily at the rain, smearing it more than moving it.

She slowed for the entrance, glanced left and right, and then pulled out, the tyres spinning a little on the wet ground.

Her phone was in her hand then, held up next to the wheel. She thumbed the station number up onto the screen and got ready to dial, to see where Minna had got with Olivia and Hugo. She needed to speak to them as soon as possible.

But before she could dial, someone called her.

She pressed the green button instantly. 'Johansson,' she said, glancing at Thorsen.

He was watching her screen closely.

'*Uh, hallå? Inspektör?*' A woman's voice.

'*Ja,*' Jamie answered, a little tentatively.

'It's Lovisa Nordahl,' she said. 'Is this a good time?'

'Of course,' Jamie said. 'What's wrong? Are you okay?' she asked, reading the timidness in the woman's voice.

'I'm fine,' she said, 'it's just … I've found something.'

'What is it?'

Thorsen sat a little straighter.

Jamie looked up, corrected her line from the middle of the road onto the right side, and then refocused on the screen.

'I found Felix's phone,' she said. 'And something else.'

Jamie felt her heart quicken. 'What did you find?'

'It's … I can't believe it,' she started, 'but it's … pills. A bag of pills. Red ones.'

'How many?' Jamie asked quickly.

Silence on the line.

Shit. Lovisa Nordahl didn't know that's what Jamie had found in Felix's room the first time.

'You don't seem surprised,' Lovisa said then, voice a little sharper.

Jamie chose her words carefully. 'We've been pursuing some leads, and we brought a suspect into custody, had reason to believe that drugs may have been involved in—'

'A suspect? Who is he?' she asked, voice strained and harsh. 'What's his name? Can I see him? I want to look him in the eye, ask him the question—'

'That won't be possible,' Jamie interjected. Mostly because someone broke him out of the station last night. But she didn't say that. 'Look, I'll update you when we get there, I'm on my way. Just, just don't do anything, okay? We'll be there soon.'

She hung up, changed down, put her foot on the floor.

Thorsen adjusted in the seat again, reached for the handle above the door to steady himself.

'Don't trust my driving?' Jamie asked, eyes fixed on the road ahead, hands on the wheel.

'I don't trust this piece of shit truck,' Thorsen replied.

'She's solid.'

'So are trees, and other cars, and brick walls,' he muttered. 'When was the last time this thing was serviced?' He looked across at her, the whole cabin juddering as Jamie shifted into fifth, the engine emitting an odd squeaking noise.

'Uh,' Jamie said, moving her head back and forth. 'You want the truth, or will a lie make you feel better?'

He grimaced, tugged on his seatbelt to see whether it would lock.

It didn't.

Jamie skidded to a halt outside the Nordahl house, the car crabbing the last few metres as the wheels locked up on the wet road.

Thorsen kicked the door open and practically leapt onto the pavement, ready to kiss solid ground.

Jamie was already en route to the front door, heading up the path.

The car was back on the drive. Christian had returned home then.

Jamie reached out and knocked.

Lovisa Nordahl opened it immediately, beckoned Jamie and Thorsen in.

They wiped their muddy feet on the welcome mat, and then entered, trailing droplets. Lovisa closed the door behind them then circled into the kitchen where Christian Nordahl was sitting at the island, a bag with a dozen or so red pills in it on the counter, along with a smartphone. His knee was bouncing, eyes already trained on Jamie and Thorsen as they rounded the corner.

Lovisa went to the far side, knotted her arms, nodded to the drugs. 'What was Felix doing?' she demanded. 'Was he on drugs? Did you know about this?'

Thorsen let Jamie speak. He'd never met the Nordahls and they didn't seem keen on introductions just then.

Jamie took a breath. Answer slowly, keep things calm. That was as important as satiating them. 'We don't know the whole story, yet,' Jamie said, keeping her hands at her side. Lifting them could be patronising, and Christian and Lovisa Nordahl did not look like they'd be patronised just then. 'But what we do know is that Felix was involved in something to do with these drugs.' She risked gesturing to the counter.

'Involved in?' Lovisa spat. '*Something to do with these drugs?* Tell us the truth.'

Well, that went well. Jamie sighed now. Fine. If they wanted the truth? She didn't have time for this. She needed the phone and the pills, and it would all come out eventually. 'We have strong reason to believe that Felix was selling drugs in order to save enough money to leave Kurrajakk.'

'Selling drugs?' Lovisa asked.

'Leave Kurrajakk?' Christian asked at the same moment. They both looked at each other. Christian cleared his throat, looked back at Jamie then.

Was Christian not surprised that Felix was selling, but was that he was intending to leave? Jamie could see Thorsen watching Christian Nordahl like a falcon. He'd not missed it either.

'Felix would *not* be selling drugs. Or be involved in that kind of thing.' Lovisa Nordahl cut the air with her hand. 'At all. He was a good boy. He was smart, and he—'

'I recovered a bag with hundreds of pills in it and about ten-thousand krona in cash from his bedroom upstairs,' Jamie said.

The parents fell quiet.

'I believe,' she went on, 'that Felix wasn't doing this for himself. I asked you, Mrs Nordahl, if Felix had a girlfriend? We have now confirmed that he did. Lena Viklund.' She looked at Christian. 'Do you know the name?'

He sort of shrugged.

'Did you know that Felix had a girlfriend?'

'I suspected,' Christian said. 'I'd heard noises – coming from his bedroom. At night.'

'You didn't say anything!' Lovisa protested. 'You didn't tell me!'

'He's a seventeen-year-old boy!' Christian practically yelled back. 'He needed some freedom! Especially with you treating him like a fucking child all the time!'

'Coming from the absentee fucking father!' Lovisa exploded. 'I'm surprised you could hear anything during the night – when was the last time you *slept*, and not passed out? We'll need to remortgage the fucking house with everything you're pissing away in the Moose!'

Jamie and Thorsen looked at each other. The Moose's Head was the local tavern. Christian Nordahl was a drinker then.

'You expect me to just sit around here all night, waiting for you to get home? Alone? I'm allowed to have a fucking life, Lovisa, you'd understand that if—'

'Okay, okay!' Jamie called, stepping forward and raising her hands. 'I know this is a difficult time, but arguing will only make things worse.' She lowered her voice. 'This is hard for everyone.'

Lovisa snorted, tears coming to her eyes.

'But we need to keep clear heads here.' Jamie looked at each of them. 'Now I need your help if we're going to solve this, alright?' She reached out, put her hand on the pills and phone. 'We're going to need to take these back to the station, have them analysed.' She met both their eyes again. Neither protested, but they both looked pretty angry.

Jamie pulled the phone and drugs towards her and put them in her pocket, risked lifting her hands a third time. 'I know this is all coming as a shock to you, and I can't imagine what you're going through right now – but if there was ever a time not to fight, this is it. Now, have you had the call from the lab in Lulea, about … Felix?' She struggled to find a tactful way to word it.

They shook their heads together.

Jamie rolled her lips into a line, nodded slowly. 'Okay, well, that should be your primary focus now. We'll follow up, and make sure they call today. In the meanwhile, we're going to keep doing our jobs, and we're going to find out who did this.'

Neither seemed enthralled by that.

Jamie let out another breath, lowered her hands. 'Mrs Nordahl,' Jamie said then. 'Where did you find his phone and the pills?'

She pointed out to the garden. 'The shed.'

'The shed? Why would Felix's phone be in the shed? Was it normal for him to go out without it?'

Lovisa sort of shrugged. 'I don't know, I don't think so.'

'No,' Christian added. 'It wasn't. Felix always stayed in touch.'

Jamie bit her lip. She pulled the phone out of her pocket now and clicked it on. The screen lit up, but there was a lock screen with a grid pattern. She'd have no luck cracking it herself. Shit.

'Do you know Felix's password?' she asked them.

They both shook their heads.

Her mind started working then. So why would Felix leave his phone in the shed, with a sample of drugs? The bag had ten pills, maybe a few more. One delivery, maybe. Shit, they didn't even know where he went missing from. Whether he was abducted, or went to meet someone. They didn't know much of anything, really.

'Why the shed?' she wondered aloud.

Lovisa Nordahl answered that one. 'Felix spent a lot of time out there – it's not as much of a shed as it is a summer house. Christian used to use it as an office, but Felix wanted to put some gym equipment in there, a sofa, a television – he went out there, played games with his friends, you know? He wanted privacy.'

Jamie nodded. 'I understand. Where did you find the phone?'

'It was on the arm of the sofa.'

'And the pills?'

'I noticed the corner of the bag sticking out between the cushions,' she said. 'I didn't know what it was until …'

Jamie nodded. 'Okay, great,' she said. 'We'll need to take a look around out there if we can?'

Christian was still. Lovisa Nordahl gave a little nod. 'It's open.'

Jamie returned it, felt Thorsen move behind her towards the French doors at the side of the room.

Outside, the sky was a flat sheet of grey, and the rain had dwindled to a mist.

It had settled over the garden.

As Jamie and Thorsen stepped out, they both shivered, the air cold.

'Summer's gone then,' he muttered, squinting upwards, as they started across the dew-slick garden.

Jamie humphed, raking the damp strands of hair off her forehead. 'Dead and fucking buried.'

23

THORSEN PUSHED through the door of the summer house at the bottom of the Nordahls' garden and held it open for Jamie.

She stepped in after him, detecting the scent of sweat and body spray. It was practically the same as what Felix's bedroom smelt like. Teenage boys. The place was maybe three metres deep by about five across. To the left there was a bench with a weighted bar across it, a rack with dumbbells, a floor-length mirror. On the right an old sofa facing a flatscreen television, a games console under it, two controllers strewn across the floor. There was little else there other than a side table with an open can of cola, and a waste basket with a few crisp packets and chocolate wrappers in it.

Jamie already knew it was going to be a bust. But she just wondered why Felix would have left his phone there. And been so cavalier about the drugs. Christian Nordahl hadn't seemed thrown by the proposition of Felix dealing them. Did he know more than he was letting on?

Did he have something to do with Felix's death? Nothing was telling Jamie that except that he hadn't reacted in the same way Lovisa had. But then again, she'd been surprised Felix had a girlfriend, too. And their own relationship didn't seem to be in the best shape. Perhaps Lovisa just had blinkers on, and Christian was more in tune with Felix. Or at least more aware of what teenage boys were liable to be involved in.

Namely girls, partying, and not telling their parents much about anything.

Thorsen didn't bother walking deeper inside, seemingly at the same conclusion as Jamie.

She withdrew the pills from her pocket and looked at them. 'Why did he have these?'

Thorsen looked at them too. 'Maybe he was ready to make a delivery?'

'Maybe. So he's out here, playing some games on his own – if Hugo Westman and Olivia Sundgren's timeline checks out – whiling away some time until he needs to make a drop-off?'

'Could be. Where were his parents?'

'Lovisa Nordahl was in work until midnight. Christian Nordahl, I don't know. But by the sounds of it, the Moose's Head.'

'So Felix was here alone.'

'Sounds like.'

'That's helpful,' Thorsen muttered, balling his hands and pushing them into his jacket.

'You said that someone was on their way from Lulea, right? To collect a sample of the drugs?'

'That's right.'

'Well, at least now we have some. And two phones. Lena's and Felix's. If they can crack them, it should at least give us an idea of what was going on between those two, and who Felix was in touch with before he disappeared. We should be getting the report from the crime scene today, too, right?'

'Hopefully,' Thorsen said.

They stood in silence. The summer house was quiet. Safe. Warm.

Neither of them seemed keen to head back into the rain.

But they had no other choice.

Because any way they sliced it, there was a killer roaming the streets of Kurrajakk, and with Felix Nordahl dead, Mats Flygare missing, and a whole writhing mess of secrets slowly coming to the surface, this thing was far from over.

In fact, as Jamie and Thorsen turned back to the door and the flat grey sky, the unease that had settled between them told Jamie that they both had the same sickening feeling.

It was just getting started.

24

IT SEEMED that Jamie's initial thought that the citizens of Kurrajakk had fled the town was wrong.

Jamie slowed down as she approached the crowd. There were maybe twenty people, milling around outside the destroyed doorway of the station.

A man broke from the crowd as they got near and lifted his hands, coming to the window. Jamie rolled it down and he leaned on the sill.

'Finally,' Torbjörn Forss said, sighing. He was the head crime scene technician from the previous morning. His thinning black hair was still sticking out behind his ears, and came to a sharp point on top of his forehead as the edges receded backwards. A widow's peak, Jamie thought it was called.

He looked at Thorsen then in the passenger seat, black eyes and swollen nose, then back at Jamie. 'You two made up then. Or maybe not.'

'Forss,' Jamie said, not even acknowledging the remark. 'Thanks for coming.'

Thorsen feigned a sneer in her periphery.

'Part of the job,' he said, not seemingly enthused to be back in Kurrajakk. 'You want to head inside, or …' He looked at the station's gaping entrance. 'Is there any real point?'

Everyone was a comedian.

'Please tell me you have the crime scene report for us to look over.'

'That depends, you got something for me?' He raised an eyebrow playfully.

Jamie drew a breath, knowing she should check it into evidence first, but coming to the conclusion there was no need, or benefit. She pulled the baggy of pills from her pocket, along with Felix's phone. 'Here,' she said, handing them over. 'And wait, there's one more.' She turned across the centre console, pulled her satchel up from behind Thorsen's seat, fished Lena Viklund's phone out of it. She'd not had chance to check it in the previous night, and she was glad of that now. If she had, it would be gone as well.

She handed it to Forss and he cradled the three items in his hands. Jamie noted that his fingers seemed strangely stubby.

The crowd in front of the station had now begun to move closer, all vying for answers, wanting to know the truth – no doubt stirred up by rumours of serial killers and mad crow-men come to life. Thorsen drummed his fingers on the sill of the window, the hard look in his eyes enough to stop them from coming any closer.

Forss held the pills up to inspect them, then shrugged and lowered them, opening the flap of his own satchel and dropping them in. 'What do you want me to do with the phones?' he asked.

'Crack them, let me know what you find?'

He scoffed. 'No shit. I mean, is there anything I should be looking for specifically?'

Jamie and Thorsen both offered an apologetic look.

'Okay then, I'll just give them a full going over. Don't suppose you have any paperwork for them?'

Again, the same apologetic look.

'Of course not,' he said, sighing and putting them in the bag as well, muttering something about 'small towns' under his breath. He came back up for air with a report in hand. 'Here,' he said, pushing it through the window.

'Autopsy report should be done by this afternoon. I'll email it over. You have internet here, right?'

Jamie snatched the report from him, teeth gritted a little. 'Do you know if the Nordahl's have been contacted to identify Felix's body yet?'

'The victim?' Forss raised an eyebrow. 'I don't know. Did you get in contact with the pathology lab to pass on the next of kin's details?'

Jamie's nostrils flared, grip tightening on the report. This was the kind of thing that a polisassistent would handle. That Hallberg used to handle. That Jamie hadn't handled in a long time. She let go of the anger, then shook her head. 'I'll get on it right away, inform the parents myself, and tell the lab they're coming.'

'If you want something done right, huh?' A second later Forss caught Thorsen's eye over Jamie's shoulder and backed away, hands raised, that same 'yikes' face he pulled in the woods making a second appearance.

When she looked across at Thorsen, she could see why.

The guy could scowl. She'd give him that.

Jamie realised something then. 'Wait,' she said, opening the door and going after Forss. 'There's one more thing.'

She turned back to the car, ready to ask Thorsen for what

she'd left out, and caught the dog-poo bag out of the air. Thorsen nodded. She'd not even needed to ask.

Forss came back over, looking at it dubiously, and Jamie dangled it in front of him.

'I hope that's not what I think it is.'

'Depends what you think it is,' Jamie said.

He lifted his hand and she dropped it in.

'Oh, it's a bird,' he said, almost too quickly.

'Do I even want to know why you know what a dead bird feels like?'

'I keep birds.'

'Of course you do,' Jamie said. 'Well, this wasn't a pet. It decided to hurl itself against my window last night. Hard enough to snap its own neck.'

'And that's … odd? What kind of bird is it?'

'A crow.'

'What kind of window?'

'Why does that matter?' Jamie's brow furrowed.

'Just curious.'

She let out a long breath. She did not have the patience for this. An ache had developed behind her ears, a high pitched buzzing going off somewhere deep in the back of her skull. 'Look, I don't quite know what the fuck is going on here – but I'm hoping that bird will tell us.'

He searched her face for a second, then nodded. 'Alright. It won't be the first bird autopsy I've ordered, doubt it'll be the last.'

Jamie just forced a smile. Asking about that was the last thing she wanted to do. 'Drive safe.'

He nodded, cradling the dog-shit bag full of bird, and headed off towards the ambling crowd.

Thorsen was out of the car now too. 'They're like zombies,' he muttered, turning to look at the townspeople.

Jamie looked over them, all shuffling awkwardly around, waiting for answers, barring the way to the station.

'You want to rock-paper-scissors to see who needs to tell them to leave?'

'Nah,' Thorsen said, clapping Jamie on the back, pretty damn hard. 'You're in charge here, right? You do it.' He flashed her a broad smile from under his blackened eyes and then set off towards the open door.

'I'm beginning to really hate you, you know that?' she called after him.

He raised his middle finger over his shoulder. 'Feeling's mutual.'

25

'WHAT ABOUT *KRÅKORNAS KUNG?*'

Jamie closed her eyes, took a breath, counted to three. 'For the last time,' she said, 'he's not real. He doesn't exist.'

The crowd clamoured in front of her as she did her best to quell them from the top steps of the station. Thorsen was at a desk behind her, going over the crime scene report.

'But he killed that boy. The Nordahl boy!' someone yelled.

'No, no, the King of Crows didn't kill anyone – because, and I can't stress this fact enough – he's not real. Okay? Everyone clear on that?'

'But—'

'No, no *buts,*' Jamie said, cutting off the wild-haired woman at the front of the crowd who'd intercepted her car the day before. 'I can confirm at this time that a murder has occurred in Kurrajakk.'

Murmurs from the crowd.

'We are currently pursuing several leads, interviewing witnesses, and gathering information. If anyone *has* any

information, or believes they may have seen something that
could be of use to us, then we'd very much like to hear it.'

The woman raised her hand again, mouth opening to
speak.

'But—' Jamie started, cutting her off, looking right at her,
'if it's not about something you *actually* saw or know – if it's
about the King of Crows, then …' She sighed, knowing that
all information could be useful, no matter how crazy it may
seem at first glance, 'then you can write it down in an email,
and send it to us, okay?'

'Email?' The word rose up from the crowd like it was an
alien word.

'Yes, the address is contact at Kurrajakk-polis dot S-E,
okay? Everyone got that?'

'Wait – what was the first bit?'

'Contact,' Jamie said.

'And then?' A face swam in the crowd. An old man with
thick glasses.

'At.'

'The word at?'

'No, the at *symbol*.'

'At what symbol?'

'No, the *at* … Jesus fucking Christ,' she mumbled,
hanging her head. 'You know what? Just write it down, okay?
Write it on some paper, and post it through the …' she trailed
off, turning to look at the obliterated doors now leaning
against the side of the building. '… just post it through the
giant hole in the front of the station, okay? We'll read them.'

More murmurs from the crowd.

'Now, everyone – go home, alright? Or to work, or wherever it is you're supposed to be,' Jamie commanded them.

'The Moose?' someone suggested.

There were more murmurs, this time of agreement.

And then they began to disperse, sidling off towards the Moose's Head.

Jamie turned away quickly, back to Thorsen, who was doing nothing to hide his smirk. 'That looked like fun.'

'Fuck off.' She came to the edge of the desk, folded her arms. 'Now, *please* tell me you found something we can actually use?'

Unfortunately, the look on his face said it all.

'No DNA recovered from the scene other than Felix's. No tracks or shoe prints indicating how either Felix or the King —' He cut himself off, cleared his throat quickly. 'How the *killer* got down into the sink hole.'

'If you're about to suggest that they *flew* in ...'

'I wasn't, but ...'

Jamie made a sort of growling noise and Thorsen went on. 'No fibres or hairs recovered from Felix's body, and nothing to suggest that he wasn't alone when he died.'

'Except for the fact that he was *murdered,* Thorsen,' Jamie said, slapping her hands on the desk and leaning over it. 'This bullshit about the King of Crows is total fucking nonsense. It's someone playing a joke! It's not real, and you can't tell me that you believe it for a second?'

Thorsen leaned back on the chair, giving himself some space from Jamie. He pursed his lips, spoke coolly. 'Do I believe that there's a magical bird-man flying through the forest dropping teenage boys on ancient Norse sacrificial altars? No. Do I believe that there's probably some lunatic out there dressed up in a damn bird costume? Maybe. I'm yet to see the costume.'

Jamie drew a breath, nostrils flaring, scratched at the table with her nails. Her bandaged right hand was throbbing.

'Once we have the autopsy report, we'll be able to make firmer assumptions. When we know how he died, what happened to him, we'll have a clearer picture of how the guy did it.' Thorsen opened his hands, voice calm. 'And once Forss has cracked the phones, analysed the pills, and your dead bird …' He nodded. 'We'll know more.'

Jamie hung her head, clicked her teeth in frustration. 'I just don't like standing around waiting for something to go wrong.'

'Ah, you're one of those detectives.' Thorsen grinned a little, laced his fingers behind his head. 'You're not going to rush out and do anything reckless, are you?'

'Me?' Jamie asked, looking up. 'Reckless isn't really my style.'

His grin widened. 'Somehow, I don't believe you.'

26

JAMIE DIDN'T LIKE WAITING AROUND for something to happen for exactly this reason. Whether she'd somehow managed to magnetise herself during her career, or she'd just really pissed someone off in a past life, she didn't know. But either way, when she stayed in one place for too long, shit just seemed to gravitate towards her. En masse.

They got the call at eleven from an angry mother who'd just been informed that the school had been shut down, and her child was being sent home.

It was the first Jamie heard of it, but not the last.

Seconds later, the phones started ringing off the hooks. Word was spreading – not just of Felix Nordahl's death, which seemed to be common goddamn knowledge now, but also of the break in at the station, the apparent coming of the end of the world, as heralded by the arrival of *Kråkornas Kung*. Fucking *Kråkornas Kung*.

Jamie ground her teeth, watching through the open station doors as people began arriving in droves – parents with their kids in tow, business owners asking whether they should stay open, if some sort of martial law was due to be declared, citizens of all ages, all demanding answers. Justice. Peace and safety in their town.

She had to quell this. Had to calm it. If they had to declare martial law, then they'd declare it.

The steps were glimmering with rain and a thin drizzle was still falling. Hands and fists danced above the jostling crowd as people yelled.

'Please, please,' Jamie called, raising her own hands. 'You need to go home – you need to let us do our jobs!'

'Tell us the fucking truth!' someone yelled.

'About what?' Jamie yelled back.

'Two kids are dead!'

Jamie was thrown by that. Two? 'There has been *one* murder,' she started.

'No! A boy was abducted from your care!'

Mats Flygare. 'At this stage,' Jamie went on quickly, 'we have no reason to believe that any harm has come to the suspect that we—'

'Liar!' Another voice now. 'You're supposed to be keeping this town safe!'

'I assure you that we're doing—'

'This kind of thing never happened when Ohlin was here!'

Jamie's jaw clamped shut so hard she was afraid her teeth would crack.

'Where's Ohlin?' Someone demanded.

'We want Ohlin!'

'Ohlin's not here!' Jamie shouted.

'Bring him back! We don't want you!'

'I'm in charge of this station now and—' Jamie started, cutting herself off as she ducked, a sandwich wrapped in cling film narrowly missing her head.

It bounced behind her and flopped onto its side next to Thorsen's desk.

His heel crushed it as he surged forward, already out of his chair. 'Who threw that?' he demanded, eyes wide and mad.

Jamie regained herself, came forward. 'Everyone, calm down!'

People were yelling now, shoving each other.

More projectiles started flying.

'Ohlin! Where's Ohlin!'

'We need Ohlin!'

Voices butted heads.

The crowd thronged.

People pushed inwards from the flanks, the crowd oozing forward up towards the steps.

Jamie and Thorsen locked eyes, both frightened – there must have been forty, fifty people there now, all clamouring, all shouting.

Jamie heard Minna scramble from her desk behind them, the chair hitting the floor, her footsteps receding deeper into the station as she took cover.

Thorsen's elbow touched Jamie's and they went forward, arms wide, baring the gaping doorway.

The bodies connected, all sweat and clawing hands, hot breath, calls for action.

Thorsen shoved them back, did his best to keep them from overrunning the station – but what they even wanted, Jamie didn't think they knew. They just wanted *something.* Some sort of justice, some sort of reassurance. But what could they give them?

Things started hitting the station now, flying past Jamie and Thorsen's heads as people lobbed objects from the back, the ones at the front crushed against Jamie and Thorsen's arms as they locked their heels into the steps and fought to keep their ground.

A window exploded to Jamie's right, a brick hitting the tiled floor with a heavy clap.

Minna screamed.

Jamie felt flecks of saliva hit her face, watched as more rocks, pieces of food, anything people had on them – came arcing over the heads of the citizens of Kurrajakk. Thorsen looked at Jamie, eyes asking what was going through her head too.

What the hell do we do now?

And then her heel slipped and she staggered backwards, up into the station. She threw her legs behind her, sliding across the floor as people surged in, their cries deafening in her ears.

A bang cut the air then, loud and sharp – a sound Jamie knew all too well. A gunshot.

The crowd ducked as one, the shouts of anger turning to those of shock.

Jesus! Someone was shooting.

She lifted her head, fumbling for her own pistol at her hip, the two guys driving her backwards both twisting their heads towards the noise.

Jamie saw him then, standing on the bonnet of his patrol car, a Smith & Wesson Model 10 police revolver in his hand, raised above his head.

Her first thought was one of amazement at the strength of the bonnet of his beaten up Volvo saloon. The second one of wonderment at how the hell he'd managed to get himself up there. The third one of disbelief that he'd fired a pistol into the air next to a crowd of people.

He looked out of breath, panting, his thick black and white beard touching his chest, his belly and flanks spilling over what Jamie assumed was a very strong and tight belt. His blotchy red cheeks shone in the grey drizzle, the smoking muzzle of his pistol still held aloft.

The crowd stared at him like they'd just seen Jesus throw the stone aside and come strolling back into Jerusalem.

He stared down at the crowd, shoulders rising and falling, face wet with rain.

Ohlin said nothing for a few seconds, then lowered his pistol, let it hang at his side.

'Everyone,' he boomed between laboured pants, 'go home.'

No one moved.

'Go home, and stay there. There's a killer roaming these streets, and anyone caught outside without a good fucking reason will spend a night in a cell!'

People looked at each other nervously.

'Hear what I fucking said? Home, now!'

Everyone jolted, then began scrambling away from the doors and onto the road.

Someone must have called Ohlin, and as much as Jamie hated it, if he hadn't have shown up, she didn't know what would have happened.

Thorsen straightened his rumpled, stretched shirt, smoothing out the creases from where someone had taken hold of it, and looked at Jamie. Hell, he looked more nervous now than he did when they were getting steamrolled by the mob.

They watched as Ohlin got down onto a knee and awkwardly rolled off the bonnet of the car.

He sidled over, pistol still hanging loosely at his side.

The people parted for him, glancing over their shoulders as he passed, as close to a gunslinger as Kurrajakk would ever get.

But a terrible police officer all the same.

'What the hell have you two done to my station?' he grunted, stepping up through the open doorway, looking at the mess on the floor – shattered glass, bricks, sandwiches, fruit – no doubt from the students' lunch bags.

Jamie and Thorsen stayed quiet, both seemingly unsure if that was rhetorical or not.

He shook his head then, sighed. 'I leave you in charge for one fucking day, Johansson, and this whole place goes to shit. Why am I not surprised?'

'I don't think that's quite fair,' Jamie protested.

He gave her a hard look. 'What's not fair about it? I told you to handle this – not stir up a damn revolt.'

'We're working hard,' Jamie added. 'We're following up on leads, doing everything right.' She cut the air with her hand. 'We're not prepared for this – we have no support, no backup, no—'

'No fucking spine,' Ohlin spat. 'You've done nothing but tell me how slick you are for four months. And the first sign of a real case and you're weak at the knees.' He feigned spitting on the floor. 'I can't say I'm shocked. I just thought you would have lasted more than a day.' He looked at Thorsen then. 'And you – I suppose you must be the new addition. Fat lot of good you're doing, either.'

Thorsen remained perfectly quiet, looked down at his shoes.

Jamie couldn't keep the look of incredulity off her face. Talk about spineless.

'So, what have you got? Other than a big fucking hole in the wall?' He turned and pointed the pistol loosely at the door.

Jamie stood a little straighter. 'We've identified the boy as Felix Nordahl – found that he was mixed up with drugs. That led us to Mats Flygare,' Jamie said, watching for Ohlin's reaction. He either didn't recognise the name, or had a good pokerface. 'During the night,' Jamie went on, 'someone broke him out of the station.'

Ohlin moved his mouth back and forth, beard bristling. 'Don't suppose you know who?'

'We would if you'd have gotten the CCTV at the station fixed like I asked, four months ago,' Jamie retorted.

He let out a low grumbling sound. 'If you were stupid enough to leave him here unattended,' he said, 'then it's your own fault.'

Thorsen had offered, but Jamie had declined that. But pointing fingers at anyone was going to do nothing now. Ohlin wasn't about to take responsibility, admitting she was at fault was only going to give Ohlin more ammo, and throwing Thorsen under the bus would … well … Jamie didn't know. He was standing awkwardly, looking at the ground like a scalded kid.

'Flygare,' Jamie said then. 'You pulled him out of school last year – scrawny, tall kid, longish hair, can't grow a moustache.'

Ohlin stared at her blankly.

She sighed. 'He was dealing pills in the school – the teachers attested to the fact that you marched in in the middle of the day, dragged him out by the neck. They never saw him again.'

Ohlin sucked air through his teeth.

'What happened? Did you get any information out of him? About who he was getting the drugs from? Anything on his supply chain, or—'

'Look,' Ohlin said, letting out a heavy breath, 'I know you think you know how this all works, but out here, the rules are different. Arresting someone, doing the paperwork, putting them in court, convictions … You do that, you put them in a cell, you get your evidence, it doesn't mean shit. We're two hundred kilometres from the nearest courthouse, and what, we're supposed to keep someone in the cell here for weeks, months? No, and if you let them go, they'll disappear, miss that date – so what's the point, eh? When you can take them out into the forest, put the barrel of your gun under their chin' – he lifted the pistol for emphasis – 'and tell them that you know where they live, and if you ever catch them selling drugs again, you'll come, and you'll find them, and you'll make sure no one else ever does. It's a big fucking forest out there.'

Jamie's mouth was doing its best to hang open. 'You can't be serious?' she asked.

'You don't like it?' he spat. 'There's the door. This was my town before you got here, and it'll be my town after you're gone.' He waggled the gun at her now.

She stayed firm, held his small, close set eyes.

'That's what I thought,' he grunted. 'Now do your damn jobs, and try not to let the town burn down in the meanwhile.' He turned then, headed for the street.

'What are you going to do?' Jamie called after him.

'Don't worry about me,' Ohlin replied, stepping down onto the street with a pained huff, 'just find the bastard who did this.'

'Ohlin,' Jamie said, coming to the top of the steps.

He paused at his car, looked back.

'You ever had any trouble with *Kråkornas Kung?*'

He opened the door, leaned on it, pistol hanging over the top. He seemed to think about it then, shifted his mouth again, beard bristling. His face was beaded with rain. 'It's a ghost story.'

'It might be more than that,' Jamie added. 'People are

scared. And we need to get a handle on it. Someone asked if he was *back,* like this wasn't the first time that this has happened.'

Ohlin stuck out his bottom lip. 'Bloome.'

'Bloome?'

'Agnes Bloome,' Ohlin called then, nodding to himself.

'What was she, a victim?'

'Town historian. She'll tell you what you want to know.'

'Wait – you know something about this?' Jamie asked, stepping down into the drizzle. 'This has happened before?'

'Agnes Bloome,' he said again, then ducked into his car with sudden urgency and wheeled backwards away from the station.

Jamie came forward. 'Ohlin! Ohlin!' she yelled, waving at him.

But he ignored her, bumped against the curb, and then sped away, tyres squealing on the wet asphalt.

Jamie slowed, then stopped, watching his car disappear in a cloud of diesel smoke.

Thorsen was at her side then.

'Fuck,' Jamie said, putting her hands on her hips. She looked up at Thorsen. 'You want to tell me what that was all about in there?'

Thorsen looked at her like he didn't know what she was talking about. 'What do you mean?'

'Fine,' she said, shaking her head. 'Whatever. Don't tell me, then.' She exhaled hard and jogged back towards the station. 'Come on, we need to find this Agnes Bloome.'

'What do you think Ohlin's going to do?' Thorsen asked, catching up at the steps.

'Honestly, I don't have a clue,' Jamie said, slotting down behind Minna's computer. She minimised a game of one-suit spider solitaire – which she looked to be screwing up spectacularly – and opened the database. 'But if his story about Flygare is true … I want to make sure we're ahead of him. The last thing we need is more bodies stacking up.'

'You don't think he was serious about that? He wouldn't actually do that, would he?'

Jamie stared up at Thorsen. He was chewing his thumbnail.

'I don't know,' she asked, 'you tell me. You're the one who's known him since you were a kid. Right?'

He stared back for a second, then offered her a strange, forced grin. 'Yeah, of course – but that was a long time ago. Things change.'

Jamie went back to the screen, raised her eyebrows a little, then started typing. 'Whatever you say, Thorsen.' She sighed. 'Whatever you say.'

27

JAMIE AND THORSEN pulled in outside the small house just after midday.

They'd not spoken on the ride over, and Jamie's mood was declining steadily. She was tired, frustrated, and ready to put this whole thing to bed.

The gate creaked open as they headed up the path, the little cottage shrouded by trees.

Thorsen stayed back while Jamie knocked on the wooden door, waiting for a reply.

The house was tired, but the frontage was filled with well-tended flowers.

A woman opened the door then, small and frail, in her late seventies, maybe more.

'Hallå, Agnes Bloome?' Jamie asked, smiling through the rain.

'Ja,' she answered, holding onto the door, head shaking a little. *'Kan jag hjälpa dig?'* Can I help you?

'Jag heter Kriminalinspektör Jamie Johansson,' she said, smiling broadly. My name is Detective Jamie Johansson. She laid her hand on her chest. 'Can we come in?'

The old woman looked from Jamie to Thorsen, then at the badge on Jamie's chest, at the one tucked in Thorsen's belt. She nodded, and then moved back from the door.

Jamie headed in, heard Thorsen follow. If he wanted to lie to her, they could go back to being strangers for all she cared. But she couldn't be bothered to think about that now.

Inside, Agnes led them into a kitchen with dark flagstones on the floor, an old-fashioned stove with hot plates on top, and a wooden counter with a Belfast-style sink. 'Tea?' she asked, already busying herself with the kettle.

'Thank you,' Jamie said, sitting at the rustic table. Sunflowers stood in a tall jar in the middle. Jamie was sure she grew them herself.

Cups clinked and teabags dropped into a teapot as Thorsen took up a position at the back wall, leaning against it, arms folded, seemingly recusing himself from the conversation before it even began. Jamie figured he'd jump back in when he thought up a sufficient excuse or lie to cover his ass.

'Ms Bloome,' Jamie began, to the woman's back, 'we apologise for dropping in unannounced like this, but we were told that you were something of a town historian.'

The woman smiled over her shoulder at Jamie. 'I've lived in Kurrajakk all my life. My mother before me, and her mother before her were the official town record keepers. They took note of everything that happened here since the town was originally founded, back in 1893.'

'Wow,' Jamie said, hoping that didn't sound too disingenuous.

'It's not an official position anymore, now that everyone has those smart-phones, and the internet and what have you,' she said, waving a hand dismissively.

Jamie cast her eyes around at the immaculately clean

kitchen, the plate rack with one plate in it, the drying rack next to the sink with one more.

'You live alone,' Jamie said, more a confirmation than a question.

'I don't have a man knocking around here,' she said, glancing back at Jamie again, 'if that's what you're asking.' Her eyes drifted to Thorsen. 'Though I'm not averse to the idea.'

Thorsen chuckled a little, gave her a weak grin.

'Though I do prefer a man who knows how to handle himself.' Agnes Bloome's eyes lingered on Thorsen's bruised face. She shrugged a little then, went back to filling the kettle. 'Men these days, not like they used to be. Years ago, a man around here would carry a gun, a knife everywhere he went … to deal with bandits … wolves … bears.' She shook her head. 'This place used to be something else.'

Jamie listened intently to the woman's rambling monologue, wondered how sharp her mind was. 'So you've kept the tradition alive, then? The record keeping?'

'In an unofficial capacity,' she said, carrying the kettle to the stove and lifting the lid with difficulty. Thorsen swooped in and lifted it for her. She thanked him. He receded to the back of the room again. 'Though,' the woman went on, 'I fear it will end with me – no children to carry on the torch.'

Jamie pursed her lips, said nothing for a few seconds.

'But I suppose if you're here, it's not a social visit?'

'I'm afraid not,' Jamie said.

'So what is it that I can tell you about Kurrajakk?'

The heat from the cast iron stove top made the air in the room thick. The kettle was already beginning to make a low hissing noise.

'I'm not sure if you've heard, but a boy was killed in Kurrajakk the night before last,' Jamie said.

'Oh, dear,' Bloome said. 'We haven't had a murder here since … I don't remember when. Years. Decades.'

'It's extraordinary – that much is certain. We're still trying to separate fact from fiction, which is why we're here.'

Bloome watched Jamie closely, the kettle starting to steam.

'Have you ever heard of *Kråkornas Kung?*' Jamie asked then.

The woman stood very still.

The kettle began to whistle.

'It's very important, Ms Bloome,' Jamie said.

The woman walked past then, out of the room.

'Ms Bloome?' Jamie called after her.

She glanced at Thorsen. He pushed to his feet and pointed, offering to go after her.

There was some shuffling in the next room.

Bloome appeared again then, tottering in with a large leather-bound book in her hands. She was making little grunting sounds and Thorsen rushed in and rescued her once more.

'Thank you,' she said resting a thin, wrinkled hand on his arm. She had thin grey hair tightly curled to her head, deep lines running from the corners of her mouth to her jawline that reminded Jamie of a marionette.

Thorsen laid the ledger on the table and turned it towards Jamie. The cover was old, and the golden writing on the front said, *Kurrajakk, 1980-2000.*

She opened it as Thorsen busied himself helping Ms Bloome with the tea. She allowed him to pour the water and carry the tray to the table while she sat next to Jamie and assumed control of the ledger.

Jamie was going from the beginning, page by page, but

Bloome seemed to know exactly what she was looking for and where it was hiding.

She flipped about a quarter of the way through, and then went forward a few pages, then back a few more until she found it.

1986. May. There was a newspaper clipping at the top of the page, the headline reading, *'Kråkornas Kung: Fakt eller Falska?'* The King of Crows: Fact or Fake?

Jamie ran her fingers down the page, seeing more clippings, a picture of a police officer holding up what looked like a bird costume. Another with a white sheet laid over a body in the middle of what looked like a field. One with a man in handcuffs being pushed into the back of a police car. The headline for that one was *En Kråka i Kedjor.* A Crow in Chains.

But none had names, just said, 'a suspect has been arrested.' There seemed to be nothing on any sort of conviction, just scant coverage of the crime and the arrest.

'What happened?' Jamie asked, looking up at Agnes Bloome.

The woman was licking her thin lips, staring at the clippings.

Thorsen put the tea down, placed a cup in front of Jamie and the old woman, then poured them each a serving. It smelt floral. Shit Jamie missed proper English tea.

She put her hands around it anyway to warm them, and waited for Agnes Bloome to talk.

'Kråkornas Kung has been around for a thousand years,' she said carefully, staring down into her tea. 'A storybook creature, like the Huldra, or Mare, or the Pesta …'

Jamie hadn't heard of a Huldra, but she knew the Mare – a creature that would sit on your chest while you slept, give you nightmares. She felt like she'd had her own personal mare for the last two years. The Pesta was a signifier of the plague – usually appearing as an old woman in black.

Jamie drew a breath. 'And *Kråkornas Kung* is a creature – like these?'

Bloome nodded slowly. 'Perhaps not as widely known, but in these parts, yes. Crows, ravens – they've always had significance in folklore here – Odin had a raven himself.' She looked at Jamie. 'But I suspect you remember your Norse history, don't you?'

Jamie smiled politely. Not as well as she'd have admitted.

Bloome laid her hands on the ledger, flat, her bony fingers smelling faintly of tea tree oil. 'They usually signify death in some way – and the King is no different. Half-man, half-crow, the story goes that a great battle took place here, and that an injured soldier fled the battlefield into the forest. He limped for miles, desperate to get away, terrified of death – something considered cowardly in Norse culture.'

Jamie nodded. She knew that much. Dying in battle was the greatest honour a man could hope for – and his soul would be picked from the battlefield by Valkyries, carried to the halls of Valhalla to feast with his fallen comrades for all eternity.

'The further he walked, the more crows began to follow – circling, watching, waiting for his death so they could pick apart his body. The man came to a clearing and in the clearing was an altar of petrified wood,' Agnes said, eyes closed, recalling the story.

Jamie felt her fingers moist with sweat, lips dry, the clearing and stump they'd found Felix Nordahl mounted on feeling eerily familiar.

'The soldier knelt at the altar, the crows filling the trees around him, and prayed, feeling himself fading. He prayed to the gods to save him – to save his life. But, angered by his cowardice, by his pleading, and unwillingness to die, the gods decided that a punishment was more befitting.

'Vines rose up from the ground and pulled the man onto the altar, bound him there. The crows flooded from the trees and dove at him, gouging with their beaks until his body was entirely marked with cuts, his clothing torn from his body.

'The soldier screamed himself raw, choking on his own blood, and then, at the end, a god appeared to him – the story varies as to who – some say Forseti, the god of justice, some say Valí, the god of revenge, others Loki – but it doesn't matter – they all offer him the same thing – they ask if he is ready to die, or if he wishes to be saved, whether his life is worth saving – whether he'll pledge himself to them in exchange for his life.

'With his dying breath, he agrees. The crows return then, and pull a feather from each of their tails, holding them in their beaks, and plug them into the flesh of the soldier. They cover every inch of his body in black feathers, using the soldier's own blood to cement the quills in place. The god reshapes him then, his arms into wings, his nose into a beak, his eyes to pure black. He breaks free of the roots, stands on the altar, and spreads his wings, turned mad by the pain of it all.'

'Jesus,' Thorsen muttered from across the room.

Jamie glanced up, then back at Agnes Bloome, who was now smiling to herself. 'He was given rule over the birds that had dogged him, made—'

'King of Crows,' Jamie finished without meaning to.

'And told to watch over the forest, to make sure that men without honour who wander in, never leave again. This was his punishment, for all time.'

Jamie sat in silence as Bloome finished, thinking about that. 'Tell me what happened in May 1986.'

'Oh,' the woman said, smiling a little, sipping her tea, 'now you are testing an old woman's memory.' She sighed. 'You can borrow the ledger, if you'd like – the clippings are all there,' she said. 'There were two deaths – a woman, and then a man. I believe the man murdered the woman – his wife – and then the brother of the woman killed the man.'

Thorsen stepped forward. 'Dressed as a giant crow. But why?'

She swallowed, thought for a moment. 'If I'm remembering right, he was never convicted of the crime – though I'm hazy on the details – there wasn't much about it in the paper – and people were a lot more superstitious back then.' She chuckled a little, sipped more floral tea.

Jamie was looking over the clippings while she spoke. She was right, it was vague.

Thorsen was talking again then. 'So a guy kills his wife, gets off with it. Then his brother-in-law seeks revenge dressed as a giant bird. Great.' He sighed.

'Is there anything else you can tell us about the crime?' Jamie said, her phone already out. She snapped a few photos of the clippings in front of her.

The old woman shook her head. 'No, but I would think that the poliskomissarie at the time would know more, though I believe he's even older than me,' she said brightly. 'Is your tea alright? You haven't touched it,' she said, glancing at Jamie.

She smiled politely, lifted it to her lips, sucked in a mouthful of the liquid. It just tasted like flowers to her, and not very nice ones. She didn't think her palate was very refined. She guessed maybe chamomile, but that would be going out on a limb. She kept her face straight anyway, and put it back down.

'Do you know where we can find him?' she asked hopefully.

Agnes Bloome shook her head.

Shit.

They were done here then.

Just further down the rabbit hole.

Jamie reflected on the story of the King of Crows as they sat. That he was charged with killing those who showed dishonour. But what dishonour had Felix Nordahl shown?

One thing came to mind immediately. Lena Viklund. The fifteen-year-old he'd slept with, gotten into drinking. Given drugs to.

Thorsen was watching her. And then, as if reading her mind, he raised an eyebrow, mouthed, 'Viklund?' to her.

She nodded briefly and he rolled his lips into a line.

They were on the same page on that, at least.

But before they could exchange anything else, Bloome spoke again. 'But,' she said, raising a crooked finger, 'There is perhaps someone who will know even more about the whole thing …'

'Who?' Jamie asked, leaning in.

'Nils Markus.'

'Nils Markus?' Jamie asked, looking up at Thorsen. He shook his head, shrugged a little. Didn't know the name. 'Who's that?'

'Kråkornas Kung,' she said. 'That was his name. The man who killed his brother-in-law.'

'He's still alive?' Jamie didn't know why she was so surprised. 'Do you know anything else about him? Does he still live in Kurrajakk?'

'That I don't know – I just remember his name, it popped into my mind all of a sudden. I remember the whole town talking about it,' she said, sighing a little. 'Back before the internet and all that, you know? Word didn't get around like it does now, but it was still the talk of the town for, oh, months.' She sighed. 'More tea?'

Jamie declined. 'No, thank you,' she said, suddenly ready to be away again. Her head felt like it was filled with broken glass, and her eyes were heavy, her mouth dry and odd-tasting from the tea. 'We need to go,' she announced.

Thorsen was already pushing off the wall. 'Thank you for the tea,' he said, offering a hand to Agnes Bloome.

She took it and he clasped hers in both of his, smiled at her.

She returned it, and then he and Jamie slipped from the room, and out towards the car.

Before Jamie could even prompt him, Thorsen was dialling the station.

28

MIRACULOUSLY, Minna hadn't forgotten how to access the polis database since Jamie had shown her that morning.

She found Nils Markus's information reasonably quickly, and Jamie was surprised to learn they weren't far away.

Though it wasn't hard to get anywhere fast in Kurrajakk. Traffic wasn't exactly an issue.

They burned down the track towards Markus's house, a lane that wound towards a grassy rise.

The old SUV broke free of the trees and onto the stony road that cut through a rough meadow up to the old farmhouse.

It was a solid, square building with little windows and an old wooden barn affixed to the lower side. The house faced across the slope, the barn at its flank, its roof lower than the main building, pushing off down the hill.

To the right, a grassy meadow fell away, a few odd goats walking around it, keeping the grass down. About fifty metres out, a rough fence made from tree boughs stretched across, beyond it a stretch of thicker grass, and then an impenetrable wall of pines. They enclosed the entire place like a palisade.

There was no wind here, but the trees moved gently around them.

A thin line of smoke drifted from the chimney of the farmhouse, but Jamie could see no car, just dark welts in the mud next to the barn where one had parked recently.

Jamie slowed next to them on the way up to the turning circle in front of the main house, and looked to see how fresh they were. Little puddles had formed from the drizzle in the deepest parts, but it was hard to tell if they'd missed Markus by minutes or hours.

She sighed and drove further up, swung around, and then parked facing the exit.

Thorsen inspected the house carefully and Jamie cast her eye over the grounds. Nothing moved except the goats in the distance. But all was silent, the layer of mist settled across the place dulling the sound of the creaking trees.

She opened the car door, heels crunching on the gravel, and headed towards the farm. Curtains were pulled across the paint-peeled windows, and the once-blue door could have done with a few fresh coats too.

Jamie thumped with the heel of her fist, knowing there'd be no answer.

She barely waited before heading down the slope towards the barn. Thorsen was out of the car too, still keeping to himself, still sheepish. He followed her all the same as she approached the double doors facing onto the drive next to the tyre marks, and shook the old wrought-iron padlock that held two ends of a chain together. The rusted links clanked but held.

'Thick chain,' Thorsen said from behind her, keeping his distance.

'Mm,' Jamie said, glancing back. 'Something in here worth stealing?'

'Or hiding.'

Jamie stared down at the lock, then sighed. No warrant, nothing to suggest anyone was in danger. No reason to kick their way inside.

She set off down the length of the barn.

Thorsen watched but didn't follow.

Jamie reached the corner, turned it. On the far side, facing into the meadow, there was a concrete slope leading down to the grass, and a pair of big metal doors set on rollers. There was no lock or handle, but there were metal support struts running diagonally across them.

And above – Jamie craned her neck upwards, squinting in the thin rain – there was an open hatch. Jamie guessed it led to a hay loft, and the hinges at the top told her the thing opened fully. It was cracked about a foot to let air circulate.

But it was open.

Unlocked.

Jamie pricked her ears, looked around.

Not a soul in sight.

Would this fly in the city? No. Wiik would have had her head for doing it. But who was going to tell on her out here?

Before she'd even finished that thought, she had her hands around the diagonal support struts, looking for a foothold. The outer frame of the door would have to do, and she pulled herself up, one foot on it, the other on the diagonal.

She tried to steady herself, found nothing to grab onto, and little to balance on.

Her heel slipped then, slick on the wet black paint, and she fell, landing awkwardly and stumbling halfway down the slope.

'Fuck,' she mumbled, rubbing her stomach and hissing. That kind of sudden stretch always hurt. Who knew getting shot in the gut would have lasting effects?

Jamie pushed the sodden hair from her face and turned, freezing.

'Need a hand?' Thorsen asked, leaning against the corner of the barn, arms folded. He raised an eyebrow.

'With what?' Jamie asked innocently.

He humphed a little, laughed. 'If you don't want me to give you a boost, would you mind giving me one?' He turned his eyes to the hatch above.

Jamie studied him for a second, then went back towards the door. 'You think I could lift your big ass?' She beckoned him over. 'Plus, I don't want to get dirt on my hands. Come on, lift me up.'

Thorsen smirked a little, feigned a bow. 'As you command.'

He had another thing coming if he thought this cutesy act was going to get him off the hook.

Thorsen half-kneeled, slapped his thigh and laid his interlaced hands on it, palms up.

Jamie went without hesitation, heel on his hand, hand on his shoulder.

He lifted her easily and her hands hit the wooden frame of the hatch.

She put her other foot on the top of the door, felt Thorsen guide her heel over his head, and then she was in, knee on flat ground, crawling through hay.

Jamie took a dusty, heavy breath, and coughed, the same sickly-sweet smell from her driveway and the station hanging in the air. It was sharper here though, more acrid, like burnt plastic, almost, or alcohol. Sharp. Enough to make your eyes water.

'Jesus,' she muttered, pulling her legs around so she was crouching.

It took her eyes a second to adjust, dim light filtering in between the slats of wood that were the walls.

She leaned back towards the hatch, squinting in the fumes, and took a gulp of fresh air before she pushed forwards.

There was a ladder on the other side of the loft, but she aimed for the nearest edge, swung her legs over, took hold of it with her hands, and then dropped over, swinging one-eighty and landing in front of the roller door.

She reached out, pushed the heavy steel latch-bar upwards, and then grabbed the handle, rolling one of them aside.

Jamie stepped into the clean air again, fighting for breath. She had a strong stomach, but the smell was enough to turn her sick.

Thorsen's hand was on her shoulder then.

She looked back, saw him staring into the interior.

Now that the door was open, she could see what he was looking at.

The centre of the barn was dominated by an old, rusted out tractor, but the entire right hand side was filled with shelves, a workbench, various scientific apparatus. And crows. Lots of them.

'Shit,' she said.

Thorsen's eyes narrowed and he stepped in.

Jamie pulled the collar of her bomber jacket over her face and went after him.

She could see now that the crows were suspended from lengths of fishing wire by little hooks driven through their bodies, their wings, their backs. Some of them were lined up on the workbench itself, some were in jars filled with liquid.

There were other animals, too – rodents, rabbits, other birds. But the crows were the thing that dominated the space.

'Jesus fucking Christ,' Thorsen muttered, looking at it all.

Jamie homed in on the central workspace, made out the tools of the trade in the gloom, all hanging neatly on the back wall. Little hooks and scalpels, curved needles, forceps, pliers. She'd seen them before – in a place not unlike this one. Her stomach twisted, eyes roving to the steel drums stacked against the back wall. She lifted her chin towards them.

Thorsen followed her gesture and headed over. He checked them, then turned back, opened his mouth to speak.

'Formaldehyde and ethanol,' Jamie said before he had the chance.

'How'd you know?' Thorsen asked.

'Taxidermy chemicals.' She turned back to the workbench. There was a crow pinned to it, wings splayed, chest opened, organs and innards removed. They were sitting in a steel bowl to the right of it. The shining pink and brown tangle of guts stared back. Like they had done from the tarmac at the Kurrajakk cross. Like they had done from the bonnet of her car outside her house.

Her stomach flipped over, eyes stinging in the fumes.

On the shelves above there were dozens of taxidermied animals, all watching her. The bodies were interspersed with beakers, glass bottles and phials. She walked right, following them, saw more apparatus – distillation beakers and glass tubing, bunsen burners and other chemistry equipment. The air was thick with their stench.

Familiar and alien all at once.

Enough to make her head swim.

Was Markus behind the drugs, too? Was this where he was cooking them up?

They'd need to catch him in the act – or at least surprise him at home and muscle their way in here. Any lawyer worth their salt would have this case thrown out in an instant over trespassing, breaking protocol.

But now that they knew … now that they knew, they could nail him.

And all this would be over.

Jamie let out a long exhale, closing her eyes.

'We need to find Markus,' Thorsen said then, appearing next to her, staring down at the disembowelled bird on the table.

Jamie only mustered a nod.

Her phone buzzed in her pocket and suddenly she was glad for an excuse to get out of there. She'd seen more than enough already.

'Johansson,' she answered.

'Inspek—'

'Ja, Minna,' Jamie cut her off. 'What is it?'

Thorsen came outside too, occupied with something else.

Jamie watched him go, not really listening to Minna. He headed down the ramp and onto the meadow, following what seemed to be a trail.

Jamie glanced back into the barn, saw that there were a couple of dark spots marking a path over the threshold, down onto the grass.

She took a few steps after Thorsen, watching him hunch forward, trace the line with his fingers.

'Say that again?' Jamie said, coming back to Minna mid-sentence.

'I said Hugo Westman and Olivia Sundgren are here with their parents. What should I tell them?'

Felix Nordahl's best friends. Shit. Why hadn't Minna told her they were coming? She ground her teeth, still watching Thorsen as he reached the wooden fence in the distance and stopped, partially shrouded in the thin mist. He touched the wood, held his fingers to his nose, then turned to Jamie. 'Blood,' he called, holding his hand up.

Jamie felt her grip tighten around the phone, then turned back to the open door to *Kråkornas Kung's* workshop of horrors. 'Tell them …' Jamie said, looking back down towards Thorsen. She hung her head, sighed, turned again, reached out and took hold of the sliding door, dragged it closed. 'Tell them we're on our way.'

29

JAMIE STEPPED BACK through the doorway to the station and shed her jacket. In and out of the rain all day, it was soaked through.

She hung it on the back of her chair, gave a quick nod to Thorsen, and he split off. It was time to divide and conquer. They needed to find out as much as they could about Nils Markus and his history. They'd gone straight from Bloome's to his farm, so while Jamie dug into Hugo Westman and Olivia Sundgren, it was Thorsen's task to learn as much about Markus as possible.

Jamie rang out her arms and stretched her shoulders, eyes still aching and heavy. God, she hoped she'd sleep tonight. She could sleep now.

And then, she was in front of the door to the interview room and walking in.

Jamie looked up, saw the dated room outfitted with a wood-veneered table, damp-black corners, and no less than five unhappy looking people. Hugo Westman was sitting at the table on the far side, still as lanky and teenage-esque as she'd ever seen. He was picking at his thumbnail. Olivia

Sundgren was next to him, arms folded, same glare as she had before, wavy dark hair hanging over her shoulders. Both were out of their uniforms.

Behind Westman was his father, Jamie guessed. Tall, thinning dark hair, a mean scowl. Sundgren's parents came as a pair. Her father was squat, with curly hair, her mother waif-thin, with greyish-brown hair and watery eyes.

They all watched Jamie as she entered.

She paused at the front of the table, put one fist into the other, cracked her knuckles, her brain faltering. What was she going to say?

'Uh,' she started, shaking her head slightly. 'Ahem, thank you for coming.'

That was met with tuts and snorts.

Okay, now she knew what she was doing. 'I'd like to speak to Hugo and Olivia individually, if I can?'

'Are they being arrested?' Westman's father asked.

'No.'

'Are they being detained on suspicion of anything?' That was Sundren's father now.

'No.'

'Are they being questioned in an official capacity as suspects or witnesses to a crime?' Westman's father again.

'You two rehearse this?' Jamie asked, the coldness in her voice apparent.

'If not,' Sundgren's father broke back in, 'then there's no need to speak to them individually. You can talk now, and I suggest you do, otherwise we're leaving, and any questions can be done in front of a solicitor.'

Alright, now Jamie was pissed.

She let out a long breath. 'You do realise I'm the one trying to *help* here? I'm the one hunting the guy who killed Felix Nordahl. Your kids should be prepared to answer questions – in fact, they should be desperate to, so we can catch this guy.' She set her jaw, met the fathers' eyes over their knotted arms. 'Or maybe you're not so keen on that because I'm going to ask them about the drugs that Felix Nordahl was in possession of. The drugs that I have it on good authority that your children were also taking, and also in possession of?'

The dads scowled. The kids looked at the table.

'I have enough photographic evidence of the two of them under the influence to detain Hugo and Olivia right now, petition a judge to grant a search warrant for your houses, order urine tests, and hold them in custody without asking them a goddamn question for as long as I see fit,' Jamie snarled. 'And when I find the pills – because I'd bet my life I will – then I'll charge them with possession, and they can kiss any hope of getting into university or finding a decent job goodbye.'

'Are you threatening us?' Westman's father replied, stepping around the table.

'I'm telling you,' Jamie said evenly, putting one hand on the grip of her pistol, 'that your kids were best friends to a boy who was chased through the forest, hacked to pieces, and then choked to death with the corpse of a fucking *bird*. So take a look at my face, and take a look at where you're standing, because I'm trying to do my job, and you're being a real goddamn pain in my ass. And trust me, that's not something you want to be.'

Westman's eyes twitched.

'Step back around to the other side of the table, give your kid some room, and stay quiet,' Jamie ordered. 'I don't want to be here any longer than you do, and I *don't* want to take time out of my day to prove to you that I'm not the type of person that says things they don't mean.'

Westman held firm, searching Jamie's face for a hint of waver.

'Dad,' Hugo said then, quietly. 'Please, I want to help.'

Westman swallowed, then stepped back, muttering something to Sundgren's father. He nodded in agreement, fired Jamie a look, and then stepped back too.

Olivia and Hugo both stiffened in their chairs as Jamie turned her gaze on them. 'Answer truthfully,' she ordered. 'Answer plainly. I need to know everything if I'm going to catch the person who did this to Felix, okay?'

Both nodded.

Jamie glanced up at the parents then. 'If there's anything you'd prefer they don't answer without a solicitor present, feel free to voice that opinion. But if you make this difficult, then it's not going to be a fun day for any of us. Okay?'

The fathers scowled.

'I'll take that as a yes.' Jamie sighed, rubbed her eyes, then sat on the chair facing the kids. 'When did you see Felix last?'

'The day before yesterday,' Hugo said.

The day before he died. 'Olivia said she spoke to him via text at the school.'

'I saw him,' Hugo said. 'Olivia wasn't there.'

'You saw him? In person?'

'Yeah.'

'What time?' Jamie asked.

'I dunno, after school,' he said, shrugging. 'We went to his house, played some video games. He's got a summer house thing in the garden.'

'What time did you leave?' Christian Nordahl had said that Felix had gone out in the evening. She needed to nail down a timeline.

'Six, maybe a little after.'

'Was Christian Nordahl there?'

'No, I don't think he was home from work.'

'Why did you leave? Was Felix going somewhere?' Jamie asked, trying to solidify an order of events.

'No, I was just going home to get some food. Felix was just chilling.'

Jamie nodded slowly. 'And you didn't hear from him afterwards?'

Hugo shook his head.

This wasn't going anywhere. She needed to change tack. 'Do you know the name Lena Viklund?' she asked.

'Yes,' Hugo said.

'Who is she?'

'Felix's girlfriend.'

'When did you see her last?' Jamie asked.

'I don't know. Last weekend, maybe.'

'The weekend just gone?'

'Weekend before.'

'With Felix?' Jamie asked.

He nodded.

'At a party in the forest?'

He waited for a second, glanced at Olivia, then nodded again.

Jamie lined that up against the timeline Gunnar Viklund laid out. He said he sent Lena away last week, so that would have been the weekend before she left. No holes so far.

'What about you?' Jamie asked, looking at Olivia. 'Did you see Lena since?'

She shook her head. 'No, that was the last time.'

'What about Mats Flygare? Know that name?' Jamie asked.

Hugo and Olivia looked at each other. 'I dunno,' Hugo said. 'Maybe. Heard it around, I think, but I don't know him.'

'No,' Olivia said. 'Same – like, maybe someone said it at a party or something.'

Jamie watched them both for a second, then took out her phone, spent a minute finding it, pulled up the photograph of Mats Flygare attached to his driver's license. It was an older photo, little grainy. But she hoped it'd work. She pushed it across the table. 'Him.'

'Oh,' Hugo said, 'that guy, yeah, I've seen him around at the parties.'

Olivia leaned in, looked, nodded as well.

'These parties, they happen a lot?'

'Every weekend in the summer, I guess,' Hugo said.

'And this guy – does Felix know him? Have you seen them talking? Are they friends?'

Hugo shook his head. 'I don't think so. Not that I've seen. But Felix … we didn't spend that much time together this summer. Not like before.'

Jamie nodded. 'Because of Lena, the drugs?'

Neither of them answered that one.

Jamie didn't want to push it. They were making progress.

'The weekend just passed,' Jamie said. 'Was there a party then?' That was just a few days before Felix died. After Viklund flushed the drugs.

'Yeah,' Hugo said.

'Felix was there?'

'Yeah.'

'He seem okay?'

'Yeah, normal … *ish*. I mean, Lena wasn't there – she got sent somewhere, he said.'

'Did Felix seem nervous, scared at all?'

They shook their heads together.

'And at these parties, was Felix selling pills?'

They kept quiet.

She needed to toe the line here. 'Okay,' Jamie said, 'you don't need to answer that one – your silence says it all.'

They both squirmed a little.

'What about Flygare – was he there? This guy?' She pointed to the screen.

'Maybe,' Olivia said. 'I think I remember seeing him – but he wasn't there all night, I don't think.'

Hugo just sort of shrugged and shook his head. 'I don't remember seeing him.'

'Anything special happen at this party? Did Felix argue with anyone, or … anything out of the ordinary at all?'

'I … I don't know,' Hugo said. 'We were …' He lowered his voice. '… *drinking,* a bit. A bit more than normal. It was … I dunno … the last one of the summer.' He shrugged again.

The way he said 'drinking' made Jamie think he didn't mean drinking at all.

'Was Felix pushing that? Harder than normal, maybe?'

Another sort of shrug of agreement.

'But nothing else happened?'

Hugo was quiet.

'Well, you got robbed, didn't you.' Olivia said, nudging Hugo.

'Shh!' he hissed.

'What!?' Westman's father practically yelled from behind.

'Shut up,' Hugo snapped at Olivia, 'for fuck's sake!'

Olivia slapped him on the arm. 'You shut up! Felix is *dead,* and you're worried about your dad finding that out?'

Hugo's mouth flapped a little, eyes filling.

Jamie shot Westman's father a look that pinned him to the wall, and then she refocused on Hugo. 'Tell me what happened.'

'I …' he started, hunching his shoulders, making himself

a smaller target for his father's gaze. 'I don't know. We got into … we were a mess …' He sighed. 'All I know is that one second I had my phone, the next … I didn't.'

'And you think someone took it? You didn't drop it?'

'We were sitting round a fire – with people we knew – we all looked – if I'd dropped it, we would have found it.'

Olivia jumped in. 'We got up to take some photos – he put it down for a second,' Olivia said. 'And then, like he said … It was just gone. Someone must have taken it.'

Jamie looked from one to the other now. Did it mean something? Did it mean anything? She recalled the photo in the dump Hallberg had sent, the one with the three of them standing arm in arm. Was that the photo they were talking about?

There was a knock at the door behind her and she turned to see Thorsen's head in the gap. 'Phone call,' he said. 'Forss.'

Jamie nodded, turned back to the room. 'I'll be back in a second,' she said, then got up and went out.

'What's up? Autopsy report back?' Jamie asked.

Thorsen guided her down the corridor a little, holding his phone out. It was on speaker.

'No,' Forss said, 'it's one of the phones. I cracked it.'

Jamie checked her watch. 'Shit, are you back in Lulea already?' He'd been gone maybe two hours, a touch longer. It was three to the city.

'No, rest-stop outside Boden,' he said. 'I started running the crack on my laptop while I was— it doesn't matter. The two phones you gave me, I cracked the shit one.'

'The shit one?'

'One's an iPhone, will take a while. The other one, the cheap Chinese thing – I'm in.'

That was Felix Nordahl's phone. The one that his mother

had found. Was it his real phone, or one just for dealing? 'What'd you find?'

'Usual drug-dealer thing – lots of numbers texting emojis, short phone calls, that kind of thing. But there was a text from a saved number – the evening before the body was recovered. About seven o'clock.'

'Okay? What did it say?'

'Need some. Meet me? Usual place.'

'Hardly enigma code,' Jamie muttered, folding her arms. 'But it's the most solid thing we've got on Felix's movements the night before he died.' She looked up at Thorsen and he nodded in agreement. 'That person could be the last one to have seen him before he was killed.'

'They could have been the one who killed him,' Thorsen added.

Jamie bit her lip, keeping her mind from running away with it. 'Forss, you said the number was saved. What name was it under?'

'Uh …' Forss said, tapping a few keys. 'Hugo Westman. You know the name?'

Jamie and Thorsen both turned to look at the door to the interview room.

'Yeah,' Jamie said, feeling her free hand curl into a fist. 'We know the name.'

Thorsen watched Jamie. 'That fit in with what he's saying?'

Jamie thought about it for a few seconds. 'Westman says his phone was stolen a few days before Felix died. They were at a party, taking drugs – going pretty hard. Harder than normal. Felix pushing the pace. Olivia and Westman think Flygare was there, too.'

Thorsen nodded. 'You think it was planned? Flygare took Westman's phone with the idea to lure Felix into the forest?'

Jamie drew a slow breath, thinking back to her first conversation at the school with Hugo Westman and Olivia Sundgren. Hugo had a phone. Had been texting under the table. 'I don't know,' she said. 'That's one theory.'

'What's the other?'

'That Hugo Westman is full of shit and that he just lied to my face.' She swallowed, feeling herself hardening.

'What are you going to do?'

Jamie was already storming back towards the interview room. 'I'm going to find out the fucking truth.'

30

J AMIE ENTERED the room with Thorsen in tow and didn't bother sitting.

She rested her hands on the table, locked eyes with Hugo Westman. 'I'm going to ask you a few questions, and if I even *think* you're lying to me, I'm gonna drag you out of that chair, shove you in cuffs, and go after you for Felix's murder. You got that?'

His eyes widened, mouth opening. He shook in the seat, looking at Olivia.

'Don't look at her,' Jamie snapped, banging the table with her hands, 'look at me.'

Olivia Sundgren shuffled out of the way a little more, like heat was coming off Jamie.

'You told me your phone had been stolen. Did you get it back?'

He shook his head, 'No, I—'

'Then why did I see you with a phone in school yesterday when I spoke to you? You were texting under the table.'

He blinked.

'Answer me.'

'It was — it's, uh, a new phone — a temporary one, while, I, uh—'

'While you what? Answer the question.' She banged the table again. Westman jumped.

'Felix gave it to me!'

Jamie stared at him intensely. 'What do you mean he gave it to you?'

'It's Felix's phone,' he repeated, looking down now, tears coming to his eyes.

His father shook his head behind him, muttered under his breath. 'Jesus fucking Christ.'

Jamie exhaled hard. 'Think very carefully, Hugo,' Jamie said slowly. 'You're telling me that your phone was stolen on Saturday night?'

He nodded.

'And that Felix gave you his phone as a replacement? Why?'

Hugo looked up, squirmed a little under her gaze. 'He said … he said he didn't need it … that he had another phone, but that … Look! It was just until I could replace it, okay? Until I could buy another one, so my dad didn't …' He turned to look at him, then shrank into the chair when he saw his father glaring back.

Jamie swallowed, stood straight. 'Here's my problem with your story, Hugo,' she said coldly. 'You say your phone was stolen on Saturday night. You then say Felix gave you his phone as a replacement. You say you saw him on Tuesday afternoon after school. You say you left him around six. There's no one to corroborate that. No one to say whether you were there at all. But I just found out that a text was sent from *your* phone to Felix's phone at seven p.m., asking for him to meet you. So explain that, please? If he knew you lost your phone, and he gave you his phone as a replacement, why would he go to meet you based on a text? Because right now, all I have are some ropy details, some stories that aren't adding up, bags of drugs and rolls of cash, and a dead teenager. And you're right in the middle of it.'

Hugo Westman's eyes filled with tears, with pleading desperation.

'So unless you can give me an alibi to tell me where you were on Tuesday night ...' She lifted her eyes to look at Hugo's father. He was a statue. He wasn't going to lie for his son. And Jamie knew that he'd already have jumped in by now if Hugo was home when he said he was.

Jamie turned to look at Thorsen.

He bit his lip, nodded slowly.

Jamie turned back to Hugo. 'Hugo Westman, I'm arresting you on suspicion of—'

'Wait!' Olivia yelled then, standing up. 'He was with me!'

'Olivia!' Her mother said quickly. 'Don't lie for—'

'I'm not! I'm not ...' she said, slumping back down into the seat. 'He was ... Felix didn't know. But we were ... we *are* ...'

'Sleeping together.' Jamie's patience with teenagers had been thin to begin with. Now it was gone.

She nodded. 'We didn't tell Felix – we didn't tell anyone – because ... because ...'

'Last year,' Hugo said, 'Felix wanted more with Olivia ... But she didn't ... So ...'

'Because you were already together?'

Hugo shook his head. 'No, but it was hard – almost broke the friendship up, you know? So this summer, when Felix found Lena, me and Olivia ...'

Fucking teenagers.

Jamie took a breath.

'That's still not enough,' she said. 'If anything – that's

more motive. Felix and you, both liking the same girl –
you're keeping it a secret, he finds out, doesn't like it … You
two argue …'

'It wasn't like that!' Hugo protested. 'Felix never knew!'

This was going nowhere. 'Where's the usual place?'

'The what?'

'The 'usual place',' Jamie repeated. 'The text to Felix's
phone from yours said to meet at the usual place. Where's
that?'

His brow furrowed. 'I, uh …'

'Tell her,' Olivia urged.

'There's a clearing,' he said. 'In the woods, near the
school – by the river. There's a falls there, it's pretty loud, no
one bothers us. Kids are always hanging out there. That's
where Felix would …'

'Just say it,' Olivia said, shaking her head, lip quivering.
'Just fucking say it. He's dead now. It doesn't matter
anymore.'

'That's where Felix would go to sell pills,' Hugo said.
'It's where we'd go to party, it's where it all happens.'

Jamie filled her lungs, turned to Thorsen. He read her
expression, folded his arms, then nodded. 'I'll go find a map,'
he said, then walked out of the room.

Jamie stood in silence, staring at the two kids. Olivia
reached out, took Hugo's hand under the table.

'You're going to mark out where this place is,' Jamie said,
her voice flat. 'And then I'm going to split you up, and you're
each going to tell me exactly where you went, and what you
did on Tuesday night.'

Olivia Sundgren licked her lips nervously, looking up at
Jamie. 'And then what happens?'

'And then,' Jamie said, putting her hands on her hips and

blinking her tired eyes, 'I'm going to decide whether either of you had anything to do with Felix Nordahl's death.'

'We didn't!' Hugo practically shouted.

Jamie looked at the pimple-chinned boy in front of her, measured him, searched him for any hint of whether there was a killer hidden behind his eyes. 'We'll see.'

31

JAMIE WAS asleep when Thorsen put a cup of coffee down on her desk.

She jolted awake, picked her head up, blinked a few times, looked around.

'Here,' he said. 'Thought you might need this. I guessed milk and sugar.'

Jamie stared down into the cup. 'You guessed wrong,' she said, picking it up and taking a long, overly sweet sip. 'Thanks,' she croaked, throat dry and tight. 'When did the door-guy finish up?' Jamie asked, nodding towards the now boarded over hole at the front of the station. The broken windows had also been boarded over.

'Wouldn't call it finished,' Thorsen said sourly, staring at it. 'Dunno, an hour ago, maybe?'

Jamie checked her watch. 'Shit, how long have I been asleep?' It had grown dark outside now. Jamie could tell through the one good window in the corner. And Minna had left for the day.

He shrugged. 'I dunno – but hey, I followed up on Gunnar Viklund's alibi, called the Moose, then called his aunt down in Malmö, no answer, left a message. Then I dug into him a little.'

'What'd you find out?

'He's a decent guy, worked at the local lumber mill for twenty-five years, got early retirement – now claims disability – workplace accident – nothing on that, though – no paperwork.'

Jamie snorted. 'I'm not surprised.'

'He seemed okay to me when he was chopping wood.'

'Looks can be deceiving.'

'Can't they just,' Thorsen said, sighing.

Jamie didn't know what he meant, but she was too tired to ask.

Thorsen went on. 'But by all accounts, no one had a bad word to say about him. Three years ago his wife, Alma, was diagnosed with cancer – he cared for her at home. She died a little under a year later. Since then, he spends pretty much every night at the Moose.'

'Including Tuesday?'

'He was there all night – showed up around five, drank himself blind, got into a bit of a shouting match with some-one, was asked to leave around midnight, had to be carried out and driven home by a friend – Olof Englander. The land-lord confirmed that, which lines up with Viklund's story.'

'An argument? With who?' Jamie asked, perking up, sucking more coffee. She did her best not to grimace.

Thorsen rubbed his eyes with his knuckles. 'I couldn't get a firm answer on that. A few names were thrown around – including Christian Nordahl.'

'Nordahl?' Felix's father. 'Him and Viklund argued? About what?'

Thorsen shrugged now. 'Don't know. It wasn't just them – a few people got involved, not clear over what, or who started it. Apparently the late night Tuesday crowd can get a bit rowdy – the landlord said that it was the first night for a week he hadn't needed to mop up blood.'

Jamie nodded. 'Yeah, things work a little differently out here. But why didn't Nordahl tell us he'd butted heads with Viklund? He said he didn't know who Felix was seeing, but Viklund knew Lena was seeing his son.'

'And he had an axe to grind – getting her into drink, and drugs.'

'You think he picked a fight with Nordahl?' Jamie asked. 'Over Lena?'

Thorsen shrugged again. 'I can call him, ask?'

'I'd rather ask Christian Nordahl, first,' Jamie said. 'He's lied to us twice now.'

'You like Nordahl for this?' Thorsen was piqued. 'His own son?'

Jamie didn't want to conjecture. They'd need to find out more about the argument before making any assumptions. She shook her head a little, pushing past it. 'What kind of shape was Viklund in when the fight started?'

'He could barely stand. Had to be carried out.'

'Drank that much?' Jamie said.

'Apparently,' Thorsen replied. 'Happens a lot.'

'With Viklund?'

'With everyone.'

Jamie didn't doubt that. 'So his alibi is rock-solid, then.'

'About ten witnesses can account for his enthusiastic presence there.'

'Honestly,' Jamie said, 'there's not a whole lot else to do here once the sun goes down.'

Thorsen didn't reply. Jamie didn't say anything more. She wondered if he drank. She didn't. Never had. Never would. She saw what it did to people when it got under their skin.

'You get anywhere with the map?'

Jamie looked down at the paper under her elbows. There was a dark splotch which she guessed was due to her drool. She covered it with her hand, pointed to a few markings she'd written on it before she'd nodded off. 'Yeah, so this is Kurra-jakk,' she said, running her finger around the town in the middle.

'I figured.' Thorsen slurped his coffee, came around to stand next to Jamie. He smelt like sweat and fading after-shave – the musky, strong kind that's all wood and tobacco and dark and heavy. His sour coffee breath washed down over her, his breathing slow and deep above her head.

'This is Felix Nordahl's house,' she said, pointing to one little circle. 'This is where Hugo and Olivia met when Hugo left Felix's.' She put her finger on another circle. 'Sundgren's grandmother's place – she's in care, the house is empty, so they've been using it to meet up.'

'Charming,' Thorsen said. 'Neighbours corroborate that?'

'Nearest house is a hundred metres away. Doubt they'd be able to.'

'I'll follow up,' Thorsen said lightly.

Jamie went on. 'And this is the place where the kids hang out, near the school.' She ran her finger into the woods out of town.

'That's gotta be, what, a kilometre into the forest?'

'That's close by Kurrajakk's standards.'

Thorsen raised his eyebrows a little.

'This is the "usual place" where Felix would have gone. So we'll head there once it's light, see what we can see.'

'We could go now, poke around?' Thorsen offered.

'No,' Jamie said, sighing. 'It's dark, remote … Do you really want to go traipsing around in the woods at night?'

'You worried about *Kråkornas Kung?*' Thorsen laughed. 'Don't worry, Johansson, I'll protect you.'

Jamie didn't join in. 'I was more concerned about trampling evidence or missing something that we wouldn't in daylight.'

Thorsen quelled his laughter, cleared his throat. 'Yeah, I wasn't serious.'

'Sure.'

'So if Felix went there at seven … Where was his body found?'

'Here,' Jamie said, putting her finger on a final circle, this one with an X in it.

'And how far is that?'

'About nine, ten kilometres as the crow flies.'

Thorsen raised an eyebrow. 'Crow jokes, really?'

'It was an accident.'

'Sure.' Another slurp. 'So how did he get from there to there?' Thorsen asked, pointing to the X on Jamie's map.

'Run?'

'Ten kilometres? Through the woods? In the dark?' He seemed dubious.

'It's doable,' Jamie said.

'Is it?'

Jamie glanced up at him. 'Yes,' she said. 'I've done it.' She looked away, casting her mind back to being run off the road into a lake in Finland, running through the forest after that, covered in blood … But that was a whole other story.

'Do I even want to know?' Thorsen's eyebrows raised.

'Wouldn't tell you if you did.'

'You're a real friendly person, anyone ever told you that?'

'Believe it or not,' Jamie sighed, 'I didn't move to Kurrajakk to build meaningful relationships with lots of new and exciting people.'

'So why did you?'

'Can we just get back to the map?'

He lifted a hand innocently, took another slug of coffee.

'His feet were dirty,' Jamie said.

'Dirty feet doesn't mean he ran ten kilometres through the woods.'

'No, it doesn't. But I'm more curious about why his feet were dirty at all.'

Thorsen waited for her to expound.

'I assume he didn't get from his house to the falls without shoes.'

'Probably not.' Slurp.

God, how loudly could a man drink?

'So why then,' Jamie asked, 'did he go there, expecting to meet Hugo, to sell drugs, and then somehow end up over here' – she dropped her finger on the X – 'with no bloody shoes on, and a crow rammed down his throat?'

'The thing that's bugging me,' Thorsen said then, putting his cup down. A single droplet of coffee ran off the rim and down onto the corner of the map. 'Is why he's spending time with Hugo Westman, then Hugo says he needs to go home for the night, and then an hour later is texting him asking to meet Felix to buy drugs.'

Jamie watched her own coffee gently steam, thinking. 'The bigger question,' Jamie added, 'is why he went at all.'

They both stared at the plywood-boarded up inside of the police station thinking on that. Thinking on it all.

Why would Felix go to meet Hugo after seeing him an hour before? How did he get from the falls to the clearing? What cowardice was *Kråkornas Kung* punishing him for?

Jamie's head was swimming.

There was more going on here than they knew.

And how did Nils Markus fit into it all? The barn was

creepy – the birds there suspicious if not damning. But were the chemicals and chemistry apparatus responsible for the pills plaguing the town? Nils Markus was the King of Crows once, but had he picked up the mantle again, or had he just given inspiration to a new generation of psycho? There'd been no sign of him at his farm, and Thorsen had found a blood trail … But what did that tell them? Was he the source of the drugs? Had Felix been there the night that he'd died?

Jamie leaned forward a little, searched the map until she found the Markus farm, slowly put her finger on it. Her eyes moved left, then right. 'Shit,' she muttered.

'What is it?' Thorsen asked, leaning down, putting one hand on the table around Jamie's shoulder so his head was next to hers.

'Nils Markus's place,' she said, 'look where it is.'

Thorsen followed her finger as she traced a line from the falls to the sacrificial site, saw that it ran right through Markus's place.

He was silent, breathing quietly now. She could see the pulse in the exposed veins on the back of his hand on the table in front of her.

'We should get back out there,' Thorsen said. 'Find Markus. Bring him in.'

'No,' Jamie said after a few seconds. 'We need to be smart about this – it's dark, we don't know the place, and this guy is dangerous, Thorsen. You saw what he did to Felix, to his brother-in-law. And we have no way to know if he'll be there now.' She leaned back, felt her hair brush Thorsen's ribs as he straightened behind her. 'We closed up the barn before we left, didn't touch anything – he'll have no way to know we were there.'

'So what do you suggest?'

She looked up at him. 'We go first thing – before it gets light. Catch him in bed, when he's not expecting us.'

Thorsen stared down at her. 'Okay,' he said softly. 'Let's do that.'

Whether he was tired too, or could just see it in Jamie's eyes, she wasn't sure. But he smiled down at her, put his hand on her shoulder, and then picked up her mug and headed for the kitchen. 'It's been a long day,' he said. 'Why don't you head home, get some rest? Call me in the morning, I'll pick you up, and we can head to Markus's place.' He reappeared in the doorway of the kitchen, hands in pockets, and leaned against the frame, filling it. 'Sound good?'

Jamie nodded. 'Yeah,' she said, rubbing her aching eyes. 'Sounds good. God knows I need it.'

He chuckled a little. 'Wasn't going to say anything, but …'

'I look like shit?' Jamie offered, standing up and cracking her back.

'You look like you've been working yourself to the bone to catch a killer.'

Jamie cocked an eyebrow, laughed. 'Translation: yes, Jamie, you do look like shit.'

Kjell Thorsen said nothing. Just smiled at her.

With his big, white teeth.

And his stupid fucking duck-egg eyes.

32

'*I'LL PROTECT you from Kråkornas Kung,*' Jamie parroted, sneering as she let herself into her house. 'Fucking Thorsen.'

She stepped into the hallway, spotted Hati immediately. He was lying at the far end of the hall, in front of the door into the garage, out of sight from the windows in the living room.

'What're you doing over there?' Jamie asked, meeting his eye.

He picked his head up, whined softly, then laid it back on his paws.

'What, shit on my bed again, have you?'

He made no sound. Didn't move.

'Oh, come on,' Jamie said. 'Do something. Growl, sidle off, bare your teeth … you're freaking me out here.'

But he didn't. He just laid there, chin on his feet, eyes moving back and forth, ears painted to his head.

Jamie drew a slow breath, watched him, then turned and locked the door, checking it twice.

Usually, she pulled her holster off and put it on the side

table. Tonight, though, she took it with her into her bedroom, and then into the bathroom, too.

She turned the shower on and as she waited for it to grow hot, she heard Hati pad in after her. She turned to see him standing in the doorway, looking up at her, eyebrows crumpled, tail hanging low between his heels.

Jamie swallowed, pulled off her jacket, and then reached out slowly for his head.

His hackles rose a little.

'Hey, it's okay,' she said softly, fingers a few inches from his nose. She glanced down at the bandage around her hand, doubted that putting it that close to him again was a good idea. And then he lifted his snout, came forward, touched the tips of her fingers gently, and then turned away.

Jamie rattled out a long breath, heart being a little faster. 'Well, that's progress,' she muttered, craning her neck around the frame to see his back end. He'd lain down in front of her bed, facing the closed bedroom door. He was still, but his eyes were wide open. And stayed that way.

Steam began to fill the room and Jamie shed the rest of her clothes, pulling her pistol from the holster and lying it on the cistern of the toilet.

As she washed herself, she kept an eye on it, ghostly and black through the translucent curtain.

But there, within arm's reach.

Loaded.

With the safety off.

Just in case.

33

HATI WAS DIFFERENT. And it was freaking Jamie the hell out.

She'd started cooking after her shower, and Hati had come and crouched at her feet, between the cooker and her shins, wedging himself in, body stiff.

The sound of a sizzling pan filled the air, and Jamie stirred the noodles on autopilot, the onion and garlic vapours burning her eyes a little. The headache that had been plaguing her all day had now receded to the back of her skull and died to a low, irritating scratching, like there were bugs inside her brain trying to burrow their way out.

Her eyes were half closed, out of focus as she stood there, spatula in hand, pistol on the counter next to her.

It was probably half-past eight – she didn't really know.

Hati rose awkwardly, pushing her back from the stove, and muscled his way free of her knees, circling behind her. She found it was less dangerous to ignore him than to try to do anything else. If he came near of his own accord he wasn't liable to bite, but if approached was about as predictable as an alligator. Mostly in the sense that he was very predictable and if you put your hand near his face he'd sink his teeth into it.

She heard his claws scrabble on the counter behind and turned, spatula in hand, ready to slap him on the head.

'Hey!' she called, raising it. And then she froze, seeing that he wasn't trying to take the raw chicken off the chopping board as usual, but instead, was standing straight, back like a pike, hackles up, his torn-up ears flattened to his head.

Jamie lifted her eyes then to the windows, to what Hati was looking at, saw the glare from the extractor fan light glimmering off it, the shine from the lamp, the reflections of her furniture there. She looked, narrowing her eyes, searching the glass, trying to see what Hati was looking at, pulling apart the images, the ghosts, the refractions.

And then she saw him.

Right in the middle, right at the glass, all black feathers and claws. A mass of crows' heads occupied the space where his face should have been, his shoulders pauldrons of layered black wings, his raised hand a writhing cluster of crows' feet, sharp, hooked little talons tapping on the glass.

Jamie's brain exploded, her eyes snapping wide, and she turned, snatched the pistol from the counter, flinging the spatula against the wall by sheer accident, and then swung back, levelling it at the window, finger already squeezing the trigger.

Her eyes tried to pick him out again, couldn't. Her finger twitched, desperate to rip that trigger back.

But then there was a flash to her right, moving across the windows. A dark shape sweeping up the length of the living room towards the back door.

She saw it through the glass there, finding the path that led down into the garden, and fleeing towards the edge of the forest, trailing feathers.

Hati went wild.

Jamie burst forwards, left hand stretching out for the handle.

She shoved her bare feet into the old running trainers that she used to let Hati out, and then she tore the thing open, dressed in a pair of sleeping shorts and an oversized hoodie.

The old wooden door banged against the wall and Jamie leapt down onto the path, the cool air stunning her lungs.

She felt Hati's tight, wiry fur brush her leg and then he bounded on ahead, loping awkwardly, as fast as his three legs would carry him. He barked, snarled, flinging flecks of drool in all directions as he scarpered towards the tree line.

Jamie picked out a flurry of black feathers melting into the shadow of the first pines, and got after it, knees pumping hard, pistol slick and heavy in her grip.

The air was ripe with that sickly sweet smell of rotten flesh, hazy and choking, thick in her lungs as she drove forward, putting her muscles to work.

She followed Hati's trail, his pale hide her guiding light as the dog tried to close ground on *Krakornäs Kung.*

Jamie kept pace with him, springing through the under-growth, knowing that she'd outrun any asshole in this town, and that this ended here. Right now.

Another flash of feathers.

Hati riled.

Barked madly.

Jamie raised her pistol, slowed momentarily, left hand flying to the grip, and then she fired three shots, close group-ing, down the corridor of trees, didn't know if she hit anything, rosettes of light dancing in her vision as the muzzle flash blinded her.

She didn't call out, didn't order the King to stop, just kept going, kept running.

She was going to run him down.

Like the animal he was.

Hati squawked. The cries of crows cut the air above.

Jamie's head was pounding, teeth throbbing.

She changed direction a little, following Hati's bright body like a firefly ahead, felt her heels sinking into the soft loam.

Another flurry of feathers.

Jamie lifted the pistol, fired again.

The shot echoed.

Kept echoing.

Cries joined it, reverberating like a cathedral choir. The shot came back then, building, thundering.

Her pistol was up again, the dim moonlight above shining off the barrel.

Crows swept down from overhead, dragged their claws through Jamie's hair, beat their wings on her shoulders. She threw her hands, up, batting them away, stumbled, nearly fell.

Pain erupted from her shoulder then and she was spinning, a tree trunk filling her vision.

Jamie landed on her back, had the wind kicked out of her, rolled, scrabbled to her feet.

She looked around. 'Hati!' she yelled, throat dry. 'Hati?' She could hear him barking. But where?

Jamie took off again, breathing ragged, heart beating oddly in her chest, out of time.

Her head swivelled as she searched the treetops, bending and swaying overhead, twisting, creaking, screeching. The air split with the chacka-chacka of gunfire, resounding through the darkened woods.

Jamie covered her ears, called out, then felt space under her feet, felt her weight shift forwards. And then she was falling, plunging through the air. She didn't think she'd even been moving, but now she was tumbling, flipping, bouncing down a slope that went on and on and on and on and then she was at the bottom, felt her bottom teeth scoop up earth, the pine needles prick at her eyes.

Jamie put her hands underneath her, forcing herself to her knees, right fist still fastened around her pistol, and looked up.

Saw him.

There.

Right in front of her.

Jamie threw her gun up, fired.

Flash, blinding.

She raked in a breath, choked on dirt, blinked, movement to her right. There!

She turned, fired again.

No, there! Left!

She swung around.

Bang.

Bang.

He was everywhere!

She kept firing, firing, firing, until the trigger rebounded off the grip.

Click, click, click.

She blinked, swallowed, tried to breathe, breathe – come on! You know how to fucking breathe – but then she couldn't. Something was around her throat, tight, peeling her off the ground and into the air, carrying her upwards.

Her feet flailed in the dark.

Her head pounded, blood roaring in her ears.

She was being choked. She knew the feeling.

Strangled.

Fists around her neck, squeezing, ratcheting tighter and tighter, forcing her windpipe closed.

And then she felt the sharpness of branches on her back, pressing into her skin as she was pinned against the trunk of a pine tree. Her eyes bulged, the bark rough between her shoulder blades.

The world throbbed black.

Her hands came up, empty – no gun – and found the black shape in front of her. Her fingers sank into it, like tar. Feathers oozed out, covered her fingers, wrists. She felt the spines stick in her skin like needles. Burrow in there, bedding there. She tried to scream, couldn't. She couldn't do anything. The King of Crows had her, was killing her. Her hands began to sink further in, deeper and deeper, the pull forcing her arms straight, straining her shoulders as he sucked her forwards, absorbing her, drowning her. He was taking her inside, pulling her into him, making her part of him, making her crow, making her – breathe!

Jamie ripped her head backwards, a sudden coldness rushing over her scalp and down her back.

She panted, spluttered, felt cold water draining from her face and hair.

Jamie looked left and right, heart threatening to break through her ribs it was beating so hard.

Her hands came into focus in front of her, submerged up to the elbows in a stream, her fingers buried in the silt, just visible in the moonlight.

She looked down at herself, dirty, on her knees at the water's edge.

Jamie coughed and spluttered, confused, disoriented.

Her body convulsed then and she vomited – spitting bile and what she guessed was stream water back into the current.

It dripped from her mouth, her head splitting, and she

flopped sideways onto her hip, running the back of her knuckles across her mouth. Jamie shuddered, cold, wet, and stared down at her hands. They were filthy from the mud at the bottom of the stream, but scratched and scraped, too. She touched her face, felt it tender on one side. Then she rubbed her throat. It was tight, sore, but it didn't feel sensitive or bruised … Had she … had she *imagined* that? No, no. It was so real. She shook her head, regretted it, then blinked again and looked up, a sudden fluttering of wings in the canopy overhead snapping her out of her little bubble.

Shit, where the hell was she?

Jamie looked around, saw nothing but darkness. The only sound was that of the water winding its way through the woods.

She tried to straighten her legs then, felt them burn like she'd been running. That much was real then. One of her naked feet stared back at her. She'd lost a shoe at some point.

Damn – and where was her gun? She looked around. Useless. It was so dark, there was no way she could …

Fear took hold then, as suddenly as she'd pulled her head from the water.

She was on her feet before she realised, looking around. More wings overhead. Her heart doubled its speed in her chest once more.

You can't stay here.

You're not alone.

Run, Jamie.

Run!

She took off again, following the stream down, stumbling and slipping and sliding through the soft mud and pine needles, arms up, protecting her face. Where was she going? She didn't know. Was she going the right way? She didn't know.

Then she saw it, a dim light ahead.

The moon? No, wrong colour. Too bright.

It grew bigger.

A straight line came into view below it.

Flat ground?

A road!

The stream disappeared into a corrugated plastic pipe that went under.

Jamie slowed, breathing hard, and scrambled up the bank onto the tarmac.

She stood, looked right and left. Of course there were no cars. This was fucking Kurrajakk.

The hair on the back of her neck stood on end and she glanced over her shoulder. Staying here wasn't an option.

Did she recognise this road? No, it was straight, unmarked, cutting through pine forest.

She looked up, willing herself to recognise something.

All she saw was the moon.

Crap.

Think, Jamie, think.

She let out a long, rattling breath, clenched her fists at her sides to stop them shaking, and then refocused. Damn, why couldn't she think straight? Her body didn't feel like her own, her mind erratic and uncontrollable.

The moon. Yes.

No, you already saw the moon.

It didn't help.

Wait, no, it'd been there when she left her house.

It rose on the left as you looked out the back door – and that meant that …

She stared up at it, then twisted to face down the road in the other direction, and started walking, not knowing if she was going the wrong way, but knowing that anything was better than standing still.

The whole walk, she couldn't get the feeling of being watched, of being dogged, of being circled by birds off her skin.

And she couldn't get rid of that damn, stinking stench of carrion either.

34

Jamie didn't know what time she got home, or at what point she recognised where she was, but it felt like she'd walked miles by the time her drive came into view.

She circled the house, limping on her bare – and now she thought injured – foot, and came in through the back door, closing it behind her.

The fear had abated, and though she was ready to collapse from exhaustion, sense hadn't left her.

Jamie reached out, knocking off the electric hob, the stir fry sitting just on the corner of it, a section of it spectacularly blackened now, and dragged a chef's knife from the block next to the sink. Then she turned the cold tap on, stuck her mouth under it, and drank deeply.

Once she was full, she stood, shielding her aching eyes from the light, and closed the door.

Inside, the air was cool, all the warmth flooded out.

She was halfway across the living room when Hati padded into her bedroom doorway and stared out at her.

He watched her for a moment, then lowered his head and went back in.

Hadn't he … Jamie glanced back at the closed back door. He never came back – he always …

You know what? She didn't even have the energy.

The next thing she knew, there was a knocking at the front door.

Jamie dragged her head from the pillow, eyes practically sealed shut, and smacked her lips. They felt dry and cracked, and the low buzzing in the back of her head from the day before now felt like someone had an icepick lodged in the base of her skull. 'Fuck,' she groaned, pushing herself to her hands and knees.

The white bedclothes were black under her. Black with dirt.

She was wearing exactly what she had been last night, and there was a chef's knife lying on the floor by the side of her bed. 'What … ?' was all she managed before the banging on the door started again.

Jamie slumped onto her side and rolled tiredly to the corner of the bed, putting her elbows on her knees, her head in her hands. She hissed, feeling her left cheek tender and swollen.

Images of the night before came rushing back then – running, drowning, sinking into black tar, having it flood down her throat, a thousand wings beating her back, a thousand claws raking at her face, her eyes, a thousand beaks gouging at her skin. She convulsed, shuddered, and then dry heaved, gagging right there in her bedroom.

She bent forward, mouth opening, and bile rose into her throat, sticking to the backs of her teeth.

A thin strand of sour liquid dripped from her lips and her whole world rocked.

'Jamie?' A voice echoed outside now. 'Jamie, you in there?'

She could see a shape moving around through the blinds. Thorsen.

Jamie forced herself up and wobbled over to the window, pulling them up.

Thorsen spotted her immediately, eyes widening in shock. 'Shit,' he said, voice muted through the glass. 'Are you okay?'

Jamie screwed up her eyes at the sunlight, pointed towards the front door.

She went into the hall, noticed Hati lying in the living room, facing the window. His good ear twitched as Jamie came out of her room, but otherwise he kept his eyes on the glass.

'Good boy,' she croaked, heading towards the front door.

She unlatched it and pushed the handle down. It opened and Thorsen stepped in, taking her by the sides of the face, cupping her cheeks deliberately as he inspected her. Her neck ached as he moved her face side to side.

'What the hell happened to you?' he asked, the worry apparent in his own bruised face. He was still sporting two black eyes.

'I … I think I ran into a tree,' Jamie said, the light still burning.

'What, on purpose?'

She pushed his hands off. 'No,' she said, swaying a little.

He grabbed her arm to steady her. 'Your phone was off,' he said.

Jamie didn't even know where it was.

'I tried calling – a bunch of times – to go over to Markus's place,' he said.

'Yeah, sorry, I …' Jamie said, pointing back into the house.

'You're covered in dirt,' he said. 'And where's your other shoe?'

Jamie looked down. She still had one on. The other was somewhere in the forest, along with her pistol. Damn. She closed her eyes, cursed herself. Her gun.

She must have got in last night and collapsed straight into bed.

'Jamie.'

She looked up at him.

He was stern. 'What happened last night?'

There was a part of her whose knee-jerk was to feed him a line. A lie. Right to his face. But what happened last night was dangerous. And Nils Markus – *Kråkornas Kung* had come right to her goddamn house.

'He was here,' Jamie said.

'Who was?'

'The King Of Crows.'

'Here? At your house?' Thorsen looked around, hand flying to the grip of his pistol hanging from his ribs. He went to move past Jamie.

She stopped him, hand on his chest. 'Hold your horses,' she said, meeting his eye. 'He's not here now.'

'How do you know?'

'Because I'm still alive. He was … he didn't try to get in – he was at the window, in the living room. My dog barked, he ran, I chased him.'

'You chased him?'

'Are you deaf this morning?'

'No, but I can barely fucking understand you,' Thorsen said roughly. 'Your mouth's all swollen and you're mumbling. How much sleep have you had?'

'Not enough,' Jamie sighed.

There was a growl behind her then and she turned to see

Hati's gnarled, scarred face hanging around the corner of the arch into the living room.

'Is that … a dog?' Thorsen asked, looking at him.

Jamie'd gotten so used to Hati's appearance, she didn't even register anymore. But Thorsen was right, he didn't look much like a dog anymore. He had been used for fighting, and he looked like he'd had a long career.

'It used to be,' she said, pushing Thorsen back towards the door. 'Now, it's just a liability. You should get out of here before he rips your arm off.'

'Hey, no, wait a second,' he said, walking backwards as Jamie drove him through the doorway.

'Wait for me in the car,' she said, 'I'll be five minutes.'

'Jamie, wait,' he called, the door closing in his face. 'I think we should—'

But then his voice was drowned out by the ringing in Jamie's ears. She turned, sank back against the door, and slumped to the ground, panting hard, out of breath.

It took her a minute to gain the strength to move, and then five more to reach the kitchen, find a packet of paracetamol, crush two under the heel of a glass, and then throw them down with some water.

She showered quickly, in water as hot as she could stand, and dressed. She found her phone on the counter next to the half-cooked, part-burnt stir-fry. And everything else was where she expected, too, except for her pistol. Which was somewhere in the forest.

Jamie stepped down onto her front path, pulling the door closed behind her, and sized Thorsen up.

He watched her keenly, leaning against the front of his BMW. 'You ready to tell me what really happened last night?'

'I told you – Nils Markus showed up, I chased him into the forest.'

'And this morning I find you sleeping in, face bruised, one shoe on, stinking dirty' – he pointed to her hip, and the empty holster there – 'and without your service weapon.'

He folded his arms now.

'What do you want, a fucking medal? You're a detective,' Jamie said bitterly, 'I get it.'

'You know,' he began, putting his hands out and moving them through the space between them, 'this thing – a *partnership* – it requires some give and take. Honesty. Trust. So why not just knock off the *I don't need anyone* crap and loop me in here – because from where I'm standing, I'm not sure I want you out there watching my back.'

'What's that supposed to mean?'

'I got a call this morning – from Ohlin.'

'Ohlin?' Jamie was surprised. He never called her. 'What about?'

'He said that someone phoned him last night, about half-past eight, reporting hearing gunfire in the forest.'

Jamie stuck her bottom lip out, shook her head dumbly. 'Practically everyone's got a gun around here. I hear gunfire all the time.'

'Cut the shit, Jamie,' Thorsen said, voice cold. 'The guy who called it in lives less than a kilometre from here. He said it was a dozen shots, maybe more, all close together. Then nothing.'

Jamie just stared at him.

'Does that ring a bell? Did you fire your gun last night?'

She stayed quiet, thinking back, coming to the realisation now that whatever had happened last night, it hadn't been real. Not totally at least. Hallucinatory, probably. Either that, or psychosis. But how someone had drugged her, she didn't know.

'This doesn't look good, Jamie.'

'I know,' she said, voice quiet. 'I chased him, I shot, I missed.'

'You chased him, you shot, you missed. And why don't I believe that's everything? You ever chased a suspect into the woods before, emptied a magazine at them, missed every shot, then stumbled home with one shoe on?'

'Something happened, okay? To me. I don't know. A trip.'

He raised his eyebrows.

'Someone drugged me – Markus. The chemicals at his farm. I don't know. Maybe he's mixing up some shit. All I know is that I went into the woods … and …' She could feel her voice cracking. 'There were birds, and they were … I don't know … And then I was falling. He was there, he choked me, I—'

'He choked you? Who? Markus?' Thorsen came forward again, reached for Jamie's chin, to lift it, to see.

She batted his hand away. 'No. I mean, I don't know. Like I said, I don't know what *was* … and what … *wasn't*. You know?'

'No, I don't. But if you emptied your weapon, shooting at someone … I know you're not liable to miss. I've seen your records. You can shoot.'

Jamie bit her bottom lip, shook her head. She couldn't trust her own memories. Her own mind.

'I'm going to ask you, Jamie – is Nils Markus out there?' He pointed to the forest. 'Is he dead? Did you shoot him?'

She didn't have an answer.

Thorsen swallowed, nodded slowly, putting his hands on

his hips, then sighed. 'Come on, I'm taking you to the hospital.'

'The hospital? What? Why?'

'Firstly, to make sure you're not concussed. Secondly, to get you a blood test, an MRI, maybe – if you're telling me that you don't know what happened last night, then we need to determine whether you were drugged, or …'

'If I'm just going crazy.' Jamie tutted, shook her head, laughed a little, eyes burning with tears. She cleared her throat, steadied herself, cleared her throat again, trying to shift the lump there. 'Fine,' she said. There'd be no arguing with him.

'Get in.' He went to the driver's door.

Jamie didn't protest or argue, she just climbed in quietly, opened the window, and closed her eyes.

As they drove, she focused on the wind on her face. Held onto it, tangible and present, and tried her best to trust herself. Trust what she could feel. Trust what her brain was telling her was happening.

But what frightened her most, was that she couldn't.

35

JAMIE TOOK a litre of saline in less than thirty minutes.

And now she was sitting in a chair with a multi-vitamin drip being fed into her arm.

They'd also taken blood, and a doctor had come and shone a light in her eyes, tested her reflexes and coordination, and then disappeared.

Thorsen had disappeared the moment a nurse had got the needle in Jamie's arm, and now it was nearly an hour later, and after ten a.m., and there was no sign of him.

Jamie's knees bounced, heels squeaking on the beige tiles as she waited for the drip to finish. She was under strict instructions not to move until it was done.

It wasn't sitting well with her.

She still couldn't quite understand how she was so dehydrated, but the nurse who'd listened to her symptoms – partially relayed by her, mostly by Thorsen – hadn't been too optimistic about it being a simple case of not getting her daily fluids.

And where the hell was Thorsen anyway?

She lifted her phone, tried him again. It rang out, went to voicemail. That made eight attempts.

Jamie exhaled hard, saw a nurse go by the open door.

'Mrs Nordahl?' she called, standing out of the chair. Jamie took hold of the bag rack and wheeled it towards the door, tube still in her arm. As she reached the threshold, she saw Lovisa Nordahl double back towards her.

'Oh,' she said, a little surprised – looking worse than Jamie felt. Her eyes were bagged, hair greasy and pulled back, skin pale and lined. 'Inspektör Johansson, what are …' Her eyes went to the drip. 'Is everything alright?'

Jamie sort of shrugged. 'Yeah, fine, I guess – waiting on some results. False alarm, is all,' she said dismissively.

'Oh.' Lovisa Nordahl smiled briefly, then let it fall. She adjusted her grip on the clipboard she was holding. 'Was there something … ?'

'Yeah,' Jamie said. 'Did you hear from the lab in Lulea afterwards?' She tried to sound gentle, apologetic almost – though the question she really wanted to know was whether Lovisa Nordahl knew that her husband had gotten into a fight at the Moose the night Felix had died.

She nodded, swallowed, but didn't say anything for a second. 'Uh, Christian is there now, he left this morning, early.'

'I'm sorry,' Jamie said. 'I can't imagine how difficult this must be.'

Lovisa Nordahl just sort of shrugged herself then, widened her mouth, like *what are you gonna do, huh?* Her job put her in front of death every day, but there was no preparing for something like this.

'I'm sorry,' Jamie went on, 'but I was wondering if I could ask you a few questions.'

'I really have to …' She started, pointing over her shoulder.

'It'll just take a second,' Jamie said, not waiting for a confirmation. 'Does the name Viklund mean anything to you?'

'Viklund?' She shook her head. 'I don't know anyone called Viklund.'

'It's a surname,' Jamie added.

A shake of the head.

'Gunnar Viklund?'

Another shake of the head.

'What about Lena Viklund?'

'Should I know who these people are?'

'Lena Viklund was the name of your son's girlfriend,' Jamie said.

Her lip began to quiver. She clamped her jaw shut, grip tightening on the clipboard. 'Well,' she squeezed out, 'I, uh, I would have liked to have met her,' Lovisa Nordahl said, searching for the words.

'I'm sorry to ask,' Jamie went on. 'I only did because your husband knew Gunnar Viklund, her father.'

'Oh, right,' Lovisa said, as though that should mean something.

'In fact,' Jamie continued, not wanting to say another word to the grieving mother, 'Christian got into an argument with Gunnar on the night Felix … went missing.'

'An argument?' She seemed confused by that.

'At the Moose's Head.'

'Ah.' Realisation dawned. Sad realisation.

'Things got heated, supposedly, they had to be separated. We have reason to believe the altercation got physical.'

There was no response.

'Did he tell you about that? Do you know why he might
have—'

'No,' Lovisa said decisively. 'I don't know why my
husband would have picked a fight with our son's girlfriend's
father.' There was bitterness in her voice. 'Just like I didn't
know Felix had a girlfriend at all. Or that he was selling
drugs. Or that he wanted to run away. Or *anything,* apparently.' Tears formed in her eyes. 'I don't know why my husband
drinks every night, or why he can't stand to be in the house,
or why we can't speak for more than ten seconds without it
turning into a shouting match. Or why … or why …' The
tears began to roll down her cheeks now. She hastily wiped
them away, looked at the ground and took a deep breath, and
then stood upright. 'Excuse me,' she said, 'I have to get back
to work now. If you have any more questions, leave a
message on my phone, and I'll respond to them as soon as I
can.'

And then she turned on her heel and walked away.

Jamie watched her leave, oblivious to Thorsen walking
towards her from the other direction.

'Hey,' he called.

Jamie turned, still holding onto the bag stand.

'You okay?' he asked, holding out a cup of vending
machine coffee.

Jamie accepted it gladly, noticed it was black this time.
He was learning. But she didn't say anything about it. She
just nodded, took a sip.

'You feeling better?'

'Much,' Jamie said, not lying. The saline and the multi-
vitamin cocktail were definitely helping.

'I just checked,' he said, taking a sip of his own, 'your
results will be a few hours. Until then, just rest up. Sit tight
and—'

'You're kidding,' Jamie said flatly. 'There's not a chance in hell you're going to sideline me here.'

'Jamie, you could be concussed – you could have a brain injury.'

'Do I look like I have a brain injury to you?' she asked, voice cutting.

He looked like he was about to say something that might have been construed as offensive. Then he registered the look on her face and thought better of it.

'And anyway, if you thought I had a brain injury, you wouldn't have just handed me this double-strong coffee.' She took a bitter sip to illustrate the point.

He reached out to take it off her. 'Then maybe you shouldn't—'

'Touch the coffee and lose a finger,' she growled, pulling it out of reach.

'Do brain injuries ever present as excessive happiness … friendliness … joy?'

Jamie narrowed her eyes.

'Then I think we're in the clear.'

She reached down, peeled the tape off her arm, and then dragged the needle out of her skin with a grimace.

'Come on, don't do that,' Thorsen said, screwing up his face. 'Jesus … Fuck, Jamie – you could have at least asked a nurse to— hey, Jamie? Jamie?'

She was already walking.

'Hey, where are you going? Jamie?' He started after her. 'At least check out, tell someone you're leaving— shit.'

Thorsen broke into a run to catch up, the door already closing behind her.

36

SHE FORGOT that Thorsen had driven, so he managed to catch up at the car.

For a second she thought he was going to order her back inside, but instead, he just unlocked it and then climbed in.

He had seemingly come to the conclusion that arguing with Jamie Johansson wasn't really an option.

'What now?' he asked.

'You got any friends left in Lulea? Or did you burn all your bridges before coming out here?'

He looked across at her, a little surprised by the barbed remark.

She hadn't meant it to come across that way, but she guessed playful wasn't really a staple in her repertoire. She was a little rusty.

He nodded after a few seconds. 'I know a few people, why?'

'Lovisa Nordahl said her husband went down there this morning to identify Felix's body. I think we should pick him up.'

'Christian Nordahl?' He did seem surprised by that one. 'Why?'

'He lied about knowing Felix was in a relationship, he got into a fight with Gunnar Viklund on the night Felix was killed. When I first spoke to Lovisa Nordahl, she said Christian told her he went out at seven, and was in bed by the time she got home after her shift ended at midnight – that Felix went out sometime during that period. I didn't press her, but the information you got from the Moose said that Christian Nordahl was tossed out at around midnight after the fight with Viklund?'

Thorsen nodded again, biting his bottom lip, thinking about it.

'Now we know that Hugo Westman came home with Felix from school, they gamed until around six, and then Westman went home. An hour later, Felix goes out. Christian told his wife he went out at seven, too. But I bet that we can put him in the Moose earlier than that.'

'But doesn't that mean his alibi is solid, same as Viklund's?'

'Yeah, but it also means he's full of shit. He and Lovisa are on bad terms, too – she said it – they can't have a conversation for more than ten seconds without it turning into a screaming match. She works long hours, isn't really at home, her husband – her words again – an absentee father, in the Moose every night, drinking himself senseless.'

'So things were bad at home,' Thorsen said, taking a slow breath.

They sat in the car park, looking out at the flat grey sky. It hadn't rained, but everything had a damp look to it and the air was heavy with moisture, like there was a storm coming. Like this was the calm before the heavens opened.

Jamie nodded. 'And we know Felix was looking to get away – looking to *run* away.'

'So what are we talking about here? Are you saying Christian Nordahl had something to do with Felix's death?'

'I don't know – his own son? There's nothing that ties him to it, but he's definitely not telling us everything. He knew about Lena Viklund – why else pick a fight with her father? There's a lot of anger there, a lot of resentment. Not an easy environment for any teenager to be in.' Jamie spoke from experience. 'So I just want him picked up, put under a little pressure. I want the truth out of him.'

Thorsen watched her for a few seconds. 'Alright,' he said then. 'I'll make a call, have him picked up when he leaves the lab. You want him brought back here, then?'

'No – let him stew for a few hours in a holding room,' Jamie said. 'He's a smart enough guy to figure out why he's there.'

Thorsen continued to watch her.

She was asking to have a father arrested as he walked out of a coroner's office after identifying his dead teenage son.

It was cold, even for Jamie. But hell, there were bigger things to deal with, and if nothing else, not having the father of their murder victim getting boozed up in the only bar in town and picking fights with other witnesses was a good thing.

'What are you waiting for?' Jamie asked then, motioning Thorsen to drive. 'Let's go.'

'Where are we going?'

'Nils Markus's house,' Jamie said. 'It's about time we arrested someone, don't you think?'

Thorsen cracked a wry smile, then started the engine. 'You know what?' he said, pulling onto the road and accelerating hard. 'You read my mind.'

37

Thorsen drove quickly.

Which made it even more of a shock when Jamie yelled, 'Wait, stop!' without warning.

'Shit,' Thorsen said, standing on the brake and wrestling the car in at the side of the road. 'What is it? What's wrong?'

Jamie pushed the door open and stepped onto the empty road, staring up at a lonely street lamp.

'Is it your head?' Thorsen asked, getting up out of the car and looking across the roof at her.

'I recognise that light,' Jamie said, pointing up at it.

'What?' He stared up at the thing too.

'That light, I remember it.'

'You sure you don't need to go back to the hospital?'

She grunted, shook her head at him. 'Behind you, is there a drainage tube going under the road, a stream?'

He glanced over his shoulder. 'Er, yeah, why?'

She circled the back of the car and jogged down the bank into the edge of the pine forest.

Thorsen watched her from the road, hands on hips.

Jamie walked forward a little, then turned back, retracing

her path from the night before. She could even still see the welts in the pine needles where she'd walked. 'This is it,' she announced.

'You're going to have to elaborate,' Thorsen replied.

'This is where I was last night.'

Thorsen squinted down the road in both directions. 'It's the middle of nowhere.'

'A few miles from my house,' Jamie said.

'A few miles from every house in Kurrajakk. Emphases on *miles.*'

She stayed at the bottom of the slope and he looked down at her.

'Fine,' he said eventually. 'I suppose we should see if we can find your gun at least.' He stepped down off the tarmac, his nice leather shoes still splattered with mud from the day before. 'You know, in case we run into one of those bears you mentioned.' He paused, held his finger up. 'And for the record, I never believed there were any bears.'

'Yeah,' Jamie said, clapping him on the shoulder and heading up the slope. 'Sure.'

They walked for around ten minutes, stopping every now and then so Jamie could make sure they were still on track. The stream split twice, and they took a wrong turn once, but eventually, the ground levelled out and Jamie found a section of bank that looked to have collapsed into the water.

She knelt, running her hands over the heel marks in the soft earth, thought back to the night before. She must have been running, lost her footing here, fallen forward, gone headfirst into the water.

A wave of nausea rolled over her – images of being picked up, choked, sucked inside *Krakornäs Kung* flooding back. Jamie closed her eyes, breathed through it. She'd been drowning. Damn, how out of it was she?

'Jamie?' Thorsen's voice was quiet, restrained.

'Yeah,' she said, picking her head up and finding him in the twilight of the forest. 'What's up?'

He was standing about ten feet away, staring across the water. She followed his eye line and froze, the nausea bounding back.

A body was lying on the ground, face down.

Jamie rose and walked slowly towards Thorsen, eyes fixed on it. It was a man. Blue wind-breaker jacket, jeans, dirty white trainers. Her heart sank, teeth chattering in her mouth as her jaw began to shake. She recognised those clothes. She'd seen them recently.

Her toe clipped something and she looked down, seeing the grip of a pistol sticking out of the leaves and pine needles that littered the floor.

Jamie stooped to pick it up, lifting her gun out of the undergrowth, cradling it in both hands.

'Jamie?'

She looked up to see Thorsen staring at her, hand out, eyes wide. 'Give me the gun,' he said gently, motioning her towards him.

Her brow crumpled. That look. She knew that look. She laughed, incredulous. 'Thorsen … no, you don't think …' Her fingers curled over the weapon. 'You're not suggesting that I …' She laughed again. It felt strange in her mouth now.

Thorsen advanced. 'Just give me the gun, okay?'

'Hey, no,' she said more firmly now. 'Listen, I didn't—'

He lunged forward then, grabbed it, dropped his elbow over her arms so that he pinned them against his ribs, and then dragged the pistol free.

Jamie stumbled backwards, still reeling.

Thorsen gave her space, faced her, ejected the magazine

and checked it, then pulled back the slide. Empty on both counts.

He kept his eyes fixed on her, pushing it into the back of his waistband. 'Don't move,' he ordered, stepping across the stream with his long legs.

'Thorsen,' she called after him. 'I didn't do this, I didn't—'

Thorsen reached the body, knelt, put his fingers against the neck. He didn't look back, didn't hesitate.

Jamie stepped forward a little to get a better look, hoped that the red pattern across the back of the blue jacket was a print and not something else.

The forest held its breath around her.

Who was she kidding. They were bullet wounds.

Thorsen hung his head, one knee on the ground, and then took the body by the shoulder and rolled it up onto its side, the white t-shirt visible between the lapels of the windbreaker soaked scarlet.

Jamie recognised him instantly, as did Thorsen.

He looked back at her, face like stone.

'Mats Flygare,' Jamie muttered.

Thorsen let the body down slowly, then rose to his feet.

'Thorsen,' Jamie started, voice catching in her throat.

'Jamie Johansson,' he started, walking back towards her.

No, no, she knew that voice – she knew that tone, that start.

'I'm placing you under arrest for—'

'Thorsen,' Jamie cut in. 'Wait.'

He stepped back across the water. 'Under arrest for the murder of Mats Flygare.' He stretched his hand out for her. 'Anything you say—'

'Thorsen,' she said again, backing up. 'Hold on.'

'Anything you say—'

'I said fucking wait!' She snatched his fingers out of the air, bent them up over the back of his hand. He twisted awkwardly, knee buckling as he tried to stop them from snapping backwards.

Jamie released and shoved him back, taking a few more steps. 'Let me explain!'

'Explain?' He spat, massaging his hand, glaring at her now. 'Explain what? How you chased him into the woods and put six bullets between his shoulders? He's unarmed, Jamie, running away from you – what the hell else did you expect when—'

'When what? I *led* you to the guy I killed?' She shook her head. 'Listen to me! Listen to fucking *logic.* I didn't kill …' She trailed off, not totally sure about that statement. 'What I do know, is that someone did something to me – Mats Flygare did something to me – he dosed me with drugs, or with … with …'

'Do you even hear yourself?'

'Yes! And I know it sounds crazy, but it's the truth. I was hallucinating – tripping. The blood tests will show it, and—'

'And it makes no goddamn difference!' Thorsen yelled now.

Silence fell like a curtain, the trunks creaking around them. 'Whether you were high or not, whether Flygare was at your house or not—'

'He was!' Jamie snapped, pointing at Thorsen. 'And I wasn't fucking *high,* I was *drugged!* Not in control of myself!'

Thorsen's jaw flexed, hands balled in fists at his side.

'You're not arresting me for this.'

He sighed, anger fighting with concern on his face. 'What else do you expect me to do? I have to. I have to put you in custody, and we need to get forensics out here – look at the body, cordon off the scene, take ballistics, swab you for GSR – you know how this works. Your word – especially when you say you don't even *know* what happened – how can I take it?'

'You have to trust me,' Jamie said. 'It was *Kråkornas Kung.*'

Thorsen closed his eyes, shook his head.

'I'm serious!'

'It obviously fucking wasn't,' Thorsen said now, through gritted teeth. 'Otherwise there'd be a man in a fucking bird costume lying there, and NOT MATS FLYGARE!' He rose to a scream for the last few words, throwing a hand towards the body across the water.

Jamie shrank a little.

Thorsen was nearly a foot taller than her, and imposing when he was angry. Which he certainly was at that moment.

'Think about this,' she said then, more measuredly, restraining herself. 'I know what I saw, okay? Before … before the trip. When I was at home. I turned, and there he is, at the window.'

'Flygare.'

'No.'

Thorsen watched her like a big cat, poised, ready to lunge again, take hold of her if she tried to run.

She had to admit it'd crossed her mind.

'*Kråkornas Kung,*' Jamie said. 'A guy in a bird costume – black feathers, the beak, the works.'

'At your house.'

'At my living room fucking window.'

Thorsen waited.

'I grabbed my gun, and when I turned around, he was already running.'

Thorsen kept waiting.

'I chased him into the forest – and then – I don't know – I started to see things – I didn't realise at first. Maybe he put something in my water supply, or ... I dunno what happened. But the next thing I know, I'm out of it, okay? Still running – and ... I shot. I think.' She swallowed, looked at the ground. 'No, I know I did. I thought ... I thought he was attacking me, so I fired, okay?'

Thorsen was a statue.

'But think about it – why come to my house, and then run? And I don't know, I don't think it was Flygare – unless he ditched the costume, or ...' She shook her head. 'No, no, because he didn't break himself out of the cell, did he?'

Thorsen set his jaw again, surveyed Jamie.

'No, exactly – someone broke him out. And the crows on the ground – it's theatre, but it's not Flygare. He's not that. He's a pusher – sells drugs to kids – but he's not got the experience, the intelligence for something like this.' Jamie nodded, seeing a glimmer of belief in Thorsen's eyes. 'And ... and ... yeah, okay, the morning that Felix Nordahl's body was discovered? In the town – there were birds. A swarm. Above the cross. And on the ground there were entrails – guts, blood. Animal pieces.'

Thorsen raised an eyebrow.

'And then that night – I didn't say anything, but something happened at my house.'

'What?' Barely above a whisper.

'Birds. They were attacking my window, or ... throwing themselves against it. And when I went outside, they were everywhere, hundreds of them – all flew away at once. And there was blood on my car, too – like the street – guts, and bones, and innards, you know? And there was someone there, watching the house.'

'You saw them?'

'No, but I felt it. And someone had to have put that shit on my truck.'

'And you didn't say anything?' He didn't look to be buying it.

'What was I supposed to say? Hey, there's a guy dressed like a giant fucking bird smearing animal organs all over the place?'

He chewed his tongue.

'I didn't want to believe it either,' Jamie said. *'Kråkornas kung,* a guy in a bird outfit – but … seeing Markus's farm, hearing it from Bloome, what happened last night, the station, the dead birds … Something screwed up is going on here, Thorsen, and we're right in the middle of it. So if Mats Flygare is lying in the woods right there, dead, bullets in his back – I have no doubt that's because he's supposed to be. If I wasn't supposed to run him down, then I wouldn't have. Someone's playing us, Thorsen. You have to see that?'

'What I see,' he said, words separated, devoid of emotion, 'is that someone is dead, and that he was shot with a gun that belongs to a police officer. And that the likely scenario, intentional or not, is that you shot him.'

Jamie had a feeling she knew what was coming.

'So tell me, Jamie – what do I do? Because I feel like if I try to arrest you – which is what I *should* do – and you know that – you're going to try to break my fingers again, or kick me in the balls, or do something, and then run like hell – and then I'm going to have to try to catch whoever's behind this, and track you down at the same time.' He sighed. 'So work with me, alright? Because I agree, there's something messed up going on here, and we're right in the middle of it. And if someone has come for you – and that's a big *if* – then I'll probably be next.' He held his hand out, in a vague *stop* signal, as though he could tell Jamie was one flinch away from bolting like a deer.

She kept his eye. 'The way I see it,' she said, 'we only have one option – and that's find Markus. If he is behind this – then we get him in cuffs, we get him in a room, and we get him to admit to it all. Flygare wasn't here by chance, alright? So either he was in the wrong place at the wrong time – which, look around – why the hell would *anyone* be out here at exactly that moment – let alone the escaped suspect we've been hunting – or' – she held her hand up as well now, to stop Thorsen from darting in – 'Markus put him here. He knew what I'd do, knew I'd chase him into the woods. All he had to do was wait for whatever the hell he dosed me with to kick in, and then put Flygare in front of me.'

'That's a big theory, nearly impossible to prove unless Markus gives a full confession,' he said darkly.

Jamie laughed sardonically. 'I guess that's the fucking point. He derails our investigation by taking out one of the detectives, puts her in a frame for murder – he got away with it once, right? What if he's trying to do it again?'

Thorsen lowered his hand, hung his head. 'Jesus, Jamie,' he said. 'You know what you're asking here, don't you?'

'I'm asking you to trust me, Thorsen.'

He thought on that for what seemed like an age. 'And if I do?'

She clenched her jaw, restrained a smile of relief. 'So does that mean you're not going to put a pair of cuffs on me?'

'Depends if you're stupid enough to try to run away.'

'I'm pretty fast.'

'Faster than Mats Flygare, apparently,' he said, dry as a bone.

'Don't joke about that.'

He offered her a weak smile now, but a real one at least.

'We have to call this in – and things will take their course. I'm not going to lie—'

'I'm not asking you to.'

'I'm not going to lie for you,' he said again. 'So whatever happens, *happens,* alright?'

'Okay.'

'And until then, you're in my custody. Where I go, you go. You don't go out of my sight, not even to—'

'Pee?'

He drew a slow breath, nostrils flaring. 'You cut people off a lot, you know that?'

'One of my many charms,' she said, sheepish.

'Yeah,' he said, pulling his phone from his pocket and dialling a number. 'I'm starting to figure that out.'

38

'FORSS,' Thorsen said as someone answered. 'Kjell Thorsen – yeah, uh-huh. Oh – yeah, no, we need you— it's urgent – right, okay … Sure, I'll send you the coordinates.'

Thorsen hung up and lowered the phone, looking slightly baffled.

'What was that about?' Jamie asked.

'It's Forss.'

'Is he coming here?'

'Yeah, he is,' Thorsen said. 'They're less than an hour away.'

'What?' Jamie was as confused as Thorsen then.

'They were already on the way.'

'Why?' Jamie stepped closer and Thorsen stiffened a little.

She read him, then backed off. Too soon.

'Uh,' Thorsen said, dropping Forss the location, 'Ohlin.'

'Ohlin?' She was even more confused now.

'Yeah,' Thorsen said. 'Ohlin's been down in Lulea – hurrying things along, I guess.' Forss obviously didn't give him much in the way of information.

'Ohlin?' Jamie repeated it, still in shock.

'That much of a surprise?'

'That he's doing his job?' She scoffed. 'Yeah, it is. But I'm not complaining. Did Forss say anything about the phones, the autopsy?'

'No, he was driving,' Thorsen said. 'Didn't seem keen to talk. Didn't seem very friendly at all, actually.'

'Well, this is the third time he's made the trip in as many days.'

Thorsen sighed, staring down at his phone as it rang out.

Jamie craned her neck, saw he was dialling Ohlin.

Then she heard the quiet, robotic voice asking Thorsen to leave a voicemail. He hung up instead.

'Of course he doesn't answer,' Thorsen muttered, blowing out a long breath. 'Guess we just wait, then?'

Jamie eyed him. 'Or we don't.'

Thorsen narrowed his eyes a little.

'You gave Forss the coordinates, right? That'll bring him right in. And he can always call if he needs directions. If he's going to be an hour, you really want to stand here while Markus is … doing who knows what out there?'

Thorsen rolled his phone over in his hand as he thought.

'Come on, it's been' – Jamie checked her watch, saw it was after eleven now – 'four, five hours since we were going to hit Markus? I know you want to do this right, but if he killed Felix, then every second we stand here is one more second he's not in a cell. Hell, maybe he's already gone, maybe he's running, and while we're waiting for—'

'Okay, okay!' Thorsen said, throwing his hands up. 'Fine, fuck! Just shut up, alright? We'll go,' he said, motioning her down the hill. 'Just please, please, shut up.'

Jamie held back another little grin, fell into step with him, and headed down towards the car.

Thorsen was in as bad a mood as she'd seen anyone, but getting Markus was their best bet of catching Felix's killer, as well as proving Jamie's innocence.

A little knot lodged itself in her stomach then. Innocence. Was she innocent? Had she shot Flygare? Orchestrated or not, was that another death she would have to add to her conscience?

She'd come to terms with the others – or at least, escaped them. Escaped to Kurrajakk to get away from them and everything that reminded her of them ...

But now, was there any more running? Was this it? Everything come back to rear its ugly head again? The death, the feelings that came with it, the weight of what she'd gone through ...

'Jamie?'

She looked up, standing next to the car in the middle of the road.

Thorsen was staring across the roof at her. 'You going to get in?'

'Yeah ... yes,' she said, shoving a lid back on whatever was trying to crawl out of her. She slid into the leather cabin and pulled the door closed. The world outside faded away, and then the trees began to blur past as Thorsen put his foot on the floor.

They sat in silence as he closed ground on Markus's house, turning into the lane as fast as the tyres would allow, and speeding up towards the house.

The stiff suspension of Thorsen's BMW complained as they hammered over the potholes and cracked tarmac, but then they were bursting through the trees and up the driveway towards the squat farmhouse and murder barn.

An old pickup truck was parked outside it, streaked with rust.

Thorsen pulled up at an angle, blocking the roadway, and got out wordlessly, pistol drawn and held towards the ground.

Jamie exited too, went after him. She thought asking for her gun back would be a bridge too far. Not like it had any bullets in it, anyway.

Euch. Not really a pleasant thought.

She clenched her fists.

Come on, Jamie, get it together here.

Thorsen glanced back, waved her down. 'Stay back, shout if you see anything.'

She advanced more slowly now, head on a swivel. She'd do what he asked, keep an eye on things, look out for Markus.

The farmhouse was dark to their left, the barn drawing Thorsen in like a moth. The once-chained side door was now open, and Jamie could see the main door facing the field agape, too.

Thorsen circled the truck and went towards the opening, moving slowly, but deliberately, weapon rising. She didn't think he'd have any problem pulling the trigger if he needed to.

Jamie approached the vehicle from behind, the old, beaten-up Toyota displaying signs of a hard life. The rusted tow-hook, however, showed fresh gouges. Shining silver scars. She knelt, ran her fingers over them. Cut, right into the metal. She stood then, glanced into the bed, saw a long chain coiled up, a few odd black feathers.

Her mind went to the door of the station – ripped off. Her first thought had been with a vehicle, and this looked to be the culprit. Had Markus loaded it up with dead birds, driven down there, torn the doors off, liberated Flygare so he didn't rat on him, then dropped a couple of birds in his wake to stoke the fires of superstition? Keep the *Kråkornas Kung* myth alive?

She moved around the pickup then, towards the door.

It was dark inside, but the light coming through the main entrance was enough to pick Thorsen out.

The smell hit her then, the same stench. Sickly, sweet, rotten flesh. She threw the crook of her elbow to her nose, choked a little. 'Thorsen,' she said.

He turned a little, standing at the far wall, to the side of the workbench littered with dead crows, and stepped to the side.

Jamie's eyes widened as she saw what he was in front of.

The King of Crows.

Or his suit at least.

She could see now in the light what it was – in all its macabre glory, the broken, mangled bodies of crows stitched together, shining and black, littered with feathers and beaks like gruesome chainmail.

Thorsen reached down, lifted the sleeve, pulling it upwards.

There was a membrane sewn to the body that spread like a wing, all covered in feathers.

Dust drifted from it, swirling gently in the shafts of sunlight, like pollen from the pines in the heat of summer.

Jamie watched it curl through the air, around Thorsen's head like a halo.

The smell intensified, even from here, and Jamie gagged, the night before flooding back, the blinding flashes of gunfire, images of the king obsessing her vision. She backed up, staggered into the open, Flygare's face appearing before her eyes, and then emptied her stomach into the mud outside the barn.

Jamie heaved, the bitter taste of half-digested coffee and bile clinging to the backs of her teeth.

She spat, wiped off her lips, and then turned back to the

barn, squinting in. 'Thorsen?' she croaked, throat tight and painful.

But he wasn't there. The suit hung lonely on its hook.

Jamie peered in, but couldn't see anything past the ancient tractor. Though she could still see the mist swirling in the air. The cogs in her mind turned, ground, and then clicked suddenly, everything making sense.

She backed up, not daring to breathe, and ran the length of the barn towards the open door on the far side. She'd be able to see in from there, be able to see where Thorsen was—

Jamie stopped, skidding in the mud.

She didn't need to look for him.

Thorsen was standing at the bottom of the ramp that faced down into the field, motionless, pistol hanging in his grip.

Jamie's heart was thundering in her chest. 'Thorsen?' she called, softly as she could.

He didn't move.

She edged closer.

'Thorsen? Can you hear me? It's Jamie, it's—'

He turned then, suddenly, like a marionette whipped round on a string. His eyes were wild, mouth open. He was pulling in heavy breaths through it, tongue flicking back and forth behind his teeth.

'Thorsen?' she asked again, meeting his eyes. 'Kjell?'

He started breathing quickly, little pants, and then brought his teeth together, bared them, letting out a low, pained growl with every exhale.

'Kjell,' she said again, putting her hand on her chest, 'it's me – it's Jamie.' Her eyes went to the weapon in his grip. 'I need you to drop the gun, okay? Just, just—'

He lifted it quickly, held it in front of his face, inspecting it minutely.

'Kjell.' Jamie was more forceful now, terrified that he was

going to blow half his face off by accident. 'Put the gun down, okay? Just throw it on the—'

And then he fired.

Jamie jumped back, the ground in front of her exploding, splattering her with dirt.

The muzzle flash danced in her eyes, the smoking barrel still held out in front of him.

And then she was staring down it.

He had it levelled right at her.

She was frozen, hands up, mouth dry, vomit still on her chin. 'Kjell, listen to me. This isn't you, okay? You've been dosed, same as me – it's … it's the King, okay? This is what he does,' she said. 'I don't know if you can hear me, but you're safe – you're *safe* – don't worry. I'm here. He can't get you, he can't—'

His head snapped around then. He searched the sky, frantic, batted and swatted at the thin air above his head, pointed the gun up, fired once, twice.

Jamie dived for cover, scrambling back towards his car.

He was out of his mind.

There were footsteps behind her.

She ran, keeping low, then slid behind the bumper.

Jamie turned, fingers, black with dirt, pressed to the gleaming fender of Thorsen's car, and looked for him.

But he wasn't there. She glanced left and right, couldn't see him.

Jamie stood, catching sight of his coat, fluttering in the distance as he ran the length of the field.

She charged after him, yelling his name.

But it was no good.

He hurtled towards the fence at the bottom – right where he'd followed the blood trail to the day before – and leapt it. Thorsen flew over, head-first, with reckless abandon, landed on his chest, and was then up again and ploughing onwards through the thickening brambles and marsh grass toward the trees.

'Thorsen! Thorsen!' Jamie yelled slowing halfway down the slope.

She sank forward, hands on knees, panting.

He was gone, swallowed up by the forest.

'Fuck,' Jamie said, standing. She couldn't chase him in – even if she did catch up, he'd be out of his mind, and armed. And with *Kråkornas Kung* lodged in his mind, there was no way she was going in there. She'd been on the other side of that experience twelve hours before. And now Mats Flygare was dead.

She had no intention of joining him.

Jamie thought instead, totally alone, unarmed, a hundred yards from a killer's house and workshop. She let out a long breath, pulled her phone from her pocket, dialled a number. Jamie held it to her ear, waited for it to connect.

'Forss,' she said, still breathless. 'Change of plan – I need you here instead.'

There was quiet on the other end, just the noise of the road under him.

'It's an emergency. Please. I'll send you the address, alright? Just, come straight here. The other thing can wait.'

He hung up wordlessly then and Jamie pulled up the location and forwarded it to him, turning slowly back towards the King's lair. How much good Forss was going to be, she didn't know – none, she guessed. At least not when it came to Markus and Thorsen, but just then, the thought of being alone scared her more than anything else.

Silence reigned all around, the sky moving more quickly now, a thousand shades of grey sliding overhead like a river.

She didn't like signs, omens, didn't buy into superstitious

shit or anything like that. But as she stood at the bottom of that slope, the smell of death still hanging in the air, the open door ahead of her, the answer to all her questions floating inside, she couldn't help feel like there was more to come. Like she was still one step behind, and that all this had happened exactly as it was supposed to.

Jamie turned back to the forest, looked for any sign of her partner. Any sign of hope.

But found nothing except darkness.

39

F ORSS ARRIVED TWENTY-THREE MINUTES LATER. And he didn't come alone.

He was driving a white van, and another pulled in behind him, followed by a beaten-up Volvo saloon painted with Kurajakk polis colours.

Ohlin.

The vans came to a stop behind Thorsen's car with a squeal of brakes, and Forss climbed out of the driver's seat of the lead vehicle. He was wearing a faded black t-shirt that displayed the name 'Dark Tranquility' on it. The intricate, gothic, jagged text indicated to Jamie that it was probably a death-metal band. She didn't know them. Though she wasn't surprised that Forss was into metal.

'*Hallå,*' she called, pushing off from Thorsen's car and raising a hand.

'*Vilken väg?*' he asked, sighing. Which way?

Jamie pointed towards the barn, but before she could say anything, Forss was snapping his fingers at his crew.

They went trudging up the hill, hard cases in hand.

'Wear masks!' Jamie called after them. 'There's a dust or something – hallucinogenic – make sure you—'

Forss waved a hand over his shoulder to signify he understood, but didn't look back.

He was in a mood.

When Jamie turned back, Ohlin was in front of her. His thick, tangled hair and beard framed his puffy red face, but didn't disguise the anger there.

'Here,' he said, slapping a thick manilla file against her chest.

He let go and it fell into Jamie's waiting hands.

Ohlin smelt like he hadn't showered in two days.

'Where have you been?' she asked, looking up at him.

'Lulea,' he grunted. 'Cleaning up your mess.'

'My *mess?*'

He snorted, hawked, then spat phlegm onto the ground perilously close to Jamie's boot. 'Yeah,' he said. 'Seeing to the boy, speaking to the pathologist, doing what you should have been doing.'

She raised an eyebrow. 'Excuse me?'

'Read the fucking report,' he said, turning away. 'Might learn something before you go around arresting people, destroying my station, whipping the whole fuckin' town into frenzy with your stories.' He raised his hands in an emphasised shrug. 'You know how many calls I've gotten the last two days?'

Jamie watched him go, gobsmacked. 'Where are you going now?'

He stopped at the door to his car. 'To stop this town from tearing itself apart, apparently.' He got in then, the whole thing rocking heavily on its old springs. Then he closed the door, spun the wheels, and accelerated out of the farmyard in a cloud of dust.

'What the hell?' Jamie muttered, blinking, unsure whether that had just happened or if it was still part of her trip.

She looked down then, at the file in her hands. Felix Nordahl's autopsy report. She lifted the cover, saw that the file was thick. Thicker than she expected. Maybe Ohlin was useful for something, after all.

Jamie glanced up at Forss's team. They were suiting up, pulling on heavy-duty filtration masks, goggles. Good, they were being careful.

She had no intention of interrupting them. And Thorsen would be out of it for a while. Who was he going to be a danger to out there? No one, she hoped. Maybe that's why he'd done it. Maybe he had enough sense to realise that – to take himself out there. She checked her watch. Midday now. A little after. Forss and his team would be a few hours, she expected. Then they'd have to go out to Flygare's body. Her stomach twinged. At least, for now, Forss knew nothing about the circumstances of that. And Jamie intended to keep it that way, at least until they'd figured a few more things out.

She'd give Thorsen a couple of hours to get it out of his system. And then, if he didn't bring himself back by three, she'd go after him. Into the dark forest. Unarmed. With *Kråkornas Kung* skulking about out there. Jamie let out a long breath. Why was this shit never simple?

Don't think about that now. Let Forss do his job. Get reading. Get ahead of this. Get into the King's mind. Find his end goal here, his angle. Is murder and mayhem all he wants? Is this just fallout? Or is he working on something bigger?

Jamie stared up at the old, quiet farmhouse. Was being out here all these years, alone, enough to drive Nils Markus mad?

She thought back to the kill, the burial site. To the story of the deserter, of the original *Kråkornas Kung*. To the Norse warrior, to the gods and their stories. To hallucinogens. To berserkers. Mushrooms, she thought. That was what they used to take, wasn't it? They would eat mushrooms, which put them into states of frenzy and rage. Which connected them to the gods.

Was that his plan? Was that his goal? To spread this all through Kurrajakk? To poison everyone? To make them all feel the fear and terror that Jamie had felt the night before? Was all this revenge? It felt like it. It felt like anger. What was done to Felix Nordahl. That was pure rage, pure evil. It would have taken a long time. It would have taken care, precision. It would have taken skill, and experience. The kind that came from putting blade to flesh for pleasure.

Her eyes drifted to the barn, to the taxidermy equipment inside, the crows, the chemicals.

Nils Markus.

What the hell are you trying to do here?

Jamie felt her grip tighten around the edges of the file, and then she looked down, swallowed, and began to read.

40

THEY CRAWLED all over the farm as Jamie read the report.

Felix had died from asphyxiation. She grimaced at that part. The cuts on his body had been made with an implement that matched the size and shape of a crow's beak. The King had dug at him with it. One cut at a time. Over, and over, and over. But for all the horror of that, he'd not died until that crow had been forced down his throat. And then he'd suffocated, choked on it.

She just hoped the *bird* wasn't alive for that part.

Jamie felt a little sick again, but ploughed on.

His blood work showed signs of extreme stress – his cortisol readings were extremely high, as were his norepinephrine levels. His dopamine and serotonin levels were raised, too, and his heart showed signs of strain. But beyond that, it was the cocktail of foreign substances in his body that told Jamie what she needed to know. Tropain alkaloids. Hyoscyamine, scopolamine. Highly psychoactive substances.

He'd been drugged, same as her – and he'd gone hammering through the forest, same as her. Except he hadn't made it out alive before the King caught up with him.

Jamie drew a long breath, thinking how it would have gone. How he'd been lured out to the falls near the school, how he'd been dosed unwittingly, then chased into the woods, tortured mentally, then physically, before finally being killed.

Jamie wondered if Flygare was there – if that's why he was so paranoid. If seeing Markus do that to Felix had set him off. Had put him in front of the door of his trailer with a shotgun in his hand in case Markus came for him next. Felix was a strong kid though, would Markus be able to overpower him alone? Even if he was on drugs?

She clicked her teeth together, watched as Forss walked down the drive towards her, mask hanging around his neck, hair moist with sweat.

He lifted his chin. 'Your boss is a real charmer.'

'Ohlin?' Jamie raised an eyebrow. 'Yeah, a sweetheart.'

He just met that with a 'Mmm'. It said it all.

'He just showed up in Lulea, then?'

Forss nodded, ran his hand over his head, his white suit pulled down to the waist, the sweat patches around his armpits extremely apparent. 'Like a bull. Rolled into the lab, shouting about this and that, demanding we get the autopsy done, get back up to Kurrajakk immediately.'

Jamie watched him. 'Did you know where you were going?'

'What do you mean?'

'When you were on the way here – where were you going?'

'I don't know,' he said. 'We were following Ohlin. Thorsen called us, so we flashed our headlights, then turned around. Then you called, and we came here, Ohlin following us.'

'So you don't know where he's gone now?'

Forss shook his head.

Flygare's place? The station? Somewhere else? What was Ohlin playing at? Did he know something they didn't?

Jamie let out a long breath, tapped the file on her thigh.

'Get everything you need from that?' Forss asked, pointing to it.

Jamie glanced down at the paperwork. 'Yeah. Not a pretty way to go.'

'Death by crow,' Forss said. 'What do you think it means?'

Jamie opened her mouth, found no words came, then just shook her head. 'I don't know. But I'd say there's no point waiting on the results to come back on those drugs, or the bird – I'd guess that what was in Felix's system is going to be what we find there. Hyoscyamine, scopolamine.'

'Potent chemicals,' Forss said. 'Psychoactive compounds.'

Jamie thought back to the sacrificial site. 'Mushrooms.'

'What's that?'

'Mushrooms,' Jamie said. 'Just thinking about where the first body was found, the Norse site. And about the crows – the suit, you know? It's a local story, *Krakornås Kung.* He was supposed to be a cowardly warrior who ran from battle … It's a long story. But it just got me thinking about the berserkers. Warriors who used to take mushrooms to enter a state of frenzy before they went into battle.'

'Psilocybin,' Forss said then.

'Psilocybin? What's that?'

'Mushrooms,' he repeated. 'Magic mushrooms – that's the psychoactive compound in mushrooms. Hyoscyamine, scopolamine, those are psychoactive, too, but not found in mushrooms. At least not that I know of. They'd produce a different reaction, anyway – more of a *rushing,* with vivid hallucinations. More of a physical effect. The way it affected Felix's chemical balance, the norepinephrine levels he was at? I'm guessing it would have come with acute paranoia, fear. I couldn't imagine what it would have been like.'

'I could,' Jamie said sourly. 'Would anyone take these things for recreational purposes?'

'In small doses, mixed with other drugs, maybe ... it's possible,' he said. 'It's hard to say what balances would produce what reactions – but you know what people are like, they'll take anything if it gets them high. The problem is, these are not exactly common substances we're dealing with. You'd need an experienced hand to process whatever plant you got them from.'

'And what plant would that be?'

He shrugged. 'I'm not a botanist.'

'Neither am I,' Jamie said. 'You don't know any, do you?'

'I don't exactly run in those circles,' Forss said, laughing.

Jamie didn't have the energy or the desire to probe into that further.

'So, uh, where's your partner?' he asked then. 'You too still at each other's throats?'

Jamie raised an eyebrow, looked over at him. She didn't recall them having become friends.

He read her expression, backed off a little. 'I just mean, he called, then you called – I wasn't sure what the deal was.'

'The deal,' Jamie said, 'is to help us catch the asshole doing this.'

He raised his hands. 'Touchy subject, I get it.'

Jamie growled, then sighed. The truth was she was worried about Thorsen. But she didn't feel like explaining their situation to Forss. 'What else have you got?'

'Uh,' Forss said, scratching the side of his head. 'The suit is something. All those crows. Yikes, and I thought I was into dead things.' He chuckled.

Jamie grimaced.

He went on. 'You were right that it's coated with a powder, like a pollen. We've bagged the suit itself, and taken samples. Looks like inhaling it would give you a pretty nasty trip. Feel sorry for anyone who's done that accidentally.'

Jamie grimaced again. 'What else?'

'We're just cataloguing the rest now, shouldn't be too much longer. We'd like to move onto the farmhouse now if we can. Is it open, or … how should we handle this?'

Jamie dropped the file onto the lid of the boot and pushed off from the side of Thorsen's car. 'I'll sort it.' She started walking for the front door, glad there was something she could kick to relieve some of the anger she was feeling.

Forss caught up with her.

'Did you ever crack that other phone?' Jamie asked then. She hadn't heard back about Lena Viklund's phone – the one that Gunnar Vikland had given them – and it wasn't in the file.

'Oh, yeah,' Forss said.

'And?'

'Clean.'

'Clean?'

He nodded, a little out of breath as Jamie powered up the slope towards the front door. 'It'd been wiped – factory reset. No memory card, no SIM, no linked accounts. I ran the IMEI number – the handset wasn't under contract, so there's nothing to tie it to anyone.'

'Hmm,' Jamie said, not slowing down.

'That strange? What were you expecting?'

'Don't know,' Jamie said, transferring her weight, lifting

her heel without stopping, and then driving it through the door in one hard kick.

It landed just next to the handle, splintered the wood, and blew the thing inwards. It swung on its hinges and banged against the inner wall.

'Jeez, remind me not to get on your bad side,' Forss remarked.

'I wouldn't,' Jamie replied.

She stepped into the darkened interior, smelt damp and mould. The house was cool, empty.

'This guy likely to be … home?' Forss asked, voice quiet.

'Hope not,' Jamie said, pressing inside. 'But I guess we'll find out.' As she moved through the rooms, she thought on Lena's phone. Did she know her father was going to take it from her? Did she wipe it because of that? Did she wipe it to protect it from her father? To protect Felix? Something occurred to her then. She turned to Forss, still hovering nervously in the doorway, hair wild. 'iPhones have that thing where if you enter the wrong passcode too many times it wipes the phone, right?'

Forss looked at her, surprised. 'Uh, no – not wipes it. Not like that at least. It locks it, stops anyone from accessing it. But that wasn't in the local memory, and it would have been if that was the case. We would have seen if someone tried to get in like that. But,' he said, lifting a hand, 'if there was a linked account, someone could have accessed it remotely and wiped it. So long as they could log in to the admin account on it.'

'So Lena Viklund could have done that from Malmö?'

'I don't know who that is, but yes. Theoretically.'

'Why do you say "theoretically?"'

'Usually you would only do that if your phone was stolen,

for example, and you wanted to protect your data from whoever had stolen it.'

'Her father took it from her, shipped her off to Malmö. Maybe she did it to stop him from seeing anything on there?'

Forss nodded. 'Yeah, sure, but there'd be a SIM in there in that case. Unless he removed it after that. But why would he?'

Jamie didn't have an answer for that one. 'I don't know,' she said, looking into the kitchen from the hallway. Something caught her eye, and she crossed the dark flagstone floor to the opposite counter. 'Speaking of phones,' she said, more to herself than anything else.

She reached out, touched the screen, saw it light up, displaying a picture of Hugo Westman and Olivia Sundgren. 'Well, guess we know who texted Felix Nordahl from Hugo Westman's phone.' She looked up, saw an empty, dated kitchen. Damn, she couldn't believe it, but she kind of missed Thorsen.

Forss appeared then, filling the space, but not his shoes. 'Want me to take a swing at that one, too?'

'Sure,' Jamie said. She already knew what he'd find, and that it would confirm what she already thought. Flygare went to the parties to pedal Markus's drugs. He took Westman's phone on Markus's order, who already had the intention of luring Felix out to the falls. To kill him. Maybe as an example to Flygare, not to cross him. The money in Felix's room – he was saving up to run. Maybe down to Malmö, to see Lena. Maybe just anywhere that wasn't Kurrajakk.

Markus must have gotten wind of that.

And he obviously didn't like it.

Forss came closer and Jamie gave him space, the sweat patches now coming with an accompanying aroma.

Her nose couldn't take any more smells.

She melted through another door into what looked to be a study. The shelves were stacked with books – everything from novels to memoirs, from history books to – she ran her fingers along the spines – horticulture.

She stopped, suppressing a wry smile, and pulled the book from the old bookcase. It was hefty, but clean. No dust. It'd been used recently. Read recently. She wasn't surprised. Markus brushing up on his facts before he designed his crow suit and poison dust, no doubt.

Jamie slotted it back into the bookcase, approached the desk in the corner. It was filled with papers – sheets filled with sketches. Of crows. Of feathers. Of wings, and eyes, and of how they could all be switched together like a disgusting jigsaw. Suit designs, she thought as she moved the papers around with her fingers. There was no need for gloves, for caution now.

This was where he designed it – where he sat and planned everything.

She moved down, to the drawers, wondering what horrors she'd find in them.

She pulled the top one open, paused, staring down into it.

There, sitting on odd wires, batteries, tools, was a pistol. A black revolver with a short, snub nose. The word 'Colt' was etched on the side. .38 Special, she thought. She always liked guns. She got that from her father.

Jamie reached in, picked it up, saw immediately that it was loaded.

Markus wasn't looking to be disturbed while he schemed then.

She weighed it in her hand, thought about her own pistol, probably still tucked in the back of Thorsen's jeans, empty. About how she hadn't charged after him because she was unarmed.

Jamie glanced over her shoulder, couldn't see Forss, and quickly pushed the pistol into the back of her own jeans, letting the hem of her jacket down over the grip.

He appeared in the doorway a second later. 'Find anything else that's *juicy?'* He twiddled his fingers in the air, eyes lighting up.

'You're strange, you know that?' Jamie sighed.

'Comes with the job.' He shrugged.

'Yeah, I can imagine it attracts a sort.'

'Coming from the kriminalinspektör incapable of cracking a smile,' he answered glibly.

'Touché,' she said.

'So, did you find anything?'

Jamie looked at him for a second, then knocked the drawer closed with her hip. 'Nope,' she said, shrugging.

And then headed for the door.

41

JAMIE STEPPED from the house and down the slope.

Forss's guys were still working on the barn and took little notice of her as she passed the door.

When she was clear, she pulled the pistol from her belt and popped the cylinder out, rotated it. It ticked ominously. The thing seemed clean, well-oiled. Looks like Markus was ready to use it if need be.

Jamie swallowed, clicking it back into the body, and held it in front of her, picking up pace.

Forss and his guys would know what to do, and he had Jamie's number if they needed anything. She guessed they'd just move on to the Flygare location when they were done here.

Though by then Jamie hoped she'd have found Thorsen and would be heading back. She didn't like the idea of him being out there alone with a gun.

As she approached the fence, she slowed, measured the steps, and then vaulted it, her midriff complaining, the old scar tissue there stretching painfully.

Jamie landed, rubbed it, and then pushed on through the reeds.

The sun was sinking lower now, there wasn't a lot of daylight left. And the darkness came quickly here. Even faster in the forest.

Jamie plunged into the trees, trying to pick out any trace of Thorsen's trail. She'd followed the broken reeds coming in, but now, everything was in perpetual twilight, the ground dark, the earth beneath even darker.

'Straight, then,' she muttered, willing her eyes to adjust, pressing deeper.

She followed what she thought could be footprints laid along a natural path, pausing every ten metres or so to listen to the forest.

It was the worst thing of all about pines, the acid from their needles killed most of the ground flora. And without it, the bugs and rodents that needed it to live were absent. No bugs and rodents, no birds. Nothing. Just silence.

A forest as close to dead as it could be.

She was just glad there were no crows there for once.

Though she didn't know if that meant she was going the right way or the exact opposite.

She walked for thirty minutes before she slowed and pulled her phone out. She had one bar. Thank God.

Jamie pulled open her map to see where the hell she was, and waited for it to load.

Her eyes ached a little at the light of the screen and she looked around. The canopy was thick here, the air still. There was no trace of sunlight. Just murk. Like being underwater.

The digital world materialised in front of her then and she squinted down to get her bearings, zooming the screen out to see where the road was – pretty much her only frame of reference.

A kilometre, maybe. She'd walked two and a half already.

Her fingers danced on the glass, and then paused.

Shit. She picked her head up.

It wasn't far.

Jamie bit her lip, glanced back over her shoulder. It wasn't exactly a yellow brick road that she'd followed, but she'd kept to what she thought looked most like a trail. And it was heading to a place she suddenly didn't want to go.

She tightened her grip on the old Colt and stowed her phone, moving forward again, this time with less caution.

It was less than an hour to sundown, and she knew where she was going now. She didn't have a doubt in her mind.

Jamie was breathing a little harder, sweat beading on her forehead when the ground began to steepen and rise towards a natural crown.

A rustle in the trees stopped her in her tracks and she looked up, seeing a dark shape flutter through the branches above.

She watched as the crow found another perch and settled next to the others.

Others.

A few here, a few there, roosting quietly.

Watching.

Waiting.

Jamie swallowed, heart beating low and fast, and pushed on again, up the hill.

As the ground rose up ahead of her and she could see welts in the bed of needles now, foot marks where toes had dug in to get up.

She could see slashes through it too, hand marks, where someone had clawed their way forward.

Thorsen? Losing his footing.

Jamie set her jaw. She didn't know if she was glad or terrified to know that she was still going the right way.

His boot marks made for good footholds, and she climbed steadily upwards, stepping quietly, trying not to spook the birds. She had two hands on the grip of the pistol now. She needed to aim true.

As she approached, a tinge penetrated the air. Thick, sickly sweet. She knew she was close then.

Her stomach turned over.

Jamie went to her knees, crawled to the crest, and stopped, listening hard.

The ground fell away before her, to a flat stone plinth in the middle of the depression. She took it in for the second time, that natural bowl with the upright stones all around, the petrified wooden altar in the centre.

But her eyes were only fixed on one thing.

There, on his knees, was Thorsen.

It took her a second to work out what she was looking at, the darkness, falling fast around her, drenched the site in premature dusk.

A shape rose up before him. He had his head hung, and it looked like pure darkness was running down his back. Tar spilling over his shoulders.

But it wasn't, it was wings.

Enveloping him in a dark embrace.

The King of Crows stood over Thorsen, hunched a little, dripping with feathers and corpses. The trees around him were alight with his army, their jet eyes catching the faintest glimpses of the fading light, a thousand tiny precious stones, twinkling as they looked on.

Jamie was frozen, watching as the King's beak curved down, brushed the back of Thorsen's head. His shoulders rose and fell as the King whispered to him.

The voice carried, no more than a guttural rumble as he spoke. Jamie couldn't make it out. But she could see Thorsen's hands at his sides, clenched into white-knuckled fists.

She exhaled, sense returning, fear bashing against the inside of her ribcage, threatening to burst her heart.

She dragged the Colt up past her hip, rested it on the ground in front of her.

Jamie stretched out, pulled her right knee up so it was level with her hip, stabilising her position.

She lengthened her arms, so the weight was on her forearms, and then levered her shoulders up to a comfortable firing position. Jamie forced herself to breathe. Fingered the trigger. Took aim. Hoped to hell the pistol shot straight.

It was a decent distance for a snub-nosed .38. Maybe twenty metres. And she couldn't see him all – just from the chest up. Shit Thorsen was big. Why was he so big?

No, she couldn't doubt herself. She had to take this shot. Had to end this now. Who knew what he was saying to Thorsen? What he was putting in his mind.

Jamie applied pressure, keeping both eyes open, measuring her heartbeat.

The trigger creaked, the hammer wheeling back. Damn, these old pistols. So stiff.

Jamie released. She couldn't risk it. If she pulled too hard, her aim could shift. No, she'd need to manually cock it. There was no way she could move position. It would take too long.

Her thumb found the hammer and drew backwards. The spring tensioned, extending as it reached full cock. And then clicked.

Loudly.

Jamie froze, eyebrows knitting together, and stared down at the King.

He wasn't moving, wasn't looking.

He didn't hear. Thank God.

And then something shifted above her.

A faint rustle of wings.

Jamie's throat tightened. She turned her head, looked upwards out of the corner of her eye. Saw a pair of tiny black orbs staring back at her. A crow. On a branch. No more than six feet up. It cocked its head, white lids flashing.

'Please,' she whispered. 'Don't.'

But it was already too late.

The crow's beak parted.

Jamie's eyes flew back to the King.

Her muscles tightened all at once, body tensing.

The crow screamed.

The King looked.

Jamie fired.

The muzzle flash split the forest in two, the report sending a thousand crows into madcap flight.

Jamie threw her hands over her head, the birds sweeping low and furious up over the rise, the space beneath the thick canopy now full with terrific movement. It rolled over her like a river, sweeping her backwards and she scrabbled to get out of the way of their scratching, flapping maelstrom.

She opened her eyes, staring upwards through her fingers, the torrent thinning, and got to her knees, pulling herself back towards the crest. Air escaped her lips as she flopped onto her belly, pistol raised again, searching for her target.

There was no body prostrate on the floor.

No dead crow.

But there was Thorsen, rising, weapon in hand.

She watched as he turned towards her, saw a flash of black behind him, a dark, feathered hand on his shoulder, a beak brush his ear.

Thorsen's pistol zeroed in on her, hand shaking.

Jamie stared back, wide eyed. No shot, the Crow fully behind him.

And then Thorsen fired.

The bullet hit the ground six inches from Jamie's elbow, blowing earth and pine needles all over her.

Shit! Jamie rolled sideways, hearing another shot.

The bullet unzipped the air above her head.

The muzzle flashes danced in her eyes as she pulled herself to her feet.

She couldn't stay here, couldn't take them both – and had no intention of putting Thorsen down to get to the King. No matter how much she wanted his head on a plate.

She'd have to dine on crow another night.

Jamie was up and running then.

She could hear footsteps behind her, ragged breath, grunting, yelling – just noise. Rage. Thorsen's rage. His intention. To kill. To kill. To kill Jamie.

She didn't need to know what the King had been whispering to him then. She already knew.

Jamie pounded through the forest. The sound of a stream to her left drew her in, her mind going back two days, to the morning this all began. She followed a stream up from the road, and that's where she would go now.

Thorsen was taller, had longer legs. He would be faster. And over uneven, difficult ground, he could close the gap.

But if she could reach the road fast enough, she could push. And she could push hard. Jamie could run, and if she could get a head start, she didn't think he'd be able to catch up. She could do a kilometre at full sprint, five in twenty-one minutes. She used to be sub-twenty, but not since her injury. Still, she didn't think Thorsen could keep either pace.

She was about to find out.

Jamie met the stream, headed down, feet sloshing in the needles.

And then she was on flat ground, bursting up into the open and onto the road.

Her breath was ragged. But she had to keep going.

Jamie turned right, knowing where she was, but not where she was going, and took off.

Her knees pumped, bomber jacket heavy and thick, jeans tight. But she couldn't risk the time to take them off.

More shouts behind her, indistinct and throaty.

Thorsen was on the road.

Another shot.

It punched into the trees above her.

Running and shooting straight was nearly impossible.

Jamie risked a glance back.

She had twenty metres on him, maybe thirty.

Night was chasing them too.

Jamie just ran.

Thorsen kept up, then flagged, then fired, then ran again, yelling more.

Sweat poured down her face.

She just kept her eyes on the yellow line that cleaved the road in two. Focused on her breathing.

Think. She had to think. Of how to do this. Of how to fix him. Because right now, she was leading him nowhere. This road ran for twenty kilometres before it reached anything resembling civilisation. Her house was back the other way, as was Kurrajakk.

She couldn't keep going forever, couldn't double back. Losing him wasn't an option either – if she did, then he could well stumble across someone else, gun in hand. And if he reached the town … No, no, that wasn't going to happen. She'd need to keep him on her, just far back enough so that he couldn't hit her, close enough so he didn't lose her.

Shit, it was all but dark now.

Fuck!

She glanced back, saw him flagging, pistol waving, breath heavy.

She didn't want to kill him.

Jamie backed off the pace slightly, the rush of blood receding in her ears.

The sound of running water replaced it and Jamie glanced right into the trees, saw another stream running out of the woods and under the road.

That was the third she'd passed now.

She glanced left then, trying to remember what was down that way. The map – what did the map show? The ground continued to fall away, gently, until …

Jamie halted then, coming to a stop, and looked back.

Thorsen was staggering forward, shoulders hunched.

She lifted her fingers to her mouth, slotted them in, and whistled.

He picked his head up, teeth bared in a mad snarl, then raised his gun.

Jamie darted sideways, off the asphalt, down into the trees.

He followed.

The forest thickened a little here and the pace was slower. Jamie picked her way forward, listening to Thorsen ploughing through after her. She followed the sound of running water, keeping the stream on her left, hoping to hell she had remembered this right.

Another glance back. He was still coming. Still murderous.

Jamie swam forward, pushing through the trees and

undergrowth, the trunks thinner, the forest denser. The rough branches scratched at her jacket, pulled at her hair.

More grunts behind her as they whipped Thorsen in the face.

At least he couldn't get a clean shot in here.

Not much further now.

She saw it then, felt it under foot.

The soft dirt ended, and her feet clipped on stone. Small at first, then solid.

The trees died away and she was on rock, an endless stretch of shimming water reaching out into the darkness ahead.

The last dregs of daylight bled from the horizon, just bright enough for this to work.

A second later, Thorsen burst from the shrubbery and stopped on the rocky outcropping, looking around. He raised his gun, scanned the water, shoulders rising and falling quickly as he sucked in ragged lungfuls of air.

And then he was falling.

Jamie came from behind, launching out of the trees, and threw her shoulder, all her weight, square into his back.

He stumbled, then lost his footing, and went over the edge.

There was a second of stillness as he fell, and then a splash as he hit the water.

It was maybe four feet down, and he didn't make a sound.

The surface boiled for a moment, then settled, swallowing him.

Jamie went to the edge, pistol trained on the point he went under, and looked over. Waited.

Five seconds. Nothing.

Ten seconds. Still nothing.

The ripples had dissipated now, the bubbles gone.

Jamie checked her watch. Twenty seconds.

Shit. Had she killed him?

Her throat was tight, heart thundering in her ears.

Jamie reached up, ready to shed her jacket, started hyperventilating to force oxygen into her blood.

And then she saw it, movement, just below the surface, two white hands, fingers outstretched.

Thorsen rose from the depths, clawing at the sky, and broke into the air, gasping and coughing.

And then he saw her, above him, and kept her gaze.

Jamie said nothing, finger tight on the trigger of the old Colt.

'What—' he started, coughing, dark, cold water rushing into his throat. 'What the fuck … are … Jamie … ?' He spat mouthfuls out, trying desperately to keep himself afloat.

'Thorsen?' Jamie asked, watching him thrash.

'Help me!' he yelled, plunging under again. A second later he was back up, going for the shore, his heavy coat dragging him down.

Jamie let herself down off the little bluff and onto a lower precipice, and got to a knee, holding her hand out.

Thorsen stretched for it, missed, went under again.

Then he was up once more, choking, spluttering, retching, and reached again.

They connected this time, and Jamie felt his skin cool against hers.

She locked eyes with him once more, opened her grip a little.

'What are you – ngghh – doing?' He sprayed a mouthful over the rock.

'Is it you?' Her voice was thin, eyes searching his face for a sign of hope.

'Who else is it going to fucking be?' He tried to yell,

grabbing her sleeve with his other hand and hauling himself to safety.

Jamie gripped then, and pulled, falling backwards as he flopped out of the water and up onto dry land.

He panted hard, resting his cheek against the stone.

Jamie got up quickly, gave him some space.

She kept the Colt in her grasp, watched him catch his breath, waited to see what would happen.

After a long time, he dragged his hands under his chin and pushed himself up a little, shivered, squinted up at Jamie through the last throes of the daylight. 'Jamie?'

'Yeah?' she asked, grip tightening on the pistol.

He looked around. 'Where the hell are we?'

42

THORSEN HAD LOST his gun to the depths, and his phone was well and truly drowned. But luckily, his car keys were in his pocket, so made it out of the lake.

Once Jamie was sure he was no longer homicidal, they tracked back to the road, and headed for Markus's farm.

Night had fallen, but they couldn't rush. They needed to keep their eyes open.

Thorsen was flagging, though, not himself. He was spent – physically, emotionally, mentally. He was huffing and panting, dragging himself along the tarmac while Jamie led, Colt still in hand.

He didn't much feel like talking – and couldn't remember anything of use. The last thing he recalled was arriving at Markus's farm and heading into the barn. Then nothing. Just fear, and a voice in his head telling him to kill – telling him to embrace the crows, embrace the darkness, to seek death as they did.

Charming, Jamie said, then pushed on.

He'd asked how she'd come up with the lake theory.

She remembered from her own trip how the stream had snapped her out of it, took a chance.

Though Jamie felt like he'd come a lot closer to drowning than she had. But that cold rush of water, that oxygen deprivation, that feeling of drowning – what it was doing chemically, she didn't know. But it was enough to break the trip at least. How much faith she had in her quick fix, though, she couldn't say. Replicating the findings weren't high on her to-do list.

It was nearly seven by the time they finally walked through the gate and into Markus's darkened courtyard.

The white vans, and Forss's team were gone.

She expected that they'd tried to call her, but her phone had died sometime between the forest and the walk back.

Thorsen fumbled his keys from his pocket as Jamie scouted the area.

Everything was silent.

'No,' she said then, coming back and taking them from him. 'I'll drive. You can barely stand.'

He managed a nod, then went to the passenger side, sagging into the seat, breathing hard like he was about to throw up.

As Jamie got into the driver's seat, she noticed her empty pistol in the door compartment. She pulled it out and slotted it back into her holster, stowing the Colt in her jacket pocket. Thorsen's eyes were shut, and either he didn't hear, or didn't care enough to open them and comment.

Either way, Jamie locked the doors, put the car in drive, and swung out of there as quickly as she could. Poking around in the dark was the last thing on her mind.

She drove steadily back towards Kurrajakk, and after a few minutes of rest, Thorsen seemed to come around a little. He wound the window down and let the cool air stream over his face. Despite his wet clothes and the chill in the air, he was sweating. Jamie knew that feeling – that come down off whatever the hell the King was playing with. Hyoscyamine, scopolamine. Tropane alkaloids. Jamie didn't even know what they were, but she knew she hated them.

'I'm sorry,' Thorsen said as they passed a sign saying two kilometres to town.

'For what?' Jamie asked, looking over at him.

He straightened up in the chair, put his face in his hands, and then rubbed roughly, slapping himself on the cheeks. 'For trying to kill you.'

He leaned forward then, shed his wet coat, started unbuttoning his shirt.

'You're not the first,' Jamie said tiredly. 'And you probably won't be the last.'

Thorsen cracked a smile, threw his jacket in the back, then his shirt. He had a white t-shirt on, and thankfully kept it on as he leaned over the centre console to fish around in the back for something.

'Doesn't make it right,' he said, head in the back seat.

'No,' she replied, 'but you couldn't help it – I can sympathise, remember?'

Thorsen pulled an old hoodie over his head and slid back into the front, looking across at her. 'Mm,' was all he said. He looked forward then, muttered under his breath. 'Flygare.'

Jamie filled her lungs. She was trying not to think about that. And it was half the reason she hadn't plugged her phone into Thorsen's car charger. She didn't feel like answering any questions from Forss like; why is there a dead body in the woods? Who shot him? Why aren't you here?

In fact, she didn't even know where she was going. Or what they were going to do next. She was on autopilot.

But as the first lights of Kurrajakk broke the darkness ahead, it became blindingly apparent. Burningly so.

'What the fuck?' Jamie said, hunching up over the wheel to get a better look.

As they approached the cross, she slowed, squinting into the flames ahead. A car was mounted on the curb at an odd angle, a raging fire billowing from its side windows, the sheet metal charred black at its flanks.

Opposite, a shop window had been smashed, the glass covering the pavement.

Jamie slowed but didn't stop, easing past the burning wreck.

There was an old furniture shop at the intersection, its wide roller shutters down, the words *'HAN KOMMER'* spray-painted across them. He is coming.

She did stop now, and her and Thorsen both kicked their doors open and stepped into the smoke-filled air. Jamie choked, coughed on it, then walked up onto the curb to get a better look at the damage.

Thorsen circled the car from behind and approached.

She glanced over her shoulder at him.

He was nudging a dead crow with the toe of his shoe. It was lying in the gutter, legs in the air, wings at odd angles, flat on its back.

Jamie looked around then, saw at least a dozen in the immediate vicinity.

The streetlights were on, but nothing else was lit.

The only noise was the crackling of the burning car, the chug of smoke as it poured from the burst windows. Its wheel was buckled under the fender – it looked like it had swerved, hit the curb at speed, snapping the axel. And then someone had … set it on fire? What the hell was going on here?

Jamie and Thorsen looked at each other.

'Where is everyone?' Thorsen asked, looking around.

Jamie checked too, shrugged. 'I … I don't know.'

The faint sound of sirens was echoing through the darkness. 'Sounds like fire are on their way at least,' he said, stepping into the road and looking out of town.

Gunfire cut the air then. A single, loud, echoing boom that rolled across the town.

Instinctively, they both ran back to the car and jumped in.

Gunfire was never a good sound to hear.

Jamie launched the car forward, the sporty tires coming in handy. They bit and slingshotted them around the corner, towards the source.

Thorsen was gripping the handle above the door, pointing through the windscreen to the melee ahead. 'Guess we found the people,' he said as Jamie stamped on the brake and sent the car juddering to a stop.

They both exited once more, facing down the clamouring crowd in front of the Moose's Head. It must have been fifty strong, maybe more.

The landlord was at the front door, shotgun in hand wrestling someone back. Shouts filled the air. People pumped fists, jostled, shoved, fought and riled like a mass of snakes. She didn't know if they were pushing to get inside, or just rioting there out of sheer magnetism.

Jamie and Thorsen both locked eyes again. damp, tired, strung-out, scared. What could they do?

The barrel of the shotgun rose in the air, four hands clamped around it, and then breathed fire into the night.

The report deafened them, flattened the crowd for an instant as a plume of white-hot flame stabbed at the sky. Everyone crouched, held their breath for a moment, then erupted again, ready to level the whole building.

Whatever Jamie and Thorsen did, they had to get that

shotgun out of the equation. They had enough shit to deal with without someone getting their head blown off.

Jamie plunged in, elbows first, fighting through the crowd.

Thorsen went in too, a few bodies across. He was tall, she could see him, but he wasn't himself, and the crowd was brutal.

Jamie felt someone grab her hair, then her collar.

She felt something crunch under her heel, looked down, saw the bulging eye of a crow, neck trapped under her boot.

She grimaced, opened her mouth to call out to Thorsen, then felt someone drag her backwards, off balance.

Jamie swung around, turned, grabbing the wrist of the woman trying to choke her with her own T-shirt. She twisted hard, jabbed the woman mid-torso with her left, right in the solar plexus. Her eyes widened in shock, and she melted backwards into the crowd, winded.

Jamie forced herself back straight again, drove through the throng of bodies, felt the wetness of sweat on the sides of her face as she squeezed between shoulders.

A quick glance – she couldn't see Thorsen. Where was he?

And then she was there, at the front, next to the guy with the shotgun. She didn't recognise him, but she could smell the booze on his skin like he'd bathed in week-old beer.

The landlord she knew – cursorily – a tough old guy with skin like tanned leather and less teeth than fingers. He was wedged in his doorway, wrestling the drunkard back.

Jamie's hands went into the fight, took hold of the shotgun – an old, tarnished pump-action – and felt it swing violently, up and down. She toppled forward, felt the stock rise up quickly under her, hit her in the stomach. Her feet left the ground, the air knocked from her chest.

She gasped, let go, stumbled backwards into the door-frame, felt the crush of bodies against her, ready to beat her down and trample her to death.

Screw this!

Jamie wrestled the Colt from her pocket, unable to breathe, and lifted it to the sky, firing once, twice, three times.

The crowd was stunned, a hundred eyes all planted on her.

'Polis!' she forced out; voice strained. 'Everyone—'

But she didn't get to finish. The landlord ripped the shotgun from the drunkard's grasp, and his eyes went to his now-free hands.

Jamie clocked him an instant too late, the word dying on her lips.

His hand balled and shot out, connecting with her cheek before she could even attempt to block.

The blow bowled her over. The pain came second, spiking through her face as she sprawled sideways, catching herself on the stone sill of the window next to the door.

Jamie glanced back over her shoulder, eyes streaming, and watched the guy come for a second taste.

She had the Colt in her hand still, and he was already too close to counter, to defend against.

So Jamie raised it. With everything she had, she twisted and shoved it upwards, ready to blow a hole through the guy before he took her head off.

But he never got there.

His elbow rose up next to his ear, reddened face swollen with drunken rage, but then he froze, and suddenly was wrenched backwards instead.

Thorsen threw him sideways into the wall of bodies, then smacked him, a heavy right cross coming out of nowhere.

A dull thwack rang out, Thorsen's knuckles connecting

with the guy's chin. His whole face rippled and folded up like an English Bulldog's, and then he collapsed to the ground in a heap.

Everyone else stood, staring at him, none wanting to try their luck.

And then Thorsen yelled, reaching behind himself and taking the shotgun from the landlord's hands without looking. He raised it above his head like a goddamn sword and bellowed loudly enough to make those in the front row recoil.

Jamie's ears were ringing from the punch, eyes struggling to focus, and she could taste blood. She didn't know what he said – it was all white noise to her – but the crowd cowered, then back pedalled, and dispersed quickly.

Thorsen put the shotgun back in the landlord's hands then, ordered him inside, to lock the doors and not let anyone in. And then he took Jamie by the arm and lifted her straight.

She stared up at him, nose still swollen from his run in with Flygare, eyes still blackened, sweating, hair ruffled. She had her hand to her own face now, feeling the skin already rising under her fingers. They must have both looked a goddamn mess.

'Come on,' Thorsen said then, dragging her back towards the car.

Jamie found her feet quickly, regaining her faculties with each step.

She walked the last few metres of her own free will and climbed into the BMW wordlessly. They seemed to have swapped places. Thorsen was now behind the wheel, and not wasting any time.

By the time they peeled away, the landlord was already back inside, and the door was firmly shut, windows dark. The only person left on the street was the man Thorsen had punched. He was on his back, holding his face, rocking back and forth, heels scraping at the pavement.

Jamie turned her head to watch the Moose and the violent drunk shrink out of the window, her hatred for this backwater goddamn town growing with every passing second.

And as the wheels of the car thundered over the dead bodies of the crows lining the streets, her hatred for the King grew with it.

43

THORSEN SWUNG them down the alleyway at the end of the block and then streaked through the lane behind the station, pulling to a sharp stop at the back door.

He and Jamie exited quickly, the adrenaline fading fast, and both dragged themselves inside.

She hit the lights while he locked the door, and then they both strode into the middle of the desks and slowed. Neither seemed to know what to do then. Silence had fallen outside the boarded up doors, but Jamie couldn't tell whether this was the start of a town-wide revolt or the end of one.

She forgot that every time she was outside the town limits, that the place was basically just unmanned. And when you threw in the liberal gun-ownership, a splash of paranoia, and a heaped helping of crazed guy in a bird costume murdering innocents, it was a recipe for disaster.

But before Jamie could think about it anymore, Thorsen was standing in front of her.

'Chin up,' he ordered, lifting his hand but knowing better than to grab her face a third time without invitation.

'I'm fine,' she answered.

He stooped a little to draw level with her eye and looked at her intensely.

'I'm not concussed.'

'I'll be the judge of that,' Thorsen said, not looking away.

'Believe it or not,' she said, opening her eyes wider just to be hyperbolic, 'that's not the first time I've been punched in the face – or concussed. I know what they both feel like.' She pushed his rising hand back down.

'Why doesn't that surprise me?' Thorsen said.

Jamie glowered at him. 'We should focus on keeping the town in one piece, rather than trading witty banter, don't you think?'

'Witty banter?' He raised an eyebrow.

'Passive aggressive comments, then. Tomato-tomato.' She brushed past him, heading for the kitchen. 'Coffee?'

'Please.'

A minute later, Jamie came back to the doorway, an ancient plastic bag of ice-cubes pressed to the side of her face.

Thorsen was leaning on a desk, staring at the boarded over doors.

She watched him for a few seconds. 'Thanks, by the way,' she said.

He looked over.

'For earlier – that guy.' She sighed. Her face was throbbing, and one of her teeth was loose. And not for the first time. She did really need to rein in the running headlong into fights with men thing. Just a little.

'He didn't look like he was about to go easy on you.' Thorsen rubbed his knuckles.

'No, he didn't,' Jamie said. 'And if you hadn't have done

that, then …' She grabbed the pistol-shaped bulge in her pocket.

Thorsen's eyes went there. 'Yeah … and think of the paperwork then, huh?'

Jamie cracked a smile. 'Yeah, that was the only thing that stopped me. Fucking paperwork. Bane of my life.'

'Preaching to the choir.'

'No, but seriously – thanks.'

'It's what partners do.' He shrugged, looked away.

It was quiet between them then, the only sound the clicking of the old kettle as it did its best to boil the water for their coffee.

'So …' Jamie said.

'So.' He tapped the desk next to his hips.

She cleared her throat. 'You want to just keep to this superficial stuff, or do you want to have a real conversation?'

'Didn't realise that was on the table.'

'That answers that then.'

'No, wait' he said, laughing, 'come on then.' He stood up, beckoned her to talk. 'Let's have a proper conversation. You want me to go first?'

'Shoot.'

'Why'd you leave the London Met?'

'Oh, right to the deep stuff, huh?'

'You wanted to talk.'

'Uh,' Jamie started, shaking her head, her knee-jerk to go to a lie. 'I, uh – there was a case. *Three* cases, actually. In a row. Bad ones.'

'That kind of comes with the territory, right?'

'I killed a girl,' Jamie said.

Thorsen's jaw flexed.

'Not on purpose – but she didn't give me a choice. She

rushed me with a knife. I had her cornered – I didn't want to. But she was going to kill me.'

He processed that, nodded slowly.

Damn, she'd never said that out loud. She clenched her hands to stop them from shaking. 'Why'd you lie about knowing Ohlin?'

Thorsen picked his head up, eyes twitching slightly.

She could see he wanted to lie, too. She hoped giving a little might get her a little. As usual, she read it right.

'I …' he began, sitting on the desk again and letting out a long breath. 'I needed to get out of Lulea.'

'Why?'

'My wife.'

'You're married.'

'Not anymore, I don't think.' He laughed a little again, this time with less verve. It died in the air. 'Separated.'

'No ring – no tan line, either.'

'Never wore one.'

'Bet she liked that.'

'She understood. This line of work – people want to get at you. The more people you have, the more there is for them to threaten to take away.'

Jamie said nothing, her silence a confirmation of that line of reasoning. Her life a confirmation of that line of reasoning.

'So what happened?' she asked after a second.

'Things got rough, then they got messy. Then there was someone else.'

'You cheated?'

'She did.'

'Oh.'

'But thanks for the vote of confidence,' he said, clicking his tongue and shooting her a finger gun.

'Sorry, it's just …' That's what had happened between her parents.

'Yeah, that'd be the usual story.' He sighed again, folded his arms. 'And in time, maybe it would have gone that way, but she found someone first, so …' He shrugged emphatically, slapped his thighs. 'So yeah, when word came down the line that they were looking for a new Inspektör in Kurrajakk, I thought why the fuck not? All I needed to do was look it up on a map first.'

'So you ran away to Kurrajakk,' Jamie said slowly, cracking a smile.

'Why the fuck would anyone else come here?' He gave a real laugh then.

'That I don't have an answer for.'

The kettle boiled away behind her, but Jamie didn't move from the frame.

'So why *did* you lie about knowing Ohlin?'

He met her with silence now.

Embarrassment. Shame. The list went on. Just to protect his pride? Just to protect himself?

Thorsen had an icy shell, but she could tell he was vulnerable beneath, once you got down deep.

She wondered if he thought the same about her.

'But hey,' he said then, standing again, 'what detective doesn't have a past, huh? All part of the job, right?'

Jamie filled her lungs, pushed up from the doorframe, offered him as warm a smile as she could past the ice pack, and then nodded. 'Right.'

She went to make some coffee, but when she reached the counter, she stopped, leaned over it, and cracked her neck.

Jamie pushed back and headed for the main office once more. 'Hey,' she said, going through the doorway. 'You want to just call it a night? We're not going to get anything else done here.'

Thorsen was sitting behind a desk, feet up, on his phone. 'Sure,' he said, almost too quickly, getting up. 'I didn't want to say anything, but …'

'You feel like you got kicked in the head by a horse?'

'Feel like I got trampled by one.'

'That makes two of us.'

'Come on, I'll give you a ride,' he said, motioning her towards the door.

They stepped back out into the cool night air and climbed into his car.

She didn't think she'd ever been more glad to be going home, even if she was scared to be there. 'What's your room like at the Inn?' she offered casually as he pulled back onto the main road.

'Like it hasn't been decorated – or cleaned – since the seventies. Why?' He eyed her.

She hated having conversations with detectives sometimes.

The buildings thinned around them, the cabin of the car quiet and comfortable. Safe. Jamie's eyes grew tired. 'I just think,' she started, 'considering our collective run-ins with the *King,* that maybe it might be prudent to …'

'Stick together?' He didn't turn his attention from the road this time.

'Exactly. And then if he does show up, at least we're both there to …'

'Watch each other's backs.'

'Right,' she said nodding.

'Just in case.' He glanced over.

'Just in case.' She nodded again. 'In the guest room.'

He chuckled a little through closed lips. 'I wasn't thinking it would have been anything else.'

'I just wanted to make sure we were absolutely clear on that.' Jamie looked at him now.

'You'll get no trouble from me,' Thorsen said, grinning to himself.

'Good, good.' Jamie watched the road. 'Oh, and one other thing – you like dogs, right?'

44

As they drove through the gate, the security light over the front door clicked on and bathed them in white.

Thorsen pulled the car up next to Jamie's police truck and killed the engine.

They both stared up at the place, a low-slung wooden exterior bungalow tucked back against the dense forest they'd come to fear. Its floor-length living room windows faced out onto a wild garden. A moss-covered driveway led around to the garage-workshop, which had now become Jamie's workout space, but it was overgrown with brambles and shrubbery that had spilled in from the once-maintained hedge. The exterior flora had grown unimpeded and threatened to engulf the house totally. Jamie had no interest in gardening, and quite liked the enclosed feeling. Like the house was protected.

Except right now, it felt anything but.

'Right,' Jamie said, breaking the silence. She got out and headed for the front door. As her feet crunched in the gravel, a deep, menacing bark echoed from inside the house.

'That'll be the dog, then,' Thorsen said, a few steps

behind her. He already had his travelling bag in hand. Though his stuff was at the Inn, she guessed that he always carried the essentials on him. He seemed like the well-organised sort. Not a patch on Wiik's anal retentiveness, but someone who rarely went into something unprepared.

Jamie fiddled with the keys, feeling the weight of Thorsen on the step behind her. 'Excuse the smell,' she said, pushing the door inwards. 'House training is still an ongoing battle.'

Thorsen just smiled as Jamie stepped inside.

The house did carry a faint aroma of undiscovered dog urine, but it also had that old smell of ancient carpets and moulded ceilings. Of someone who smoked in there decades ago. Of someone who died there.

Hati walked out of the living room and paused, looking at Jamie. He cocked his head, tail rising. A wag was a little too much to ask.

Then he noticed Thorsen.

His remaining ear went back, and he growled, lowering his scarred head.

'Hati,' Jamie said authoritatively, stepping forward. 'In,' she ordered, pointing back to the living room.

The dog looked back at her, knowing what she wanted but fully defying the instruction.

'It's okay,' Thorsen said, sliding in past Jamie. 'I'll give him a wide berth.'

'That's probably wise,' she said. 'It's, uh, last door on the right. First one is my room, second is the bathroom, you're on the end. Clean sheets are in the cupboard in the bathroom, towels too. I've got my own bathroom, so …' she said awkwardly.

This was the first time that Jamie had welcomed a house guest since … ever. Shit. She wasn't exactly the social type, she realised.

Thorsen gave another nod. 'I'll figure it out,' he said, walking down the corridor.

He completely ignored Hati. He let out a low growl, lips peeling back over the few teeth he had left.

'Oi,' Jamie called, pointing at him.

He looked up at her.

She kept his gaze.

Thorsen passed, and then the dog sidled back into the living room.

The door to the guest room closed then, and Jamie was alone.

She let out a slow breath, turned, locked the door, checked it, and then headed for her own room. She was dying for a shower, and a good meal.

Jamie kicked the door closed behind her and went to her bedside unit, kneeling in front of it. She opened the bottom drawer, exposing the wide, flat electronic gun case. She typed her code into the keypad – her father's birthday – and lifted the lid.

Inside, there were two moulded depressions. One was empty, but perfectly fit the SIG Sauer P226 semi-automatic pistol in her holster. The other contained a matching P229 Compact pistol. A smaller version of her service weapon. Four magazines were lined up around the two pistol spaces and in a box nestled in the corner of the case was a box of 9mm ammunition. Hollow points. They bloomed on impact, reduced punch-through, and the chance of shooting the thing behind what you were aiming at. Designed to hit something and stop, they were the safest type of ammunition, used the world over by militaries, police forces, and civilians for home defence.

They had what was called *stopping power.* The ability to put someone down.

Jamie slipped the P226 from its holster on her hip and ejected the spent magazine. Evidence or not, there was no way she wasn't going to carry it loaded.

She rested the weapon on the case and opened the ammo box, thumbing rounds into the magazine until it filled up. Fifteen 9mm rounds. Fifteen shots.

Fifteen bullets with the King's name on them.

Jamie grimaced then. Or Mats Flygare's.

She shook that thought out of her head, slotting the magazine back into the pistol and banging it into place with the heel of her hand.

Then she laid it on top of the bedside cabinet and pulled out the compact P229, and a loaded magazine. The P229 took a ten-round mag. But it wasn't for her.

A knock at the door behind her grabbed her attention and she dropped the lid of the case closed. It latched automatically and she stood, turning, pistol still in hand.

'Yeah?'

Thorsen opened it and stuck his head in, catching sight of the pistol first. 'Don't shoot,' he said, stepping inside. 'I come in peace.'

'You'd better,' Jamie replied.

He smiled, then hooked a thumb over his shoulder. 'There's no hot water.'

'What? Should be – might take a while to pull through. Just run it for a bit.'

He nodded, then lingered.

'Everything okay?'

'Yeah,' he said, lowering his head a bit. 'It's just … today.'

'A hell of a day.'

'Yeah. And, uh – Flygare.'

Jamie watched him.

'I just wanted to say … I know you didn't …' He met her eye then. 'What I mean is, I know that you didn't *mean* to, if you did, you know …'

'Kill him?'

He just stared at her.

'Whatever happened,' Jamie said, walking over, loaded pistol in hand, 'it is what it is – and that's fucked up.'

'You can say that again.' He chuckled, then sighed.

'Here,' Jamie said, turning the pistol over and proffering him the grip. 'That is, if I can trust you with it?'

'Do you?' he asked.

She studied him for a moment, the apologetic duck-egg grey eyes, the tall frame, shoulders hunched, back soft. 'Yeah, I do.'

He accepted the pistol, their fingers touching for a moment before Jamie let her hand fall.

'It wasn't your fault, what happened – I don't blame you,' she said.

'But do you forgive me?' He lowered his head, looked up at her.

'For what?' Jamie laughed. 'You can't run for shit, and you can't shoot for shit either, apparently – so there's not much to really forgive you for. I was never in any real danger.'

He held the pistol in both hands, laughed again. 'Sure, whatever you say.'

'Now get out.' Jamie pushed him on the arm, back through the door. 'If you're not going to take a shower, then I will.'

He nodded. 'Yeah, of course.' He held up the pistol a little. 'Thanks for this.'

'Well, yours is at the bottom of a lake. So it was either

that, or …' She pulled the old Colt from her pocket and held it up.

'Do I even want to ask where you got that?'

'Best not.'

'That's what I thought.' He looked down at the pistol in his hands. 'This works great. Though, I don't suppose you have anything bigger, do you?'

Jamie just shook her head. 'Goodbye, Thorsen. Oh, and make sure you don't leave that anywhere,' she added, nodding at the gun. 'The dog's a thief.'

He laughed, then realised she was serious. 'What, he'd steal a gun?'

Jamie held up her dirty, still-bandaged hand. 'How do you think I really got this?'

45

When Jamie killed the shower, the sounds of gnashing, snarling, and crashing reached her ears.

For a second, she didn't know what the hell it was, and then it dawned on her.

She stumbled from the slick bathtub, swearing, and grabbed a towel, wrapping it around herself as she raced into the bedroom and out into the hall, expecting to see blood splatters up the wall and Thorsen and Hati locked in a fight to the death.

And for an instant, that's what she thought she was looking at.

Thorsen was flat on his back, with Hati on top of him. Thorsen had his hands in Hati's neck, and the dog's head was whipping back and forth, teeth clapping together, trying to get at Thorsen's face, except ... his tail was wagging?

There were all manner of alien noises coming from her dog, but the thing that she couldn't wrap her head around was that he was *playing* with Thorsen.

He'd been with her four months and he'd never once accepted a pat on the head without trying to bite her hand off.

'Ah-hem,' Jamie said, dripping onto the carpet.

They stopped wrestling and Thorsen pushed Hati off. He landed, tottered on his three legs, then regained himself, grinning up at Jamie, tail still wagging, tongue lolling from his mangled jowls.

'Sorry,' Thorsen said, getting up tiredly, 'did we disturb you?'

'I'm feeling pretty fucking disturbed, yeah,' Jamie replied. 'What the hell are you doing?'

'Playing,' he said, shrugging a little. He reached down, ruffled the skin on Hati's scruff roughly, without looking or hesitating.

The dog relished it.

Jamie didn't have any words.

'I'm, uh, good with dogs,' Thorsen said. 'He just … needed some guy-time, I think.'

'Guy-time?' Jamie arched an eyebrow.

'Yeah, some dogs are guy's dogs, you know? Need some rough play to show 'em who's boss.' He lifted his fists like a Victorian boxer and cycled them in the air.

'Right …' Jamie said, sighing. 'Well, seeing as you two are such good friends, he can sleep with you tonight. Just bear in mind, he wets the bed.' She turned, flicked her hand over her shoulder.

'That's fine, so do I,' Thorsen called.

'I'm gonna finish my shower now.' Jamie closed the bedroom door behind her, leaned back against it, and shook her head in disbelief. Then, bitterly, the surprise was replaced with jealousy. Jamie sighed, flexing her bitten, raw hand, and then went back into the bathroom to dry off.

After that, the night passed uneventfully.

Thorsen showered quickly – and Jamie guessed Hati was

in the bathroom with him because there was no sign of him in the living room.

Jamie cooked dinner; a bolognese with two-days-past-its-date minced beef that either Thorsen didn't realise smelled a little questionable, or was too polite to say anything about.

By the time they came to eat it, they were both spent. Thorsen so much so that Jamie could see the bags under his eyes through the bruising.

They both scraped what was left of their meals into Hati's bowl and went to bed by nine, ready to put the day behind them.

But by twelve, Hati was barking again.

Jamie sat upright in bed, eyes stiff and heavy, sweat under her jaw, and grabbed her pistol off the bedside.

Hati's thunderous barks rang through the wall, and by the time Jamie got to the hallway, Thorsen was already there.

Hati was at the windows in the living room, against the glass on his hind legs, barking upwards at the sky.

Jamie blinked herself clear, glanced at the clock on the wall in the kitchen. Damn, was she ever going to get any sleep?

Between Hati's barks, she could hear the cawing of crows. A symphony of calls that overlaid, building to a muted roar beyond the sanctuary of the house.

Thorsen was at Jamie's shoulder, pistol in his hand, too.

He looked over at her, and she at him, eyes going to his neck, to his quickened pulse.

Hati shoved his way between their legs then and into the hallway, running towards the front door.

He pulled up short and leaned back into a braced position, barking and snarling at the wood.

Jamie was so done with this.

She strode forward, snatched up a slip lead from the coat hooks next to the door and threw it back to Thorsen.

He understood immediately, and looped it over Hati's head as Jamie unbolted the door and clicked the security light on.

Cold air rushed in and chilled Jamie's bare legs, her sleeping shorts fluttering gently in the breeze. Gooseflesh came up on Jamie's arms and she shivered, squinting into the night.

The stone was cold under her feet as she stepped out, felt Thorsen's hand on her shoulder.

He stepped past her, Hati on the end of the lead up on his hind legs, growling at the darkness.

Jamie lifted her pistol, the calls of a hundred crows ringing down from above. The brilliance of the security light caught the underside of their sleek bodies, making them glitter and flash as they wheeled in low circles.

'There!' Thorsen said, lifting his pistol too, Hati's lead firmly in his left hand.

Jamie saw him then, standing between their cars – shadowed by her truck. No more than ten, fifteen metres away.

She watched the muscles roll in Thorsen's forearm as he put tension on the trigger, and then lifted her hand and gently pushed his weapon down.

He looked over his shoulder at her.

The King was just standing there, his legion above, sounding his arrival.

But he wasn't doing anything.

Jamie could make out the curve of his long beak, the face a mask of feathers, the posture hunching, the cloak flowing, all death and theatre. But he wasn't doing anything.

And Jamie wasn't about to play the next round of his goddamn game.

She drew breath into her body, tasted his sickly-sweet poison on the air, his stench, and called out. 'Markus!' she yelled. 'This is over!'

He just stood there.

'We know who you are,' Jamie went on. 'We're coming for you!'

Thorsen watched her out of the corner of his eye, muzzle still trained on the King.

There was no reply, just the screams of the birds and Hati's echoing barks.

Jamie narrowed her eyes. 'Get down on the ground,' she ordered. 'Make this easy on yourself!'

But he had no such intentions.

Before Jamie even saw him move, something was flying through the air.

She reacted instinctively, throwing her pistol up, pushing the breath from her body.

She fired one, deliberate shot, and saw the limp body of the crow that he'd thrown blown into two pieces, a plume of shimmering dust erupting from the carcass as the bullet ripped through it.

The body fell to the ground between the cars and the house, leaking dark black onto the stones.

There was a moment of stillness as the muzzle flash faded from the air, and then a torrent of birds all plunged into the space. Black bodies swirled, screeching as they attacked the ground, the stench of the King stinging Jamie's nostrils.

They shielded their faces from the sudden onslaught of wings and beaks.

Hati lost his fucking shit.

The dog twisted himself up in in the lead, tossing saliva

everywhere as he scrambled to get out of the way and tried to bite at them simultaneously.

A mad, sharp cackle cut through the clamour, and a dark shape flew past to their right, darting around the edge of the house – the same way that the King had run the night before. The same way that Jamie had chased him.

Thorsen, eyes wide with rage, moved to follow him, but Jamie's fist was firmly in the back of his T-shirt.

'No,' she said, holding onto him.

'He's right there!' Thorsen protested. Hati agreed.

'It's what he wants,' Jamie said, voice calm now. 'Trust me, I took that bait last night.'

'But now there's two of us,' he said, blind to it.

Jamie kept her hand on him, moved to go inside, letting the birds dive-bomb their fallen brother all they liked. She wasn't buying into the spectacle of it anymore. She refused to.

'We can end this,' Thorsen said, reluctantly moving over the threshold.

'We're not rushing in there, both armed, just to get dosed again. You can't tell me you think that's a good idea?'

He opened his mouth to speak, but the sense of it seemed to be prevailing.

'Look, if he comes in here,' Jamie said, 'we'll blow his damn head off. You have my word on that.' She waggled her gun in the air for emphasis. 'But charging into the woods at night is a dumb fucking idea.' She kicked the front door closed. It killed the din of the crows' beating wings.

Thorsen swallowed, drew a slow breath, then sighed. But he didn't tell her she was right.

He just reached down, slipped the lead over Hati's head, and met Jamie's eye as the dog loped into the living room to stand watch at the glass.

'I'll stay up,' Thorsen said then. 'Keep an eye out.' He turned, followed Hati.

Jamie locked the door, hearing the armchair facing the window squeak as Thorsen sat down into it.

She peeked around the corner, seeing that Hati had already gone over and curled up at his feet. Thorsen's hand was just visible on the arm of the sofa, laid over his pistol, finger slowly drumming on the barrel.

For a second, she wanted to stay up as well. But then, she didn't. If Thorsen was on watch, then Thorsen was on watch. It was good enough for her.

As she went into her bedroom, she heard his voice. 'Get some sleep,' he called. 'I'll wake you if anything happens.'

Jamie slowed, but didn't stop, and didn't respond.

She just closed the door, and went to bed.

And then, before she knew it, she was asleep.

46

JAMIE WOKE AT SIX, the smell of coffee in the air.

It was just light, and when she walked out of the bedroom, Thorsen was in the kitchen, busying himself with breakfast. Hati was asleep on the sofa, and the early morning sun was coming in through the windows.

She had to do a double-take, the vision of a quiet nuclear life overlaid perfectly over her own shattered shit-show version. Then she noticed the loaded pistol on the countertop, the dozen dead crows on the grass outside, and the three-dozen sitting in the surrounding trees like sentinels.

And all was right with the world.

'Coffee?' Thorsen asked, turning with the pot of drip-filter in his hand.

'Please,' Jamie said, rubbing her eyes. She felt like she looked like shit. But Thorsen didn't look much better. 'You want to get some sleep? Could probably grab a few hours now if—'

'I'm good,' Thorsen said, putting the pot down on the counter and reaching for a pair of mugs off the tree.

'You fell asleep in the chair, didn't you?'

'Hati would have woken me if anything was wrong.' He poured out two cups. 'Not like you stayed awake either.'

Jamie just accepted her coffee, hid her smirk behind the cup, and took a long, bitter mouthful. Shit that was good.

'So,' Thorsen asked, reaching for the pistol, 'ready to hunt Nils Markus the hell down today?'

Jamie took another sip, then grinned, this time unabashedly. 'You read my mind.'

'Good. I made eggs. Hope you like scrambled.'

'My third favourite kind.' Another sip. 'After poached and fried.'

'Are there any other types?'

'No,' she said, shrugging. 'But it's the thought that counts.'

They pulled in outside the station just after seven, and rolled to a stop.

There was still shattered glass on the ground, but at least the riot hadn't persisted into the night. The sun was shining weakly, a thin layer of morning mist hanging in the air. This late in the year Jamie thought the sun would be too weak to burn it off and take hold of the day. Hell, it'd probably rain again before lunch. But at least for now the weather was playing ball.

They exited Jamie's truck and stepped down into the quiet street. It was eerily still. There were no cars, no pedestrians. Nothing. The place was a ghost town.

But that suited them – there was a mountain of work to get done, and a killer to track down. Markus was running wild, but just barrelling around the town with their lights flashing wasn't going to help. They needed to be smart about this. He wouldn't go home, or at least, if he had, he wouldn't stay there. Forss and his team would have ransacked the house and removed everything of note, so Markus would know the place wasn't safe.

Shit, Forss. Jamie dug her phone out of her pocket and powered it on. She'd charged it all night but hadn't switched it on yet.

She didn't know why – maybe she just wanted one more hour of peace before the shit hit the fan again. And didn't it just.

The second her screen came to life, notifications cascaded down it. It buzzed angrily in her hand as fifty backlogged messages and missed calls all arrived at once.

'Someone's popular,' Thorsen said, approaching the front doors.

Jamie tossed her keys to him, thumbing through the messages. 'Okay … okay … okay …' she muttered, going through Forss's updates. 'Right, so they cleared Markus's farm, then went on to the second location.'

'Flygare?' Thorsen asked, unlocking the doors.

'Yeah,' Jamie said. 'Uh … couldn't get hold of me … called Ohlin … couldn't get hold of Ohlin.' Jamie glanced up.

Thorsen tilted his head to the side, made a clicking sound with his tongue. 'Big surprise.'

'So … Looks like Forss called in a coroner to deal with the body … our friend Vardeman.'

'Oh yeah, he was a fun guy,' Thorsen laughed.

'I assume you're being sarcastic?'

'You assume correctly. Coffee?'

'Please.' She picked her head up, following him inside. 'You keep making a habit of that I'll start thinking it's all you're good for.'

He went wordlessly to the kitchen.

Jamie went back to her phone. 'Looks like he arrived late,

removed the body, and Forss … is still in town.' Jamie pursed her lips, didn't read out the last text which said. *'There's a car on fire in the middle of your town …'* It was followed up with a lonely question mark ten minutes later. Then there was nothing. 'Forss is staying at the Inn,' Jamie called. 'I'll let him know we're here.'

Jamie typed out a text and hit send.

'You think we should work out a story for what happened last night?'

'Other than *my partner got inadvertently dosed with a potent psychotropic, ran off into the woods, then tried to kill me?'* Thorsen poked his head around the door.

'Yeah,' Jamie sighed. 'Something *other* than that. If we want to keep our jobs, that is.'

'Honestly,' Thorsen said, disappearing again. 'I could go either way.'

When the boarded over, semi-repaired door opened at three minutes past eight, Jamie thought it would be Forss. At worst, Ohlin. But instead, Christian Nordahl walked in.

And he didn't look happy.

Jamie was hunched over her desk, combing through old paper records, looking for any sign that Markus owned or had connections to another property, or anyone else in town.

So far, she'd found absolutely nothing.

'Mr Nordahl,' she said, standing up, not really keeping the surprise from her voice. 'What are you—'

'You had me arrested?' he spat, closing the space between them quickly.

Thorsen was out of his chair behind Jamie now and made a point of putting his hands on his hips in a way that emphasised the holster hanging from his ribs.

Jamie held her hand up, showing Christian Nordahl that he'd come far enough, and he seemed to take the hint.

'We didn't have you arrested,' Jamie replied coolly. 'We simply asked the Lulea polis to bring you in to clear up a few inconsistencies in your story.'

'Inconsistencies? In my story?' he asked, scoffing. 'You know my wife won't fucking speak to me? She thinks I murdered our son!' he yelled, beating on his chest.

'Did you?' Thorsen asked from behind Jamie.

She motioned him to shut up.

'No,' Nordahl replied, devoid of emotion. 'I didn't.'

'Considering you're here,' Jamie said, taking a seat behind her desk and proffering the one opposite to Nordahl, 'I suspect that they didn't hold you for very long. And considering we didn't get a phone call from them, they didn't get anything out of you.'

'They had no grounds to hold me. Because I didn't fucking do anything!'

'I'll ask you once to keep your voice down. We're having a conversation – a civil one, and if you want to keep it that way, I suggest you control yourself.' She gestured to the dark bruise that had formed on the side of her face, then pointed over her shoulder at Thorsen's bruised, scowling face. 'Look at us – we strike you as a pair of detectives with any patience this morning?'

He settled himself, clasped his hands in his lap. 'I just want to know *why* you had me held, and what you think these inconsistencies are? I've been nothing but helpful, truthful, and—'

'Except you haven't.' Jamie sighed. 'You haven't been truthful, at all. Because the first time we spoke, you said you saw Felix the afternoon before he disappeared. Except the timelines don't match up, and we have a witness who says *they* were with Felix, and saw no sign of you that afternoon. You also said that you were home by ten, but multiple people place you at the Moose's Head well *after* that, picking fights with other patrons.' Jamie leaned forward. 'Now, your wife has already told us that you've got a bit of a problem. And that you and her have problems. And considering that you lied about seeing Felix that afternoon, about what time you got home, and then you lied about not knowing that Felix had a girlfriend, I'm inclined to believe exactly nothing that comes out of your mouth. So, if you want to know why we had you picked up, it's because you lied to a police officer when questioned about a murder. On several occasions.' Jamie offered him a brief, polite smile, then sat back. 'Does that answer your question?'

Nordahl's knee began bouncing. 'Okay, look, I'll tell you the truth, alright?'

'That would be pretty helpful.'

'That night ... Felix and I ... we fought.'

'Fought? Physically?'

Thorsen got up now and came over, leaning against the next desk with his arms crossed.

'No, no,' Nordahl said, 'not at first, at least.' He sighed. 'I ... I knew. About the drugs. And about the girl – the Viklund girl.'

'You knew who she was?'

'Not until her father attacked me,' he said sourly. 'But I knew that Felix was seeing someone.'

'It sounds like you and he weren't all that close.'

'We used to be. We used to be great. A family, you know?'

'So what happened? How do you get from happy family to ... this?'

'You know how it goes,' he said, brushing it off a little.

'Kids get older, they don't want to spend time with their parents anymore. I used to take Felix to something five nights a week – football, gymnastics, basketball, judo, whatever it was. He did it all. But then, he stopped playing, and I didn't know what to do with myself.'

Jamie folded her arms too. He'd get no sympathy from her. 'So you started going to the Moose.'

'Lovisa always worked long hours. I didn't know what else to do.'

'Right, so tell me what happened the night that Felix disappeared. And be specific this time.'

Christian Nordahl took a deep breath, steeling himself. 'I got home at about quarter past six. Felix was out in the summer house, playing games.'

Jamie nodded. That lined up with Hugo Westman's story. They'd been out there, gaming, and then he'd left at six. He could have just missed Christian Nordahl.

Nordahl went on. 'I stuck my head in, asked if he was okay. He grunted, as teenagers do.'

'Grunted? Was your relationship like that generally?'

'We didn't speak much – not lately, at least. And every time we did, it just seemed to turn into … shouting, you know?'

Lovisa Nordahl had said the same thing.

Christian Nordahl didn't strike Jamie as especially repugnant or horrible. But sometimes, you just get sick of someone. And it was clear that he was unhappy, drinking every night. She doubted he and his wife slept in the same bed. And unfortunately, these things were like snowballs. They just continued to build and grow and gather speed until they hit something and exploded. And now, with Felix gone, she guessed that a big goddamn snowball had just hit a brick wall. Their marriage wouldn't recover. How could it?

'So you stuck your head in, said hi, he grunts, then what?'

'I asked if he wanted anything to eat, another grunt. I said something, probably, I don't know what.'

Thorsen grunted now, disapprovingly.

Christian shook his head. 'Sorry, I mean – I said, I think, something like – you spend all your fucking time out here, rotting your brain, why don't you read a fucking book or something?'

'And what did he say?'

Nordahl squirmed. 'He said, um – and you spend all your time in the fucking bathroom, masturbating to porn on your phone, messing things up with mum, why don't you try going a day without a drink?'

Jamie raised an eyebrow. She guessed that wasn't an off-the-cuff insult. 'And then?'

'And then I went inside.'

'And got a drink?'

No denial came.

Jamie sighed. 'Okay, so tell us what happened next, because we know Felix went out, and we know you went out, so tell us about the fight.'

'It was about fifteen minutes later – I was inside, and Felix came in and went upstairs. Then he came down with his schoolbag, headed for the door.'

'You stopped him?'

He nodded. 'I told him to, but he wouldn't, so I went to the door, closed it before he could get there, blocked the way.'

'Then what happened?'

'I asked him to tell me where he was going, to show me what was in the bag. I didn't *know* what was going on at that point, but I suspected something.' He drew another shaky breath. 'But he wouldn't show me, so I tried to grab it, we pulled it back and forth, he pushed me, the bag split open, and money and drugs fell out.'

'What kind of drugs?'

'Red pills, a bag of them – a big bag. And rolled up bank notes.'

Jamie thought back to her first exploration of their house. That's what she'd found in Felix's room. And if he thought he was going to meet Hugo Westman to drop off some more supplies, then that matched up.

'And that's when you fought?'

'I grabbed for them,' Nordahl said, 'Felix shoved me. I grabbed him, he threw me up against the wall – he's so big now – he was so big …' His voice began to crack.

'Mr Nordahl,' Jamie urged him.

He nodded. 'I told him … I told him that if he walked out of that house with those drugs … that he wasn't welcome back. That he could go and live with his … his little slut girl-friend …' He broke down then, sobbing into his hands. 'But that was it! He grabbed the drugs, the money, walked out! I watched him go … I just *let* him go … And now he's … now he's …'

'It's alright, Mr Nordahl,' Jamie said slowly. 'It's okay.'

'But I didn't kill him – okay? That's why I didn't say anything! Because I knew you'd think that … that I had … but why?' He shook his head. 'Why would I kill my … my own … Felix … Why would I do that?' His voice cracked, tears forming at the corners of his eyes. 'I didn't, I swear! I wasn't a *good* father – at the end – but … but I loved Felix, and … and …' He broke then, doubling over, bawling into his hands.

Jamie sighed and closed her eyes, letting the anger that had flared in her subside. 'You know you've held our investigation back *days,* Mr Nordahl.'

'I know, I know,' he blubbered. 'I'm sorry.'

Jamie looked over at Thorsen, who was glaring at the man.

She looked back at Nordahl then. 'Okay, so after that, you went to the Moose, right?'

He managed a nod.

'I'm going to need you to get your shit together, Mr Nordahl. Zero patience, remember?'

He sniffled, picked his head up, then nodded, lip quivering.

'How long was it before you had an altercation with Gunnar Viklund?'

'Uh, I don't know – he was there when I arrived, and he didn't say anything all night, and then I guess maybe around eleven, I caught him staring at me, drunk. Really drunk.'

'And did you know at this point that it was his daughter that Felix was seeing?'

'No.'

'And did you know *him?*'

'I knew who he was, but we weren't friends.'

'Just drank in the same place.' Jamie leaned forward, elbows on the desk. 'Tell me how it started.'

'I was at the bar, getting another drink, and then he was there – he said to keep my son away from his daughter ...' Christian Nordahl looked at the ground. 'I may have told him to fuck off.'

'And then?'

'And then he grabbed me – by the collar – told me my son was a lowlife piece of shit, a drug dealer.' He scoffed a little, made a sort of snarling face. 'Told me I needed to stop him seeing his daughter, and I realised then that it must have been Felix's girlfriend.'

'Who swung first?'

He looked sheepish.

'You were wound up, angry with Felix, yourself, I get it. Did anything else happen?'

'Some other people got involved, he was shouting about Felix, about how he'd ... how he'd ... forced her to ...'

Jamie watched him, motionless.

'And then he said that I needed to make sure he didn't go after her ... that he'd sent her away, to protect her from Felix ... to Gothenburg ... and that if he caught him trying to contact her—'

'Malmö,' Jamie said then, cutting him off.

'I'm sorry?'

'You said Gothenburg. Gunnar Vikland sent his daughter to Malmö, to live with his aunt.'

'Malmö, then,' Nordahl said, shaking it off. 'Whatever. He said that if he caught Felix trying to contact her, he would—'

'Did he say Gothenburg to you?'

'I don't ... I don't know ... Maybe, but he was drunk ... I was drunk ... He could have. It was loud, other people were involved. I don't really remember ...' He sighed, put his head in his hands. 'I got thrown out after that ... and then ... then I went home. To bed.'

He fell quiet and Jamie looked over at Thorsen again for his reaction. He was still scowling.

'You can go,' Jamie said then, turning back to Nordahl.

'I can ... what?' he said, picking his head up.

'You can go,' Jamie repeated.

'Jamie ...' Thorsen interjected.

'Get out, Mr Nordahl. Go home.' She got up to emphasise that she meant right now. 'And if I find out you've been at the Moose's Head before this investigation is over, I'll throw you in a cell. Stay home, don't leave, and don't leave town. We'll be in touch for your official statement.'

Nordahl got up, shuffled towards the door.

'And tell your wife the fucking truth,' Jamie called after him.

He paused at the threshold, glanced back, but didn't say anything. And then he was gone, out into the early morning sun.

Thorsen was next to her then. 'What a piece of shit,' he muttered.

Jamie bit her lip. 'All fathers do their version of their best,' she said quietly. 'But it's rarely right.'

Thorsen's brow creased, trying to work that one out.

Jamie didn't have the time or the energy to explain, to talk fathers and upbringings. That was a very large can of worms for another day.

Maybe another century.

And right now, they had more pressing matters. Like finding Nils Markus.

Except, as Jamie sat down at her desk, her brain was elsewhere.

She pulled out her phone and dialled.

'Who you calling?' Thorsen asked, still on the next desk over.

'Forss.'

'Why?'

She sighed. 'I need him to tell me what he found at Markus's farm yesterday.'

'Can't it wait?' Thorsen asked. 'He said he was coming in this morning.'

'No, it can't.'

Thorsen stood, reading the immediacy in her voice. 'Why not?'

'Because I have a feeling about something.'

'About what?' He came closer now.

'That all the evidence gathered from his farm will tell us Nils Markus is *Krakornås Kung.*'

'And that's a ... *bad* thing?' Thorsen wasn't following this one either.

Jamie's heel tapped on the tiles as she waited for Forss to pick up.

'God,' she said, chewing her thumbnail, 'I fucking hope not.'

47

'INSPEKTÖR,' Forss answered, sighing. 'I'm on my way in –
can't this wait? I'll be there in five—'

'No, it can't,' Jamie said quickly. 'I need to know what
you found at Markus's farm yesterday.'

He sighed again, and Jamie heard the clicking of his indi-
cator as he pulled in at the side of the road. The Kurrajakk
Inn was a little over a kilometre from the station – and Forss
was right, just a few minutes' drive. But this couldn't wait.

'Okay,' he said, tapping something – Jamie guessed the
password into his laptop. 'My notes say … we catalogued
several chemicals, mostly congruent with embalming and
taxidermy practices, uh … we catalogued the apparatus there
… we took samples of the powder on the suit … is there
anything specific you want to know? There's pages and
pages.'

'The apparatus,' Jamie said. 'Tell me about it. What was
there?'

'Distillation equipment, mostly,' Forss answered. 'I don't
really know what you're asking?'

'Markus was making the powder from plants – there were horticulture books in his house.'

'Right?'

'What process would someone use to extract psychoactive substances from plants and then turn it into a powder?' Jamie asked. She could feel Thorsen watching her.

Forss was silent for a few seconds. 'Uh, it's not really my strong suit …'

'Just make an educated guess,' Jamie urged him.

'I would think you'd want to dry the plant, take the part of which has the highest concentration of those chemicals, and then pulverise it – and if you could, then find a way to separate out the substance, usually with the introduction of another chemical, a binding agent or catalyst even, depending on whether you're trying to remove the substance itself, or the contaminants. Why are you asking?'

'Because I want to know if Markus's set up was equipped for all that.'

'I don't know, is the simple answer,' Forss replied. 'Much of the equipment we found had been boxed up. It's possible – but it's also possible that some of the equipment may have been broken, or removed. All of this will be in my report,' he added. 'I don't really see what's so pressing?'

Jamie held the phone from her ear, looked up at Thorsen. 'Did you ever get hold of Viklund's aunt in Malmö?'

He shook his head. 'No, she never responded to the messages.' He stepped closer then, knelt at the corner of her desk, massaged his mouth, looking into space. 'You like Viklund for this now?'

Jamie bit her lip. 'I don't know. Thanks, Forss,' she said, bringing the phone closer to her ear again. 'See you in a minute.' She hung up then, turned to face Thorsen. 'It just struck me as strange that he'd say Gothenburg to Nordahl, when he told us Malmö.'

'Every word out of Christian Nordahl's mouth since this all started has been a lie. And he was blind drunk that night, so I don't think that it's really much to go on.'

Jamie rocked on her chair, looking over his head, thinking. 'No, it's not. But … I don't know.'

'He's got a rock-solid alibi, too. Hell, he had to be carried out of the bar that night and driven home because he couldn't stand up. And we know that Christian Nordahl went to meet the King at seven, right? Which is exactly when Viklund was in the Moose.'

'But we know that the king wasn't working alone. Luring Felix out there and killing him like that was a two-person job, at least.' She looked at him now. 'And it was out of character for Viklund to get that drunk. And on a Monday night? And why pick a fight with Christian Nordahl too unless to reinforce his alibi? Why lie about *where* he sent his daughter? You don't mix up where your sister lives.'

'Unless Christian Nordahl remembered it wrong,' Thorsen offered.

Jamie looked at the ground. Something didn't feel right. 'Flygare could have lured Felix out to the falls while Viklund was cementing his alibi at the Moose.'

'And then that scrawny drug addict chased Felix Nordahl ten kilometres through the woods, stripped him naked, then hacked chunks out of him before ramming a bird down his throat?'

'We know Felix died in the middle of the night. Plenty of time for Viklund to sober up and get out there.'

Thorsen wasn't disagreeing, he was just testing Jamie to see if the theory was watertight. 'So say it *is* Viklund. That he recruits Flygare. Then Flygare gets busted, so he recruits

Felix to replace him. Felix starts coming around, he takes a liking to Lena. They get close. Viklund finds out, loses his shit. Lena and Felix plan to run away together. Viklund gets wind of it, so he lays down a plan to stop Felix once and for all.'

Jamie nodded along slowly.

'He has Flygare swipe Hugo Westman's phone during the party to get Felix to come to the falls. Then he doses him, chases him into the woods and waits for Viklund to show up.'

'Then Viklund puts Felix on the altar, tortures him for a few hours, and finishes off by choking him with a fucking bird.'

Thorsen raised his eyebrows, let out a long breath. 'It would explain why Flygare was waiting in his trailer with a shotgun in his hand. Seeing something like that would screw anyone up.'

Jamie nodded again. 'I'm thinking Viklund goes out there to check on Flygare, make sure he knows not to talk, he's already gone.'

'Locked up in our cell,' Thorsen added.

'Viklund comes looking, bursts in here all suited up, drags Flygare out, figures out his next move …'

'Then comes to my house, doses me, lures me into the woods, and puts Flygare up as target practice.'

'Two birds, one stone.' Thorsen met her eye. 'Sorry.'

Jamie shrugged it off. 'So how does Markus fit into it?'

'As a smoke screen,' Thorsen said. 'Maybe Viklund knew about the King of Crows case, and had the bright idea to use Markus as a patsy. To put him in a frame so we're looking in the wrong place.'

'It's smart. Especially with his alibi already established, and with how helpful he was when we first met him – giving us Lena's phone.'

'Which led nowhere. Just another false trail.'

'But he must have known we'd go looking for Markus.'

'Yeah, and we're yet to find him. Remember the blood trail down the field the first time we were there? Viklund shows up there, gets into it with Markus, he makes a run for it … Viklund catches up with him … then …'

Jamie sat upright, laced her hands on top of her head. 'And then he stages Markus's farm. The birds, the horticulture books, Westman's phone … all planted to make us think it was Markus.'

Thorsen seemed to be coming around to the idea. He stood then, wheeled in circles, one hand on his hip, other in front of his face. 'So he takes Markus out of play, knowing we'd come for him, frames the guy, and sends Lena away before any of it even happens because he knows she's the only one who could point the finger at her own father.'

'Except … did he? He told us Malmö, he told Nordahl Gothenburg. But we can't get hold of his aunt, and the phone he gave us was a blank. Forss said it was clean – factory clean. No SIM card, no memory card, no linked accounts, nothing on cloud storage.'

'So not even Lena's phone then.'

'I don't think so.'

'So what,' Thorsen said, laughing, 'he's just got his own daughter chained to a pipe in his basement, or … ?'

As he met Jamie's eye, his laughter died in the air.

Everything was still between them for a second, and then Jamie and Thorsen both leapt towards the door.

Thorsen got there first, flung it open, cleared the steps, heels crunching on the shards of glass. Jamie was right on his shoulder, and they split around the nose of her truck, ripping the doors open simultaneously.

She climbed in and jammed the key into the ignition,

shoving it into gear and mashing her foot into the accelerator all at the same time.

The gearbox complained loudly, then caught, and the SUV slingshotted forward.

Jamie looked up, catching sight of Forss crossing the road having just parked his van opposite the station.

He held his hands up, satchel over his shoulder, shaking his head in disbelief, and presumably anger.

But Jamie and Thorsen couldn't have cared less just then. If they were right, then a girl's life could be hanging in the balance.

If it wasn't too late for her already.

48

THERE WAS RARELY a need for sirens in Kurrajakk.

And today was no different. Despite them hammering along at nearly double the speed limit. Any faster and Jamie thought the body panels on the truck might peel away. The wheel was juddering alarmingly under her grip. Though she said nothing to Thorsen, just kept her foot flat to the floor.

She had no intention of alerting Viklund to their presence before they arrived. She wanted to catch him unawares, and though she would have loved to have beared down on the place, sirens blaring, and kicked the front door in – if that gnawing sensation in the pit of her stomach was anything to go on, they might be chasing the King of Crows back to his nest.

And what awaited them, Jamie didn't know.

The adrenaline was still pumping, but that didn't mean the gravity of the situation ahead eluded her. And nor did it elude Thorsen. He had one hand firmly on the door, fist clenched around the handle, and the other balled up on his knee, which was jigging furiously.

Jamie slowed, the brakes forcing the car to rock unevenly

as she approached the junction, and then she gunned it back onto the next straight, the whole truck swaying like a turning ship as they went.

This was Viklund's road, and the plastic-leather wheel under her fingers was slick with sweat.

'Pull up short,' Thorsen said, voice low and hard. 'We should go in on foot.'

Jamie couldn't help but agree, and let off the gas, pulling the truck in on the verge. The tyres fought for grip, then locked, sending a cloud of dust into the air.

They both exited, quiet and determined, and unholstered their pistols simultaneously. Both held them up, both pulled back the slide, falling into step at the edge of the roadway, and then both let go, the dull metallic click of a bullet slipping into their respective chambers the only sound.

The forest had fallen quiet around them, the sky an unmoving and bulging grey mass above, gnarled and rippled.

The sun had faded, the fog lifting to a low ceiling, pressing down on them with the weight of a pending deluge. There was no let up as summer sank into autumn. Rain, sun, rain, sun, as good as breathing.

They were just between waves.

Jamie and Thorsen spotted the mailbox first, quickened their pace, muzzles to the ground.

Thorsen made a sharp, measured whistling sound, then motioned Jamie down off the verge and into the trees. Come in from the blind side of the house. Good call.

She followed him in, stepping quickly and cautiously, acutely aware of the rustling of her bomber jacket, of the squeaking of her boots.

Thorsen neared the property line, waved her down behind, and they both sank a little lower, the compact two-storey cottage with a rough exterior and stone tiled roof coming into view through the brush.

They waited there, looking for signs of movement, saw none.

Thorsen motioned Jamie forwards again and they crept from the trees and onto the grassy frontage, the ground soft under them.

Jamie spotted the chopping log, the axe Viklund had used when they'd first met up standing upright, blade lodged in the scored surface.

Thorsen followed her eyes, paused for a moment, then pointed around to the far side of the house like a Navy SEAL commander.

She nodded her confirmation, checking the near side one last time – seeing nothing except overgrown weeds, an impassable barrier.

The curtains were drawn in the downstairs windows, the door a solid slab of wood. But they snuck all the same, moving as silently as they could.

Jamie readjusted her grip on her pistol, measured her breathing, and pressed on.

As they reached the far corner, Thorsen fell in behind Jamie, waited for her to check, trusted her eye. She peeked, saw an open space, a stone path through an unkempt lawn penned in by trees. Towards the back of the house she saw old vegetable plots, ancient green-bean structures that had been claimed by brambles, a score of wildflowers at the edges, before the grass gave way to the overhang of pines.

But there was no movement, no sound. And there was no car here, either. Maybe Viklund was out? She hoped so.

Jamie motioned Thorsen on and he stepped out, pistol up, covering the space. He strafed a few paces into the open, paused, listened, and then gave Jamie the signal to follow.

She stuck close to the wall, walking the length of the house towards the next corner, while Thorsen kept strafing, opening up that angle, getting a view of the back garden.

'Tss,' he said, a short sharp sound more than a word that made Jamie freeze, four feet short of the corner.

Thorsen hovered like a giant wasp, hunched forward, pistol close to his body, waving gently like a poised stinger as he assessed whether to use it or not.

Jamie kept her eyes on him, waiting for his sign.

Then he relaxed a little, nodded for her to go on, and came in closer.

Jamie's heart was hammering. Damn, she hated this. She left Stockholm to get *away* from this shit. And now here she was, in the goddamn quagmire again, weapon in hand, hoping to hell she didn't eat another bullet.

She got to the corner as Thorsen reached her shoulder, and looked around it, cheek against the cool white stone.

Clear.

The back garden was open, an old, rusted washing line standing at a skewed angle in the middle of a rough lawn.

A set of stone slabs led from the back door to the forest behind, and through a blanket of blooming yellow flowers. Their heads were wide, their dirty yellow petals streaked with black veins, their centres dark black spots. Jagged leaves collared the heads, the long stems curving over like the tails of scorpions. They waved gently, a slow breeze winding through the trees. And then Jamie smelled them – their stench all at once familiar and enough to twist her stomach into knots.

Sickly sweet. The smell of death.

Everything crystallised in her mind then.

It was these flowers – dried, ground, extracted, concentrated. Whatever they were, it was what was in the pills, in their heads, flowing through their veins.

The sound of breaking glass, heavy footsteps, and then a thudding door snapped Jamie and Thorsen out of it and she felt his hand on her shoulder then.

She looked back at him, saw he was looking around the corner, pointing at a cellar door with the nose of his gun. An old pair of wooden doors laid at an angle, paint peeling from them, a loose chain coiled at the base.

They waited for a few seconds, then stepped out, keeping low and quiet.

The windows at the back of the house were curtained over.

But the cellar was open. All they needed to do was lift the door.

Thorsen slowed at it and Jamie moved past, towards the back door. She reached up, took hold of the old-fashioned brass handle and pressed it gently. The metal creaked softly, as it moved, but the door wouldn't budge. Locked. Shit.

Her eyes went back to the cellar.

Only way in.

Jamie exhaled.

Think of Lena. She's trapped in there, Jamie told herself. Get a fucking grip.

Jamie swallowed the bile rising in her throat, raked in a deep breath, and scuttled back towards Thorsen.

She gave him a quick nod and he lifted one of the cellar doors open.

The smell of the flowers flooded out, stronger, more concentrated. Jamie's eyes rolled in her head, mouth wetting with saliva. She waited for the smell to pass, and then leaned over, staring down the narrow, steep stairs into the dusty depths.

The last thing she wanted to do was go down there.

But they didn't have another choice.

Shit, she wished she had a mask … something. Anything.

With the feeling of the pollen thick on her skin, Jamie pushed the crook of her elbow against her face and lifted her leg over the jamb, letting her heel find the top step.

It held, taking her weight, and then she was going down, stepping slowly, deliberately.

The weak sunlight died above her as Thorsen began his descent too, and then suddenly they were both on the ground, staring into the basement.

It was the entire width and length of the house, the floor above propped up with old stone and mortar pillars.

The floor was all earth and uneven rock, and the ceiling was floorboards, cobwebs strung from them like tinsel at the most sinister Christmas party Jamie had ever been to.

They both squinted into the darkness, a dim lamp burning somewhere at the far end.

The air was thick with dust that Jamie feared to breathe in.

Thorsen seemed to be in the same camp and motioned her onwards.

Though the stench of the hallucinogen was heavy in the air, the dust felt like mould, damp, the mixture creating a cocktail of death and decay.

They took different paths, circling around the columns towards the lamp, both pausing halfway when they saw what they were walking towards.

Along one side of the basement, a long workbench had been set up, and was filled with chemistry apparatus. There were beakers and distillation tubes, pestle and mortars and bunsen burners, large round glass jugs with long spouts, evaporation trays – everything you'd need to turn flowers into drugs. One of the flasks had been smashed, shards of glass lying on the bench and floor in equal part. That was the sound they heard.

'Tss,' Thorsen said again, grabbing Jamie's attention.

She looked over, saw him standing in front of rows and rows of flowers hung up to dry. They were suspended from the ceiling in lines. Hundreds of them. Enough to dose the entire town.

He lifted his chin then towards the corner and Jamie's eyes widened. She hadn't seen him there in the gloom, but against the far wall, next to a staircase leading up into the house, was a man in a chair.

He was older, in his late sixties, and thin. He had a tuft of grey hair on his head, a loose white shirt on that was stained with food. He was strapped in – hands and ankles, and by the stench coming off him, hadn't been allowed to leave that seat to relieve himself.

Jamie grimaced, held her breath, and zipped over, lowering her pistol and reaching out. She pressed her fingers to his neck, felt a weak pulse and looked over to Thorsen, nodded. He was alive. But barely. His skin was grey and sallow, even in the dim light from the lamp on the work-bench. He was dehydrated, and either asleep or unconscious. She guessed the latter considering he hadn't roused when touched.

She didn't think he'd hold on for much longer.

But who was he? Jamie stooped a little, lifted the old man's chin until she could see his face.

And though she didn't know him, the realisation dawned.

She looked over at Thorsen again, saw his focused, grey eyes shining in the half-light.

'Nils Markus,' she mouthed.

His eyebrows lifted a little in surprise, lips parting to say something. But before he could make a sound, the floor-boards above Jamie's head creaked and dust rained down on her.

They both froze, looked slowly upwards, distinctly aware for the first time of the stark truth.

They weren't alone in the house.

49

Nils Markus would have to wait. Whether he had anything to do with Felix Nordahl's death, or if he was just a pawn in Gunnar Viklund's twisted game, they couldn't focus on him now.

If Lena Viklund was in the house, she wasn't down here.

Thorsen motioned Jamie over and she walked towards him, ducking carefully under the drying flowers.

He guided her, and then touched her arm, signalling her to wait while he took the first step up the stairs into the main house.

For a second, she thought she should do it, but Thorsen was more than capable.

He moved cautiously, lithely for his size, and was at the top in seconds. A plain wooden door stood there, a manual bolt on the inside straddling the jamb. Thorsen reached for the tarnished knob, shrouded in the shadow of the staircase, and turned gently, resting his shoulder against the wood, pistol raised in his other hand, ready to lead the charge through the gap.

He looked down at her and Jamie readied herself, pistol raised once more.

Thorsen cracked the door, paused, listened.

Jamie's heart was in her mouth.

He let out a slow breath, nodded slightly. His fingers readjusted on the grip, the sweat that had beaded on his temple glistening softly in the light spilling through the doorway.

Jamie followed him up, and as she neared, he pushed inwards, teeth bared as the hinges squeaked.

She froze.

They waited.

Nothing.

Silence.

No movement.

No footsteps.

No screams or yells or attempts to flee.

Jamie didn't know if that was worse or better.

Thorsen stepped forward, already too far gone to come back, and Jamie, despite everything in her body and mind telling her not to, followed.

The air in the house was close and warm, the windows and doors sealed closed.

Jamie filed into the hallway next to Thorsen, the back door ahead of them, the stairs rising above.

She tapped him on the shoulder, signalling that she'd check the front of the house, a room opening up to the left of the front door. He gave her a nod and waited as Jamie traced forward, approaching the entrance into what she guessed was a dining room.

She got to the corner, hovered, listening for any movement, and then poked her head around the open frame.

A sparse dining room stretched out, an old wooden table

occupying it, overflowing with magazines, mail, books, papers, pens, and other junk. There was another door that led towards the back of the house off the room, and Jamie guessed it had to be a kitchen or living room.

She backed into the hallway again, turned to face Thorsen, who was still waiting to proceed towards the doorway in front of him.

He watched her for a signal, and she gave him a nod, pointed him onwards.

Thorsen let out a long, measured breath, moved his head side to side to stretch his neck, and then shuffled forward.

She watched him go, checking over her shoulder so she wasn't snuck up on, noticed that the front door was bolted shut. And padlocked. Screws had also been driven through the wood and into the frame, sealing the thing completely.

A shiver ran down her spine.

Ahead, Thorsen reached the doorway.

Jamie held her breath.

He stepped into the gap, covering the room, then looked at her, nodded.

Clear.

Jamie was about to move when she felt the weight of eyes on her. Her pistol swung upwards to face the stairs, ready to fire. But it wasn't Gunnar Viklund looking down. It was a teenage girl.

Lena Viklund was fifteen, with straw coloured hair that streamed over her shoulders and halfway down her midriff in natural waves. She had dark, blue eyes, and deep bags cut into her cheeks. Her skin was pale, fingernails chewed down to the quick, kneading the fabric of her dirty sweater. She stared down at Jamie wild eyed and fearful.

Jamie stared back, heart hammering.

This was a girl who was a prisoner in her own home.

Jamie swallowed, extended a hand.

The girl shrank a little, tucking her feet under her on the step.

Jamie beckoned.

The girl shook her head.

Jamie moved to take the first step and the girl shook her head harder, brought her finger to her lips, urged Jamie to shush. To be silent.

From the corner of her eye, she could see Thorsen, standing in the opening to the living room. He was looking back at Jamie, who was mimicking Lena's motion, finger to her lips. Stay quiet.

It only meant one thing. Gunnar Viklund was here.

Thorsen nodded, gestured to the room ahead of him, then gave a quick 'okay' sign with his hand before bringing it back to the grip of his gun. The room was clear. But for how long? Where was Viklund? On the far side of the house? Upstairs?

Jamie looked back at Lena Viklund, smiled warmly, reached to the chest of her bomber jacket and flattened the fabric around the polis badge. She nodded to reassure her and offered her hand again.

Come on, please.

The girl didn't move.

For God's sake! I'm trying to save your fucking life!

Jamie could feel Thorsen watching her.

He moved back towards the back door behind him, keeping his weapon trained on what Jamie thought had to be the kitchen – the room connecting the dining room and the living room. Jamie watched out of the corner of her eye as he reached for the handle, jiggled it a little, found it locked. He ran his fingers up the frame next to the lock, glanced up at Jamie. More screws? Were they all trapped in here?

Lena Viklund was in front of her then, standing on the

bottom step, bare footed. She held out her hand and took Jamie's, her skin cool and clammy.

A wave of relief rode through Jamie and she was immediately moving. No time to waste.

She led the girl back through the hallway towards Thorsen, towards the basement door. That was their exit.

But when she reached it and tried to open the thing, Lena Viklund pulled away.

Jamie turned to her, losing the girl's hand. She brought them to her chest, stared at the basement door, shook her head violently, screwing up her face in terror.

'Hey, hey,' Jamie mouthed, risking the quietest whisper she could muster. Her hands were up now, trying to calm the girl. 'It's okay, it's okay, alright? We're polis officers,' she said, gesturing to Thorsen. 'We're here to save you.'

She shushed Jamie again, shaking her head, terror in her eyes, and an instant later, Jamie knew why.

'Leeeeeena,' came a cold voice from the room in front of Thorsen.

She heard the clack of Thorsen's gun as it snapped to attention, and she whirled round to face him. He was staring into the room, hands locked around the grip of his pistol.

Jamie reached behind her without looking, found Lena's arm, and dragged her forward so she was shoulder to shoulder with Thorsen, a wall to protect the girl.

Jamie's pistol raised next to her partner's, Lena Viklund cowering behind them, and homed in on Gunnar Viklund.

He stepped slowly from the kitchen doorway into the dilapidated living room. There was a grubby old carpet worn down to the threads, a sofa that looked like it'd been pulled out of a swamp, and empty alcohol bottles and cans strewn everywhere.

Viklund's pace was slow, measured, his dark eyes moving

from Jamie to Thorsen and back. He didn't look scared, but Jamie didn't feel like she was staring at a monster either. She'd seen evil – the look of evil in a man's eyes. The emptiness. The void. But Viklund didn't have that look. Not like Jamie had seen before.

He stopped two steps in, thick black hair and beard wild around his head. For a second, Jamie thought the hair continued down onto his shoulders and back, but then she realised it wasn't hair at all.

He was wearing a cloak. A shining, shimmering black cloak adorned with thousands of layered feathers. He reached slowly to his head.

'Don't move!' Thorsen yelled, jerking his pistol. But Viklund didn't seem to hear him, or at least didn't seem to care.

He kept reaching, and closed his fingers – his shaking fingers – around the hood pooled at the nape of his neck, and dragged it upwards.

'Viklund!' Thorsen roared again. 'Stop! Get down on the ground, hands flat! Do it now!'

'Is this what you want?' he muttered, pulling it over his head. It fell into place, cascading down over his forehead and painted expression, the heavy mask of crows' beaks and eyes, assembled into a sharp, black hook, sending shivers down Jamie's spine.

Her brain was whirring. Thorsen was yelling. She was just trying to make sense of this. What was he doing?

'Please, I don't want to … Don't make me do it again …' he said.

'Viklund!' Thorsen kept yelling.

She wished he'd shut up so she could think! Something was wrong. This wasn't right.

Viklund's hand raised then, reached slowly for the

mantlepiece above the fireplace to his left, took hold of the thing there, dragging it slowly off.

She couldn't see his face anymore, but Jamie could swear she heard whimpering. A stifled cry.

The thing dropped, hung loosely in his grasp. A glove – a black, leathery glove that he pulled onto his hand with what seemed like reluctance.

'Drop it, now! I'll fucking shoot!' Thorsen was screaming. Loud enough to make Jamie's ears ring.

As Viklund raised it, Jamie saw the apparatus for what it was. The knuckles had been fitted with crows' heads, their breaks hanging from the ends of his fingers like talons. They clicked as he moved his fingers, and Jamie imagined them digging into Felix Nordahl's skin. That's how he'd done it. How he'd tortured Nordahl.

'How cruel,' he said, looking directly at them with a thousand glinting eyes. 'How cruel you can be … Lena.'

Jamie froze.

Thorsen's brow crumpled, and he looked at Jamie, sensing the same change in the air as she did.

She felt a tap on her shoulder and turned to face Lena Viklund, knowing it was already too late.

The girl's hand was out, in front of her face, laid flat, palm up, on it, a mound of yellow powder.

She blew, hard, and sent it into the air in a thick cloud, right into Jamie and Thorsen's faces.

Jamie reeled backwards, Lena's high-pitched, wicked laugh ringing in her ears.

Her nostrils burned; her eyes burned.

She staggered and stumbled, hitting the wall behind with her shoulder, hacking and coughing violently.

There was a grunt to her right and she forced her eyes open, looked for Thorsen, saw that Viklund was on him, arms around him from behind, claws digging into his chest. Thorsen howled and bucked as the crow lifted him from the ground, keeping his arms pinned to his sides, tearing at his skin with the beaked glove. His legs flailed, looked for any purchase, found none as Viklund kept him in the air.

Jamie's mind stuttered as she tried to work out what was happening. Why was he carrying him? Why was he holding him?

It dawned with what little brainpower she had still working – he was waiting it out, waiting for the drugs to kick in, for the flowers to take hold again.

She looked around for Lena, saw nothing, an empty hallway, heard feet pounding stairs, the door to the basement swinging wide.

Jamie choked, spat phlegm and bile onto the boards and lifted her pistol, screwing one eye closed, watching the barrel wave in the air.

She levelled it towards Thorsen, tried to hold her breath, looking for any sort of steadiness. Thorsen's heel caught the doorframe and he kicked backwards, causing Viklund to spin around.

The second black filled her vision, she fired. Mostly on blind instinct.

She kept the weapon aimed low, pulled the trigger twice.

Muzzle flash lit the room.

The report didn't even reach her ears, just the ringing that came after. She blinked eyes still on fire, and saw Thorsen on his knees, coughing viscously.

Something blinked next to her and she felt pain in her arms, the feeling of something whipping her skin.

Jamie gasped, spun to the floor in the hallway. Her hands

swam in circles in front of her, blood running down her wrists, deep scratches running over the backs of her knuckles.

More footsteps then, the basement door rebounding off the wall.

He's gone, she thought. Viklund is gone.

Jamie searched for her dropped gun, saw a blood trail leading across the boards and over the threshold down to the basement. Her mind reached a conclusion on what had happened as she laid her hand on it. She'd shot Viklund – maybe Thorsen – and he'd fled, knocked her down, slashed at her on the way past.

Her body seemed unresponsive as she tried to get to her feet, her arms and legs like heavy logs, cumbersome and stiff. 'Thorsen!' she called out, voice hoarse. Blood was pounding in her ears now.

'Jamie,' he said between coughs, crawling towards her, trying to get his legs under him.

She held her hand out and he grabbed it, fingers sliding across her bloodied skin.

'Viklund,' he said, shaking his head, blinking hard, trying to focus.

They'd both been dosed though, she knew that.

How long before it took full effect, she didn't know. A minute? Two? Three? Was there any fighting it?

'He's running,' Jamie said, trying to steady her breathing, throat tight. 'But I hit him.' She pointed to the blood. 'We can get him.'

She lurched towards the door, felt Thorsen's hand on the back of her jacket as she took the top step.

'Lena?' he asked, helping her down and steadying himself at the same time.

'She ran,' Jamie said, not knowing what the hell had just happened.

Viklund's words – is this what you want? Is this what you really want? She thought he meant them, but did he mean … Lena? She was a part of this. Somehow. How cruel she could be … What did he mean?

But they needed to get Viklund first. Whether Lena was guilty or not, she still thought Viklund was the one who killed Felix, who'd abducted Nils Markus – made him make the suits. Plural. One at Markus's house to throw them off the trail, the other here.

They swam through the cellar, picking up pace, following the shaft of sunlight filtering down on the other side.

Jamie fell into the steps, climbed them on all fours like a dog, and then flopped into the open air, gasping for breath.

Thorsen was next to her, pulling her up, both of them fighting the flowers as hard as they could.

There was blood in front of them, shining black on the pale grass, leading into the trees.

Jamie looked at it, saw it swirl in technicolour like oil on the surface of water.

Her balance failed her and she stumbled two steps to the right.

Thorsen reached out, snatched for her arm, and missed.

Jamie nearly fell, nearly dropped her gun.

She shook her head, slapped herself on the cheek, didn't feel it. Damn this shit was strong.

She ground her teeth instead, flexed her hand around the pistol, focused on feeling the stipple effect of the grip. Focused on the feeling of pain in her bleeding hand. On the cool air on her face.

For an instant, she had clarity. And she used it.

Jamie barrelled forward, pistol raised.

Thorsen panted along behind.

She knew now, that whatever she saw, whatever she heard

– she couldn't trust it. She had to hold on to reality, to her idea of reality. She knew what a pistol felt like in her hand. It was her anchor. The grip, the weight, the tension of the trigger. Things which were ingrained in her. Things which would keep her plugged into reality. Point the gun, follow the gun.

Jamie kept running, following the trail of blood splattered on the bed of dead pine needles, and with the last shred of her working mind, hoped that Thorsen would be able to do the same.

To hold on to something real.

And when the time came, to know the difference between that and everything else.

50

JAMIE SLOWED, the blood trail snaking in front of her.

Her mouth had gone dry, her eyes heavy, a fizzing steadily growing somewhere in the back of her brain. She reached down and fumbled her phone from her pocket with unwieldy hands, dropped it.

It bounced on the bed of pine needles and she fell to her knees to grab it.

Thorsen loped past, paused by a tree, leaning against it, panting hard. He was gnashing his teeth, rubbing his forehead with his hand – aggressively, kneading the skin around, chuffing like a bull every few seconds as he did his best to fight off the hallucinogen.

Jamie mashed her screen, not bothering to pick the phone up, and managed to get it unlocked, one eye locked closed to limit the double vision. It took her a few precious seconds to get the phone app open, but she managed to, and scanned the list of swimming names for the one she called last. They were screwed out here alone, and she knew from experience this trip was liable to last a while. She didn't even bother searching for Ohlin, she just called Forss instead.

The phone began ringing as Thorsen started staring upwards, head whipping around as his brain succumbed to the poison.

'*Vad vill du den här gången?*' he answered grumpily. What do you want this time?

'Mmmmmbbbbb – tttnnnnnnggghhh—' Jamie started, her tongue and lips nowhere near her control.

'Inspektör?' his voice was immediately more concerned. 'Is everything alright?

'Fwwwooooorrsss,' she forced out through gritted teeth. 'Hwwwellllppp …'

'Inspektör Johansson? I can barely understand you. What did you say? You need help?'

'Kittel … fjalll …' she squeezed out, 'heeaaadd t … t … Kitt … ehhh … fwah …'

'Kittel … fjall? Head to … ? Where are you?'

'Nnnnggghhh … . nowww!' she yelled, with everything she had. Above her, Thorsen was going wild. His eyes had widened, pupils like black holes in his face. He lowered his body, free hand held out like a claw, and then he took off ahead of her.

Jamie left the phone, the call still running, and scrambled after him, her mouth tingling. Your gun. Focus on your gun. The grip. The undulations under your fingers. The weight of the metal. The smell of the gun grease and steel.

She breathed through it, picking up pace, counting her steps. Making her mind listen.

Thorsen was lurching from one trunk to the other in front of her, a black line of blood still running beneath their feet. But Jamie didn't know if it was even real.

Thorsen stumbled, Jamie made up ground.

He was just ahead now.

She felt like she was in stilts, and it was hard to ignore the fact that the grey sky had now turned a deep, throbbing shade of purple and gold above her.

Jamie jumped then, her brain making her feel like she was swimming through tar. But the impact was real enough.

Her shoulder struck Thorsen square in the back and he collapsed forward, Jamie on top of him and dragged her knees up around his ribs, to try and keep him pinned. What her plan was, she didn't know, but Thorsen was losing his grip on reality and she'd already seen what that looked like when he had a gun in his hand.

Jamie lunged up the length of his body, snatching for his weapon.

Fuck he was strong! He bucked like a horse, trying to roll over, nearly throwing Jamie off.

But she was on his arm, her free hand around the barrel.

He lurched sideways and they were tangled then, like snakes. Everything felt strange and elongated like they were records on a player and someone had turned down the spin speed. Sound stretched out and dulled, the swaying canopy bent over and then sprung back like lengths of kelp on the seabed.

And then the gun went off, filled her vision with stark white, launched a bullet into the air.

Pine needles rained down on them.

Jamie yelled – or maybe it was Thorsen – she couldn't tell.

The pistol fired again, Thorsen's hand still around the grip, Jamie's around the barrel.

The report cut the din, then echoed, growing and diminishing and growing and diminishing until Jamie's teeth chattered in time with it. A wave of nausea rolled through her.

A third shot.

Pain then. Blinding pain in her fingers, on her palm. She

released the gun, held her hand in the air, felt it throb and sting, vibrating like it was on fire. The skin was red and enflamed, burned by the heated barrel.

She swore, lost her grip on Thorsen, and he threw his elbow back. It hit her in the ribs and the pair blew apart like opposing magnets.

Jamie rolled on instinct, Thorsen going the other way, and they both scrambled to their feet, Jamie cradling her injured left hand, right still around her own weapon.

There was a moment of stillness, and then they were facing each other.

Their eyes met, two strangers. Jamie saw no recognition in his eyes. She was looking back at a stranger, too. Fear erupted in her, mouth salivating uncontrollably.

Th … Thuh … Her mind tried to work.

She saw her raised pistol between them, realised she was pointing it right at the guy in front of her.

Her pistol.

Her pistol.

Her pistol.

The grip. The stippled grip. The weight. The barrel. The sights. The steel. The smell.

She blinked.

Thorsen! That's who he was.

But then, he wasn't alone.

A black shape was at his side, dark hands on his shoulders, long claws sliding down his chest.

The thing moved behind him, a head of eyes, all blinking at once, a hundred beaks all clacking and snapping as it moved next to his head. Began speaking in a voice unlike any she'd heard. A hundred crows, a writhing mass of them, all whispering at once in his ear.

Thorsen's face contorted in pain, the voice growing.

And then he raised his gun, pointed it at Jamie.

No!

The voice grew, louder now.

'No!' Jamie yelled this time. 'Don't!'

She didn't recognise her own voice now.

The head of crows stopped, looked at her then, blinked, an army of translucent lids flashing across the surface of the eyes all at once.

Jamie shuddered.

And then it whispered something else.

And Thorsen slowly brought the gun to his own head, pressed the muzzle against his temple. Beads of sweat ran down his cheeks to the corners of his jaw, his eyes still black voids, his face still twisted up in anguish.

The birds spoke to her then, low and alien. 'Is this what you want?'

Jamie could smell blood, thick in the air.

They spoke again. 'For him to kill himself?'

'No!'

'No?' The heads laughed, shimmering and jostling together. The eyes were fixed on her again then, unblinking, terrific. 'What about you, then?'

A cold wind enveloped Jamie, choked the air from her for a second, and then she felt the birds at her own shoulder, pecking and picking at her skin, their feathers rustling in her ears. 'You cannot resist,' they muttered, a thousand tiny voices all as one. 'Give in to it. Give in to the King ...'

Jamie stared at her own gun, still pointing at the man in front of her. At ... at ... She blinked. Focus on your pistol. The weight. The feel. Thorsen. Yes. Thorsen! That was his name.

'One of you must die ...' the birds whispered. 'This is the word of the King ... and the King must be obeyed ...' The birds all chattered and laughed, their voices sharp in her mind, stabbing at it.

Jamie ground her teeth. Pain lanced through her jaw. Focus on your gun. Your gun.

'Take him,' the birds commanded. 'The head.'

Jamie's pistol raised, her hand not her own. She could see birds under it, flapping and pushing her wrist into position until it was at head level.

She looked down the sights, saw the man in front of her right between them.

He had a pistol pressed to his temple.

Was he going to shoot himself?

The forest pulsed around them, like they were inside a giant ribcage. The forest breathed. In. Out. In. Out.

Jamie tightened her grip, felt the ripple of it under her fingers. The stipple.

Thorsen … Thorsen … The word bounced around her skull.

'Kill him …'

'Thorsen,' Jamie muttered.

'Kill him …'

'Thorsen … Thorsen …'

'Kill …'

'Kill … Thorsen …'

'Yes … Yes … That is the word of the King …'

'Kill …' Jamie whimpered. 'Kill Thorsen …'

Laughter erupted behind her, sour and insipid, enough to make her skin crawl. The crows bit into her shoulders, pressing on her. She felt their breath hot on her neck, their beaks tugging at her hair, all whispering death in her ear.

Her grip tightened on the gun.

Her left hand clenched at her side, still throbbing, still burning.

'Kill him.'

Jamie closed her eyes.

'Kill him.'

Her hand jerked and she fired.

'Kill him!'

She fired again. Again. Again. Again. Again!

The pistol flew backwards suddenly, over her shoulder, and Jamie drove the red-hot, still-smoking muzzle right into the mass of crow heads.

A wailing, agony-riddled scream filled the forest, and Jamie's eyes shot open. She gasped, the man in front of her still standing, eyes closed, pistol against his forehead. He was shaking. Above his head, there were half a dozen white welts in the trunk of the pine tree he was standing in front of. Bullet holes.

Jamie dropped her gun and lunged forward, knowing only that she needed to save this man.

Her hands closed around his gun and tore it from his grasp, hurling it into the woods with everything she had.

She grabbed his face then, fingers digging into the hair behind his ears, and his eyes opened.

They stared at each other, the mass of crows still writhing around in pain behind her.

'Thorsen,' she said, voice strained.

He searched her face.

'Thorsen,' she said again, swallowing, and then she stepped back, turned to face the King's messengers, clawing their way along the ground. Her hand lifted and she pointed to them, a word forming on her lips which she didn't have any will not to say, but didn't resist either. 'Kill.'

Thorsen stepped past Jamie, shoulders raised, hands coiled into fists, and then plunged them into the wicked mass of wings and feathers.

The crows shrieked.

Thorsen lifted them clear of the ground with both hands, looked over his shoulder at Jamie.

She swallowed, heart racing in her chest, and then gave into the darkness, nodded.

Thorsen lowered his head, sucked in a deep, howling breath, and drove the mass of crows right into the trunk of a waiting tree.

They fell quiet, slumped to the floor, and lay still.

'Thorsen …' Jamie whispered.

He turned.

Silence reigned, the forest throbbing around them like the soundless beat of a great heart.

She held her hand out.

He approached.

She leant her head against his chest.

Slowly, tentatively at first, his arms enveloped her.

And in the distance, rose the first echoes of approaching sirens.

51

JAMIE WAS SITTING in the Kurrajakk hospital waiting room with her hand around an IV bag stand for the second time in a week when Christian Nordahl's mother walked out of the Intensive Care ward and cleared her throat.

Jamie opened her eyes and lifted her head. It felt like an axe had been buried in it.

The fluids were doing a good job of stripping the drugs from her system, but the aftereffects were still in full swing. Thorsen was sitting opposite her, slumped back in the chair, asleep. She didn't know if he'd taken the brunt of Lena Viklund's dose, or if the repeated exposure had given Jamie some sort of tolerance, but it seemed to be hitting him harder than it was her.

'Thorsen,' she called, knowing he'd want to be woken for this regardless of how he was feeling.

He roused slowly as Jamie got to her feet and glanced at the clock. It was nearly seven in the evening now. They'd been brought in before midday.

Lovisa Nordahl had her hands around a clipboard and looked stern. No, actually, she looked angry. She was even more drawn than before, but now, her face was a painting of cold rage. Probably because she'd spent the last few hours caring for the man who'd killed her son.

'He's awake,' she said, with as much venom as Jamie had ever heard someone muster.

Jamie gave her a nod, rolling her tongue around her dry mouth, and moved slowly across the small room, giving Thorsen a quick kick on the boot.

He jerked awake, having fallen back into a stupor, and blinked, looking up at Jamie. His eyes had returned to normal now. Big, grey. He stared up at her for a few seconds, unmoving. Jamie wondered how much of what had happened had stuck with him.

She had snatches – she knew they'd chased Viklund into the woods, that she'd come face to face with Thorsen, pointed a gun at him, that he'd held his own against her head. That the King had been whispering in their ears, that they'd nearly killed one another.

That Forss and Ohlin had somehow found them …

Thorsen got up, wobbled a little, and steadied himself.

Shoulder to shoulder they ambled into the corridor and down towards a room at the far end. There was no officer posted outside the door because there wasn't one to post. But Viklund was half dead and practically lame anyway thanks to Jamie.

Lovisa Nordahl pushed the door open and Jamie and Thorsen filed in, dragging their stands with them. Lovisa Nordahl stood in the corner of the room.

'Mrs Nordahl, you can't be in here.' Jamie offered the woman a smile. Though she thought she wanted to hear this, she didn't.

She hovered, then exited wordlessly, watching Viklund as she closed the door.

As soon as it clicked shut, Jamie turned to face the man.

He was lying on his back, both wrists handcuffed to the rails of his bed. His left leg was suspended in a cast – Jamie's shot in the house had torn through his calf. It was surprising to the doctor who'd seen to him that he'd been able to walk on it at all, let alone escape. Though the details of exactly what happened in the house were foggy at best.

Other than his leg, it was his face that had taken the brunt of the punishment. His right eye was completely destroyed. Jamie supposed that was what happened when someone rammed a hot muzzle into it. The eyeball and eyelid had been burnt – 'melted together' was the term the doctor had used when they'd first come to update Jamie and Thorsen on his condition. It was hidden beneath a white pad, but the doctor said he'd never see out of it again.

The left side wasn't much better. It was swollen and blackened, his face bandaged. Apparently, his eye socket and cheek had been fractured, and his eye had suffered a hyphema, a bleed, which had caused practically all the white to disappear and be replaced with a deep mauve.

Jamie figured it was par for the course when you got your face rammed into a tree by someone the size of Thorsen.

Though she didn't feel a shred of guilt.

The guy deserved all of it.

And more.

He watched them from his 'good' eye, thin lips twisted into an ugly grimace through his dark beard.

'Gunnar Viklund,' Jamie said after a few minutes.

He remained silent.

'We're going to need you to tell us everything you know.'

More silence.

'We have time,' Jamie said, 'enough evidence to make sure you're never going to see daylight again, and a county-wide alert out for Lena. She'll be picked up soon enough, and I can promise you that I'll be doing whatever I can to have her tried as an adult ...' She watched him closely. 'Unless there's anything you'd like to tell us that could ... lessen the harshness of her treatment?'

He lay perfectly still, his heart monitor beeping steadily.

Jamie kept an ear out for any changes.

Thorsen just stood quietly, either not up to speaking, or happy to let Jamie take the lead.

'Viklund,' Jamie said again, 'we need to know the truth. Tell us why you did it. Tell us what happened – to Felix Nordahl. To Mats Flygare. To Nils Markus. Two people are dead and Markus is in the other room fighting for his life. So by the end of the night, we could be getting ready to charge you with three counters of murder. Do you understand what that means? For you? For your daughter? What she did to us, running away ... she's going to be charged with being an accessory to murder. Are you sure you want your daughter to live with that for the rest of her life? It's not too late. You can still help her.'

He just stared back at Jamie.

She wasn't going to get anything from him. She knew that.

Viklund wasn't stupid. He knew he was entitled to legal counsel, whatever happened. That a charge would be a charge, not a conviction. That in reality, they had no evidence against Lena Viklund at all.

Gunnar Viklund's words to her were clear enough, though – *is this what you want? How cruel you can be.* Could a fifteen-year-old girl really be the one masterminding this, behind it all?

Could a fifteen-year-old girl be the leader of a town-wide drug ring? Of a conspiracy of this size? Flygare, Nordahl ...

Were they her pawns, too? Taking Hugo's phone … planting it at Markus's house. Using it to lure Felix to the woods … then taking his phone, planting it in his own summer house? She would know where to go, would know his parents' schedules from experience … Did she come up with her own 'disappearance' down to Malmö? How could a daughter twist her own father up like this? Make him *kill* … for her. And for what? To what end?

Jamie had a lot of questions. But it didn't seem like Gunnar Viklund was going to answer any of them.

'Come on,' she said then, touching Thorsen on the arm. 'Let's go.'

He turned slowly and led the way out of the room.

'We'll be speaking again, Mr Viklund,' Jamie said, looking back at him. 'I hope those cuffs are comfortable. You'll be wearing them for a while.'

She closed the door then and stepped into the corridor. As she looked up, she caught Lovisa Nordahl's eyes. The woman was standing a little way down, arms folded, eyes full and shimmering with tears in the halogen strip lighting.

Jamie swallowed, holding her gaze, and then looked away.

She had no answers for her.

She had nothing.

52

Three days passed.

Painfully slowly. Gunnar Viklund was remaining silent and hadn't requested legal advice. He hadn't requested anything. He'd not said a word. To anyone. In three fucking days.

Nils Markus had also not woken up. His blood work showed high levels of the same drugs found in Felix's body, and in both Jamie and Thorsen's, too. And combined with his dehydration, they said that it had caused swelling to his brain. He'd be in a coma for who knew how long. He might never wake up, the doctor said.

Forss and his team had ripped the Viklunds' house apart, collected samples, and catalogued everything. And Flygare's autopsy had been carried out the day before. Which meant they were liable to receive both sets of paperwork this morning.

And to top it all off, there was no sign of Lena Viklund either.

Jamie was not doing very well, and it was slowly dawning on her that this was probably their plan all along.

And that the father-daughter *King and Princess of Crows* team knew that Jamie and Thorsen were coming and made preparations. They pumped Markus full of drugs to kill him so he couldn't talk. And knowing that Jamie had killed Flygare … all they had to do was wait for that result to come through and the whole investigation would be thrown into jeopardy. And that wasn't even considering that over the course of it, that the two lead detectives had been under the influence of a powerful hallucinogen.

Could their reporting really be trusted?

Jamie was tapping her nails on the table, watching the phone.

'Hey,' Thorsen said, appearing at the side of her desk with a cup of coffee. He put it down.

Jamie stared down into the black liquid.

'Thanks,' she said, picking it up, holding it in her hands. Letting it warm them.

She looked up from the desk to watch the glaziers fit new doors on the station.

Perhaps the only good thing to come out of this whole case was that the station was getting a little bit of TLC. The place was a dump – to put it nicely. And Jamie wasn't looking forward to a winter with single glazed windows. At least now she'd be warm, if she kept her job that was.

The other good thing – and Jamie used the word 'good' loosely – was that Ohlin had actually had to do *his* job.

They'd regarded him as completely absentee through the entire case. But he'd actually been back and forth to Lulea to hurry up the autopsy and forensics results, had been holding things together in town while Jamie and Thorsen were chasing down leads, and had been liaising with the fire and ambulance services when things got out of control. Which was all the more impressive considering the guy couldn't *spell* the word 'liaising'. But that's how he worked. People knew him, they called him. And he'd spent the entire time making sure the place didn't tear itself completely apart. He still did a pretty shitty job considering the way things had gone, especially outside the Moose. But still, she had to admit that it probably would have been a lot worse if he *wasn't* there. But that did come with a fair amount of derision. Which Jamie didn't really feel like taking, but pretty much had to considering his input into the inquiry into Flygare's death could be the difference between her being relieved of her position in the Swedish Polis Authority and being tried for murder.

'You know watching that thing isn't going to make it ring,' Thorsen said.

Jamie peeled her eyes from the phone, not even realising she was staring at it again.

'No, but if I wish really, really hard …' Jamie said, looking up at him, 'then maybe the coroner's office at Lulea might burn down and destroy the autopsy report and all the evidence before anyone has a chance to read it.'

Thorsen offered her a wry smile but said nothing.

'When I want something to happen,' Minna said, spinning round on her chair, grinning, her freckles bright against her pale skin. 'I buy a perch from the monger, take its guts out and throw them into a fire. Then I pray really hard. And sometimes it works.'

Jamie and Thorsen stared at her in disbelief.

Then Thorsen spoke, taking the words out of Jamie's mouth. 'This is the weirdest fucking town I've ever been to in my life.'

Minna was still grinning. 'It's not uncommon – a lot of families do things like that around here. It's from the old ways.'

'The old ways?' Thorsen enquired, his face saying against his better judgement. 'You mean like the old *Norse* ways?'

Minna nodded. 'Yeah, it's not like we pray to the old gods or anything,' she said, shrugging then. 'But it's, like, one of those things, you know? You throw fish guts in the fire and you wish really hard and maybe it happens.' She turned around then and went back to whatever 'work' she was doing.

Thorsen's eyebrows were practically in his hairline they were so high. He looked down at Jamie and she just shook her head. There was no way she was going to join this conversation.

Her phone started buzzing on the desk then and she snatched it up, hoping it was Forss dialling her directly. It wasn't.

'Hallberg,' she said, a little surprised. 'Hi.'

'Jamie,' Julia Hallberg, one of Jamie's old colleagues from Stockholm – and for a brief time, her partner – said. 'How are you? I saw the news – three dead in Kurrajakk, Jesus. That the case you called me about?'

'Uh-huh,' Jamie said tiredly. 'Unfortunately, yes.'

'Damn, this shit just seems to find you wherever you go, doesn't it?'

'Tell me about it.'

'Anyway – I just wanted to check in, see how you were, if there was anything else I could do? I never heard back from my last email and you didn't return my call, so I wanted to make sure that you got the file.'

'With the pictures from Nordahl's account? Yeah,' Jamie said. 'Thanks, they were really helpful.'

'What about from the other accounts?'

Jamie sat up a little straighter now and Thorsen read the tension in her.

She laid the phone on the table, put it on speaker. 'What other accounts?'

'Uh … Something Westman, and Olivia … Sundgren, I think? I got into their accounts, sent you a dump of the photos there, along with the older photos from Nordahl's account, too. I put them in a secure cloud folder, sent you the links. You didn't get them?'

'No,' Jamie said, not angry at Hallberg, but more at herself for not following up on this. She'd been so wrapped up in the case. She was already tapping on the keyboard in front of her, waiting for the ancient PC to pull up the email client. 'Hold on,' she said, navigating through login. Her account was linked to her phone, but nothing from Hallberg had come through, she would have seen it. 'When did you send it?'

'Uh … Four, five days ago? The day after I sent the first one.'

Jamie scanned up and down the spartan inbox. The last email she'd received was the first one from Hallberg. 'No, nothing, are you sure you sent it?'

'Yeah, I am … Hang on …' There was shuffling as Hallberg moved her phone around. 'Yeah, here it is. It definitely sent … hang on …'

'What, did it not go through?'

'It was just a couple of links – maybe the system flagged it as SPAM. Can you check your junk folder?'

Jamie's teeth were clenched hard as she double-clicked junk and waited for the screen to reload. And then there it was.

She opened it quickly, saw three links, and opened each in a new tab.

'Got them?' Hallberg asked then.

'Yeah, found them,' Jamie said, already going into the files to display the photos. There were hundreds.

'Great – I hope they help! They have the geotags on them, dates, any tagged accounts, captions, it's all in the metadata.' Hallberg sighed. 'I miss working with you, Jamie. I hope you're happy up there.'

Jamie stopped scrolling, looked down at her phone. 'Thanks, Hallberg, me too,' Jamie said, holding her voice steady. She didn't want to comment on the rest.

'Alright then …' Hallberg said after a few seconds. 'I've got to get back, but, er, yeah – let me know if you need anything else. You can always call if you do. Bye.'

She hung up, leaving Jamie with Thorsen's eyes on her and a whole load of new images to keep her mind off the impending bad news.

'I like her a lot better than Wiik,' Thorsen said then. 'That guy is a bit …'

He trailed off when Jamie fired him a hard look.

Thorsen cleared his throat and moved behind Jamie, folding his arms.

She went back to inspecting the photographs, focusing on Nordahl's first. They were much the same as the sample Hallberg sent her. Lots of photos with Hugo and Olivia, lots of selfies, and a lot of photos with Lena Viklund, too. The girl looked a lot prettier here – her long wavy hair clean and shiny, her skin bright. She was wearing shoes, too. She looked like a normal teenage girl. But she wasn't tagged in any of the photos, while Hugo and Olivia were. Which Jamie guessed meant she didn't have an account of her own.

She read through the captions. Love. Love. Love. Love. Can't live without you. Love. Love. Shit, Felix Nordahl wasn't a poet, but he was laying it on thick.

Jamie let out a long breath, leaned back in her chair, and rocked gently.

'What are you thinking?' Thorsen asked, reading over her head.

'I don't know,' Jamie said.

'Bullshit.'

She sighed, leaned forward, hands on the desk. 'Okay, so Lena Viklund – sociopathic criminal mastermind or victim?'

'You asking me or yourself?' Thorsen stepped around beside Jamie, perched on her desk. 'Let's do one, then the other,' he said. 'Victim.'

'Okay, so Gunnar Viklund is the one behind the drugs. He recruits Flygare to sell for him, Flygare gets booted from school, so he recruits Felix to replace him, runs the two of them at the same time. Expansion. Right?'

'Sure.' Thorsen nodded.

'How does he recruit them?'

Thorsen rolled his head back and forth. 'Lena's in school with both of them.'

'So he gets his daughter to do it for him, bring them in close, he gets them excited about the money … it works, right?'

'I suppose.'

'And in that scenario, Felix decides he wants out, plans to run away with Lena, Viklund gets wind of it, kills Felix, busts Flygare out of the station, abducts and frames Markus … All the while keeping Lena prisoner in the house.'

'Right.'

'And the doors were screwed shut.'

'Right.'

'But she disappeared before Gunnar Viklund did. And when I tried to take her through the cellar, she refused to go.

And remember what Viklund said – about her being cruel? She kept us there.'

'To what, toy with us?'

'Let's consider the other scenario, then.'

'That the fifteen-year-old girl is the one behind all of this?'

Jamie paused for a few seconds to mull that over. 'Just for the sake of argument.'

He let out an exhale. 'Okay, go.'

'So, in this scenario, Lena is the one behind the drugs.'

'How would she—'

'The *how* isn't important. Let's think *why.*'

'The *how* isn't important?'

'Humour me.'

Another sigh.

Jamie licked her lips. 'Viklund doesn't work, does he?'

'No. He claims *Bostadsbidrag* and disability for his back.'

'He look like he had a bad back when he was chopping wood to you?' Jamie asked.

'They never do unless a welfare inspector is sniffing around.'

'And he's a regular at the Moose.'

'Yep.'

'And that house look like it was in good condition?'

'A shit-hole. Think that's the technical term.'

'Right. So then maybe Lena's trying to make provisions for herself. Maybe the drugs are a way of securing her future. And we know from her involvement with Felix she was interested in older guys …'

'You think her and Mats Flygare?' His eyebrows went up again. 'That's a leap.'

'My father always said a leap and a lead were only one letter apart.'

'Your father? I thought you said he wasn't polis?'

Jamie met his eye, brushed it off. 'Whatever, the point is that if she got under Flygare's skin, whether she *liked* him or was just using him … He could have sold the drugs for her, that's all I'm saying.'

'And when he got kicked out of school, she turned her attention to Felix?'

'Right,' Jamie said. 'Except Felix had bigger plans. He wanted to leave, was planning on it, squirrelling away drugs and money so he could go.'

'To escape?' His face changed. To one of serious consideration. 'To escape Lena? You think he saw through her act?'

Jamie stared at the screen again, at the pictures of Lena and Felix together, laughing, kissing, holding each other. 'That doesn't look like an act to me.'

'She had everyone else fooled – us included.'

'For thirty seconds,' Jamie snorted. 'It's not like we really had chance to think about it before she turned on us.'

He held his hands up. 'Alright, so what are you saying then?'

'I think …' Jamie did think. She took her time. 'I think that maybe it started off like that – that she was just using Felix. But then things changed, got serious. I think that maybe she bit off more than she could chew, didn't expect to, didn't mean to, but she fell in love with him. And I think when that happened, Felix wanted to run away with her, take her away from it all. Especially if she was playing the victim – making out that her father was the one behind it.'

'So, he starts squirrelling all this money away, and then when he's got enough, he tells Lena they're leaving? Springs it on her. She realises then that he wants out of their operation, and Kurrajakk. So she … kills him to cover her tracks and stop him talking?'

Jamie swallowed, staring at the pictures. 'No … I don't think so.' She stood then, grabbed her jacket off the back of the chair. 'Come on, we're going for a drive.'

'A drive?' Thorsen asked as Jamie headed for the door. 'What about your phone call? Forss?'

She threw the Kurrajakk Polis bomber around her shoulders, didn't look back. 'He has my number. He'll be able to reach me if he needs to.' And then she ducked out past the glaziers and into the weak September sun.

53

JAMIE PARKED the SUV on the unnamed stretch of road and got out.

Thorsen took one look around and then realised where they were. 'All these roads look the same,' he commented, circling the truck.

'You get used to it,' Jamie said, stepping down into the verge and then heading up into the forest. They walked for a few minutes until she found the same summer-dried trickle of a stream and followed it to the rim of the bowl.

Jamie and Thorsen stood above the ancient site, staring down at the blood-stained stump and stone plinth in the centre for the third time. The scene of Felix Nordahl's murder.

'What are we doing back here?' Thorsen asked, looking around disdainfully. This had been the place he'd first run into the King. Jamie just didn't know which one. She hadn't ruled out it being Markus too, yet. And she knew there were at least two suits. And she could have sworn she'd seen more than one of them the night she'd chased Flygare into the woods.

Jamie shuddered, shook it off, and walked down towards the stones.

Thorsen followed, pausing at the edge of the plinth and watched as Jamie began circling the stump, mind ticking away.

He gave her space.

She appreciated it.

After two laps, she stopped. 'Torture,' she said then, looking up at Thorsen across the altar. 'Suffocation. Cowardice.'

'Uh … the less popular follow-up to *Live. Laugh. Love.*?' Thorsen offered.

'Ha-ha,' Jamie replied. 'No – think about the kill. There's anger here, hatred.'

'I think that's fair to say.'

'The killer—'

'Gunnar Viklund,' Thorsen interjected.

'The killer,' Jamie reiterated. 'We don't know it's Viklund – not alone at least. Felix wasn't a weak kid. It'd take a lot to subdue him.'

Thorsen just sort of shrugged. He couldn't disagree.

'The killer pinned Felix down – used that glove that Viklund had, with the beaks, and gouged at his skin. It would have taken … minutes? Twenty? Thirty? There wasn't an inch on his skin that wasn't cut. And then, after all that, they would have rammed a crow down his throat – held it there until he died. How long would that take? Three, four minutes? And there were no ligature marks on him, so I think he was held down, not tied.'

Thorsen watched her carefully.

'That's not a one-person job.'

'What are you saying?'

Jamie approached the stump, stood at one side, mimicked

holding an arm in place. 'Gunnar Viklund.' She switched sides, mimicked holding the other arm. 'Mats Flygare.' She jumped up on the stump then, crouched as though she was straddling a body. 'Lena Viklund.'

'You think Lena did that? Not Markus?'

Jamie turned, holding herself in the crouched position, massaged her lips with one hand, forearm of her other resting on her knee. 'If it was Lena Viklund who did this to Felix, she had the help of her father and Mats Flygare. But it still doesn't tell us why. This is the first time that they've killed anyone. And we know they've been selling this shit for more than a year because Flygare got kicked out of school because of it.'

'So what does 'cowardice' have to do with it?'

'Agnes Bloom said that the *Krakornås Kung* myth was rooted in Norse myth. She said that the King was a warrior who fled the battlefield. A coward. That the gods *punished* him for being a coward.'

Thorsen stuck out his bottom lip, folded his arms. 'Felix Nordahl was planning to run away from Kurrajakk.'

Jamie stepped down off the altar. 'Right. So, what if we've got it backwards then?'

'How do you mean?'

'Well, what if Felix Nordahl didn't want to run away *with* Lena Viklund. What if he wanted to run away *from* Lena Viklund.'

Silence fell between them then as Thorsen rolled that over in his head.

'What if Felix *did* love Lena – what if he wanted them to go together, but she didn't want to, couldn't—'

'Or maybe he found out she was a psychotic little manipulator and drug kingpin?'

'Or that.' Jamie sighed. 'He wants to leave, she won't, he tries to go anyway, makes plans to run away ...'

'She thinks him a coward ...'

'The timeline fits if they broke up,' Thorsen said. 'Felix was at that last party with Westman and Sundgren alone. Maybe that was his goodbye to them.'

'Westman said they did drink harder than normal. Maybe he was drowning his sorrows.' The theory held water, she couldn't deny that.

'And you said he had money stashed away. And if Westman wanted to buy some pills, more cash the better if he's about to leave Kurrajakk.'

She bit her lip. 'But ... Felix gave Westman his phone. Westman said Felix told him he didn't need it. So, he must have known he lost it. So why would he go to meet Westman if he knew it wasn't Westman?'

Thorsen contemplated that one for a second. 'Well, it was the only number saved, wasn't it?'

Jamie nodded. 'So maybe it's not Westman's number at all. Maybe Lena just saved his name afterwards before she planted the phone to make it *look* like it was Westman.'

'And then planted Westman's real phone at Markus's house to frame him. I don't think we ever compared those numbers,' Thorsen said.

'So, Lena texts Felix's dealer phone from a random number, lures him out there on the premise of selling one last batch before he takes off.'

'She surprises him.'

'And does her powder on the hand party trick.' Jamie held her hand up, blew over her palm.

'Felix takes off into the forest ...' Thorsen said.

'Lena and Flygare chase him down while Viklund is at the Moose shoring up his alibi ...'

'He knows what's coming, doesn't want to go through with it, picks a fight with Christian Nordahl … Tells him to keep his son away from Lena …'

'Jesus Christ,' Jamie muttered. 'Gunnar Viklund was trying to *warn* Christian Nordahl.'

'Because he knew what was coming.'

'Except it was already too late.' Thorsen let out a long breath. 'That's a lot of conjecture.'

'But it all fits.'

'It's still not worth a damn unless we can get Lena or Gunnar Viklund in a room to confirm it.'

'Hang on,' Jamie said, pulling her phone out. She dialled Forss's number, waited for him to pick up.

He did. *'Hallå?'* he sighed.

'Forss, it's Johansson.'

'Johansson …' he said, not hiding the groan in his voice. 'I'll send the report over when it's ready. And … and … you really shouldn't be calling me right now. Not with Flygare's autopsy …'

'Yeah, yeah,' she said cutting him off, 'I know, but I need to know something about Gunnar Viklund's house right now. You can send the report in full when it's ready then.'

'I'm really coming to enjoy our phone conversations.'

'Tell me about the Viklunds' house,' Jamie said again, ignoring the sarcasm.

His chair squeaked in the background as he leaned back. 'What do you want to know?'

'Was there anything there to suggest an interest in Norse religion or mythology?'

He scoffed. 'Was there anything to suggest …' He laughed then. 'I'm guessing you didn't go upstairs?'

'Didn't really get the chance before we were drugged and forced to hold each other at gunpoint.'

'Fair enough.' He cleared his throat. 'Viklund's bedroom was filled with stuff – books, knick-knacks, wood carvings, notes and notepads, little shrines, you name it, it was there.'

'That was Gunnar Viklund's room?'

'Yep.'

'You sure?'

'Double bed, men's and women's clothes in the wardrobe. Fairly sure. The other bedroom wasn't far behind though – smaller, the collection less extensive, but a bit more macabre if anything.'

'Macabre?'

'You think it's normal for a teenage girl to collect bird skulls and animal teeth?'

Jamie grimaced.

'About par for the course for a psycho-killer's house, though. In my experience at least.'

'You've seen a few?'

'This isn't my first, let's say that.'

'You got any photos, of the Viklunds' rooms?'

'You know what my job entails, right?'

'Just send them over, would you?'

'Your wish is my command,' he drawled, tapping away at his keyboard. 'Oh, while I have you, we had an identification on the flowers outside the house, same as the ones drying in the basement. Henbane.'

'Henbane?' Jamie repeated for Thorsen's benefit. He was standing close enough to overhear the conversation no doubt.

'Yeah, it's a wildflower, highly poisonous if ingested in its natural form. The petals and bulb are rich in the compounds found in the refined drug – those tropane alkaloids – hyoscyamine, scopolamine.'

'Does it grow here, in Sweden?'

'Rarely – but the patch outside the Viklunds' house was

cultivated, looked after. That number of flowers, as well as the number they had in the basement – it'd be enough to drive the whole town crazy.'

Jamie swallowed. Was that their plan? Did they intend to do that? To spike everyone, send everyone into a murderous, paranoid rage?

'Photos should be with you now,' Forss said. 'Report shouldn't be far behind, and the autopsy results should be back today or tomorrow. The full report will be quick, I think. Ohlin's up Vardeman's ass like one of Vlad's war-pikes.'

'You really have a way with words, you know that?' Jamie sighed, pulling her phone away from her ear and opening the email Forss had just sent.

She scanned through them while he waited in the background, showing Thorsen. Everything Forss said was true – the skulls and teeth, plucked crow or raven feathers, candles and shrines, books and books on Norse mythology … and in Gunnar Viklund's room, the double bed with a floral spread, the wardrobe filled with women's clothes, the dressers still lined with nail polishes and make-up, all covered in dust, but still there, right where …

Something occurred to Jamie then.

'Thanks for that,' Jamie said quickly to Forss. 'I'll call if I need anything else.'

'I'm sure you wi—'

But he didn't get to finish before Jamie cut him off and jogged past Thorsen.

'Where are you going now?' he called after her.

But she was already gone.

54

'YOU WANT to loop me in on the game plan here?' Thorsen asked as they pulled into the hospital car park. 'If we're going into Viklund's room again—'

'We're not,' Jamie said, killing the engine and getting out.

A few minutes later, they got off on the second floor. Thorsen stepped out of the elevator after Jamie, glancing up at the sign above. *Onkologi.* Oncology.

'Something you're not telling me?' he asked, stopping under it.

Jamie paused, looked back. 'You said that Viklund's wife died, right?'

'Yeah, that's right,' Thorsen replied. 'I might be of some help if you tell me what you're thinking?'

'I don't know what I'm thinking yet, but hopefully, in a few minutes, I … Hey!' Jamie said as a doctor walked out of a nearby corridor junction.

The woman stopped, looked up. She was in her fifties, had dark hair pulled back into a low bun at the nape of her neck. 'Can I help you?' she asked, eyes going to the badge on Jamie's chest.

'*Inspektör Jamie Johansson, Kurrajakk Polis,*' she said quickly.

Thorsen caught up then. 'Kjell Thorsen,' he added, giving a quick nod.

The doctor nodded back. 'How can I help?' she asked tentatively.

'Have you been a doctor here for a while? In oncology?'

'Twenty years. What's this about?'

'Do you remember a patient …'

'Alma Viklund,' Thorsen jumped in, figuring out where Jamie was going with this. 'She was diagnosed with cancer three years ago. She passed away two years ago.'

Jamie banked on Kurrajakk being a small town, then. That there weren't so many patients that the doctor wouldn't remember.

Her brow furrowed as she thought. 'Alma Viklund … Ah, yes,' she said, smiling briefly. 'I do remember her. Her diagnosis was quite late, and unfortunately the treatment didn't have a great effect. If I remember rightly, she underwent a course of chemotherapy, but when we received the results of her scans, she elected not to continue with it. She refused the second round. I don't think we saw her after that.'

'And when she did come in,' Jamie started. 'Was she alone? Did her husband come with her?'

The doctor stared into space, delving into her memory. 'Erm … No, I don't think so. I'm fairly sure that there was a girl with her. A teenage girl. Does that sound right?'

Jamie looked at Thorsen, then back at the doctor. 'Did they seem close?'

'I think so. She never missed an appointment. Always held her mother's hand. Stayed by her side the whole time. I couldn't imagine how hard it must have been for her. She was maybe twelve, thirteen at the most.'

'Thank you,' Jamie said then. 'I'm sorry, you must be busy – we'll find you if we have any more questions.'

The doctor nodded again, then walked away at pace and entered a room down the hall.

Jamie turned back towards the elevator, walking slowly, mind piecing it all together. Thorsen watched her. She had no doubts that he'd formed his own conclusions, but he was waiting for her to articulate her theory.

She hit the call button and waited.

'Inspektör?' she heard from behind.

Jamie and Thorsen turned in unison to see Lovisa Nordahl, Felix Nordahl's mother standing there in the corridor.

'I thought it was you,' she said, coming forward a little, wringing her hands out.

'Mrs Nordahl,' Jamie said, smiling softly. 'How are you?'

She held her hand out, shrugged. 'You know, trying to keep busy.' She swallowed. 'I just wanted to say … thanks, you know? For catching …' She pointed up to the ceiling, meaning the third floor, the ICU where Gunnar Viklund was still recovering, chained to his bed.

Jamie just nodded. There really wasn't much to say. Especially since she thought there was still more to do. No, she *knew* there was still more to do.

'I don't know if you would want to … or if you *can* … but, it's … it's Felix's funeral tomorrow. They released his body to us now that …' Her voice began to crack. 'We wanted to …'

'Of course,' Jamie said, stepping forward and putting her hand on Lovisa Nordahl's arm. 'Of course we'll come.'

Lovisa nodded, eyes filling with tears, and then turned away, disappearing down the adjacent corridor before she broke down.

Jamie turned back to Thorsen, the elevator now there and waiting for them.

'Where to now?' he asked.

Jamie lifted her finger, went to speak, then stopped. Everything finally clicked.

Her mouth twisted into a smirk, and then she lowered and shook her head. 'Fuck,' she muttered, laughing a little. 'Jesus Christ.'

'What is it?'

'I think I finally figured it out. Why Lena did what she did. Why she *is* how she is …'

'And that's funny … why?'

'Because it wasn't me that solved it.'

Thorsen stared at her.

'It was Minna.'

55

THEY PULLED in at the Kurrajakk cemetery and exited the car, letting themselves through the rusted iron gate and heading across the manicured grass.

'So you're saying Minna figured it out?' Thorsen asked, trailing behind Jamie as she walked between the headstones, looking from one to the next to the next. He had his hands in his pockets, and seemingly was just along for the ride now. She didn't know if that meant he trusted her, or if he could just see that Jamie was basically a freight train at this point and it was a case of jumping on board or getting left behind.

'Well, let's not give her *too* much credit,' Jamie said over her shoulder, stopping briefly to check out the name on one of the headstones. She crossed it off and kept going. 'But she did say something interesting.' Jamie turned now. 'You know when she said that a lot of families around here do things like burning fish guts … well, it got me thinking about the site, about Felix, about everything. Torturing someone is one thing, but to what end? Was it purely for the twisted pleasure of it, or did Lena *want* something out of it?'

Thorsen put his hands on his hips. 'You're saying you think Lena Viklund sacrificed Felix Nordahl.'

'I'm saying it seems like an awful lot of effort to go through and a heck of a coincidence considering the books, the shrines, the theatre of this whole fucking mess if she didn't.'

Thorsen stared down at Jamie. He was a whole head taller than her. 'I don't know, Jamie. Ritual sacrifice ... It's ... Do you really believe that she thought it would have accomplished anything? The flowers, the costume, the murder ... yeah, it all points to the Viklunds not quite playing with a full deck of cards ... But the drugs? They were running an operation out of that basement. If anything, I think all this other *stuff,* the performance, the birds, the outfits ... I think that's just ... for show. I think it's all fiction to disguise the fact that their drug ring was coming apart at the seams.'

Jamie stared back at him.

'You disagree,' Thorsen said.

'Let's just focus on finding Lena first. Then we can get some answers.'

Thorsen cracked a grin. 'You're that sure?'

Jamie said nothing, didn't move, didn't nod.

'Alright then,' Thorsen said, laughing. 'After you.'

'Okay.' Jamie nodded. 'Keep an eye out for a yellow flower.'

'A yellow flower?'

'Yep. Henbane. I think Lena Viklund will have come by here and laid one on her mother's grave.'

'That's a big guess,' Thorsen laughed. 'What are you willing to bet on that?'

'Oh, I don't think you want to bet on it.'

'And if I do?' He folded his arms, puffing his chest out.

'Then you'd be confirming that you're stupider than you look.' Jamie sighed, stepping out of the way and pointing to a headstone four down and two to the right. 'Because I can see it from here.'

56

It was raining.

Big, heavy droplets pelted down from the flat grey sky, thundering against the raised umbrellas that formed a dome over Felix Nordahl's grave.

Everyone stood and watched as the casket was lowered into the hole, the bearers' black shoes splattered with mud as they stood by.

Jamie's eyes swept the faces of the crowd. She saw the Nordahls, side by side, but a million miles apart. There was Hugo Westman and Olivia Sundgren, standing shoulder to shoulder, holding hands. Their parents were behind them.

Jamie spotted the teachers from the school, among them was Inger Holm the English Teacher, and Mr Ledman, the geography teacher that had come on to Jamie. He kept looking over. She didn't meet his eye.

Otherwise, it was kids and parents, people she didn't recognise. But from the turnout, Felix was as popular as people said.

As the vicar spoke and people cried, Jamie let her eyes drift to the distant rain-shrouded tree line that bordered the cemetery. She shifted her weight, her boots squelching in the soft grass. Her black jeans were soaked, the white shirt and black sweater she was wearing damp under her woollen pea coat. She thought it best to ditch the polis uniform, out of respect, but also so that Lena wouldn't spot her so fast if she showed up.

She hadn't yet.

Despite Jamie's intuition on the flower being right, Thorsen still thought that Lena wouldn't show her face in Kurrajakk, that she'd be running for the hills.

Jamie disagreed. She thought Lena was broken. Cruel, violent, without remorse, yes, but not well. The picture that had formed in her mind, the way her father had reacted to her presence in the house, the way her mother had passed, the way the photos with Felix made her look, the way that the bedrooms were upstairs … they were all painting a picture of Lena in Jamie's mind, and before any of the homicidal tendencies, she saw a girl who wasn't whole. Who was alone. Who was angry. So very fucking angry.

It didn't earn her any forgiveness, or sympathy. But Jamie hoped it would help them catch her.

The casket reached the bottom of the grave, the vicar said his peace, and then slowly the crowd began to disperse.

Jamie stayed in place, Thorsen next to her, holding the wide black umbrella above their heads, her eyes fixed on the trees ahead.

'You still think this is the right call?' he asked, voice low.

'I do,' Jamie said, gaze unflinching.

'Alright then,' he sighed. 'Let's get this over with. Before I get even wetter.' He moved his feet, heels squeaking against the wet leather of his boots. 'If that's even possible.

·   ·   ·

Night fell quickly, but the rain didn't abate.

A single streetlamp next to the cemetery cast a dim glow over the nearest headstones, but died beyond.

The rain was coming down in sheets, crackling on the roof of Thorsen's BMW. Jamie's polis truck would be too easy to spot.

Thorsen drew a breath, then sighed, looking at the clock on the centre console. It glowed in the darkness, read 8:19pm.

'We've been sitting here for seven hours,' Thorsen said. 'She's not coming, Jamie.'

Jamie was looking out at the cemetery. 'A little longer.'

'How much longer?'

'You head off if you want, I'll stay here,' Jamie said.

'This is my car.'

'You've got an umbrella.'

He fell quiet, adjusted himself in the seat, champed his lips. Jamie was thirsty too, but there wasn't much room to pee in here and giving themselves away by going outside was the last thing they wanted to do. So they were on a drinks embargo.

She could tell Thorsen was getting angsty. But she didn't much feel like playing eye-spy or making idle conversation. She'd fallen into a cool focus, eyes planted on the cemetery. On Felix Nordahl's grave.

'Fine,' Thorsen said, folding his arms. 'Wake me in the morning when she hasn't shown up.' And with that he leaned his head back and closed his eyes.

It wasn't morning, but it was late when Jamie shook Thorsen awake.

'Hey,' she said.

He opened his eyes and sucked in a deep lungful of air, sitting up. 'What is it?' he asked, blinking himself clear.

'I think I see something.' Jamie's voice was quiet and restrained.

She'd been sitting in total silence for over four hours.

It was now nearing 12:30am.

'What is it?'

'If I knew that,' Jamie said, 'I wouldn't have woken you.' She nodded out of the window. 'See it?'

Thorsen squinted, trying to make out whatever Jamie was talking about. 'I don't see … Wait.'

Jamie did wait.

Thorsen's silence and stern expression confirmed Jamie's thoughts.

'On you,' he said.

Jamie opened the glove box in front of her and pulled out the two pistols there – the two that Forss's team had recovered from outside the Viklunds' house. The one she'd dropped and the one she'd thrown out of Thorsen's reach.

'Here,' she said, giving him the P226. 'You can have the big one this time.'

He smirked a little, taking it while Jamie pulled back the slide on the P229 Compact, and chambered a round.

'Ready?'

He nodded.

They exited the car and stole across the road, onto the pavement, and through the open cemetery gate.

They knew their way to Felix Nordahl's grave, and both took wide routes, ready to close in from both sides.

Jamie lost sight of Thorsen quickly, the rain hiding their approach.

Her heart was beating quickly, the droplets cold on her scalp as they soaked through her hair. Her eyes stung as the rain splashed off her cheeks, her footsteps muted by the symphony of it hitting the grass and gravestones.

Felix Nordahl's headstone swam into view, Jamie's eyes adjusting to the darkness.

She slowed, waiting for them to pick out the scene fully, waiting for the black shape in front of it to form into a fifteen-year-old girl.

Jamie stepped cautiously, weapon raised, pulling a pen-torch from the pocket of her jacket and holding it in her off-hand under her wrist. She took a breath, waited until she was close, and then clicked it on, drowning Lena Viklund in light.

The girl froze, on her knees, hunched over in front of Felix Nordahl's headstone, knees black in the loose soil.

'Lena Viklund,' Jamie called, squinting through the rain. 'Don't move.'

Lena Viklund didn't. Her long, straw-coloured hair spilled from her head in long strands, touching the earth in front of her. She had her hands clasped amongst it.

Jamie's eyes went to them, her grip tightening on her weapon. 'Let me see your hands,' she commanded.

Thorsen materialised from the darkness on the other side, moving unheard. He watched Lena, ready to fire if need be.

Lena Viklund did nothing, her hunched back rising and falling gently, jerking every few seconds as she sobbed.

Jamie kept her weapon trained on the girl. 'Let me see your hands,' Jamie said again, stepping closer. 'Now, Lena.'

Slowly, the girl slid them out from under her hair, pushing a drenched yellow flower through the dirt until it rested against the untarnished stone that bore Felix Nordahl's name. 'It didn't bring her back,' she said, her voice swallowed by the sound of the rain.

'Lena,' Jamie said. 'Stay right where you are. Don't run.'

'He was going to leave me too ...'

Jamie looked down at her, the water painting her tattered t-shirt against the sharp ridges of her exposed ribs but said nothing more.

And neither did Lena Viklund.

She just knelt there, whimpering, weeping into the sodden ground.

Jamie lifted her head, looked across Lena's back at Thorsen.

She nodded once and Thorsen understood, slowly lowered his weapon.

Jamie kept hers trained on Lena as he reached for a pair of handcuffs.

He drew them out slowly and unlocked them, the shining steel catching the faintest glimmer of light from the distant street.

Jamie kept her weapon on Lena, her guard up.

Thorsen approached slowly, handcuffs raised.

And all around, the rain just kept falling.

57

'Is Nils Markus dead?'

Jamie and Thorsen looked at each other, both still soaked through. Neither was expecting that question. Especially not from the bedraggled fifteen-year-old girl in front of them.

It was correct procedure to wait for someone to be with her – a family member, or someone from social services to make sure that Lena wasn't being exploited or treated unfairly.

But it was the middle of the night and that would take hours, maybe days. And they needed answers now.

'No,' Jamie replied. 'Why do you ask? You were trying to kill him, weren't you?'

Lena looked up, face dirty and thin from spending four days in the forest. 'We weren't,' she said. 'We just … He wanted to … He was going to tell …'

'Tell?'

She nodded, a child suddenly, wide-eyed and frightened. Jamie had a flashback to the Viklund house, to Lena blowing dust in their faces, the malice in her eyes in that moment. A different girl from the one fidgeting in front of them, cuffs clinking on the table, drowning her wrists.

'Who was he going to tell?'

She shrugged, like a child. 'I don't know – someone … the polis?'

Jamie narrowed her eyes, inspecting the girl in front of her. The girl who had been in a *sexual* relationship with Felix Nordahl.

She needed to be careful.

'What was he going to tell us?'

'That … that we did a bad thing to Felix.'

'What did you do to Felix?' Jamie asked.

She looked up at them, lip quivering. And then she cried, bent forward, let the tears mark the table as proof.

Thorsen touched Jamie's arm and she looked over. He lifted his other hand, motioned her to ease off a little.

She nodded, leaned back so she was less imposing.

'Nils Markus is going to make a full recovery,' Jamie said, lying easily. 'In fact, he's been quite talkative.'

Lena Viklund's head shot up now. 'Can I talk to him?'

'I don't think that's a good idea,' Jamie said.

'What did he say?'

'Why don't you tell us your side of things? We know your father killed Felix. That's what happened isn't it?' Jamie met her eye.

She looked back at her, eyes big and dark, like saucers. She nodded slowly, as if deciding whether to go all in or fold on the last card.

'How do you know Nils Markus?'

'He … he was a friend of my mother's,' Lena said, cautious now.

'Right, we knew that,' Jamie lied again. 'Markus said as

much. Tell us about your mother – you and her were close, weren't you?'

She nodded. 'Yeah, we were.' Her lip started quivering again.

'Can you tell us what happened after she stopped getting treatment at the hospital?'

Lena's eyes widened a little bit but she hid it well, feigning ignorance like a pro. 'We, uh …'

Fuck, Jamie wanted to lean on her. Wanted to make her talk. She was lying through her goddamn teeth. It was plain as day to see. But she couldn't. And she definitely didn't need to give the SPA any other reason to fire her. The only reason she was here now was because the Lulea pathology lab were dragging their heels on the Flygare autopsy.

'She … she …' Lena started.

'She turned to religion? The old ways.'

Lena nodded slowly, weighing Jamie up.

If she wanted to play this game, she'd lose. Jamie had a good pokerface, and she could keep the smile she was wearing all night if she had to.

'The medicine that the doctors gave her wasn't working any more,' Lena said, her voice moving into a higher register, like a little girl's. She hunched her shoulders up a little, too, squirmed in the chair. Oh, she was good.

Jamie restrained a smirk. 'What happened then? How did she find the site, in the woods?' Jamie took a swing. 'With the tree stump, the altar.'

'She … she found a map, in an old book about Kurra-jakk,' Lena said then, knowing she had to give them something. 'We went up there … She would pray.'

'She would pray.' Jamie nodded. 'And were her prayers ever answered?'

Lena said nothing.

'How did she pray? Did she sacrifice things? Animals, maybe?'

Silence. But no denial.

'What about the flowers? Did your mother plant them? We saw old vegetable plots in the garden, but they hadn't been used for a while. Did your mother used to grow things? She was good at it, wasn't she?'

Lena looked from Jamie to Thorsen and back.

Thorsen had his arms folded. He was watching Lena like a hawk, not buying a word of her story either.

'How did she meet Nils Markus?' Jamie thought then about the path leading from Markus's house to the site. The one she'd followed Thorsen down. 'Did they meet at the Norse site?'

Lena said nothing, then gave a tiny nod. Just enough to keep Jamie and Thorsen satiated.

'Was Markus interested in the old ways, too?'

Lena swallowed.

'They were friends? Did they get close?' Jamie imagined it – the absentee father abandoning his wife. The pair of them, Lena and her mother, looking for a cure. For hope. For anything.

Jamie remembered the horticulture books in Markus's house then.

'Did he tell your mother about the flowers?'

'They started growing there … after she started praying. It was them … they listened …'

'And Markus told her what they were?'

'Yes …' she whispered.

'Did he help her prepare them? Help her use them?'

Another nod.

'For the pain?'

One more nod.

58

When news broke that Lena Viklund was in custody, things happened quickly.

Gunnar Viklund's solicitor delivered a written statement where he fully admitted to the murder of Felix Nordahl, the abduction of Mats Flygare from polis custody, and conspiracy to supply a controlled substance. It said nothing of Lena, listing the reason for murdering Felix Nordahl as an argument that escalated unforeseeably.

There was no way he could plead manslaughter on that charge. But it still left a sickening taste in Jamie's mouth that he'd even attempt to.

And it was made all the worse as Lena Viklund was guided out of the station by protective services, ready to be taken into custody as a minor and placed in psychiatric care. Jamie's recommendation that she remain restrained and under constant supervision was met with raised eyebrows.

Jamie leaned against her desk, Gunnar Viklund's statement screwed up in her hand, scowling as Lena walked past.

The girl didn't stop, but did look up at Jamie through her hair, lip curling into a triumphant smirk.

Jamie felt her blood pressure rise just at the sight of it. But she still wasn't sure why. Why Lena had *let* herself be brought in. Why she hadn't tried to run. Why she hadn't made *some* attempt to do … *something.*

The paper in her hand was the only thing she could think of. That getting caught would force her father to accept all the guilt for what had happened, or watch his daughter be dragged through the courts and tried for murder too.

Was that it? Did she know that for all his faults, for all the things he'd done, that he wouldn't let his daughter be tried for it? He deserves everything he gets … That's what Lena had said. Did letting herself get caught ensure that her father went down for this? Was she forcing his hand? To accept responsibility. To finally accept responsibility …

And then the girl was gone, put in the back of a car ready to be transferred to Lulea and a secure ward there for evaluation.

Jamie hung her head. This was all fucked.

And now, Gunnar Viklund wouldn't be far behind. As soon as he was declared fit to travel, which was any day, he'd be taken to the county jail in Lulea to await trial.

Nils Markus was still unconscious and was the final piece of this puzzle. Was he victim, or instigator? Was he really a friend of Alma Viklund? The horticulture books, the taxidermy, the history of *Krakornås Kung* … He was no saint, and his credentials made him the perfect person to fill that role. Flygare and Felix were the pushers, poisoning the town. Gunnar Viklund the muscle. Nils Markus the engineer who had the means and the knowledge to prepare the drugs, the suits, to draw the birds to where he wanted them.

She'd spent the night reading. Reading up on crows. To her, they'd always meant death. In Norse mythos, they represented knowledge, memory, truth. Ravens were Odin's messengers, who brought him information. They were highly intelligent creatures, highly social. They formed family units and complex social structures. And if one member of the murder died, they would flock to the body, circle around it, wheeling and crying, warning other crows of danger. Or maybe singing their death chorus, lamenting their fallen brother or sister. Their father. Their mother.

Jamie remembered her boots crunching on the entrails in the middle of the town cross. And then what was smeared across the bonnet of her SUV outside her house. Dead crow. Nothing but nature. Nature and theatre.

And at the centre of it all, the director – the meek, mild-mannered, broken-minded fifteen-year-old girl that no one would see coming. That they hadn't seen coming. And that was going to dance circles around the doctors and polis officers that dealt with her if they weren't looking for it.

Which Jamie suspected they wouldn't be.

And all that added up to this playing out *exactly* as Lena Viklund wanted it to. The screws in the doors at the Viklunds' house. They weren't there to keep Lena Viklund in, they were there to trap Jamie and Thorsen.

They were never supposed to leave. Never supposed to get away.

And if they hadn't Jamie didn't know what would have happened. Kurrajakk would probably have burned to the ground by now.

So, what came next?

Gunnar Viklund was going to prison.

Felix Nordahl was dead for wanting to live his life. There was cruel irony in that. But was he really innocent in all this? Was he a victim, or as much a part of the problem as Mats Flygare had been?

Flygare … Jamie grimaced. A drug-dealer. A low life. But

did he deserve his end? Six bullets in the back while he ran through the forest? That had been the fate Jamie had made for him. He'd tormented her, lured her out there … And Jamie doubted of his own choosing. He was just a pawn. Bait. Target practice. He was dead because Jamie was *supposed* to shoot him. She was confident of that. But it didn't ease the sickening heat festering in her guts over it.

So where did that leave them? Custodians of a town plagued by superstition, by paranoia? One that almost came close to its end? What would have happened if they'd not gotten out of Lena Viklund's house? How far would she have taken this? Would she have laid every single person in town on that altar one by one, watched the life drain from their eyes with glee, just to try and bring her mother back? Or maybe it was under her mother's orders. Lena said she never left her. Was there a voice in her head, guiding her? One that was telling her what to do, what to say …

Jamie had no answers and knew that their last best hope to get them was lying in a hospital bed in a coma.

'Coffee?' Thorsen was at her side, suddenly, pushing a cup of black into her hand.

'Thanks,' she said, taking it.

'Bite marks are healing nicely,' he said, nodding to her right. They were still visible, but had scabbed over now and were much less inflamed than they had been. But they still throbbed, especially against the warmth of the mug.

'Mmm,' Jamie said, lifting the cup to her mouth. It was no consolation.

'I know you're not seeing it this way, but this is a win. Gunnar Viklund is going down for Felix's murder, and with our written reports, Lena Viklund is going to be sleeping in a padded room for years to come.'

Jamie didn't reply. She just watched the car pull slowly

away from the curb, Lena Viklund's eyes fixed on hers until it disappeared.

'With all the evidence we have,' he said, 'there's no way she gets out of this. I promise you that.'

'I don't know if you can,' was all Jamie said.

Thorsen sighed. 'And once Nils Markus wakes up, he'll tell us his side of things – and if he was Alma Viklund's friend, and he was just a victim in all this, then his testimony will help us put Viklund away … or if he was in on it all along … well, then we'll nail him to the fucking wall with the rest of them.' Thorsen lifted his own cup, waited for Jamie to clink hers against it.

She reluctantly obliged.

'We caught the guy, Jamie,' Thorsen went on. 'And his deranged, murderous daughter too. Bonus.'

Jamie drew a slow breath. 'I'll celebrate when it's over.'

'Somehow I doubt that,' Thorsen said, turning away and heading for his desk.

A minute later the door opened in front of Jamie and Ohlin walked in, practically waddling, his black and white beard and hair a stark contrast to his red face. 'Johansson,' he grunted, a folder in his hand, 'the bane of my life.'

Jamie checked her watch. 'Before midday,' she said. 'Getting an early start are we?'

'Watch it,' he growled, pulling up short of her and holding out the file. 'Here.'

'What's this?' Jamie asked, trying to keep her voice even.

'You know what it is.'

She read the words on the front of it, saw that it said Lulea Pathology Centre, stiffened a little. 'Thanks for hurrying this up,' she said, the bitterness in her voice not well hidden.

'Hurried up?' Ohlin put his hands on his hips indignantly. 'I'm the *only* reason it took this long.'

'I don't understand …'

'I held it up as much as I could,' he said, 'in the vague hope that you might be able to catch the bastard responsible for all this in the meanwhile.'

'You … *delayed* the autopsy?' Jamie was staggered.

Ohlin shook his head, tsked. 'You're welcome. I hope it wasn't in vain?'

'No,' Jamie said. 'It wasn't. We got him.'

He studied her, then just made an 'Mmm' sound. 'Well?' he said after a few seconds. 'Aren't you going to read it?'

And find out that I killed Mats Flygare? Give you the satisfaction of putting me in cuffs right here in *your* station? 'Of course,' she said instead, testing that pokerface of hers to the limit.

She lifted the flap, read the words, struggled to comprehend them. They swam around the page, her heart hammering against the inside of her ribs.

'Jesus, can't you read?' Ohlin grunted. 'It says that Mats Flygare died of a massive heart attack.' He snatched the file back off her and scanned down the page with a pudgy, nail-bitten finger. 'The report says that his system was over-flowing with scopolamine, hyoscyamine, and enough amphetamine to launch a rocket into outer-goddamn-space. Forensics report says that his tracks show he was running through the forest, and then suddenly collapsed. His heart damn well exploded with all the drugs.' He closed the file with a slap. 'And then some idiot walked up and put seven nine-millimetre rounds in his back.'

'He was already dead?' Jamie croaked, her throat and mouth dry as a bone. She was in shock.

Ohlin sighed. 'That's usually what happens when

someone *dies* of a massive heart attack, yes.' He moved his mouth back and forth, whiskers bristling, and then scratched his chin roughly. 'The forensics report that came back on that bird outfit recovered from Markus's farm showed seven bullet holes that matched up with the wound-pattern on Flygare's body, too. Which suggests that someone found him in the forest, stripped the stupid thing off him, and then hung it in Markus's barn.' He scowled at Jamie. 'You know none of this weird shit happened before you arrived. What are you doing? Close your mouth. You look simple.'

Jamie did, blinking, still trying to come to terms with what she'd just been told.

That she *didn't* kill Flygare.

By sheer dumb fucking luck.

Ohlin sighed again. 'It's abundantly clear now that this place just isn't capable of functioning properly without me.' He walked past Jamie then. 'Hey, you,' he called.

Thorsen stood up at his desk. 'Sir?'

'There a fresh pot of coffee on?'

'Yeah, it's—'

'Good, now get back to fucking work,' Ohlin snapped, waving him off and walking towards the kitchen.

Jamie turned to look at Thorsen, who appeared to be grinding his teeth, hands clenched in fists at his sides.

There was a loud, school-girl sigh from behind her then and she turned again to see Minna on her chair, facing them, grinning as usual. 'It's so good to have him back in the office, don't you think?'

'Yeah,' Jamie growled. 'He's a delight.'

'I hope he'll be around more.'

'God,' Jamie said, taking a hot, bitter sip of coffee. 'I fucking hope not.'

EPILOGUE

Lena Viklund sat in the hallway that led to the back door of the Bjornsson Juvenile Hospital just outside Lulea.

She was on a secure girls' ward that required a keycard to get out of. It was staffed around the clock by nurses and support workers and couldn't be escaped.

The door that she was sitting just ten feet away from led into a private garden surrounded by ten foot walls. But it caught the sun in the morning. Not that Lena had been allowed out there yet. She hadn't said a word to the doctors that had spoken to her. But had asked one of the nurses if she could go outside.

The nurse hoped that it might make this sweet young girl feel more comfortable. That it would be a positive step to help her open up, to reveal the trauma that had happened to her. After all, what harm could it do? She'd read Lena Viklund's admissions notes, of course, but believing that this girl was anything except in need of love and care was difficult to imagine.

The nurse exited the consulting psychiatrist's office and walked the length of the corridor.

Lena Viklund didn't look up, but she heard her approach.

'Lena?' the nurse said, voice soft. 'Would you like to go outside now?'

She held out her hand and Lena took it, eyes fixed on the floor.

The nurse led her to the door, lifted her keycard and ran it through the reader.

Lena watched through her hair.

The magnetic lock opened, and the nurse pushed through, leading Lena by the hand down the stone steps and onto the lawn. It stretched to the back of the enclosed space and ended at a patch of exposed earth where shrubs and other flowers were growing.

'Shall we walk?' the nurse asked.

Lena offered a meek nod.

They began, moving slowly around the perimeter.

'Will I be able to come out here on my own?' Lena asked, voice dulcet and girly.

'Yes, in time,' the nurse replied, 'if you help us under-stand what happened to you. We hope that you'll be able to spend all the time you want out here. Would you like that?'

Lena nodded, said nothing more.

They reached the far corner and began moving along the line of shrubs.

Lena stopped then, pulled on the nurse's hand. 'Flowers,' she said.

'Yes, that's right.' The nurse smiled. 'Flowers. There are all kinds here. See?'

Lena nodded, tugged her hand free, and collapsed to her knees, the shapeless, oversized clothes they'd given her making her look even more frail than she was.

The nurse looked down at her, leaning over the bed,

smelling the nearest flower – a purple geranium. Lena lingered there.

'Would you like to stay a while?' the nurse asked.

Lena nodded.

'Okay, I'll just be over there, alright?' She pointed towards the hospital, thought giving Lena a little space might be good for her.

Lena watched her recede through her hair, moving slowly from flower to flower, smelling each one. Purple. Red. Pink. Orange. Yellow.

She glanced over at the nurse again, saw that she was almost at the steps to the back door now.

Far enough away.

Lena Viklund reached up slowly, and pushed her finger into her mouth, outside her back bottom molars to the deepest part of her gum and hooked it around the tiny lumps there.

She withdrew them slowly, looking down at her upturned finger, wet with saliva, dotted with three seeds.

And then she turned them over and pushed them into the earth among the yellow flowers, closing the rich, moist soil around them.

She rose then, and walked back towards the hospital, stretching out her hand to the waiting nurse.

'I'd like to come out here again,' Lena said, offering her the smile she'd been waiting for.

The nurse grinned back, resisted the urge to hug Lena. 'I'm sure that would be okay.'

After all, what could be the harm in that?

AUTHOR'S NOTE

I always leave a certain period of time between finishing the novel and writing the author's note. In fact, it's usually the last thing I do before the manuscript is uploaded and the book launches. An author's note, for me, is a way to reflect on the book, but also a way for me to connect with you, the reader.

We have a strange relationship, but it's one I find fascinating. You know that it's not real, it is *fiction,* after all. But it's the story that keeps you engaged. Keeps that suspension of disbelief active. Stories are magic in that sense. But for me, the thing I truly love, the thing I find most rewarding about this whole thing is speaking to you guys and seeing what you take away from it that wasn't my intention.

I love hearing how you guys take Jamie and what you extricate from her. Because Jamie is part narrator, part central character, she's rarely referred to in the third person by any kind of omniscient point of view. So you'll get something like, 'Jamie was bored of the conversation,' rather than, 'Jamie was the type of person who was easily bored by these kinds of conversations.' The difference may seem innocuous, but what it does is make Jamie a person to be defined by you through her actions and thoughts, rather than a person I define to you.

I know who Jamie is to me.

But I find it so special that Jamie is something different to everyone.

If you read the last author's note, you know I had a few minutes of madness and tried to keep Jamie from you! Tried to take her elsewhere. I now realise that she's not mine to do that with. Jamie belongs to you, the readers. If she occupies a space in your brain or even in your heart, she's as much yours as she is mine. So if that's the case, take solace in the fact that she's going to be around for the foreseeable!

And honestly, now that I've decided that is the case, it's a relief. A weight off. December is a really tough month for authors — especially those self-publishing. To put it into perspective, my advertising costs doubled this December. But my sales did not.

It's because of Christmas and all the other books releasing.

But now Jamie is coming on the 31st, which means that the pre-orders that are delivered on that day will likely save me from burning through my entire nest egg! As such… Well, Jamie to the rescue!

Now, enough of that stuff. Enough puncturing the bubble and breaking the fourth wall. Let's talk *Death Chorus!*

Since I began the prequels back in… April of 2020 — wow, that long already… I've been learning. Learning to write crime, and also learning what kind of crime I wanted to write.

I feel like I touched on it in the prequels, hit my stride with *Angel Maker,* and then got off track a little with the sequels. They were thrill rides, that much I know, but they didn't have that *something* that I feel I captured with *Angel*

Maker. Angel Maker was a special book to me for lots of reasons, and I feel like that resonated with the readers. So when it came time to reflect on what came after *Old Blood,* I took some space from Jamie and her stories to think about what that was and how to capture it in whatever I wrote next.

New starts are always easier. You've got a new place, new characters, a whole new playground to cause mayhem in. But I couldn't keep giving Jamie a new start every time. Not totally, at least. But it got me to thinking — thinking about how I could take the things I loved about the two trilogies — that sense of continuity and linked stories — but blend it with the excitement of the new start. How I could write true stand-alone novels that favour the readers who have been with me from the start. How I could take all the parts you love, all the parts I love, and keep distilling this formula, this recipe, to something... perfect. And I use that term very personally. Perfect to me, in that it feels *right* to write. That it has the right balance of crime, procedure, character, action, pace, mystery, and a neck-snapping twist.

Someone pointed out to me that their favourite novels of the series were *Idle Hands* and *Angel Maker* because they had the heaviest psychological elements.

I pored over the definitions of psychological thrillers, and found them to be varying, but invariably linked to psychology. Either told from the point of view of someone under psychological stress or torment, or focusing on the psychological elements of a mystery or villain in the case of mystery or crime novels, or a novel that utilises narrative devices like dissolving realities, a blurring of reality and surreality as a result of a distortion of the narrator or protagonist's mind, or even just a novel that uses fear, suspense, angst, or any other negative emotion as a part of the story.

All in all, if a book gets in your head, it's a psycho thriller.

Is that what I am? A psycho thriller writer with a crime veneer? I didn't know. I don't know.

But I was amenable to the idea, and started to consider it.

Mo Hayder passed this year.

When I heard that, I went to my bookshelf and looked at her novels. I really enjoyed reading them. Loved the sense of fear and dread and confusion she was so good at crafting. I also love Blake Crouch's writing, and he does a lot with surreality, too.

And as always, thinking of other great stories got the gears churning.

Death Chorus began with a vivid scene in my head, like it always does. That scene is chapter one. In every book. And once it's created, I let the story unfold from there. You get to experience the mystery with Jamie, and she is the perfect conduit through which to channel this new-found psycho experience.

I love plunging the reader into the chaos of the story, into the melee. Putting you right on Jamie's shoulder and inside her head, so you're dragged along whether you like it or not, seeing, experiencing, feeling what she does.

And when I brought these new ideas to the existing methods I had, I realised that psychological thriller was probably the next natural step in that distillation. Bringing to the forefront the things I'm already doing that readers like, and allowing those other elements to fizzle out and take a backseat. This is how I'm working. How I'm discovering a way of making these novels better with each one.

It's a lot to unpack, and I know that these notes can feel quite scatterbrained at time, and that's because they're freeform, an outpouring from my mind and fingers that tell the story of the story.

I have a hell of a long way to go before I'm done — and not just finished — but before I'm done distilling this thing down to what I want it to be. It's a process that will never end, because as I continue to write, my idea of what kind of writer I want to be always changes. But what I do know, is that I always want the next one to be better. That I always take on board reviews and feedback and build on what I've done before in order to keep chasing that ideal — whatever it may be.

With your help and support, *Angel Maker* climbed all the way to thirtieth in the entirety of the UK Kindle Chart! It was rubbing shoulders with Michael Connelly, James Patterson, Lee Child, LJ Ross, MW Craven, Jo Nesbo, JD Kirk, Angela Marsons, and so many more writers that I consider to be operating on a whole other level from me. That was humbling, truly so. But it was also inspiring. And so when I really started writing *Death Chorus* I felt like I had all the tools and the fire to put something together that would crystallise all of my plans.

And I hope it did.

I think it's the best Jamie yet. And I don't say that with any sort of hubris — I simply look back at the mistakes of the last books and believe I avoided some of them here! And if it's not better, then at least this one is less worse!

Jamie's off on another adventure next. *Quiet Wolf.* The title will make sense once you read it. After the excitement of *Death Chorus*, Jamie is growing bored. So when the chance to do a favour for Wiik comes knocking, she jumps at it, much to Thorsen's dismay.

They'll head north, to the remote mountains, where dark secrets lay in wait...

And while new villains are coming, don't think I've forgotten about those who have come before. Those whose stories are still unfinished, whose endings are still unwritten.

I know some of you are probably wondering what happened to some of your old favourite characters? Well, you won't have to wait to long to find out. I won't say any more, but in the next few books, there'll be some returns, some shocks, some twists, and plenty, plenty more crimes for Jamie to solve.

Read on to learn more about *Quiet Wolf,* but for now, hopefully you're satiated and have had your Jamie fix for a while.

See you on the other side of 2021, folks! 2022 is going to be a hell of a year.

Morgan

QUIET WOLF

DI Jamie Johansson Book 5

All is quiet in Kurrajakk. So when a call comes in from Wiik, Jamie's old partner and the current head of the violent crimes department at Stockholm Polis HQ, she leaps at the chance to stretch her legs.

Wiik has a personal favour to ask — his ex wife's sister has gone missing, along with her husband and daughter.

The Boehmans were driving into the night, heading for the border, and then… they vanished.

Local polis have turned up nothing and are of no help. Before Wiik can even ask, Jamie is already on it.

When Jamie and Thorsen arrive in the quiet border town of Ettranger, it doesn't take long for them to realise things something isn't right there. An inept twenty-six year old is running the polis station, there's been a spate of unreported missing persons, and there are rumblings of a strange community living out on the lake, shut off from the rest of the world.

When Jamie and Thorsen discover a crash site on the

road, they converge on a place known only as The Farm, hoping to find the missing Boehman family safe and sound.

But with winter closing in, the nights freezing, the land-scape untamed, and the animals that stalk it it just as wild, Jamie and Thorsen will need to stick together if they hope to exhume the truth. But will that truth be enough? What secrets are hidden at the Farm? Where are the Boehmans? And is it already too late… to save them, to call for help, to get out alive?

Quiet Wolf is available now on Amazon.

ACKNOWLEDGMENTS

I just want to say thank you to all of those who continue to support this journey. Honestly, most of the time, I don't really know what I'm doing and nor do I ever feel like the next one will be any good. I take advantage of you readers by bouncing ideas off you, throwing unfinished, unpolished, and poorly thought out samples at you, and then ask you way too many questions about them! But you're always there, and always so willing to help. And for that, I can't say enough thanks. You may not always agree with my methods, my choices, or my decisions, but you never fail to bring an energy and enthusiasm that keeps me going.

So thank you — you know who you are. And you know I couldn't do this without you.

ALSO BY MORGAN GREENE

Printed in Great Britain
by Amazon

41328912R00239